T0155176

HONEY
AND
LEONARD

MARK PAUL SMITH

Virginia

Previously published in 2016 by Christopher Matthews Publishing under ISBN 9781938985812

Published in 2019 in the United States by BQB Publishing
(an imprint of Boutique of Quality Book Publishing Company, Inc.)

www.bqbpublishing.com

978-1-945448-47-8 (p)
978-1-945448-48-5 (e)

Library of Congress Control Number 2019947818
Book design by Robin Krauss, www.bookformatters.com
Cover design by Rebecca Lown, www.rebeccalowndesign.com
Edited by Caleb Guard
Author photo by John Sorenson

PRAISE FOR HONEY AND LEONARD
AND MARK PAUL SMITH

"Smith (*Rock and Roll Voodoo*) takes on the topic of love in one's twilight years in this uplifting tale. Widow Honey Waldrop and widower Leonard Atkins begin the novel happily in love despite Leonard's battle with the early stages of Alzheimer's and his scheming niece Gretchen's insistence that she keep power of attorney over him. But when Leonard's blood work shows an unusually high level of arsenic, Honey becomes a person of interest for allegedly poisoning him. The couple flees the law in favor of a romantic trip to Paris, insisting that the arsenic is from Leonard's years of working with pesticides on farms, and their story becomes international front-page news, billed as "the Bonnie and Clyde of love." Their love grows as they navigate newfound fame, failing health, and a foreign city; memory lapses and greedy heirs vying for inheritance money add depth. Though the prose is somewhat stilted, the premise is refreshing enough to keep readers engaged. Smith imbues his story of elders in love with plenty of rakish charm."

— Publisher's Weekly

"The story of Honey and Leonard was beautiful. It is a story of love and its importance on every level of life. The portrayal of the condition of Alzheimer's disease was very eye opening. I enjoyed reading this book."

— NetGalley review

"This was such a beautiful story. It was a reminder that love is all important . . . through everything. It was an eye opener re: Alzheimer's and all the effects."

— NetGalley review

This book is dedicated to my father, Maxwell Paul Smith, who died of Alzheimer's Disease in 2006 at age 82.

SPECIAL THANKS

To my "Honey," Jody Hemphill Smith. To my editors, Caleb Guard and Brenda Fishbaugh. And to Terri Leidich, founding mother of BQB and WriteLife Publishing.

OTHER BOOKS BY MARK PAUL SMITH

Rock and Roll Voodoo

The Hitchhike

ONE

HONEY REMOVED HER EYEGLASSES and blinked in disbelief.

The tree-lined street in front of her house was jammed with fire trucks, police cars, an ambulance and several governmental vans. Uniformed people were everywhere. Most of her neighbors had come out to see what was happening. Honey felt her heart begin to race as she noticed the yellow police tape being stretched around her two-story, brick home.

"Leonard!" she screamed as she began running toward her front door. "Leonard! Oh, no!"

She made it through the crowd and the yellow tape and halfway up her front steps before a burly detective in a brown suit grabbed her with both arms. "Oh, no you don't, lady. This is a crime scene. You can't just come charging in here."

"But this is my house!" she cried as she realized the futility of her struggle.

The detective released her from his bear hug and held her by one wrist so he could get a better look at her. "Is that you, Mrs. Waldrop?" he asked.

"Yes, it's me. You know it's me, Davey. You delivered my newspapers for ten years. Now, let go of me," she wiggled out of his grasp. "What's happened to my Leonard?"

"He's going to be fine. The medics are with him now. I'll take you to him if you promise to stay with me and not rush in like you own the place."

"I do own the place."

"Bad choice of words on my part. It is a working crime scene at the moment. I'm still Davey but you'd better call me Detective Perkins for now. I'm in charge of the investigation."

"Crime scene? Investigation?" Honey raised her voice. "What have they done to my Leonard?"

As she waited for the detective's explanation, Honey noticed all activity around her home had come to an abrupt standstill. Everyone was staring at her. Detective Perkins offered her his arm and began escorting her into the home.

"Why is everybody staring at me?"

As if in answer to her question, the front door banged open and out came two medics carrying Leonard on a gurney. He looked quite pale and was strapped down for safety. He managed to raise his head slightly when he heard Honey calling his name.

"What happened?" Honey asked as the detective let her get close enough for conversation.

Leonard looked confused and alarmed as he shook his head and said, "I have no idea. They said I have to go with them."

"Where are you taking him?" she demanded as the medics continued toward the ambulance. "You've got him all doped up. What's going on here?"

The detective had to grab her arms again as she attempted to grab the gurney. "Come on now, Mrs. Waldrop. He's going to be fine. You've got to let him go so they can take him to the hospital for testing and observation."

"Don't you 'Mrs. Waldrop' me. And take your hands off me, Davey. This is police brutality."

The detective let her go as Leonard was taken away and loaded into the ambulance. Honey didn't try to follow. A tight circle of uniforms had gathered to see if she was going to make enough of a fuss to get handcuffed. Being surrounded, Honey wisely decided to change her approach.

"Davey," Honey said, "I mean Detective Perkins. Perhaps you and I could go inside so you could tell me exactly what is happening."

The detective appeared relieved by Honey's more cooperative attitude. "That is an excellent idea. Let's do go inside. But let me warn you, there are quite a few folks in there and they're searching your home."

"Can they do that?"

"Yes, I'm afraid so. We've got a search warrant signed by the judge. Here it is. Take a look."

"How can they take Leonard out of my house if he doesn't want to go?"

"Adult Protective got a court order to have him removed. Here, look."

Her eyes glazed over the documents in emotional shock.

Honey was glad the detective had warned her about the search. Once inside, she was devastated to see people in hazardous materials suits with masks and plastic gloves going through every drawer and cupboard. She was disoriented by the time she and the detective settled into the breakfast nook in the kitchen. It felt like aliens had invaded her home.

"I'm sorry," she began, "this is all just too much."

"No, no. There's no need to apologize. I know how hard this must be for you, and let me start off by saying I don't believe a word of it. Not one word."

"Believe a word of what?"

Detective Perkins took a long look into Honey's eyes and

sighed deeply. "Okay. Here it is. Leonard went in for some blood tests recently, and it looks like he's been poisoned. That's why they sedated him and put him on a stretcher. Apparently, the doctors wanted him immobilized for the trip to the hospital."

"What?" Honey's eyes widened. "Who would poison Leonard? He doesn't have any enemies. Neither one of us do. We've only been dating a year come Halloween. He's been a farmer his whole life."

The detective waited for her to continue with a look of sympathy in his eyes. Suddenly, Honey realized what was going on. "Oh, my God, you can't think it was me."

"No, I don't think it was you," the detective attempted to calm her. "I've known you and Doc Waldrop, rest his soul, my entire life. And I know you and Leonard have been having a wonderful time together these past few months."

"All of North Manchester, Indiana, seems to know everything about us," Honey scoffed. "My husband was the finest doctor this town ever saw. I loved him dearly, but he's been dead nearly five years. And now, Leonard Atkins is the best thing that ever happened to me. You can put that in your report. Everybody else seems to be taking notes. You'd think people would have better things to do than gossip about a couple of old folks falling in love. It's 1992 for heaven's sake. Old people are taking over the world."

"This isn't about gossip, Mrs. Waldrop. Leonard's been poisoned. The blood tests prove it. Don't worry, I'm not going to arrest you today. I just need to ask a few routine questions."

"*Arrest me today?*" Honey gasped. "That sounds like you might arrest me in the near future."

"No, at this point, I'm not even saying you're a suspect."

"So what am I?"

"You're what we call a person of interest."

"Oh, good Lord," Honey began to cry. She wasn't one to break down easily because she'd seen a lot of sorrow in her day. But tears were getting the best of her at this point. It felt like everything she loved was being taken away. "This is like some terrible television program," she said as she wiped her eyes with a cloth napkin.

As the detective took her hands in his to try to comfort her, a person in a hazmat suit came up and said, "Detective Perkins, we've searched the kitchen and the living room and the bathrooms. We've got samples.

"Better check the basement," he said.

"Oh, yes," Honey said, "by all means, check the basement. That's where I keep all the poison."

"Now, Mrs. Waldrop . . ." the detective began.

Honey removed her hands from his and began to regain her composure. "No, I'm fine. Go ahead. Search anywhere you like. I'll help. This is preposterous. There is no poison in this house. Come on; let's check my closet upstairs. That's where I keep my makeup. If I had any poison, which I don't, that's where I would keep it."

"Good idea," said Perkins. "That's more like it. We do appreciate your cooperation."

"It doesn't look like I have much choice," Honey grumbled as she and the detective went up the carpeted steps with one of the hazmat suit people.

Her walk-in closet was the size of a large bedroom. It was filled with a long lifetime of a wealthy widow's clothing and accessories. She had more than two hundred pairs of shoes and a hat for nearly every day of the year. Each side of the room had a vanity desk with a large mirror and drawers filled with make-up and lotions and perfumes and hairsprays.

"This ought to keep you and your boys busy for a good long time," Honey said as she looked up to the detective. "I've got shoes in here older than you."

"I'm sure you do," Perkins said as he took Honey back downstairs to the kitchen nook.

"I know who's behind all this," she said once they sat down.

He waited for her to continue.

"It's Gretchen. Gretchen Atkins, Leonard's niece. She's been taking care of his money. Or should I say stealing his money. He gave her Power of Attorney once he started having problems with his memory after his wife died. He's rich as Croesus, you know."

"I've heard that."

Honey paused, catching herself. "Now don't you dare think I would hurt my Leonard for his money. I've got more than enough of my own, thank you. The doctor left me well off when he died, and I've been doing quite fine by myself. You can ask my broker."

"Why would Gretchen be behind this?"

"She doesn't want me in the picture. I ask too many questions. I told Leonard he never should have signed over Power of Attorney to her. And I told Gretchen he could revoke it any time he wants. That's why she's trying to get guardianship on him. She wants him found mentally incompetent, so he can't revoke her Power."

"How do you know all this?" Perkins asked.

"Leonard's at my house more than he's at that pathetic nursing home she put him in. She calls it independent living. I call it independent dying. I know he has some problems with his memory, but he's getting better. I'm taking good care of him."

She looked at Perkins to make sure he was paying close enough attention. "Anyway, Leonard brings his mail over for me to help him go through it. I saw the petition to establish guardianship over Leonard that Gretchen filed with the court. Her lawyer sent him the legal notice."

"How long ago did this happen?"

"It wasn't more than a week ago. And I'll tell you what. Leonard's prepared to fight it. He doesn't need a guardian as long as he has me. And if he does need a guardian, it'll be me, not her. She's stealing his money. She doesn't care about him. She just wants his money. Look at the car she's driving. It's a brand new Toyota. I've been told her big new house is paid for. She doesn't make that kind of money teaching fifth grade."

"So why would she want to poison Leonard?"

"He doesn't have a will. Gretchen's the only family he's got left. If he dies, it all goes to her. Leonard and I were going to get a lawyer to do a will and revoke that Power of Attorney, but now she's trying to say he's not competent to sign anything."

"Is he competent?"

Honey's face lit up as she formulated her response. She was still a beautiful woman. She had Liz Taylor in her eyes and Katherine Hepburn in her shoulders and hips. Her family came from Mobile, Alabama, where she'd been the queen of her high school senior prom. It was a storybook life until she lost her only sibling, her brother, on a bombing run over Germany in World War II. After that terrible loss, she started volunteering in the hospital, treating many returning veterans. She was a good worker, but she got in trouble a time or two for flirting with the patients. The doctor was tall and handsome. He swept her off her feet at a time when she was looking for a hero. They married after the war and moved north to his home state, Indiana.

Honey could pour out Southern charm like maple syrup turns Southern grits into a decidedly Northern dish.

"I'll tell you how competent Leonard is," she told the detective. "Last Saturday night, he showed up at my door with a dozen roses and took me to dinner. His shirt was clean, his shoes were shined and his hair was strictly Valentino. We had a perfect, Italian night out."

"Did you drive?"

"No, I let him drive my Cadillac. I hate to drive, and he's still an excellent driver. He sold his Oldsmobile two weeks ago and he's looking for a new one. He's between cars."

"How did he get to your house?"

"He walked. He's in good shape, I'm telling you, mentally and physically. The nursing home is right down the street from my house, about a quarter mile."

"I know he's got a valid driver's license," Perkins said. "He got a ticket last month for running a red light."

"That was that stupid light out on South Mill Road. I was with him. We were in his old car. There was nobody on the road. He always runs red lights when there's nobody coming. He's got a mind of his own."

"There was somebody on the road."

"If you want to say that policeman was on the road. He was hiding behind the gas station, just waiting for someone to run that light."

Perkins laughed. "Let's get back to the point. How do you suppose Gretchen would poison Leonard?"

"I have no idea."

The detective waited patiently for her to continue. Honey knew what he was doing. He was waiting to see how she would attempt to incriminate Gretchen and unwittingly shine light on her own activities and motives. She wasn't going down that road.

"What makes you think Leonard was even poisoned?" she asked. "He didn't look that bad on the stretcher. He was fine last night and this morning when Dorothy Anderson picked me up for our Wednesday bridge luncheon."

"We have blood test results that show he's been poisoned."

"Poisoned with what?"

Perkins shook his head and said, "I'm not supposed to tell you that."

"Why, Davey Perkins. Don't you Sherlock Holmes me. You

can't come in and tear my house apart and call me a murderer and then not tell me what kind of poison we're talking about. Besides, if I did it, which I most definitely did not, and wouldn't even think about even if I hated him, which I don't—I love the man dearly . . . Now wait, where was I going with that?"

"You were saying, 'If I did it.'"

"Oh, right. If I did poison Leonard, I would already know what the poison was, now wouldn't I?"

The detective smiled slightly as he said, "I guess that's right. And, anyway, I know you wouldn't poison anybody. So I'll tell you. It was arsenic."

"Arsenic!" Honey was visibly shocked. "That sounds so positively evil. Where would I get arsenic?"

One of the hazmat suits interrupted to ask, "How much of the medicine cabinet do you want us to analyze?"

The detective got up to supervise the search and said, "Don't worry, Mrs. Waldrop. It won't take much longer. I'll make sure we don't take anything you need on a daily basis. By the way, are Leonard's meds in the same cabinet as yours?"

"Mine are on the right, his are on the left. You can read the names on the bottles. And, Davey, please, stop calling me 'Mrs. Waldrop.' You make me feel as old as I am. You're a full-grown man now. You may call me 'Honey.'"

"Yes, of course, Mrs. Waldrop . . . I mean, Honey."

Perkins chuckled in embarrassment and went off with his people, leaving Honey alone with her thoughts. She was more than worried. She was being accused of trying to murder the man she loved. She knew she hadn't done anything wrong, except maybe let too many people know she and Leonard were happily in love and living together.

What makes people so nosey? And why do they love a scandal? Oh, that's right. It's good old-fashioned entertainment.

How could she prove her innocence? And what about Leonard? She was more worried about Leonard than anything else. She kept seeing the confused look on his face as they took him out on the stretcher. The more she thought about it, the more she realized there was only one thing she needed to do. Go find Leonard.

She got up to make some Earl Grey Tea for herself. She needed to think. Going to see Leonard might be problematic. For one thing, she hated driving. For another, there must be rules against attempted-murder suspects going to see their alleged victims in the hospital.

She could get in to see him. They would have taken him to Wabash County Hospital, fifteen miles away. She knew everybody there except the new folks. She had been president of the Women's Auxiliary when her late husband had practically run the place. She got on the phone to call Dorothy, her bridge club friend.

Dorothy answered after the first ring and said, "My goodness, Honey, what's going on over there? I had to drop you off a block away. I should have stayed with you. Now, I hear Leonard's been murdered and you're the number one suspect. How could anyone even suggest such a thing? Don't worry. I'm your alibi. So are all the girls at bridge club."

"Dorothy," Honey said. "Leonard is not dead. The police say he's been poisoned but they know it's not me. They're still here, searching the entire house."

"Oh, thank God! Is he going to be okay?"

"I'm pretty sure he will," Honey said. "Now, listen. I need a ride to the hospital right now. I've got to be with Leonard. He needs me."

There was a long pause on the line.

"Honey, I'm not sure I can do that. I'm not sure you should do that. Are you under arrest or anything like that?"

As Honey was contemplating her status, Detective Perkins walked back into the room. "I'll call you right back," Honey said as she hung up the phone.

"Who was that?" Perkins asked.

"That was Dorothy."

"Don't tell me you're trying to get a ride to the hospital."

"How could you know that?" Honey was a little surprised the detective was such a master of the obvious.

Perkins was 6'3" tall and weighed 260 pounds. His last sixty pounds had landed in his belly. Now, Honey, at 5'4", 115 pounds, was playfully poking her right fist into that belly. "How could you know that?" she repeated.

"Honey, please." He backed up a step to avoid her poke and said, "You know I can't let you go see Leonard. We're in the middle of an investigation here."

His denial stung like someone trying to slap some sense into her. Honey sat back down at the kitchen table, collapsing like a deflating blow-up doll. All the fight drained out of her. She put her arms on the table and put her head down and began to weep softly. "I need to go see him. I need to take care of him. He needs me. What will he do without me?" She raised her head. Tears had smeared her makeup. "Won't you take me to him? Please. He's all I've got."

As Honey's voice was approaching a wail, Karen Lindvall, the duly-elected and first female prosecutor in the history of Wabash County, walked in and informed Detective Perkins that she was taking over the crime scene investigation. The prosecutor was a blonde, tough-talking, 55-year-old woman of beautiful, Swedish descent. She paid no attention to Honey at first, electing to inform the detective of his many mistakes in gathering evidence. "You can't have people running around from room to room like this," she scolded. "We'll have one team for each room. And, by the way, we'll be focusing on the kitchen. This is a case of poisoning. All the food and liquid needs to be tested."

The prosecutor virtually kicked Detective Perkins out of the room, then turned to Honey and softened considerably, "Come here, Honey, and give me a hug. I know how hard this must be. And don't worry. I know you didn't do it. We've known each other too long."

"I helped you get elected," Honey sobbed into her shoulder. "We had a big fund raiser right in this house."

"That's got nothing to do with it," Lindvall said. "This is woman to woman. I know you and I know Leonard. It's a small county. I know how much you love him. But you've got to admit, it does look bad, Leonard getting poisoned while he's shacking up at your house."

Honey backed away from the hug, dried her eyes and said with a sniffle, "I wouldn't call it 'shacking up.'"

"You can call it whatever you want," Lindvall chuckled. "Now, listen, I know you want to go see him. And I'm going to authorize that, okay? I probably shouldn't but I'm going to do it anyway. What are you going to do? Machine gun him to death in his hospital bed?"

Honey's eyes turned hopeful. She couldn't believe her ears.

Lindvall handed Honey a handkerchief. "In fact, I'm going to let Perkins escort you to the hospital. I need to get him out of here anyway. He's like china in a bull shop."

"Thank you, thank you, thank you," Honey gushed as she threw her arms around the prosecutor.

"But you've got to promise me you'll stay with the detective at all times. And don't say anything to anyone about the case. I know you'll cooperate with this investigation any way you can and I've got a feeling I'm going to need you. By the way, Leonard's doing fine. They're keeping him overnight for observation, but he's showing no signs of trauma. So, go see him, and when you get back we'll talk about what he's been drinking and eating."

"What about the arsenic?" Honey asked.

The prosecutor looked back with steel in her eyes, "Who said anything about arsenic?"

Honey looked like a little girl getting caught stealing candy.

Lindvall softened her stare. "Never mind. I know. Don't you believe a word he says."

With that, the prosecutor spun on her high heels and stormed out of the kitchen, shouting, "Perkins!"

Leonard was sitting up in bed, flirting with two young nurses, like everything was right with the world. The man looked many years younger than his age. He had a full head of silver hair and laughing blue eyes with bushy eyebrows Honey could never get him to trim. His jutting jaw and powerful forehead made him look tough and stubborn but he was mostly gentle and kind. He was an excellent dancer. Most of his best moves came from square dancing as a young man.

"Step aside, girls," Honey said as she moved quickly to him. "This is my man."

"Honey," Leonard said as she buried herself in his embrace. "Where have you been? I've been looking all over for you."

"I can see how hard you've been looking for me," Honey said, gesturing to the nurses. "Ladies," she said as she disentangled herself from Leonard's embrace, "could we have a little privacy?"

The nurses politely left the room. "Who's this?" Leonard asked as he noticed Perkins for the first time.

"This is Detective Perkins. I've known him most of his life. We used to tip him the most of anybody on his paper route. Isn't that right, Davey?"

Perkins nodded but said nothing. He was still smarting from Honey spilling the beans about the arsenic. He took out a note pad and pen and said to Leonard, "I've got a few questions for you, Mr. Atkins, if you don't mind."

"You're a detective, huh?" Leonard asked as the two men shook hands. "I'm glad to meet you, but if you don't mind, I've got some questions for you. Starting with why the heck did you haul me out of Honey's house on a stretcher? And what's this about me being poisoned? I don't feel poisoned. Look at me. I've been ready to get out of here since they drugged me up and brought me in. Now they say I've got to stay all night. What's going on?"

"Funny you should ask that question," Perkins said. "I can't talk about the investigation but I do need to know if you are able to understand your situation."

"He wants to know if you're competent, mentally," Honey interrupted.

"You sound like my niece, Gretchen," Leonard said to Perkins. "She wants the court to declare me incompetent so I can't revoke the Power of Attorney I gave her."

"What do you mean by that?"

"Okay," Leonard began with a deep sigh. "My wife died two years ago, and I had a real rough go of it. She was all I had, so when she was gone I didn't know what to do. I lost it for a while. I guess it's what you call grieving.

"Gretchen is my niece, the only family I have left. She took over my finances after my wife died. I gave her what's called a Power of Attorney. That means she can run my life any way she wants until I revoke that power. A Power of Attorney is something you can always revoke. That's what her lawyer told us, anyway. Now that I want to revoke the Power, Gretchen and her lawyer are trying to get me declared mentally incompetent. They've petitioned the court to get a guardianship over me."

"And you can't sign anything or revoke anything if you're not competent," Perkins concluded.

"Absolutely," Leonard said. "And that includes writing a will, which I have never done. Stupid of me, I know. I just never got around to it. Besides, I always thought my wife would live longer than me. Then she got the cancer and left me alone.

"My wife and I only had one child. Her name was Emma. She drowned back in 1942. She was only seven years old. Gretchen was at the pond when it happened. It wasn't Gretchen's fault, but I know she always blamed herself. She became like the daughter I lost after her mother and father died. Gretchen's father was the only family I had left. When he died, Gretchen was all I had and I was all she had."

"So how can she say you're incompetent?" Perkins asked.

Leonard looked at Honey before answering. Honey nodded and he continued cautiously. "I do have a problem with my memory and the doctors at the nursing home are saying it's Alzheimer's. I don't know if they're right, but I do know I've been getting better since Honey and I got together."

"What's Gretchen doing with your money?" the detective asked, continuing his inquiry into Leonard's competency.

"I've got a feeling she's hiring lawyers and surveyors to help her sell off parts of the farm. I've heard some rumblings about a new housing addition coming in. Every time I ask Gretchen about it she won't give me a straight answer. In fact, it seemed for a while there that nobody wanted me to know what was going on."

"And then you found me," Honey said.

"That's right, pumpkin."

"What about your brother? Once he died, didn't his share of the family farm go to Gretchen?" Detective Perkins asked.

"Over the years, after our parents were gone, I gradually bought out my brother's share. He and his wife were terrible with money and he was a pretty bad drinker," Leonard said. "In the end, he didn't own any part of the farm. I know Gretchen was never happy about any of that."

"Well then," Perkins began, "you sound pretty darned competent to me. But let's start with the obvious. What is your date of birth?"

"That's easy. August 12, 1916."

"And that makes you how old?"

"75?"

"Leonard," Honey tried to help.

"No helping please," Perkins said.

"Okay," Leonard said, "I might be a little older than 75. I'll tell you, it's 1992 now and I was born in 1916 so that would make me how old?"

"You want to borrow my pen and paper?"

Leonard took the paper and was able to determine he was 76, not 75. "That's an honest mistake," Leonard said. "The years go by so fast anymore I can't keep track of them."

"At least you know what year it is now. Can you tell me today's date?"

Leonard looked helplessly at Honey, who shook her head to show she couldn't help. Then he looked back at Perkins and said, "I'm afraid you've got me on that one. If I had to guess, I'd say it's sometime in September."

Honey said, "That's right."

"No helping," Perkins warned. "What day in September?"

"That I couldn't tell you. And before you ask, I don't know what day of the week it is either. That doesn't make me incompetent. It just means I'm not working, so keeping track of the days isn't so important. I don't get weekends off like you. Fact is, I never got weekends off. Farming keeps you busy seven days a week. Why don't you ask me something important like who's the president?"

"Okay."

"It's George Bush. But he won't be president for long. There's an election coming up, and I think this kid from I forget where, some southern state, is going to win."

"What's his name?"

"I think his name is Clinton, but don't hold me to that."

The questions went on until Perkins got a pretty good idea that Leonard was not only competent, but also quite clever at hiding his memory problems. Anything he couldn't remember he wrote off as unimportant.

Leonard repeated his birth date three times over the course of the interview. The sooner he got to a competency hearing, the better off he would be. Repeating oneself is the first of many bad signs to come.

Honey was certain that Leonard's memory problems were caused by grief over his wife's death and the stress caused by Gretchen's legal maneuverings. She was also convinced that the more time Leonard spent being in love with her, the better off he would be. Honey was in denial. She decided not to tell the detective about the time Leonard fell asleep watching television at her house and awakened to shout at her, "Who are you and what are you doing in my house?"

A nurse came in to say dinner was on the way and to ask if anybody else wanted a meal. Right behind her was a chunky woman in a business suit who announced in a Spanish accent, "I am Maria Gomez from Adult Protective. Are you Leonard Atkins?"

Before Leonard could answer, Ms. Gomez looked at Honey and said, "And you must be Honey Waldrop."

"What's this about?" Perkins asked.

"Who are you?" Ms. Gomez glared at Perkins.

"I am Detective David Perkins of the Wabash County Sheriff's Department. I'm in charge here."

"Not any more," Ms. Gomez snarled. "Read this."

Perkins took the document and reviewed it.

"It's an emergency restraining order issued by Judge Jonathan Fee of the Wabash Circuit Court," Ms. Gomez explained, "the court in charge of Gretchen Atkins' petition to establish guardianship over Leonard Atkins. This order clearly states that Honey Waldrop shall have no contact with Leonard Atkins, either directly or indirectly, pending the outcome of the criminal investigation regarding the poisoning of Leonard Atkins."

"What does this mean?" Honey asked.

"It means you must leave this hospital room immediately," Ms. Gomez said. "If you choose to not comply, you will be charged with invasion of privacy, a Class D Felony, punishable by up to three years in jail."

"You can't do this," Leonard said, struggling to get out of bed. "I know my rights. Tell her, detective. She can't just march in here and tell me I can't be with my woman."

Perkins looked at Honey, who was beginning to lose her color, and said, "I'm afraid she can, Mr. Atkins. This court order is basically a no-contact order. Judge Fee has signed it. Honey, I'm afraid you and I are going to have to leave."

Honey fainted on the spot. She hit the bed first, which broke her fall, then slid to the floor before anyone could catch her. Besides a few bruises that would show up later, she was not injured. Fifteen minutes later, she awoke on a gurney in the nurses' station down the hall from Leonard's room.

"Where am I?" she asked while trying to bring the ceiling into focus. Detective Perkins' concerned face came into her view.

"You're in the hospital. You fainted in Leonard's room. Don't try to sit up. You've got a tube in your arm. It's an I.V. The doctor thinks you might be dehydrated."

"I never got a chance to drink my tea," Honey said, struggling to sit up. "Where's my Leonard?" She flopped her head back down on the pillow, "Oh, yes, it all comes back to me now. They kicked me out of his room because they think I poisoned him. What am I going to do Davey? What can I do?"

"For now you need to rest and try not to worry."

"Who was that woman who came in with the court order?"

"That was Maria Gomez, one of the toughest women you'll ever meet. She works for adult protective and she's seen enough abuse of the elderly to put her on the warpath forever."

"Didn't you tell her I would never hurt my Leonard?"

"I don't think she much cares what I think," Perkins said. "Don't worry, the investigation will prove you're innocent."

"I thought I was innocent until proven guilty."

TWO

THE FRONT PAGE banner headline of the North Manchester Herald screamed, "Waldrop Home Searched for Poison." Beneath the headline was a four-column photo of Honey's house, wrapped with yellow tape and surrounded by emergency vehicles.

Honey had spent a fitful night at her home after being released from the hospital. She was up and waiting for the paper when it arrived at 5:30 a.m. The news hit her so hard she nearly fainted again. Breathing deeply, she returned to her kitchen and drank a tall glass of water and took a blood pressure pill before sitting down to read the story. She was still in her robe.

"Oh, my goodness," she cried out to the empty house, "this sounds like something out of *The National Enquirer!*"

The story read:

Leonard Atkins was rushed to Wabash Memorial Hospital yesterday as technicians searched the home of Honey Waldrop for clues in an apparent case of poisoning.

Mr. Atkins is a retired farmer from Wabash County and Ms. Waldrop is a highly regarded community leader in North Manchester. Mr. Atkins had been placed in the nursing home for memory issues, but The Herald has learned that the two have been living together in Ms. Waldrop's home for several months. He is 76 years old; she is 77.

"They just had to put the ages in," Honey grumbled. She had always loved to see her name in the paper and it had been printed many times over the past fifty years as she led one charity event after another. This was the first time anyone had revealed her age. She knew the whole town was atwitter over two older folks getting romantic, but this was really too much. Having the world know her age was almost as bad as being accused of attempted murder.

The story continued:

Wabash County Prosecutor, Karen Lindvall, said no charges have been filed in the case and stated Ms. Waldrop is not a suspect, but does remain a person of interest. Lab results from food and medicine and cosmetics removed from the home will not be available for at least two weeks, Lindvall stated.

Wabash County Detective David Perkins would not comment on what kind of poisoning is involved in the case, nor would he comment on any possible motive.

"Two weeks," Honey howled at the newspaper. "I'll be lynched in the town square by then. And Davey makes it sound like I've got some motive he can't talk about."

Honey threw down the newspaper and got up to make herself some tea and oatmeal. All she could think about was Leonard. His favorite saying was, "Be happy with what you got." She could hear him saying it in her mind. She could see him too, handsome devil that he was. She could even smell him in her mind. He always smelled like Old Spice deodorant. Honey loved everything about that man.

"Be happy with what you got," he loved to say. "That's the only way to be happy. Some folks, you could give them a million dollars and all they'd want is another million dollars. They can never be happy. The only way to be happy is to be happy with what you got."

"Well, I'm not happy with what I've got," Honey said as she paced back and forth from the kitchen to the living room, wondering what in the world she was going to do.

She paced until 8 a.m., plotting her next move. She knew what it would have to be. It was probably too early, but she dialed the number anyway.

When the going gets tough, the wealthy call their stockbrokers.

Surprisingly, she got Jim Tech on the phone and immediately poured her story out, beginning with, "They took Leonard away," and ending with, "I'll do anything to get him back."

Tech knew something was seriously wrong as soon as Honey launched into her tale of woe without the usual social small talk as an introduction. She was a misplaced Southern belle, after all. Somewhere in her rambling and excited story, he heard the words "police" and "search warrant" and "poison."

"Honey, slow down, please," he said. "Are you telling me the police got a warrant and searched your home because they think you might have poisoned Leonard?"

"Yes," Honey sighed. "That's what I'm telling you."

There was a long pause on the line. Honey waited for Tech's analysis, amazed he could so quickly get to the heart of her problem with one question.

"Did you read the paper this morning?" she asked.

"I don't take the North Manchester paper," he said. "Was it bad?"

"Was it bad?" Honey cried. "I'm front page news like some triple-ax murderer."

"Honey, Honey," Tech tried to calm her. "Settle down. It's going to be okay. You didn't kill anybody, did you?"

"Jim, I can't take this. After all I've done for this town. How can they treat me like this?"

"I'll tell you what. I'm glad you called me. I know exactly what you need to do."

"You do?"

"Yes, without a doubt. You just sit tight and wait by the phone. You're going to be getting a call this morning from somebody I highly recommend. He's a criminal defense attorney from Fort Wayne by the name of Robert Nimmo."

"Good, I don't want anybody from North Manchester handling this case." Honey wrapped the phone chord around her hand several times. "The lawyers here believe everything they read in the paper." Nearby Fort Wayne was definitely the big city compared to North Manchester.

"I'm innocent," Honey said, trying to be brave as she swung open the front door to usher the forty-two-year-old attorney into her home. It was a little after noon. "Thank you for coming so quickly and on such short notice."

"We got lucky," Attorney Nimmo said. "I had a trial scheduled for today that was continued to a later date. I've got some time."

"Good," Honey said. "So, as I was saying, I really am innocent. Do all your clients say that?"

Nimmo laughed as he shook her hand and looked into her eyes with a confidence Honey found instantly reassuring. "I only represent the innocent." He was as tall as Detective Perkins but much more trim. His hair and beard were a little long, but well-trimmed and with enough gray to show experience. His suit was expensive, and his dress boots with side zippers were well shined. She noticed his briefcase was Oleg Cassini with gold trim as he laid it on her dining room table and snapped it open to take out a writing tablet. He was handsome. He didn't wear glasses.

"I usually don't make house calls," Nimmo joked, "but when Jim Tech told me about you I figured I might as well check out the scene of the crime."

"There's been no crime committed here." Honey said.

Nimmo sat down, picked up his pen and continued in a more sober tone. "I know, I know. Sorry about that. I'm just using a little comic relief here to help you lighten up. I know how hard this must be for you. But let me tell you, everything's going to be all right."

Honey stepped into the kitchen as he spoke and returned with a dishtowel in her hands. She was wringing it so tight it looked like she might tear it in two. "Are you sure?"

Nimmo leaned back in his chair and took a deep breath. "Yes I am sure. But listen, before I start asking you a bunch of questions like some cop, let me tell you where we are. No charges have been filed against you. It's my job to make sure charges are never filed in this case. In other words, I'm here to nip this case in the bud. Good attorneys plea bargain, better attorneys charge bargain."

Honey pulled out a chair and sat down across from the attorney. "What do you mean by that?"

Nimmo put down his pen and folded his hands in front of him with his elbows resting on the arms of the chair. "I mean we're not going to sit around and wait for them to file a criminal charge against you so we can then negotiate a plea bargain. We're going to do our homework now so they never file charges in the first place. Then we'll make the newspaper print that news as big as today's story."

Honey clapped her hands and stifled a squeal of glee. "I like the way you think."

Nimmo leaned forward and put his elbows on the table. "I know the prosecutor. That doesn't mean she'll bend the rules to give me special deals. She's good that way. She doesn't do favors for her friends. We've known each other for years. She's a fair person. Apparently, you two know each other quite well?"

Honey began bouncing in her seat. "Oh, yes. I've known her since she was a young lawyer. She got mad when I knew it was arsenic they said poisoned Leonard."

Nimmo picked up his pen and began writing. "Arsenic, huh? Sounds kind of old school, don't you think? Who would want to poison Leonard Atkins?"

Honey stood up and walked around the table to put her hand on Nimmo's shoulder. She smiled tightly and whispered. "Nobody would poison Leonard. In fact, I don't think he was poisoned at all. I think Gretchen is making this up. And now she's got a no-contact order or something that says I can't even go see him even when he needs me."

"Hold on, slow down. Who's Gretchen?"

The attorney nodded and took notes as Honey told him the story of Leonard's niece, Gretchen Atkins, trying to get him declared incompetent so she could maintain control over his estate.

"You know," Nimmo said, "I do enough estate litigation to know the vultures often start circling long before anyone dies."

"That's the thing," Honey said. "He's not even close to dying. He's only seventy-six. That's young these days. It's one year younger than me, and let me tell you, I got a lot of living left to do and so does Leonard. And we intend to do it together."

Honey put both hands on the table. "Mr. Nimmo. I need you to do something for me right now, today. Something you might not want to do."

Nimmo looked up at Honey, surprised by the urgency of her tone and the determination of her movement. "I'll do what I can. What is it you want me to do?"

Honey stood up straight and folded her arms across her chest. "I need you to go see Leonard. He's already back at the nursing home, I checked. Now, they've got him in assisted living. He was in independent living, but they moved him to more secure quarters because of all the trouble. I can't go see him, but you can. I need you to tell him I love him and I need you to tell him I'm going to get him out of there."

"I'll go see him for you," Nimmo said. "And I'll do it as soon as we're finished here. But don't talk crazy about getting him out of anywhere. Even I would have trouble defending you on that one."

Honey gave Nimmo a look to make him realize she was capable of doing just about anything at this point. Her strong eyebrows arched high over hazel eyes that shined fiercely. Her nose was sleek but solid. Her jaw was firmly set. She came from a long line of stubborn women. Her proud Southern family had buried its wealth in a cotton field to hide it from the Union Army during the last year of the Civil War. Her grandmother still thought the South should have won the war.

"What are they going to do?" she asked. "Throw me in jail? I've got news for them, especially that Gretchen. She's the one who belongs in jail for doing this to us. I'm not going to live the time I've got left without the one man who has finally made me realize how truly fulfilling life can be."

Honey's voice cracked as she broke down and started to cry. Nimmo stood up and gave her an extended hug. "Now, now, Honey. Don't be sad. We're going to get him back for you. Don't worry. It won't even take that long."

"How long?"

"A week or two, maybe a month."

"That's too long. They'll kill him by then. Every time he gets mad about being in there and away from me they give him more drugs. That nursing home is nothing but a pill factory. They dope him up so much he doesn't know where he is. They're going to kill him."

"Nobody's going to kill him," Nimmo tried to console her. "But why don't you think he was poisoned?"

"He was fine when I left him yesterday morning about 11 a.m. And, if you must know, he was even a little frisky."

"Frisky?"

Honey looked over her glasses at the younger attorney and said, "We're not dead yet."

"Of course, I mean, good for you . . . good for him."

Honey laughed at his embarrassment and decided to change the topic. "You're my attorney, right?"

"I will be as soon as you retain me."

"Oh, yes, I almost forgot," she said as she took her checkbook out of her purse and dashed off the check. "I understand it's five thousand for now. Is that correct?"

"Correct," Nimmo said as he took the check.

"Don't worry, it's good," Honey said. "As Jim Tech probably told you, I have more than enough money to get by."

Nimmo put the check in his briefcase as he let her continue. "So, now that you're my attorney, you can't tell anyone what I tell you, is that right?"

"That is correct. It's called attorney-client confidentiality."

"Fine, then let me tell you, I fully intend to rescue my Leonard from that horrible nursing home. That means it's going to be your job to keep me out of jail. That's your job anyway, isn't it?"

Nimmo looked at her with a stern frown. "Before you do that, let me go talk to him. If he's competent and he hasn't been poisoned, we might be able to keep the charges from being filed. And, since the no-contact order is based on criminal charges being filed, we can probably kill two birds with one stone."

"How can they have two cases against me at one time?" Honey asked. "Isn't that double jeopardy?"

"There are two kinds of law in America," Nimmo explained. "One is criminal law. That's where the state punishes people for committing crimes. The other kind of law is civil law. That's basically where people fight about money. The criminal case has not been filed against you yet. It's under investigation. On the other hand, the civil case has been filed. That's the one where Gretchen is seeking to have Leonard declared incompetent so she can keep controlling his money."

"I'm glad you understand all this," Honey said.

A ray of afternoon sun shined through the curtains in Honey's dining room and illuminated her face. Tears were glistening in her eyes, but her chin was still squarely set. She looked much younger than her age as the sun lit up her blonde hair and smoothed the wrinkles on her face.

"It's not just Gretchen who doesn't want us to be together," Honey said. "It seems like the whole town is jealous of what we've found in each other. It's like they think old people shouldn't be dating and having romantic times. I know they call me an old fool behind my back. They just can't stand it that we're in love. Unhappy people hate happy people!"

Nimmo couldn't help but laugh. "You said a mouthful there. And while you're at it, you might add that short people don't like tall people and fat people definitely hate thin people."

Honey laughed with him. It felt good to finally feel some emotional relief. She liked this lawyer. He didn't take himself too seriously. As she was contemplating the new and satisfactory relation with her attorney, there came a knocking on Honey's front door. She looked at Nimmo and said, "Who could that be?"

"If it's the press, don't say anything," Nimmo said as he followed her to the door.

Honey opened the door to find herself staring into a television news camera with a reporter saying, "I'm Andrew Lockner from WTHR in Indianapolis. Any comment on the poisoning of Leonard Atkins?"

Before her attorney could intercede, Honey launched into what sounded like a well-prepared response. "Leonard Atkins has not been poisoned. He's my good friend and I ought to know. I'm Honey Waldrop and I most certainly have done nothing wrong. I love Leonard, and now they won't even let me go see him. There are people who are after his money and they want me out of the way."

"Who's after his money?" the reporter asked.

Attorney Nimmo managed to get between Honey and the reporter and said, "I think that will be more than enough for today. Ms. Waldrop is my client and she has nothing further to say."

"Have murder charges been filed against your client?"

"No charges have been filed," Nimmo said as he hustled Honey back inside her house.

"Did I say too much?" she asked once they sat back down.

Nimmo hugged her tightly. "You said way, way, way too much."

Honey relaxed in his arms before backing out of the embrace. "Why can't I tell my side of the story?"

Nimmo put his hands on her shoulders and looked her closely in the eye. "If you go on camera about how innocent you are, it makes the prosecutor file charges to prove the search was justified."

Honey's eyes widened. "Would they do that?"

Nimmo took his hands off her shoulders and backed away to look out the dining room window. "Probably not just to prove a point. But the more this thing gets in the public eye, the harder it will be to make it go away. I don't know if you noticed those reporters are from Indianapolis. That's the state capital, a hundred miles away. This story is obviously catching fire and you, my dear, only fan the flames with your comments."

He drew the curtains together so no one could see inside.

THREE

HONEY WAS GETTING READY for bed when she heard someone knocking on her front door. It was after 9 p.m., but it could still be another reporter. In the three days since the story broke, she had been approached by all kinds of media people. The story had struck a vibrant chord in the romantic soul of the heartland. Even *The Chicago Tribune* dispatched a reporter to get the inside story of the elderly lovebirds in trouble with the law. Ignoring the advice of legal counsel, Honey had let the *Tribune* reporter in to proclaim her innocence and her undying love for Leonard.

As the knocking on her door continued, she knew it wasn't a reporter. That knock was more than familiar. That was a "shave and a hair cut, two bits" knock. She knew who was on the other side of her door before she unlocked it.

"Leonard," she gushed as he took her into his arms. He was barefoot and still in his pajamas. "What on earth are you doing here? How did you get out? Where are your shoes?"

"Piece of cake," he said as he kissed her hard on the lips and hugged her tightly around the waist. "Bed check is at nine and my room is on the first floor. They don't lock the windows. No one will know I'm gone until breakfast."

"Did you forget your shoes?"

"No, they make too much noise. I didn't want to go clip clopping down the sidewalk."

Honey took his big hands in hers. "Get in here before anyone sees you."

Leonard stumbled and had to catch himself on a chair as he came into the living room.

"What's the matter?" Honey asked. Leonard was not a clumsy man.

Leonard sat down in the chair and ran his fingers through his hair. "Oh, I'm sorry, Honey. They've been drugging me up pretty bad in there. They keep making me take pills I don't even know what they are. I think they're putting something in my cottage cheese. It doesn't taste right and they serve it with every meal, even breakfast. I'm telling you, I had to get out of there before somebody poisons me again. And I had to see you."

"You are a sight for sore eyes," Honey said. "You look a little tired but you're still your same old handsome self. You know they won't even let me come see you? They're still saying I poisoned you." Honey took a seat on the arm of his chair. She held his head in her hands and put her nose to his nose, "What are we going to do now? If you're on the run and I let you into my house, that makes us both fugitives."

Leonard kissed her on the forehead and then on the lips. "Oh, no, I know. I shouldn't have come here. I don't want to get you in trouble."

"Too late for that," Honey said as she rose from the chair and began dancing around the room. "I've been in trouble with you since our first kiss at the Halloween benefit party for the United Way. Remember how you danced us behind the pillar and took my breath away?"

Leonard got up and began waltzing with her. "Like it was yesterday. You came as Marie Antoinette and I came as a scarecrow. It wasn't even a date. We met at the party. We spent a lot of money that night trying to out-donate each other."

"It was for a good cause," Honey said, kissing him again.

"What do we say?" Leonard prompted.

"Love is grand," they said together.

"I never knew it could be this good," Leonard said as he brought her in, cheek to cheek. He stopped the waltzing to kiss her again, slowly and softly and passionately. "And you always taste so good."

"I just brushed my teeth," Honey laughed. "Lucky for you."

"Lucky for you, too. I brushed right before I crawled out the window of that damned nursing home." Leonard laughed with her and then fell silent.

"What are we going to do, sweetie?" Honey asked as she collapsed her head into his body.

Leonard wrapped his arms around her. "I've been thinking a lot these last few days. I don't like what they've done to us, keeping us apart and all. It's not right. It feels like the police have taken over the world. This never would have happened in the old days."

Honey waited for him to continue.

Leonard had to sit down for another dizzy spell. Honey ran into the kitchen and got him a tall glass of cold water. Leonard drank it down in one motion and handed the empty glass back to Honey. "Your lawyer came to see me a couple days ago. Nice guy, good dresser, but he says this mess could take weeks or even months to clear up. I'm not ready to wait that long. So, I've been thinking. Maybe it's time you and I take a little trip."

Honey gasped and put both hands over her mouth. "I've been thinking the same thing. I'm tired of people telling me what to do. Oh, Leonard, I can't believe you're talking like this. You know I'll follow you anywhere. I'm sick to death of this little town. I can't even go shopping anymore without people looking at me like I'm some kind of criminal. Even Doty doesn't want to go out with me.

Besides, I've been stuck here since 1946. I'd say that's more than long enough."

"You know we're going to have to leave the country because of all this legal mess," Leonard said. "We need to go someplace where they can't find us."

Honey pushed him playfully on the shoulder. "They can't find you incompetent if they can't find you at all."

Leonard stood up and took a wide, athletic stance as he regained his bearings and balance. He raised his right arm in the air and proclaimed in full, theatrical voice. "Let's go to France. I always wanted to go there. My friends went there because of the war, but I couldn't go because I had to stay home and farm."

"Let's go to Paris and kiss on the top of the Eiffel Tower!" Honey shouted as she bounced up and down.

Leonard kissed her like they were already there. He dipped her until her hair touched the floor then he raised her up and over his head by her armpits. Once he set her down, he took a step back and put both hands on his hips. Then he put his hands on his knees as the dizziness returned. He was slightly out of breath. "Now, wait a minute. Before we really do this, we'd better talk it over. We could both end up in jail."

Honey grabbed his arm to steady him. She wasn't worried about his breathing or the dizziness. She had just felt his full strength, and she was beginning to be carried away by her own. "I'm starting to feel like this little town is nothing but one big prison cell. The last time a man swept me off my feet I ended up in North Manchester, Indiana. It wasn't romantic at all. I didn't know anybody. The doctor was working around the clock. We never had children and everybody always thought we were strange for not adopting. I worked my tail off to become a leader of this community and look what little thanks I get for all my efforts. They're trying to throw me in jail, for Heaven's sake.

"So, I don't see what's to talk over at this point. I want to get swept off my feet and end up in Paris with the man of my dreams. This might be my last chance for romance. I say let's do it now. I don't need to talk about it. I've been playing it safe my whole life and look what it's gotten me. I've got half the population of a small city pointing fingers at me behind my back. I'm more than ready for a change of scenery."

Leonard had stood up straight and regained his breath by the time Honey finished her harangue. He decided to be the voice of caution one last time. "This is a pretty important decision for us to make on the spur of the moment."

"Oh, no," Honey shook her finger in his face. "This decision has been a long time coming."

◆

By 3 a.m. that morning, Honey and Leonard were on the interstate and headed for the Indianapolis International Airport. It had taken them several hours to get on the road. They had some emotional catching up to do. For starters, they took a steamy shower together. Leonard needed a little freshening to get rid of the nursing home smell. They both got wet removing each other's clothes. As the shower washed away their troubles, he sang "Stardust" to her, word for word and note for note, as she washed him playfully. He was a good singer. She stroked his behind. It felt perfect to have him back. The legal consequences of leaving the country and becoming a fugitive with him barely crossed her mind.

Honey loved the water and soap because it washed away their wrinkles, much like Leonard's beautiful baritone singing washed away the years. She wore only a brassiere in the shower to keep her breasts from sagging. Sex for them was not quite the same as it had been in their youth. The emphasis was no longer on pounding penetration, yet they still thrilled to each other's touch and taste. The sudsy shampoo smelled like sweet romance.

The pure joy of loving human contact never gets old.

Honey had decided fairly early in the relationship to give oral sex a try, even though it had never been part of her long marriage to the doctor. She'd read about it for years. She was curious.

Leonard eagerly followed suit. It didn't take long for each of them to wonder why they hadn't tried this sensual technique much, much sooner in their lives.

The two of them laughed together like true lovers during their reunion shower. They dried each other off and got under the bed sheets for a delicious cuddle. Leonard fell asleep. Honey let him snore while she hastily packed one small bag for two. She grabbed their medications and toiletries and some underwear. They didn't need heavy baggage to haul. They could buy new clothes in Paris.

While packing, Honey got a surprise glimpse of her near naked self in the full-length mirror on the back of her bedroom door. Oh, it was tragic. The skin under her neck and arms had wrinkled and was sagging slightly. Her legs and stomach looked like crepe paper. Tiny purple and red veins were beginning to take over. Age spots and tiny moles were all over her like nagging insects. She was glad Leonard wasn't seeing her in this light. And how much worse would she have looked without the bra?

She caught herself pouting. It didn't seem fair. She felt young and in love. Life felt fresh and free. Her courtship with Leonard had been a whirlwind. But the mirror said she was old. The reflection actually frightened her. Not so much because she was afraid to die, but because it looked like her body would not be able to carry her much farther down the road. Or, worse yet, it would break down and force her into the clutches of assisted living.

Honey scolded her image in the mirror. "If I was the only one this was happening to, I would be even more mad than I already am."

She got dressed and began looking more fit and firm with each piece of clothing she added.

Leonard was sleeping peacefully in bed. He looked as much the worse for wear as she did, but somehow, it didn't seem so shockingly bad on him. She awakened him with a kiss on the forehead, reminded him where he was and helped him get dressed. She convinced him she should drive since he was still a bit groggy from the nursing home drugs. She hated driving but they had to get going and be in a hurry about it.

Honey could barely see over the rear seat of her Cadillac as she carefully backed out of the garage. Leonard got out to shut the overhead door. Honey had misplaced the automatic door opener months earlier.

"Goodbye cruel world," Leonard said as they drove out of town.

Honey laughed and slapped her right hand on the dashboard. "You do realize, sweetie, that we are now fugitives from justice? My lawyer's job just got a lot tougher."

"You know how lawyers spell justice?" Leonard asked.

"M.O.N.E.Y.?"

"No. J.U.S.T. U.S."

Honey turned her head to look at him briefly before returning her attention to the road. "Ooh, that's good. I haven't heard that one. I thought I'd heard all the lawyer jokes. But, you know, I like my lawyer. He says once they figure out I didn't poison you, there will be no reason for the no-contact order. So I say, let them work it out while we're in France."

"You do realize, pumpkin, we'll be homesick in no time."

"That's fine. We'll deal with it at that time. Right now, I'm sick of home."

She did not realize what a fire their departure would light in the plus-size bellies of Leonard's niece, Gretchen Atkins, and Maria Gomez from Adult Protective.

Honey did understand they had precious little time to make a clean getaway out of the country. She also had a sinking feeling that neither she nor Leonard would have the slightest idea what to do once they reached the airport.

Leonard settled into a thoughtful silence as Honey eased onto Interstate 69 south and managed to set her cruise control at what she thought was a cautious 65 mph. Unfortunately, she took her foot off the gas as she was fumbling with the cruise control and ended up setting her speed at an illegally slow 45 mph. She couldn't see the speedometer because the steering wheel was blocking her view. She could barely see over the wheel. They rolled on into the night for an hour at reduced speed. Leonard remained preoccupied as the occasional truck roared by with a long pull on its air horn.

"Why are these trucks going so fast?" Honey asked as she continued to fail to realize her own speed. "And why are they honking at us?"

When Leonard failed to respond, Honey became concerned and grabbed him by the shoulder. "Sweetie, what's the matter? You haven't said a word in thirty miles. What's the matter? You don't want to go to France? I thought you always wanted to go there?"

"It's not that," he finally murmured as he turned to look out the passenger window.

"I know what you're worried about."

"I'm not worried."

"Yes, you are. I can tell by the way you won't look at me. You're worried because we don't have any luggage. That's it. You think I forgot to pack your bag. You don't need to worry. I kept it light but I got all your medicines—the heart pills, the blood pressure and your inhaler. When they searched the house, the police didn't take medications they knew we needed on a daily basis. Between the two of us, we've got enough pills to open a pharmacy. All we really need is our medication, and I've got it all."

It took a few moments before Leonard explained, "No, I'm not worried about anything. I'm too old to worry. Worrying never did anything but waste my time."

"So, what's the matter?"

"I'm ashamed," Leonard said.

"Ashamed? Ashamed of what?"

Honey waited for two whole minutes before Leonard finally confessed, "I don't have a passport."

"A passport?" Honey asked. "Is that what's got you in this deep, dark mood? A passport? You are a silly, silly boy. Don't you remember we got our passports before that evil niece of yours put you in the nursing home? You remember. We went down to the post office together and filled out all the paperwork and then we went out to that Chinese restaurant on Pearl Street and had the best egg rolls ever."

"Yes, yes, I do remember now. Those egg rolls were great. I remember the egg rolls now, but I've got to tell you, I don't exactly recall the post office."

"Yes you do. You said that one old lady on the most wanted poster reminded you of me."

"She did. She was ornery. Not near as pretty as you but she looked just like you when you're about to get your way."

"See, you do remember."

Leonard looked at Honey, tears welling up in his eyes. He didn't want to say what he knew he had to confess. When he finally spoke it was in the unsteady tone of a man who had just received a terrible medical diagnosis.

"I'm glad to hear we've got passports. That's good. What's bad is that's a pretty big thing I don't remember. I know you want me to remember. But I'm telling you, I can't see it in my mind. I can see the egg rolls and the wanted poster but I can't see anything about passports. It scares me to death, Honey. I can't see it. No matter how hard I try, I can't see the passports. The worst thing is, knowing I don't remember the passports makes me wonder what else I don't remember."

Honey kept her eyes on the road and reassured him. "Don't you be afraid, Leonard Atkins. You're just tired and all doped up. What you need is some rest. You go ahead and take a nap. It'll all come back to you when you see the passports. I've got them in the bag I packed for the two of us."

As she spoke, a semi driver honked his horn as he blasted by in a rush of displaced air that shook the Cadillac and jolted Honey back to the task of driving. She looked in her rearview mirror and saw a car following too closely with its headlights blinking off and on and little blue and red lights flashing.

"Leonard," she said. "There's a fire truck right behind us."

Leonard craned his neck to look behind and said, "That's no fire truck, Honey. That's the police. How fast are you going? Oh, no. They're going to find out who I am and send me back."

He looked at the speedometer. "Good grief, Honey, you're only going forty-five miles an hour. Speed up to sixty five, maybe they'll let us keep going."

By the time Honey was up to fifty five, two backup units had arrived to participate in the suspicious, low-speed chase.

"Better pull over," Leonard said. "Looks like the jig is up. Somebody at the nursing home must have sounded the alarm."

"How could they possibly know it's us?" Honey asked.

"The license plate is in your name, and they know I'd be with you," Leonard said.

Two more police cars arrived and helped surround Honey and Leonard as the Cadillac came to a squeaking stop on the side of the off ramp Honey had used to exit the highway. Officers from the city, county and state jumped out of their squad cars with side arms drawn and took cover behind their vehicles. The state trooper behind them barked through the speakers in his car, "Get out of the car with your hands in the air. Get out of the car now. You are completely surrounded."

Honey and Leonard struggled out their respective doors, blinded by the spotlights and more than a little stiff and sore from the drive. "It's okay," Leonard called out with his hands in the air. "We don't mean to make trouble."

It became instantly apparent to the nervous police officers that they had intimidated a harmless, elderly couple. The ad hoc swat team lowered their weapons and began to laugh in relief, teasing the state trooper who called in the chase and making jokes among themselves like, "Better search these two. They look like big time drug dealers. We'd better call in the dogs."

The police were having a regular party at Honey and Leonard's expense until Honey started crying in embarrassment and put her hands on her knees, pleading, "Won't you please turn off those lights? They're hurting my eyes."

Leonard ran over to help her and shouted, "Haven't you boys had enough fun for one night?"

The lights went out in a hurry and the cars began to leave. Eventually, the original state trooper was the only one left on the scene. He felt so bad he didn't even give Honey a warning ticket after she explained she'd been having trouble with her cruise control.

"I'm sorry about the guns and the lights," he said as he checked her license and registration. "We've been having lots of trouble with drug traffickers in these parts lately. One of our officers got shot last month. You were traveling so slowly we thought you must be on drugs."

The trooper checked Leonard's identification. "You folks really shouldn't be driving at night. There's a Holiday Inn right over there. You can see the sign. Why don't you get a little sleep and try again in the morning? By the way, where are you headed?"

"Just down to Indianapolis to see our grandchildren," Honey lied like a pro.

The trooper wrapped up his investigation without further inquiry. It would still be several hours before Leonard was reported missing.

Once they were back in the car and buckling up their seat belts, Honey said, "I thought for sure they knew it was us."

"They did know it was us," Leonard said. "They just haven't figured out we're on the run. I guess that no-contact order isn't in their computers."

Neither Honey nor Leonard could make much sense out of the confusing, green information signs as they rolled into the Indianapolis Airport. Leonard was driving. He had taken over driving after the police stop. He and Honey hadn't checked in to the hotel as suggested by the police. They both knew there was no time for anything but a quick bathroom break.

It was nearly sunrise and traffic was already so heavy in Indianapolis that Leonard didn't dare slow down. He was getting frazzled but trying hard not to show it. The drive around the Interstate to find the airport was a harrowing ordeal for someone used to small town streets. It was five lanes of speeding traffic with cars merging in and out for no apparent reason. Honey was no help at all.

"Slow down, sweetie, so I can read these signs. I don't know if we need to go to the terminal first or the parking lot first. What's the difference between long term parking and short term parking?"

Leonard decided to take refuge in the Hertz rental car lot. At least it had a sign he could understand. He parked the car, turned off the ignition and slumped his shoulders in exhaustion. "This could be the end of the line, pumpkin. I'm starting to think this whole thing might be a bad idea. If you want to know the truth, I'm amazed we made it this far. We got dumb lucky with those cops who stopped us, and that was nothing compared to trying to find this crazy airport. And by the way, they're doing bed check at the nursing home right about now."

Honey looked at him with the patient smile of a woman who knows she's going to get her way. "Are you done?"

Leonard couldn't help but lighten up. He'd seen that look before.

"In the first place," Honey said, "here we are at the airport. We made it. You should be happy. In the second place, there's no such thing as dumb luck. We're not dumb but we are lucky. We're lucky to be together, and you, sir, are lucky to be with someone as wonderful as me. And nobody's luckier than a little old damsel in distress." She finished with a Southern drawl that made him laugh.

"So what are we going to do now?" he asked.

Honey checked the contents of her purse, put on some lipstick, gave him a sweet kiss on the lips and opened her door. "Watch me work," she said as she got out of the car and shut the door.

Leonard watched her out the window until she disappeared into the rental car building. He chuckled to himself as he lowered down the power seat to take a nap in "naptown," everybody's nickname for Indianapolis. He was exhausted from the night and none too optimistic about the coming day.

Within five minutes Honey was back with a tall, blonde flight attendant in tow. She knocked on the window to awaken him. "Leonard, would you please get out of the car and say hello to Julia. She works for the airline and she just happens to have a co-worker who is flying to Paris this morning."

Julia was only too happy to help. She had a grandmother about Honey's age. Before Leonard really knew what happened, the flight attendant had helped them park the car in long term parking, taken the shuttle bus with them to the terminal, helped them book two tickets to Paris, upgraded them to first class at no extra charge and introduced them to her friend Jennifer at the boarding gate.

Julia handed Honey and Leonard off to Jennifer like they had been planning the transfer for days.

"I can't believe you two didn't have any bags to check," Jennifer laughed as she gave Honey and Leonard a quick course in boarding the plane. "As soon as they announce first-class boarding, you two go up to that woman. She'll take your tickets. I've got to get on board now but I'll see you after takeoff."

"Now, there goes a lovely young woman," Honey said as they watched Jennifer disappear into the boarding bridge.

"I don't know how you do it," Leonard said as they settled into their seats to wait at the gate. "I do know one thing. I am the luckiest man alive. There's nothing better than watching you pull rabbits out of the hat."

He gave Honey a kiss on the cheek and began searching the pockets of his pants and sport coat. Honey had resigned herself early in their relationship to the fact that Leonard would always be searching for his wallet.

"I've got both our passports. Look, I'm putting them in this little pouch I wear around my neck," Honey said. "Don't you remember them now?"

Leonard shook his head to indicate a sad no.

"Our driver's licenses and credit cards are in there too. Everything else we need is in this carry-on bag. And we both know you don't carry a wallet anymore."

"Oh, right," Leonard said. "Good, good. I don't want to try to keep track of all that stuff. But there is one thing I need to tell you, pumpkin."

"What's that, sweetie?"

He looked at her like he didn't want to confess.

"Come on now, sweetie. You can tell me."

It took Leonard a while but he finally blurted out, "I've never been on an airplane before."

"Oh, my stars," Honey said, looking at him to make sure he wasn't joking. One look in his eyes told her he was serious as an oxygen mask. She had to be careful about his male ego. Why wouldn't he have told her this before?

"Then this is a big day," Honey recovered. "I can't believe I didn't know that. How have you never been on a plane?"

"It's not that I didn't want to go," he said. "The wife would never go. She never went anywhere except to church. After she died, I just . . ."

"Now, now, there's no need to explain. Lots of people have never flown. This just makes it that much more exciting. Doing something you always wanted to do is pretty much what we're all about, isn't it?"

Leonard nodded in agreement, and a smile began to morph out of his stern countenance.

"You are in for the time of your life, Leonard Atkins. Remember what a thrill riding the train used to be? Well, flying is like taking the train, only you blast off into the sky like a spaceship in the movies. I haven't flown since a couple years before the doctor died. It's a wonderful experience. You go up and up until you're through the clouds, and then the sun is shining bright. It's so invigorating."

Leonard looked like he was trying to get in the mood but he was a little pale. The notion of flying was already making him airsick.

Honey handed him a Milky Way bar. "Are you scared?"

Leonard unwrapped the chocolate bar and took a big bite. "Scared wouldn't be the right word. I am a little nervous and excited but I'm not scared. I guess I'm amazed to actually take a plane ride. I've wanted to ever since Lindy took The Spirit of St. Louis all the way across the ocean."

"When was that?"

Leonard chewed thoughtfully on the chocolate. "That was in May of 1927."

"I'm amazed you remember the month."

"Oh, yeah. I was ten years old, almost eleven. I was just starting to pay attention to girls. Lindbergh was the biggest thing that ever happened. School was almost out for the summer, and we were listening to 'Ain't She Sweet' on the radio whenever we could get a channel to come in clearly. 'Yes I ask you very confidentially, ain't she sweet?'" Leonard sang loudly enough for people nearby to notice. Honey hugged him hard. She loved the way he remembered all the lyrics to the best old songs. If they ever had to go through a competency hearing, all he'd have to do is get up to sing a song or two.

Leonard was still humming "Ain't She Sweet" as they boarded the plane and took their large, leather seats in first class. They buckled up just in time for the flight attendant to bring them each a tall, thin glass of champagne. The rest of the passengers shuffled to their cheap seats in the rear.

Leonard looked puzzled as Honey clinked his glass in a toast.

"What's with all this?" he said, turning around to watch the flight attendant drawing the curtains on the economy class. "Why's she closing the curtains? Look back there. Those people don't have big seats like we do. I'll bet they're not getting champagne either. What's going on, Honey? What did we do to deserve all this?"

"Every age has its compensations," Honey said. "People take care of us because we're old and in love. Why do you think Boy Scouts help little old ladies across the road?"

Leonard fumbled with his seat belt. "I don't feel old. The last time some kid tried to help me at the store I told him to get lost."

Honey clicked the seat belt into its socket. "Boy Scouts help old people so they can feel good about themselves and do their duty and earn merit badges."

"And so they can look good doing it," Leonard groused. "But what I'm talking about is this class thing. I don't know what happened to the America I grew up in where everybody was supposed to be equal."

"I know, I know," Honey said. "People with money get all the breaks. But you worked hard all your life to become wealthy and now you're quite generous."

"Well, we never had much when my brother and I were growing up. Now that I've got money, I don't really feel that much different." He turned around again to look back at the people in economy class. "It doesn't feel right that some people get champagne and some don't."

The 747's engines began to roar as the plane started being towed backwards. Leonard had the window seat. He pressed his face against the glass. "Honey," he said, "we're going backwards and this thing doesn't have any wings. Look, I mean it. This thing has no wings."

"Don't be silly, Sweetie. They're towing us backwards. Look behind us, you'll see the wings. We're too far in the front of the plane to see them unless you look way back. Look way back. Do you see them?"

Leonard looked toward the back of the plane. "Oh, yeah, I see them now, but this thing still doesn't look like it should be able to fly."

Honey could feel Leonard tensing up so she tried to distract him. "Now, where is that lovely Jennifer? Excuse me miss," she said to the flight attendant with the champagne. "Where is Jennifer?"

"You mean our Jennifer, the flight attendant?"

Honey shook her head. "Yes, she helped us with our boarding passes."

"She's in the rear of the aircraft. Would you like me to get her for you?"

"No, that won't be necessary right now," Honey said. She turned to Leonard, "See, sweetie, Jennifer's on the plane. She knows everything will be fine, so don't you worry."

Leonard put on a brave face as the plane taxied into takeoff position and waited. A bell rang. Then two more bells chimed. The engines whined to a fever pitch, and the plane began shaking as it turned onto the runway and stopped again.

"I suppose they're waiting for clearance to take off," Leonard said.

"Oh, my, you do know a lot for a first time flier."

After much too long a wait for any nervous flyer's comfort, the plane started rolling forward and began picking up speed. Honey grabbed Leonard's hand and they both squeezed tightly as the plane lifted off and began gaining altitude at a steep angle. Honey made no comment but she could see Leonard was holding his breath. He had his eyes mostly closed except for the occasional sideways glance out the window.

Once the plane began to level and Leonard had opened his eyes, Honey said, "See how easy? Isn't this the best?"

Leonard relaxed his grip and let out a sigh of relief. Honey thought for sure he was going to begin complaining about something to cover up the emotions he had just experienced. Instead he said, "You know why it's better to die in a plane crash than in a nursing home?"

Honey laughed, glad to see he was in good humor. The flight attendants and several passengers had heard the set up and were waiting for the punch line. Honey was only too happy to play straight man, "No, why is it better to die in a plane crash than in a nursing home?"

"You only crap your pants once in a plane crash."

FOUR

THE EXHILARATION of his first flight, combined with several glasses of champagne, put Leonard in a storytelling mood. Honey sighed deeply and relaxed. His stories always made her feel like a little girl, especially the ones about the old days. She and Leonard had completely forgotten about being fugitives. Yet, at that very moment, their absence was being duly noted.

It took the nursing home until 10 a.m. to call the police. They searched the premises thoroughly before calling in what might have been either an escape or a kidnapping. The Wabash County police had launched several costly manhunts in recent years only to locate missing persons in on-site closets or trashbins.

Once Prosecutor Lindvall heard the report of Leonard's absence, she drove directly to Honey's home to investigate. She didn't need a search warrant. Honey would invite her inside.

The front door was locked. No one answered the four-chime bell or her persistent knocking. Now she might need a warrant. Or, she could say she was worried about Honey being injured inside and unable to answer the door.

The back door was closed but unlocked. "Anybody home?" she called out as she entered cautiously. Nobody answered, even after she loudly repeated the question.

The house was neat and tidy but unoccupied. It smelled like an apple pie had recently been baked. The prosecutor began looking for clues. In the upstairs bathroom, she found Leonard's wet pajamas hanging on a hook outside the shower. She laughed out loud as she thought about Honey and Leonard playing in the shower. "Good for them," she thought as she went down the stairs and through the kitchen to check the garage.

Once she realized the Cadillac was gone, the prosecutor used Honey's kitchen phone to call the sheriff. Much as she loved Honey and the thought of her romance with Leonard, the prosecutor had a job to do, and right now that job was to find Honey and Leonard. She didn't think to notify the airports. She was fairly certain the two lovebirds would be found cruising the country roads around Leonard's farmland. He owned hundreds of acres although he no longer farmed the land himself.

Maria Gomez from Adult Protective heard the news nearly as quickly as the prosecutor. She was in the sheriff's office with Leonard's niece, Gretchen Atkins, by noon. The two were complaining loudly to the receptionist that not enough was being done to locate Leonard. Sheriff Donald Peterson decided it was time to come out of his office. He buttoned his shirt and adjusted his badge as he walked to the counter. "What can I do for you ladies?"

Gretchen leaned over the counter and raised her voice. "For starters, you can find my uncle. He's off with that Honey Waldrop. She's kidnapped him for sure."

Sheriff Peterson wasn't about to be intimidated in his own office. He leaned into Gretchen close enough for her to smell his coffee breath. "What makes you say that?"

Gretchen leaned back as Mrs. Gomez stepped up to enter the fray. "We heard the prosecutor checked Honey's house and her Cadillac's gone."

Now it was the sheriff's turn to step back. He looked over his shoulder and then back at Mrs. Gomez. "Where'd you hear that?"

Gretchen leaped back into action. "It's all over your radios."

The sheriff held both hands up, palms out. "Maybe she went grocery shopping."

Gretchen hissed in his face. "The only shopping Honey does is for rich old fools who don't know a gold digger when they see one coming."

"I'd be careful calling Leonard Atkins an old fool," the sheriff said. "He's been a friend of mine for more than forty years and he's not that much older than me."

"That doesn't change the fact that you got a missing person report on him from the nursing home more than two hours ago," Ms. Gomez said.

"She tried to poison my uncle." Gretchen stomped both feet. "And she's run off with him in violation of a court order."

The sheriff half smiled at her temper tantrum. "Who says they're together?"

"Anybody with half a brain!" Ms. Gomez shouted.

With that, the sheriff stiffened and escorted the two women out of his office, advising them he would arrest them for interfering with a police investigation if they continued to insult his intelligence. He had a woman in each hand. "We'll do everything we can do to locate Leonard."

As they were leaving the building, Gretchen said loudly enough for the sheriff to hear, "Looks like we'll have to track them down on our own."

The sheriff shook his head and walked back into his office. He knew their complaints were valid, but that didn't mean he had to listen to them.

Gretchen had plenty of resources to organize a search. As Leonard's Power of Attorney, she had access to his entire fortune. She resolved to take matters into her own hands.

Once Gretchen and Ms. Gomez were gone, the sheriff called in reports from his officers. Nobody had located Leonard or Honey, but one deputy had learned that an elderly couple had been detained briefly in the middle of the night, heading south on the Interstate.

"That's it," the sheriff pounded his desk and addressed his chief deputy. "They're headed for the airport in Indy. Better notify the Federal Aviation Administration and Airport Security." As he leaned back in his high-back leather chair, the sheriff mused out loud. "You got to love Leonard. I'd have thought he was too old for this kind of tomfoolery. Guess he's proving me wrong again. He always was a straight shooter but he never did give a hoot about the law.

"By the way," the sheriff called out to the chief deputy, "wait a couple hours before you call the airplane people. No harm in giving Leonard a little head start."

Meanwhile, Leonard was telling stories at 30,000 feet, halfway to New York City and a flight connection to Paris, France.

"When I was a boy, working the farm with my daddy, we had to deal with what they now call the Great Depression. We didn't call it that, at first. Nobody knew how bad it was going to be or how long it would last. I remember asking my father about the stock market and what it was that made it crash. We were baling hay at the time. He stopped our Farmall tractor right there in the middle of the field. I knew it was important. He sat down and talked to me like I was a man. I couldn't have been more than fourteen years old, but he talked to me like a man. And, for the first time, I saw fear in his eyes. I'd never seen daddy afraid before, but this time I could feel it in my bones. Especially when he talked about how we could lose the farm if the bank in North Manchester failed. That's the first time I knew that even a farmer needed a bank to get along.

"Anyway, I didn't understand much of what he tried to explain, but in the next couple of years things got real tough all over. Our house was less than a quarter mile from the railroad tracks that went to Chicago. Lots of guys riding the rails in those days, and it didn't take long for word to get around that my mother would feed anybody who came to her back door and asked for food. Daddy never let them make camp on our land but he didn't stand in the way when momma fed them. Some days she'd feed more than a dozen men, and not just scraps. She fed them steak and eggs and biscuits with gravy and gave them big glasses of fresh milk. Even let them get water and clean up at the well behind the cow barn."

Leonard looked over Honey's shoulder and could see his fellow passengers were listening. He raised his voice so they wouldn't miss his conclusion. "We never got robbed, not once. Those guys were all decent men, looking for work. Daddy hired a few of them for short-term work."

"What about your mother?" Honey asked. "What did she say about her free kitchen?"

Leonard leaned back in his seat and lowered his voice to a reverential tone. "My mother was a generous soul. She taught my brother, Daniel, and me what she called the secret to a happy life."

"You mean the secret to happiness?" Honey asked, loud enough for most of the first class section to hear.

"That's right, the secret to happiness," Leonard said, making her wait for it.

Honey giggled. "Well, come on. I'm sure we'd all like to know. What is the secret to happiness?"

"You already know it," Leonard teased.

Jennifer, the flight attendant, came up from the back of the plane, "What's this I hear about the secret to happiness?"

"Leonard was just about to tell us," Honey said, hugging her. "I'm glad you're here to hear it."

Leonard grinned and held out his hand for Jennifer. "Now, I forget what we were talking about."

"Don't you do that to us," Honey laughed, pushing his shoulder.

Leonard sat up straight in his seat, smiling as he realized several rows of passengers were listening. "All right. Here it is, the secret to happiness. Are you sure you're ready?"

Honey beamed as she took his hand. "Yes, we're more than ready."

Leonard raised her hand like she had just won a boxing match. "Okay then, here it is. The secret to happiness is to help other people."

Honey beamed at Jennifer, who passed on the smile to the passengers who had tuned in to the Leonard show.

"I think that is absolutely correct," Jennifer said. "It is that simple. I always feel best about myself when I'm helping someone else."

"Then you should feel pretty good about yourself," Leonard said, "for all the help you and your friend gave us today."

"You've been an angel," Honey agreed.

After landing in New York City, Jennifer helped Honey and Leonard make their way to the next boarding gate. They were almost too late for the flight to Paris so they boarded immediately. Leonard looked around to see if any law enforcement agents were around to apprehend them. "I can't believe we're getting away with this trip to Paris. I thought they'd have us by Indianapolis. We haven't been covering our trail at all. We bought the tickets in our real names."

"What's the worst they could do to us if they did catch us?" Honey asked.

"They could keep us apart."

"Oh, dear. Then we'd better keep moving," Honey said.

Their plane from New York to Paris had leveled off over the Atlantic Ocean before the Wabash County Sheriff's Department called the F.A.A.

Maria Gomez used her adult protective credentials to convince the Federal Bureau of Investigation that an elderly man had been kidnapped and was in mortal danger. It didn't take the F.B.I. long to discover Honey and Leonard's flight plan. They tried to make arrangements to have officers lie in wait in Paris, but French officials were less than enthusiastic about becoming involved in the case. The French never did like Americans telling them what to do. And an elderly couple flying to Paris didn't seem like much of a threat to national security.

Honey and Leonard had no trouble sleeping through most of the flight to Paris. Being up all night and topping that off with several glasses of champagne put them out like a light. Honey slept with her head on Leonard's shoulder. He rested his head on top of hers. The flight attendant threw one blanket over the two of them.

Once they landed in Paris, Jennifer helped them through customs and got them a cab, saying to the driver, "Hotel Frontenac, please."

"You've got a reservation for two nights," she said to Honey as they hugged goodbye. "And you've got my number at the airline. They can always track me down. I'm off to Singapore so I won't be seeing you for a while. I'll look you up next time I'm in Indianapolis. Goodbye, Leonard, take good care of our girl. Have a wonderful time in Paris."

Less than an hour after saying goodbye to Honey and Leonard, Jennifer found herself being interrogated by a stern, baldheaded man from airline security. She told them she had never met a more delightful couple. She also said Leonard seemed in complete control of his mental faculties and that Honey was in no way exerting control over him.

"Am I in trouble for helping them?" she asked.

The security man ran his fingers through the hair he no longer had. "Not as long as you didn't know they were on the run."

The cab driver took off in a hurry. Honey squeezed Leonard's arm. "Can you believe it? Here we are in France with our own French driver, heading into Paris. It's a dream come true. Our dream is coming true."

"You are my dream come true," Leonard said as he kissed her tenderly. "I never met a woman who could make things happen as fast as you. I don't know how you came up with those airplane girls. I don't know what we would have done without them."

Honey snuggled closer. "Somebody else would have come along. Don't you see, sweetie? We've got love on our side."

Leonard caught the driver checking them out in the rearview mirror. He patted the man on the shoulder. "Hey, there. Thanks for the lift. Do you speak English?"

The driver shook his head yes and no at the same time. "A little bit."

"That's all we need," Leonard said. "We're looking for the Eiffel Tower."

"Yes, yes, I take you there," the driver said. "Is near hotel."

It didn't take long before Honey and Leonard were surrounded by the magic of Paris. By the time the Eiffel Tower came into view, Honey was bouncing on the seat like a little girl.

"There it is. Oh, my stars, there it is. It looks like a postcard. I feel like I'm floating into a postcard. The Eiffel Tower looks even prettier than the pictures. It's taller than I thought it would be. And look at all the buildings. They look like fancy birthday cakes. And the cafés with the awnings. Everything looks so French. Oh, my, we'd better get to the hotel fast. I'm so excited I'm going to wet my pants."

The driver must have understood her body language because he got them to the hotel in a hurry. Honey paid him in French currency and tipped him handsomely. Jennifer had helped her exchange quite a bit of money in the airport.

They checked into the hotel, found their room and fell into bed with their clothes on for an exhausted nap.

Leonard awakened in a golden room. He sat on the edge of the bed and wondered where he was. The sun was streaming through a tall window, making the flocked wallpaper glow. He thought he might be dead. Everything was so peaceful and full of light. It felt like he might be in heaven.

He didn't notice Honey still sleeping in the bed. The window had captured his attention. It was outlined in shining silver, its see-through curtains flowing in a slight breeze as if beckoning him with the outstretched arms of angels.

Suddenly, and for no good reason, he was afraid of the window. Its allure became menacing and it began to feel like a trap. He began to feel cold.

Where am I? What has happened to me?

He checked his arms and legs to make sure he still had a body and got up slowly to move away from the window. He heard his mother calling him from far away.

Why is mother calling?

The voice seemed to be coming from the window. Despite his fear, Leonard moved toward the sound of his mother's voice. The window and its curtains sucked him into the light of his own confusion. His heart was racing as he looked through the window screen and tried to understand where he was and what he was doing there. It was a terrible feeling, not knowing.

The scenery was no help at all. It was totally unfamiliar and unnerving. He was lost, inside and out, until he heard the soothing voice of his mother. "Leonard, it's time for bed."

"Mother, where are you? I can't see you."

"I'm right here. I'm always with you. You know how much I love you. But it is time for bed."

"I need to see you so you can tuck me in and give me a kiss goodnight."

He felt a kiss on his forehead and then heard the voice say, "Sleep tight, my son. You don't need to see me. Sleep tight. Tomorrow's going to be another big day."

"What's happening to me?" he asked his mother. "I feel like I'm losing my mind."

"Don't worry about losing what you think is your mind," his mother said softly. "The mind is much more than you think. We all become a part of it eventually."

"When we die?"

"Nobody ever dies," his mother said. "We simply escape the illusion, the prison, of self."

"So what do I do until then?"

"Be happy with what you got."

Leonard chuckled at hearing her favorite saying. He didn't sound like himself. His half-laugh sounded like it was coming from far away.

His mother's voice felt comforting. Then she was gone, without saying goodbye. He was alone again. He felt like someone else, someone he didn't know, someone he wasn't supposed to be. He couldn't remember who he was. His mother was gone. He could no longer feel her love. He was sweating and confused. Nothing made sense.

His anxiety began to rise until he heard what he thought was his mother's voice again. This time it came from behind him. He turned and saw a woman in his bed. It wasn't his mother at all.

I know this woman. I know I know her. Why can't I recognize her?

"Leonard, it's me. It's Honey. Wake up, sleepy head. You're dreaming."

He could feel the woman shaking him and calling herself "Honey." He still couldn't remember how he knew her. She helped him sit down on the bed and brought him a glass of water. He gulped down the entire drink and looked at the woman sadly.

"Thank you. I needed that. I thought you were my mother. Who are you? Are you an angel?"

"Leonard, it's me, Honey. We just flew to Paris and now we're in our hotel room. You just woke up. You're a little confused. Don't worry, you'll be fine."

Leonard looked out the window from his seat on the bed and saw his mother waving to him from the curtains. She was young and beautiful. As he waved back, she disappeared. His mind began to slowly refocus. The woman who brought him the glass of water was talking about things he didn't understand. He wasn't really listening to anything she said. He was straining to hear the voice of his mother again.

"She's gone," he said. "Mother's gone."

Honey got him up and off the bed and walked him back to the window. Her warm touch started to bring him back to reality. It took a while but the woman began to convince him they were in France.

"Come into the bathroom," she said. "I can prove it. Look

in here. See that thing that looks like a toilet but isn't a toilet at all? That's a bidet. You know about these. Look, it has water that comes up from the basin to clean your bottom. You've never seen one of these in Indiana, have you? That's because you're in France now. This is a bidet, and we're in Paris. I'm Honey, and you love me. Just remember, do not go to the bathroom in the bidet. That's not what it's for."

Leonard had to laugh at her presentation, and as he did, he began to remember who she was. His memory came back to him like frames in a reel of film that start off as still pictures and then gradually turn into fluid motion as the reel speeds up.

"Honey," he said as he recognized her. "I thought you were my mother."

Honey pulled her hair back into a ponytail and then let it fall over her shoulders. "I am definitely not your mother."

Leonard blinked his eyes as he watched her hair play. "How long have I been gone?"

Honey took his hands in hers. "Not that long. How long have you been awake? I was sleeping."

Leonard was deeply shaken. These mental lapses were getting to be as bad as seizures. He never knew when they were coming and he never knew how long they would last. His biggest fear was that the next one would take him out for good. And that would take his love away.

What is wrong with me?

He knew he was repeating himself a lot. Honey always told him about that. And he knew he was having trouble coming up with words when he needed them. All that was normal for a person his age. What he didn't know was when he would suddenly feel lost and afraid again.

Honey directed him to sit on the bed and sat down beside him. "Do you remember how we got here?"

"Not really. I mean, wait a second. I do remember the Eiffel Tower. We were in a taxi. Yes, we were coming from the airport and there was that lovely young woman, what was her name?"

"Jennifer."

"Ah, yes, Jennifer. She was pretty much our guardian angel for the entire flight. Where is she now?"

Honey jumped up and turned to face him, taking his head in her hands. "See, your memory is fine. All it takes is me to bring it back. Do you remember why we came to France in the first place?"

"Yes, I do," Leonard said as he began to regain his confidence. "My niece Gretchen is trying to get me declared incompetent and she's trying to get you charged with murder."

"Attempted murder," Honey said. "You're still alive. And you're my star witness."

His face lightened up. His frown turned into a wry grin. Suddenly, the light bulb turned on in his troubled mind. He looked at Honey as she tried to talk him back into his own memory. Now, he knew what she was doing. Now, he knew what she'd been up to all along.

"You're about ten steps ahead of me," he said.

Honey danced backwards into the bathroom entrance. "Make that twenty steps ahead."

Leonard stood up. "No, I see what you're doing. We're taking this trip so you can prove I'm competent and so you can prove you would never try to hurt me."

"Well, at least now I know you're competent," Honey said. "I was beginning to think you thought we were just running away."

Leonard looked at her and realized he had never loved anyone so deeply. She could change in an instant from his favorite little girl into his most cherished lover. He loved her every incarnation. She kept him on his toes, emotionally, physically, and intellectually. She gave herself to him unconditionally and would accept nothing

less in return. The best thing about her was that she loved him
with all her heart. That made him feel quite a bit better about who
he was and what he was doing.

"I never ran away from anything in my life," Leonard said.
"It just started looking like it was high time for me to take you to
Paris. I didn't run away from that nursing home. I walked away.
I made a choice. *We* made a choice. We chose love and we chose
Paris, and now, here we are, together in Paris. It's magic, I tell you.
It's pure magic."

Honey embraced him. "Take me dancing, you big, strong,
beautiful man."

"Let's take a shower first. Paris can wait."

———————

Honey and Leonard asked for no directions at the hotel desk before
floating out, hand in hand, onto the exciting streets of Paris. In two
blocks they found themselves on the Champs-Elysees, marveling
at the grand avenue and the sculptured walls of the buildings
along the way. Stone carvings of human faces and fruits and
lutes decorated every nook and cranny of the historic structures.
Restaurants with outdoor seating were everywhere. The smell of
pastry was in the air. Most of the cafés had all the chairs facing the
street.

"Looks like theater seating," Leonard said. "Must be some
kind of show going on."

"We're the show," Honey laughed as she took him in both
her arms and pressed her face into his chest. "It's love on parade.
Everybody wants to see that."

They passed a young couple dressed completely in black. They
weren't arm in arm or even holding hands. They were much too
Goth for any show of affection. Honey had to throw herself against
Leonard to get him to stop staring.

"Did you see that girl?" he asked after they had passed. "She has rings all over her face, rings on her nose, rings on her lower lip and rings on both her eyebrows. She looks like a cannibal headhunter."

"That's the new thing," Honey said. "Kids don't just pierce their ears anymore. They pierce everything."

Leonard stopped dead in his tracks, horrified at the thought. "You mean all that jewelry was holes in her face?"

Honey nodded.

"How can she eat? How can she wash her face? My Lord, how can she blow her nose? Wouldn't everything come out the hole?"

Honey laughed.

"No, really, I'm not kidding. Did you see her? She had rings on her eyebrows. Big ones. They have to get in her eyes. Why would anyone do that?"

"They're just kids, sweetie. They're out to change the world. They do things to shock their parents. It's perfectly normal. We did it too. We had Benny Goodman and swing and the jitterbug and dance marathons."

"There's nothing normal about putting metal through holes in your face," Leonard snorted. "And I never did the jitterbug until after the war."

Honey grabbed both his hands and started dancing, pushing him away, then pulling him back, and then twirling completely around with one hand in the air. Leonard put his complaining aside and got caught up in the moment; spinning and strutting his own dance moves. In an instant, they felt young again, leading each other around an ornamental light pole and putting on quite a dancing demonstration as they pranced into the street together. Traffic slowed to avoid and admire the impromptu performance. Their dancing wasn't as fast or energetic as it had once been, but they still looked good, even in slower motion. They'd danced enough together to be able to spin each other completely backwards and around while still holding hands.

The couple dressed in black had returned and stood on the sidewalk watching the older folks having a good time dancing. Honey saw them gawking and broke away from Leonard to grab the young man by both hands. At first, he stiffened in surprise, but Honey was not about to take "no" for an answer. He couldn't help but follow her back into the street, dancing quite smoothly along the way.

The young girl held out her tattooed hands. Leonard forgot his prejudices for the moment. He took her hands and was soon spinning dance moves with her like the air was filled with big band jazz music. Traffic had now stopped completely. Leonard started singing. So did Honey and the younger dancers. Each was singing a different song, but it didn't matter. The two couples moved around each other like they were finalists in a dance competition. The four of them even joined hands for a jitterbug circle. Their spontaneous joy was catching. A waiter from the nearest restaurant waved a towel over his head with a hoot. Drivers got out of their cars to cheer them on. A small crowd of onlookers assembled on the sidewalk, amazed to see the generations coming together through the language of dance.

Horns began to blare from trucks in the rear of the backed-up line of traffic. The dancers twirled each other back to the side-walk.

The young man was the first to run out of breath. He'd been the most energetic dancer. His hipness had been yearning to bust a move for way too long. He danced like a dog off the chain, a dog with plenty of sexual energy to burn.

The two couples wound down the dancing, breathing hard and laughing. Each of them was pleased and satisfied to have participated in such a joyous, surprise event. They had brought their own little corner of Paris to a standstill.

The celebration conversation couldn't last long because of the language barrier, but they communicated quite well with hugs and high fives. They said goodbye for a short time and then walked away. No phone numbers were exchanged. Their dance had been a once-in-a-lifetime happening.

Something important had happened to the younger couple, although they were only beginning to feel it. Their impromptu jitterbug with the older couple had given them a glimpse of something they had previously regarded as corny and unattainable. By the time they walked away, the Goth couple was holding hands. Their days of being tragically cool and detached were over, although they hadn't realized it yet.

Honey and Leonard sat down for a coffee and lunch. A break in the action was what they needed. They would be paying tourist prices for the meal but they didn't really care.

"See now, sweetie," Honey said. "She was a lot more interesting and sensitive and fun than she looked like at first."

Leonard shook out the folded napkin and placed it on his lap. "The girl was so beautiful when she smiled. Now, if she'd only get rid of all those piercings."

Honey broke off a piece of French bread and handed it to Leonard. "It won't be long until she's having babies of her own. Nothing like a child grabbing at your face to make the piercings go away."

Leonard laughed at her imagery. He thought for a moment and commented, "Those kids could dance. Where did they learn to jitterbug?"

Honey reached for the butter. "Everybody knows how to dance. We just had to give them a little encouragement. By the way, did you see they were holding hands when they left?"

"I did notice that. They'll probably get married and settle down and have four kids and always talk about that crazy, old, American couple in Paris that made them fall in love."

"Don't laugh," Honey said. "Love is contagious."

After a delightful quiche lorraine meal, Honey and Leonard had a little trouble getting up and out of their chairs. Their muscles had gotten stiff from sitting down and eating after the dance work out. Laughing at each other's groaning, they did a few painful stretches, loosened up, and began walking down the Champs-Elysees to the circle around the Arc de Triomphe. The luxury specialty shops held no attraction for them. They were more interested in the canopy of clipped horse chestnut trees that lined their path.

Leonard was determined to see the Arc that had welcomed parading armies from Napoleon III to Charles de Gaulle. "The best thing about it," he said, "is The Tomb of the Unknown Soldier from World War I. That's right beneath the Arc. It has an eternal flame."

Honey grabbed his arm and stopped him in his tracks. "How do you know all this?"

Leonard crouched down so he could look her in the eye. "I love to read. All my life I've loved to read. What? You think farmers don't read? Ever heard of *The Farmer's Almanac*?"

Honey laughed and marveled at her man's ability to dredge up tidbits of historical information from things he'd read years earlier. How strange that he could know so much at one moment and forget so much in the next.

As Honey and Leonard arrived at the circular traffic jam around the Arc, cars from all directions were forming a seamless web of horn-blowing, tire-squealing chaos. It looked like a merry-go-round that was spinning too fast to catch a ride. The smell of burning grease and gasoline hung in the air like a sooty fog. They didn't know about the underground walkways beneath the traffic that allow pedestrians safe passage to the Arc. All they knew was the Arc was right in front of them in all its glory and, by God, they were going to get to it, traffic be damned.

"Sweetie," I don't think this is a good idea," Honey said as he grabbed her hand and prepared to make a dash.

Leonard kept his eyes on the traffic. "Nonsense, pumpkin. What's that you always say about helping little old ladies across the street? Just let me help you. These cars will stop. All we need is a break in the action."

Honey assessed the situation. Both she and Leonard were wearing cross-training footwear, the same shoes that had just jitterbugged on the Champs-Elysees. They were both still pretty mobile thanks to their dancing and swimming and yoga classes. But they weren't fast runners by any means.

The cars are only going twenty miles an hour. They could stop in time, couldn't they? So, why not make a dash for it? There are four lanes of traffic. All we really have to do is take it one lane at a time.

"Okay, let's go for it," Honey said.

"Look, here we go, come on," Leonard urged as he pulled her onto the cobblestone circle to make it through a break in the traffic.

Honey moved quickly to keep up and immediately tripped on the uneven surface of the road. She felt herself flying into a major fall until Leonard grabbed her right arm to keep her from going down and to keep them both moving forward. He heaved her up like he was throwing a bale of hay onto a wagon.

By the time she regained her balance and was finally standing upright, they were stopped and stuck between the second and third rings of traffic from the center. They were surrounded by blaring horns. The air was chokingly thick with the stench of internal combustion. Cabs and cars and trucks were swerving dangerously to avoid hitting them.

They realized it had been a terrible mistake to try and cross through this much traffic. Honey couldn't see any way out of the predicament they had gotten themselves into. The drivers were negotiating a tight circle so they couldn't see pedestrians until it was too late to stop.

"Leonard!" Honey screamed as an overloaded lorry screeched on its brakes and went into a sideways skid, stopping less than two feet from her face.

"He's blocking for us," Leonard yelled as he pulled Honey across the final two lanes of traffic.

The lorry had formed a barrier across the two inner lanes of traffic. Cars screeched to a stop to avoid hitting the lorry. One cab slammed into the rear dual tires of the stopped truck but didn't do any damage.

"*Vive la France,*" Leonard shouted from the safety of the sidewalk island as he held up both arms to indicate a touchdown had just been scored.

The lorry driver grinned wildly as he straightened out his truck and got going again with a gear-grinding lurch. He flashed the peace sign as Leonard screamed, "You saved our lives! You're our hero!"

Honey went to find a place to sit down. She felt too light-headed and nauseated to be exhilarated by their narrow escape. She still saw the truck about to run them over. She could still smell the burning rubber from its sideways slide. She began to feel uncertain about the escape to Paris.

"I don't know if this trip was such a great idea," she said as they sat down on a green, wooden bench.

Leonard realized it was his turn to take up the slack. "You sound like me in the Indianapolis airport. You slapped some sense into me when I was down. Now, what am I going to do to get you back on track?"

He hugged her as they both tried to catch their breath. "I'm sorry I dragged you into all that. I wasn't thinking right. Here I am, having a ball dodging traffic, and you're scared to death. I am sorry. I should have my head examined."

"At least you caught me before I hit the bricks, face first," Honey said. "I'm always surprised by how strong you are. If you hadn't grabbed me, I would not be sitting here talking to you. Those crazy drivers would have run me over a dozen times."

She took a couple deep breaths and looked up at the blue sky as she started getting herself back together. She began speaking in an exaggerated southern drawl. "No, I won't think about how close I came to meeting my maker. I think I'll just be grateful to my knight in shining armor for saving me on the streets of Paris, France."

Then, she turned serious and said, "You know what's good about us, Leonard?"

"I know a bunch of things."

"No, what's good about us is when one of us gets down the other one always seems to be up. We're a good team that way. We balance each other out. It's not always me who has to be strong. All my years with the doctor, rest his soul, it was always me who had to take the lead. I mean, he was the boss at his work, but when he came home, it was always me who had to make the rest of our lives happen. With you, it's just . . . I don't know. We seem to do things together."

Leonard took her hand and kissed it. He seemed lost in thought.

Honey tried to bring him back. "What?"

Leonard sighed deeply and looked at her with tears welling up in his eyes. "It's odd you should talk about your marriage like that. You know, I loved my wife dearly, but I swear that woman never took the lead on anything, especially after our daughter died. Even cooking. She was a great cook but she always asked what I wanted and then she made it. I'm glad it's not like that for us. We're a team. Don't you think it's perfect we're getting a second chance to work things out?"

"Yes, I do, Mr. Atkins. Yes, I do," Honey said, standing up. "Now let's go see that eternal flame you've been talking about."

FIVE

THREE SEPARATE FORCES were in pursuit of Honey and Leonard by the time they were dancing and dodging traffic in the streets of Paris.

Gretchen Atkins, Leonard's niece and Power of Attorney, hired a private investigator out of Indianapolis named Adam Wolfe. She paid Wolfe a $10,000 retainer from Leonard's checking account and let the investigator know there was more where that came from. Wolfe was on a plane to Paris the day after Honey and Leonard's departure.

It took two days for Maria Gomez from Adult Protective to convince the FBI to put an agent on the case. That didn't have any immediate impact on the chase. The agent soon realized the French police would be no help at all in locating the elderly lovebirds in flight. In fact, once *The Chicago Tribune* reported Honey and Leonard had fled to France, the French news media picked up the story in a big way. Honey and Leonard were front-page news, breaking news, their faces and names all over the paper and on every television channel. French readers and viewers and radio listeners were cheering for the elderly couple, laughing at the fools in the USA who were trying to capture them. It took a week for the French police to get motivated and that was only after the press started making fun of them and calling for the Pink Panther to get on the case.

The third force after Honey and Leonard was the reporter

who made their love story front-page news in the first place, Jack Crumbo of *The Chicago Tribune*. Never, in his twenty-five years of reporting, had one of his stories caught fire like this one. It was old folks in love. It had elder law and criminal consequences.

Any new angle he could come up with was making headlines across the nation and flooding his publication with reader response. After breaking the story, he developed news sources through several trips to Honey and Leonard's hometown. He quickly became the recognized expert on North Manchester, Indiana, and its most intriguing couple.

Television reporters were interviewing Crumbo about every aspect of the case, particularly the alleged poisoning of Leonard and the no-contact order against Honey. Two publishers and an agent called about possible book deals. Someone from The American Association of Retired Persons offered him a job.

It didn't take long for Honey's Attorney, Robert Nimmo, to take his case to the press. Nimmo had been a newspaper reporter before law school, so he knew it would be best to give an "exclusive" to the guys who buy ink by the barrel. He met Jack Crumbo of *The Chicago Tribune* at a North Manchester park the day after Honey and Leonard's unscheduled departure

Nimmo was leaning against an Oak tree when Crumbo parked his 1984 Chevy Caprice and got out of the car to stand up stiffly. "Attorney Nimmo I presume?"

Nimmo walked to the car and shook Crumbo's hand. "That's me. Better known as Honey's lawyer. Thanks for coming on such short notice. You're the only one I trust with what I've got to say."

Crumbo grabbed a reporter's notebook and a pen out of his car. "Why don't we grab a picnic table and you can tell me all about it."

The two men walked a few yards to the nearest table and sat down on opposite sides. Nimmo looked over his shoulder and returned his attention to Crumbo. "I'm sure you're wondering why I called."

Crumbo put his pad on the table and held his pen at the ready. "I'm not in the business of making guesses."

Nimmo shifted his weight on the bench and shook the table slightly.

"The first thing you need to know is Honey did not poison Leonard."

Crumbo put down his pen. "Imagine a defense attorney telling me his client is innocent. I'm shocked. So, forgive me if I remain skeptical. Everybody tells me Honey didn't do it but nobody can prove it. And Gretchen Atkins keeps talking about Leonard's blood tests with the high arsenic levels."

Nimmo leaned across the picnic table. "Okay, we're off the record, right?"

"Right."

"This is strictly confidential?"

"Absolutely."

"Good," Nimmo said. "Because here it is. Proof that Honey did not poison Leonard."

Crumbo picked up his pen.

Nimmo looked over his shoulder again and began whispering. "I've got a good friend who's a forensic pathologist. I've hired him on the case, and he knew right away what it was."

Crumbo looked around the park and smiled. "What are you talking about? And why are you whispering and looking over your shoulder?"

Nimmo straightened up and began speaking in a normal volume. "All right, maybe I don't need to be such a secret agent. But attorneys can get in trouble for talking to the press about a case that's under investigation. Anyway, here it is. My forensic expert said the high levels of arsenic in Leonard's blood are most probably the result of his life as a farmer."

"I don't get it," Crumbo said as he began writing furiously in his notebook.

"Yes, you do. Farmers spend their life around pesticides. In the old days, the pesticides were loaded with arsenic. That's why Leonard has arsenic in his blood. Because he's a farmer, not because anybody tried to poison him."

"Whoa. That's a hell of a story, right there," Crumbo said. "I'll have to get my own pathology source since I can't quote you. That shouldn't be too hard. How long until your guy can go public with this?"

Nimmo stood up from the table and lit a cigarette. "It's going to take a while, weeks probably, maybe months. Getting the blood from Maria Gomez and Adult Protective will be tougher than stealing Dracula's midnight snack."

"Why not just take Leonard's blood?" Crumbo asked.

Nimmo looked at him to make sure he wasn't joking. "You mean you don't know?"

"Know what?"

"Honey and Leonard left town last night, early this morning. The sheriff called me a couple hours ago, looking for them. Now, I'm hearing the cops stopped them on the highway late last night and let them go because they didn't realize they were on the run."

Crumbo began fumbling with his own cigarettes and lighter and pen. "Holy shit. Where are they now?"

"I'm not sure. I heard something about a flight to Paris, but you'd better check that out with the sheriff."

Crumbo finally got a cigarette lit. "Paris, as in France?"

Nimmo lowered his voice again like he was Deep Throat in Watergate. "You got it. Evidently, they got tired of being kept apart in Indiana."

"What about the protective order?" Crumbo asked.

Nimmo became stern. "Honey is in clear violation if she's with him. It's a D Felony in Indiana, up to three years in jail. They charge it as Invasion of Privacy."

Crumbo thought about the legalities as he took a deep inhale on his cigarette and turned his head so as not to exhale in Nimmo's face. "What about Leonard?"

"Leonard's not doing anything wrong. The protective order is against her seeing him, not him seeing her. All he's doing is allegedly getting kidnapped and that's not a crime."

Crumbo couldn't believe the scoop he was getting. He asked flurries of questions and took copious notes before he had to leave to confirm the outrageous story. As he was heading toward his car, he asked Nimmo, "Why didn't you stop them?"

Nimmo held his hands up like he was being robbed. "They never told me they were leaving. All of a sudden, they were just gone. They left before I could get them news about why the arsenic was in his blood."

———————◆———————

It took two hours for Adam Wolfe, Gretchen's investigator, to connect with the taxi driver who had transported Honey and Leonard to their hotel in Paris. Wolfe was confident that tracking down an elderly couple would be child's play for him after his twenty years as a homicide detective in several different cities.

Upon landing in Paris, he hired the first attractive, bilingual woman he met and paid her enough to immediately quit her job at one of the airport bars. Wolfe and his new employee interviewed taxi drivers at the airport and found their man quickly. He recognized Honey and Leonard by the photos he was shown.

The driver accepted Wolfe's $150 bribe and proceeded to drop off the investigator and his interpreter at the wrong hotel on the opposite side of town. This would be the first of many bum steers Wolfe would get from people who had been charmed by Honey and Leonard's story and instinctively wanted to protect them.

By the time Wolfe suspected the taxi driver had misled him, he also realized the driver might have been pretending to recognize Honey and Leonard in order to make some easy money.

The investigator called back to Indianapolis from a pay phone to have his office do a credit card check on Honey and Leonard. Gretchen had provided him all the necessary account numbers and information. No Paris charges popped up. Honey was paying cash for everything.

Wolfe and his interpreter, Simone, began the tedious process of checking out all the hotels in Paris. It didn't take long for them to realize they had much in common. This was Paris and neither of them had a significant other. Simone was 15 years younger than the 50-year-old Wolfe. She was blonde, vivacious, and athletic. By the fourth hotel, she was beginning to remind him of a French movie star whose name he couldn't remember. Before he knew what was happening, the investigator was becoming more interested in chasing Simone than he was in completing his assignment.

———

Honey and Leonard set out walking from the Arc De Triomphe to The Louvre but ended up taking a cab. Honey could tell Leonard's feet were starting to bother him. He never complained, he just walked more slowly.

The ride was a welcome relief for her as well. They'd been running around Paris like a couple of teenagers on Spring break. Once the novelty of being in France began to wind down, the jet lag started taking its toll. They'd only slept a few hours in the last two days.

The back seat of the cab smelled delicious to her, like Cognac, good cigars, and French bread. The city of light and love rolled by in a kaleidoscope of statues and flowers and famous paintings come to life.

"Everything feels so bright and colorful," she cooed as she put her head on Leonard's shoulder.

"This is even better than I thought," Leonard agreed. "The whole street is one big art show. Look, there's a statue every twenty yards. Some are modern and crazy and others look like they're three hundred years old."

Honey caught the driver staring at them in the rear view mirror. "We love your city almost as much as we love each other," she said.

The driver laughed and began giving them detailed descriptions of the sights along the way. It didn't matter that he spoke little English or that he usually despised American tourists. Honey and Leonard were lighting up the back seat of his cab. The Frenchman became most animated when they came upon the Luxor Obelisk in the center of Place de la Concorde. He managed to explain, in broken English, that the 23-meter erection of yellow granite had been imported from Egypt in the 1830s.

"It reminds me of you," Honey said to Leonard.

"On a good day," Leonard laughed, "with some help from you."

The driver drove them around the Tuileries Gardens and chatted excitedly in French about its centuries of history and unparalleled public beauty. Honey and Leonard didn't understand a word he said, but they marveled at his smooth, French accent and apparent depth of knowledge. They decided not to walk the gardens. The cab was too perfectly comfortable.

Upon arrival at the Louvre, Honey managed to pay and tip the driver in the French francs she had exchanged earlier. "This is like funny money," she said as she folded her remaining stack of embellished bills back into her neck pouch.

Leonard was staring in disbelief at the glass and metal pyramid that had nearly taken over the classic French architecture of the world's most famous art museum. I.M. Pei's Louvre Pyramid, surrounded by three smaller, glass pyramids, completely dominated the courtyard. Honey gasped in disbelief as she took in the object of modern art.

Leonard was so stunned he couldn't move. "It looks like aliens have landed."

Honey took him by the hand. "What on God's green earth have they done?"

Leonard refused to follow her lead. "They've ruined everything. That's plain to see."

Honey kept tugging on his hand and arm. "Now, Leonard, let's not be old fuddy-duddies."

The cab driver, seeing their shoulders sag in disappointment, got out of the car to agree with them in no uncertain terms. He pointed at the modern structure and held his nose and spit on the pavement. He looked at Honey and Leonard and shrugged his shoulders as if to apologize on behalf of the people of France. Then his expression lightened and he said, *"c'est la vie,"* as he got back in his car and drove away.

Leonard finally started walking. "You must have tipped the hell out of that guy."

"I don't know how much I gave him but it was at least twice the price of the ride. He was so nice."

Leonard looked at the cab driving away. "Brutal art critic."

Honey waved goodbye. "I love the way they say 'c'est la vie.' What, exactly does that mean?"

"It means, 'That's life.' And I'm glad you asked because that's about the only French I know."

Honey threw her arms around him and hugged for all she was worth. "You know a lot about the world for a farm boy from Indiana."

"You know more than me," he said as he squeezed her back.

The two lovers savored their embrace at the center of the world's art. Honey finally broke the silence and said, "You know, that new art in front of the old building is a little like you and me."

"What do you mean?"

Honey swung his arm as they continued walking. "I mean, we're old, like the buildings, but we're new together, like the glass pyramid."

"I hope we don't look as stupid as that thing."

"Some people think old folks falling in love is ridiculous," Honey said. "They don't understand love. They think it's for young people. They think love has to have perfect skin and sexy, short dresses. They think old people should just get out of the way and die. They don't seem to realize that, one day sooner than they think, they'll be as old as us. And it's been so long since most of them have been in love that they forget how wonderful it feels."

Leonard held her as she continued, "You know, I'm not sure I was ever really in love until I met you. I mean, I loved the doctor. He was tall and had broad shoulders and he was smart. But I think I was more in love with the idea of being a good wife than I was with him as a lover. That's when we were young and trying to have children. We tried everything but nothing worked. The doctors told us everything seemed fine, but for some reason, we never had children. We never talked about adoption. I don't know if having children would have been good or bad for us. I burned way too many dinners waiting for him to come home late from the hospital."

"I never felt the way I feel now," Leonard said, helping her change the topic. "Running away to Paris with you feels like we've died and gone to heaven. Everything has a warm, rosy glow to it. My heart feels like it could bust right out of my chest. When I look in your eyes . . ."

"What?" Honey cooed as she took his hands in hers.

"I feel young again."

"This is better than feeling young," Honey said. "I never knew what to do when I was young. I was always worried about making a mistake. Now, I know what I've been missing."

Leonard stopped walking. "What have you been missing?"

Honey kissed him quickly on the lips. "Being in love with you."

"You know, now that I think of it," Leonard said, "maybe that glass pyramid doesn't look so bad. At least it's something new. It's interesting. And it sure isn't keeping people away from the museum. Look at that line of people waiting to get in. It curves around and loops. It must be a three-hour wait."

"That line is not for us," Honey said. "I've waited in enough lines for one lifetime."

Honey and Leonard walked down to the Seine River to begin their hike to the Notre Dame Cathedral. Fighting crowds at the Louvre seemed pointless when the entire city felt like a giant art museum. The Pont Royal with its five elliptical arches connected the Right Bank with the Left Bank. Open-air boats floated down the river with eager tourists pointing at everything they saw.

Despite the scenery, the intrepid couple was getting tired of walking by the time they crossed the ancient Pont Neuf to reach the island heart of medieval Paris. People kept pointing them in the direction of Notre Dame and saying it wasn't much further. It seemed to take forever to get there. Finally, they walked around a corner and there it was, in all its glory, the Notre Dame Cathedral.

Ornate, Gothic arches supported sharply sloped roofs beneath a towering spire, populated by greening copper statues of the twelve apostles. Honey and Leonard craned their necks in awe. They were no longer tired. "I feel like I'm walking back in time," Honey said as they began to stroll around the bell towers and gargoyles and flying buttresses.

"And I am Quasimodo," Leonard said.

"Who?"

"You know, Quasimodo, *The Hunchback of Notre Dame*. I always identified with the hunchback. He had to stay in the church and ring the bells. It was like me having to always work the farm. He falls in love with Esmeralda, a gypsy street dancer. You are my Esmeralda."

Honey halted the walk. "Wait a minute, big boy. Esmeralda could never love Quasimodo because he was too ugly. I don't want to be her."

Leonard took her in his arms. "To tell the truth, I don't remember much about the book except the hunchback ringing the bells. That, and I always wanted to see this place. Now that I'm here, it feels even bigger and better than I imagined all these years. Usually, you go places and they don't turn out to be as good as you thought they'd be. This place is way better than the book."

"You know," Honey said, "The more I think about it, the more I would be honored to be your Esmeralda. Having you love me is all I need. I'm just glad you're not a hunchback."

"Perfect," Leonard said. "But you know there's a little hunchback in each and every one of us."

"What do you mean?"

"You know," he said, "the part about you that isn't quite the way you want it to be. The part you don't like about yourself. It can be physical or mental. The point is, we're all in our lonely tower from time to time."

"Ringing our bells?"

"You got it, pumpkin. Ringing our bells. And you can ring my bell anytime you want."

———————

By the time the sun was setting and they were having dinner at a chic bistro, Honey was beginning to have trouble with Leonard. He seemed edgy and paranoid. He was upset that the menu was in French.

"Leonard, we are in France. People speak French here. It's not the waiter's fault you can't read the menu."

Leonard was getting downright cranky. "Oh, come on, they know lots of English speaking people will be trying to order off this menu. They ought to have English subtitles."

As if on cue, the waiter brought a menu written entirely in English. He handed it to Leonard like a patient teacher tutoring a child with special education needs. Without a word, he spun on his heels and went on to the next table. His forced silence and stiff body language were as sarcastic as a snooty French waiter can be.

"Do you believe that guy?" Leonard said. "He's just begging to get no tip at all."

"Now, Leonard, let's not spoil our dinner. At least we can read the menu now."

He seemed somewhat appeased as he turned his attention to the menu. But he couldn't concentrate on the selections. He kept peering over the top of the menu and looking over Honey's shoulder and out the window.

Honey turned around to see a small group of people across the street, standing on the corner.

"Who are those people?" Leonard asked. "They keep looking over at us. Do you think something's going on over there? They look like they're up to no good."

At first, Honey thought he might be teasing her. Then she realized he was serious. "Those people are waiting for the bus, Leonard. That's all they're doing. Now, stop worrying and let's order a bottle of fine French wine. I've been waiting a long time for this moment."

Leonard turned sullen as he let Honey order the wine and then dinner. Honey tried to be cheerful. Even the waiter tried to be entertaining as he delivered artfully prepared meals and said, "Bon appetit."

Leonard tried to lighten up and enjoy the meal but he couldn't stop looking out the window. As darkness fell, the street reflections on the window seemed to confuse him.

"We'd better get out of here," he said as they were finishing the main course. "I don't like the way things are shaping up."

His tone frightened Honey. For a moment, she became caught up in his paranoia. Were they in danger? Was the bistro about to become the scene of a crime?

She looked around and gathered her thoughts. Leonard is having one of his moments. Spotting the waiter, she signaled for the check. "Leonard, I think it's time we took a little walk. The evening air will do you good. We'll get some ice cream someplace nice and take a cab back to the hotel."

Leonard hardly heard her as he got up abruptly and headed for the restroom. He disappeared, but as Honey was paying the bill, she saw him walk out of the men's room and head straight out the front door of the restaurant without so much as looking in her direction.

She tipped the waiter well as he asked if everything was all right. He had seen Leonard becoming increasingly agitated throughout dinner and had watched in disbelief as Leonard walked out the door by himself.

Honey quickly gathered her money, glasses, and purse and headed out into the street to catch Leonard. He was already a block away and headed for the river. "Leonard!" she yelled as she began trotting after him. "Wait for me."

He didn't seem to hear her but he did slow down and eventually came to a stop at a concrete railing overlooking the Seine. Honey was out of breath by the time she caught up to him. "Leonard, what's wrong? Why did you leave me? Couldn't you hear me calling for you?"

Leonard seemed surprised to see her at his side but at least he recognized her. "Honey, where have you been? I've been waiting for you here by the river. Look, isn't it beautiful the way the street lamps reflect in the water? And see the party boats serving people dinner on their cruises. We need to take one of those boats."

"Leonard you just walked out on me at the restaurant. You left me alone to pay the bill. How could you do that? Do you even remember doing that? When was the last time you took your blood pressure medication?"

Leonard rubbed his temples with his fingers. "Remember my medicine?"

Honey grabbed his hands. "No. Do you remember that we just had dinner at a restaurant?"

Leonard looked perplexed, apparently searching his memory. "Now that you mention it, I'm not that hungry. But I could use a little dish of ice cream. I'll bet it's good here."

Honey raised her eyebrows, lowered her head and looked Leonard in the eye. "Where are we?"

Leonard put his arm around her. "We're in Paris, you silly pumpkin. You know where we are."

Honey felt relieved and confused at the same time. How could he know he was in Paris and not remember the restaurant and walking out on her? For the first time, she began to think his memory problems might be more than she could handle. The blackouts and bouts of paranoia frightened her.

"Come on," she said, "let's get you to bed. It's been a long day. We're both tired. I'll get us a cab and we can find some ice cream near the hotel."

SIX

IT WAS 1942. Gretchen Atkins watched her cousin, Emma, swim toward the center of the farm lake. All she could see was wet, red hair and stroking arms. Emma was 40 yards from the shore. Both girls knew it was deep out there but they didn't know how deep. They had been taught to always stay close to the shore. Gretchen was 6 years old and Emma was 7. Emma was Leonard Atkin's only child. Gretchen was the only child of Leonard's brother, Daniel.

There were no adults supervising. Gretchen's mother had left for a moment to bring back lunch. This gave the girls a chance to break the rules. The double dare was for Emma to swim to the middle, dive down and come back up with muck in her hand to prove she'd been to the bottom.

Gretchen stayed in the chest-deep water before the drop off to marvel at her cousin's bravery. The lake wasn't large enough to have a name but it was way too big for children to swim across. She wasn't as strong a swimmer as Emma. A part of her hoped her cousin would get tired and have to turn back. If Emma made it to the middle and came up with muck in her hand, it wouldn't be long before Gretchen would have to take up the challenge. That's the way it was. Whatever Emma did first, Gretchen had to do second.

Emma made it to the middle and yelled for Gretchen to come join her. "Come on, it's not too far, you can do it."

"I'm not coming until you show me the muck," Gretchen yelled back.

"Chicken," Emma shouted as she took a deep breath and dove for the bottom.

Gretchen watched as the surface of the lake became smooth again. Emma went under for a long time. She was down for 10 seconds, then 20, then more than 30 seconds. She was under for too long. *She should have come back up by now. The lake can't be that deep. She can't hold her breath that long.*

Just as Gretchen was looking around to locate the rowboat, Emma came popping up with a splash and a yell. She had muck in her hand and she was slapping the water in triumph. But she kept splashing too much. Something was wrong. She sounded like she might be trying to scream, but Gretchen heard her own name being called out in a choking gurgle.

Emma was in trouble. She'd swallowed too much water coming up for air and she was panicking. Her head disappeared beneath the water again. Bubbles were coming to the surface. Gretchen ran for the rowboat. Her father had recently taught the girls how to row. By the time she had both oars in the water, Emma had popped back up but with no sound this time. Her splashes were noticeably weaker.

Gretchen started rowing for the middle with all her might. One of the oars came out of the oarlock, throwing her back and off balance. The boat nearly tipped. She shivered and shrieked in anger as precious time was lost trying to get the oar back into place. Looking over her back, Gretchen screamed Emma's name and called for help. No one was close enough to hear. The last she saw of her cousin was a hand, barely above the surface, finally letting go of the muck from the bottom of the lake.

By the time she got to where she thought Emma had gone under, Gretchen was afraid to jump in. The water looked murky and evil. She was hoping Emma would bob back up and she could grab her. The water was still. She looked around and screamed in desperation. No help was coming. It was up to her to save her cousin.

Gretchen held her nose and jumped into what felt like a watery grave. She let herself go deep down into the lake and opened up her eyes. There was nothing to be seen. Visibility was ten feet at best. She let herself keep sinking but she had to come up for air before she felt the bottom. She inhaled too much water coming up and had to grab the boat to cough out the water and clear her head.

She put her head under water and thought she saw a body floating 10 feet under and a short distance away. She swam to the vision with her eyes open. She knew she was running out of time.

There was nothing there. It must have been a reflection. She swam back to the boat, more careful not to swallow water upon resurfacing.

Gretchen screamed again when she saw her uncle Leonard running toward the lake. "Uncle Leonard, Uncle Leonard, Emma's under the water! I can't find her."

Leonard hit the pond running, determined to save his daughter. Gretchen's father, Daniel, was close behind and dove in as well. In a few powerful strokes they were at the boat and began diving frantically for the bottom. After the first few dives, they took off their pants and shirts and boots. Gretchen hung onto the side of the boat, sobbing. Leonard and Daniel were soon by her side, catching their breath.

The men dove down again and again, coming up empty-handed every time. The crying little girl had too much time to think. On a hunch that wouldn't go away and kept getting stronger Gretchen decided to go down one more time and search directly under the boat. She let herself sink, feet first with her eyes closed, about eight feet into the water. It felt like Emma was calling her name. She couldn't hear anything. It was more like a voice inside her head. She felt like she was dreaming, or dying herself.

As soon as she opened her eyes, she was face to face with her cousin. It was a scene from a horror movie. Emma's lifeless eyes were wide open and her mouth appeared frozen in a silent scream. Their noses were almost touching, like looking closely into a mirror. But one side of the reflection was no longer living. Gretchen was so shocked she took in half a lung of water.

Life's terrible tragedy was communicated in that moment. Gretchen came face-to-face with death at much too young an age. She was so frightened and repulsed by what she saw that she pushed the body away and tried to escape to the surface. She took in even more water as she swam up for air.

On the surface, she coughed until she could speak, and then grabbed her father's shoulder. "She's right down under the boat, Daddy. But she's not there anymore."

The brothers retrieved the body and swam it to shore. Leonard rolled his daughter over on her stomach and picked her up by the waist to drain her water. Too much brownish liquid came out. He rolled her over and started mouth-to-mouth resuscitation. Daniel started pushing on Emma's chest.

Gretchen stood on the shore, hoping for a miracle, but knowing her cousin was gone for good. She had never seen a dead person before. The body didn't look like Emma anymore. Something magical had left and the corpse no longer looked human. The little pink bathing suit looked strangely out of place.

She had never seen her father or her uncle cry before. They worked desperately on Emma's body for what seemed like forever. Daniel was the first to give up. He finally had to pull Leonard off his daughter's body. The two men hugged and sobbed into each other's arms. They took Gretchen into their grief circle and squeezed her tightly.

The loss of her cousin would remain forever in the back of Gretchen's mind, waiting for the least little trauma to bring it to the forefront. Her childlike faith in God went missing that day and never came back.

Nobody ever blamed Gretchen for Emma's death, but she always blamed herself. She had thrown down the double dare and then been unable to save her cousin.

The drowning took the wind out of Leonard's marriage. He and his wife never had another child. They celebrated Emma's birthday every year with a sadness that could find no consolation. Leonard threw himself into working the farm and investing his profits in stocks and commodity futures. His wife never got over her grief, although she learned to hide it by working around the farm and volunteering at church.

Gretchen was raised an only child. After her mother had several miscarriages, her parents gave up on having more children. When Gretchen was 21, her mother died of cancer. Her father's drinking got worse after that. He died at age 55.

After Leonard's daughter drowned, he paid special attention to Gretchen, his only niece. She was the bright spot in his life. He taught her how to drive a tractor and ride a horse. She learned how to milk cows and bale hay. Leonard paid her college expenses and took her on business trips to Chicago and Kansas City. They became increasingly close over the years, especially after Gretchen's father died from alcoholism.

Gretchen had several boyfriends over the years but she never got close to marriage. She was too much of a loner. Her interest in farming faded as her teaching career took over. Try as he might, Leonard could not convince her to carry on the family farm.

By the time Leonard's wife died, Gretchen had become the daughter he lost fifty years earlier. It was only natural that he would trust her with his business affairs when his memory started playing tricks on him. He gave her his power of attorney without question. He had been consulting with Gretchen on dealings and investments for years.

Gretchen grew to consider Leonard's money as her own. After all, she was his only heir.

By the time Honey Waldrop came into the picture, Gretchen had misappropriated at least $750,000 of her Uncle Leonard's money. She paid off her house and bought a new car and took expensive vacations. Worst of all, she was secretly turning a good portion of Leonard's farm into a housing development. She had announced her early retirement from teaching the week before she realized her Uncle Leonard had a new romantic interest.

Gretchen was more than jealous of her Uncle Leonard's affections for Honey. She was accustomed to being the center of his world. Now, she had slipped to an unacceptable and much too distant second on his social list. And she was certain that Honey would discover the embezzlement and help Leonard revoke his power of attorney. He could also draft a will that would diminish or eliminate Gretchen's stake in the estate.

Gretchen had slipped into near panic mode by the time she convinced her uncle to move into the nursing home. Her plan was to pay the doctors there enough to declare him incompetent. That way he couldn't rearrange his legal affairs. Her fear of getting caught stealing flipped a switch in Gretchen's mind. The lights dimmed on her love for Uncle Leonard and left her alone in the darkness of envy and jealousy. Emma's horrible death mask made regular appearances in Gretchen's troubled dreams.

Then Leonard's routine blood tests showed high levels of arsenic. What a gift for Gretchen's plan. This was exactly the evidence she could use against Honey. Gretchen went to the authorities and accused Honey of poisoning Leonard..

Leonard had become increasingly distrustful since he had been talked into the nursing home's independent living facility. He didn't like living there and had decided to move out. Gretchen knew he was spending more and more time at Honey's house. Honey was clearly winning the battle for her uncle's affections.

Honey and Leonard had played right into her hand by breaking the law and fleeing the country. Gretchen could not believe her good fortune. But, even as she was wondering how Honey and Leonard could be so legally naive, she had a nagging feeling that, the longer they were on the run, the worse her position became. She knew her Uncle Leonard better than anyone, and she knew he was mentally competent more often than not. Her only hope was to get Honey out of the picture. The best way to do that was to get her convicted of a crime. It didn't matter if it was kidnapping, attempted murder or violating the no-contact order. With Honey gone, she could somehow convince her uncle that her "investments" had been in his best interest.

SEVEN

O N THE THIRD DAY of Honey and Leonard's escape, Gretchen called the office of her investigator, Adam Wolfe. After getting his message machine most of the morning, she finally spoke to his assistant. "No, we haven't heard from Mr. Wolfe today, but I'll have him call you as soon as he checks in."

"You tell him it's almost 5 p.m. where he is, and he should have called me long before now. He promised to check in with me at least three times a day."

Two hours later, Wolfe called Gretchen. He and Simone had spent a night on the town and ended up sharing a room and each other until dawn's early light. Even so, he had news to report. "Honey used her Visa Card to rent a new, 1992, Ford Taurus, around noon today, Paris time."

"So where are they now?"

"I have no idea. They rented it for two weeks. The desk clerk said she overheard something about the French Riviera."

"What about the police?"

Wolfe paused to formulate his response. "You told me not to contact the police until I found them."

Gretchen's tone ratcheted up from annoyed to nasty. "Well, now that you've let them out of Paris, we're going to have to change our strategy, aren't we?"

"I suppose so." Wolfe knew he was in no position to fight back.

"Now, listen carefully. I want you to go to Giverny. That's where Leonard will go. He always wanted to see Monet's gardens."

"Who's Monet?"

"Monet is only one of the most famous Impressionist painters of all time. Don't tell me you haven't heard of him," Gretchen said, beginning to wonder if she'd hired the right man.

"Oh, that Monet," Wolfe bluffed. "Of course, I've heard of him. I'll get right over there and keep you informed."

———

Leonard drove the rental car and found Monet's house and gardens at Giverny without incident. It was only 75 km up the A13 from Paris. Leonard was chatty the whole way. The paranoia of the night before had long been forgotten. He was having a great day on his way to doing something he had wanted to do his entire life. He was keenly aware, however, that he and Honey were probably being followed, if not chased.

"Yep. Two nights in that hotel was enough," he said to Honey. "We've got to keep moving if we don't want to get caught."

Honey turned around to look out the rear window. "Do you really think they're after us?"

Leonard chuckled at her sudden paranoia. "No doubt about it. I'm amazed we've made it this far. I'll bet the police are looking all over Paris by now. Too bad for them. We're gone."

Honey pulled down the passenger sun visor to check her makeup in the lighted mirror. "What about Gretchen?"

Leonard put both hands on the steering wheel and pushed himself back in the seat. "You know, that girl has turned into the biggest disappointment of my life. I thought she loved me. I know she did. I hope she still does. The terrible truth is she's fallen in love with my money. We've been through a lot together. But she just can't handle me being with you. That doesn't make any sense. I mean, the girl is my brother's daughter. After he died, she became more like my daughter. So, I can't understand why she wouldn't just want me to be happy. She knew what a train wreck my marriage was after we lost Emma."

Honey flipped up the visor and turned to look at him. "Leonard, I've got some bad news for you. News you already know but won't admit to yourself."

"What?"

Honey touched his right arm. "Gretchen's been stealing your money and she doesn't want me helping you find out about it."

Leonard stopped pushing against the steering wheel. His shoulders slumped as he hung his head. "I can't believe that. I can't believe that's true. She's a good girl. But let's not talk about it anymore." He straightened up in the driver's seat. "We need to savor this moment. Here we are at Claude Monet's place. Can you believe it? Here we are, parking our fancy rental car in the lot outside Claude's house. Come on, let's go see his gardens and the paintings and the places he used to have breakfast and drink wine and go to bed."

Honey and Leonard walked, hand in hand, to Monet's house and went on the inside tour first. Honey's favorite part, by far, was the bright, yellow dining room. "Oh, Leonard, it's so beautiful. Who would ever think to make a dining room this gorgeous yellow?"

"Monet was all about color," Leonard said. "You know, it's funny. People look at paintings and they want to impress everybody with their knowledge of art history and compare this artist to that artist. All they need to say is, 'Hey, I love the yellow.'"

They went outside in the bright autumn sunshine and strolled down the sloping gardens of daisies and poppies and rare flowers; down the central aisle, covered by iron arches for climbing roses in the spring. "You don't need to talk about art," Honey said. "You need to feel it. Like we're doing now. We don't need to decide which flower is the most beautiful, we just need to appreciate the whole garden."

"I'll tell you what we need to do," Leonard said as they entered the underground tunnel to make their way to the water garden. "We need to create our own garden back home."

"But we're not painters."

Leonard lifted her slightly by her left arm. "We'll invite the painters over so they can wander the paths and mingle with the flowers and paint things the way they feel them."

"What if they feel like cutting off their ear?" Honey clutched him tighter.

Leonard laughed, "Then we won't invite them over."

"Poor Vincent," Honey said. "He was so unhappy."

"I'll bet he was happy when he was painting. His work always makes me feel good about myself. Like this place does."

Honey gasped as they came out of the tunnel and approached the water gardens. "Look, there's the Japanese bridge and the Wisteria and the lilies. Oh, my stars, it's even more beautiful in real life."

As they walked the paths around the water, Leonard told Honey a little about Monet. "You know, when he died in 1926 he was 86 years old. Some of his best paintings, the water lilies, were done in his eighties. You know what that means?"

"What does that mean?" Honey said as she pulled her gaze away from the pond and looked at Leonard.

"It means the best is yet to come," he said as he gave her a big hug. "It means we're still a couple of kids who can go anywhere we want and do whatever we want. It means we're young and in love."

Honey couldn't help but laugh with him in his enthusiasm. "I can't argue with you. I do feel young in this perfect garden with you."

"You know the critics called his work Impressionism when he was a young painter. They meant it as an insult. But he loved the term and used it until the word became the name of an entire movement in painting."

"So why do they call it Impressionism?" Honey asked.

"Because it's not realistic. It goes beyond that. Monet and his buddies started painting the effects of light with broken color and rapid brushstrokes. Some of the stuff almost looks fuzzy. They called it plein air because they painted in the great outdoors and they weren't afraid to add a little emotion to the canvas."

Honey grabbed his arm to interrupt. "How do you know so much about art?"

Leonard thought about the question for a moment before he answered. "I don't know that much about it, but my mother was an artist. She painted in oil on big canvasses. She painted the great outdoors and everything in it. We'd come in from the fields, and there she'd be, doing a painting of the barn with a cow in front of it. Or painting a vase of flowers, catching the light just right in the evening sun. I used to love her work."

"Do you still have any of it?"

"You know, that's the darndest thing. I don't have a single painting. She died when I was twenty-two and all the relatives swooped in, and then there were no more paintings. They sold them, the vultures. Dad gave the rest away. He couldn't bear to look at them. Her death was hard on him. It was hard on my brother and me too. She died of lung disease. She was a smoker, so was Dad. Once she got sick she made me promise to quit, and I did. My brother, Daniel, tried to quit but he couldn't do it. They didn't even call it cancer back then. It was quick, though. One day she was fine. Three months later, she was gone."

"Oh, Leonard, that's so sad."

Leonard got back on his art history track. "Monet was her

favorite painter. She had a book of his work that she always kept on the coffee table in the living room. I used to love looking at the pictures of his paintings. They always felt so far away and romantic and colorful. Funny thing, now that I'm here, this place reminds me of home. It's really a lot like the farm. Look at the rolling hills and the trees and all the beautiful things growing. We could be back in Indiana."

"Don't tell me you're getting homesick."

Leonard kissed her on the forehead. "No, I'm not homesick. Home is where you are."

"What a perfect thing to say."

Honey and Leonard lingered in the gardens for another hour but eventually began walking toward the car. "It's time to hit the road," he said. "We can't stay here too long. Gretchen knows this is the first place I'll visit."

As they were leaving the gardens, a young woman came up in an excited rush and asked them to sign a copy of her newspaper. Honey put her glasses on to see the paper. She couldn't read the headlines but it was impossible to miss the photo of her and Leonard, it took up much of the top half of page three.

"What does it say?" Honey asked the woman. "Do you speak English?"

"Yes, I do. Oh my, it is really you. Please sign my paper. Here's a pen. You are going to be famous in France."

"What does the headline say?"

"Oh, yes, excuse me. It says 'Elder Lovers Flee to France.'"

Honey signed the newspaper as Leonard said, "Like I said, it's time to go. Looks like the French papers are picking up the story and photos from *The Chicago Tribune*." Then he turned to the young French woman and said, "Tell anyone who wants to know that we're headed for Amsterdam."

Honey and Leonard got in their car, and Leonard drove

back to Vernon and across the Seine River. Honey looked at him quizzically. "This doesn't look like the way to Amsterdam."

Leonard laughed like a spook show host and stepped on the gas. "Who said anything about going to Amsterdam? We're about to get lost in the French countryside, headed south for the Riviera. You in?"

Jack Crumbo landed in Paris three days after Honey and Leonard had arrived. Despite the raging popularity of the story, it had taken him that long to convince *The Chicago Tribune* to pay for his trip. He had no idea how to find the senior lovers on the run. They could be anywhere in France, or Europe for that matter. So, he did what any journalist would do. He went to the main offices of a Paris daily newspaper.

His *Tribune* credentials opened all necessary doors, and he was quickly introduced to Corbin Lacoste, reporter in charge of the exploding Honey and Leonard story. Lacoste was thrilled to meet the man who initially broke the story and eager to share what few leads he had as to the couple's whereabouts. Fortunately for Crumbo, Lacoste spoke excellent English.

Lacoste stood at attention and nearly saluted his American counterpart. "I am so happy to meet the man who turned a love story into international news."

Crumbo shook his hand. "It wasn't international until you guys picked it up."

Lacoste walked Crumbo over to his desk. "Look at these clips from all over. Here's the London story, here's Stockholm. And look at this—it's even in Tokyo. Reporters from all over the world are picking up your story. You're a hero."

Crumbo laughed aloud at that comment. "All this means is I've got a lot more competition."

Lacoste offered Crumbo a seat. "What's Leonard like? Is Honey really in love with him? Did she try to poison him? Where did a farmer get all that money?"

Crumbo sat down and took a closer look at all the articles. "That's too many questions. You've got to ask them one at a time." He was pulling rank on Lacoste, who was twenty-eight years old, seventeen years Crumbo's junior.

Lacoste didn't mind. "Yes, yes, I am sorry. Please just tell me about Leonard. Tell me everything. I want to know it all."

"Tell you what," Crumbo said. "I'll tell you the most important facts about the story if you agree to help me find Honey and Leonard. But you've got to agree to keep it off the record until I give you the okay."

Lacoste was so delighted to be partnering with Jack Crumbo and *The Chicago Tribune* he was bouncing up and down. At nearly six feet tall, Lacoste was a couple inches taller than Crumbo and in much better physical condition. Crumbo was carrying an extra thirty pounds around his midsection.

"Okay, then," Crumbo said. "Settle down. Here, have a seat. People are watching." Indeed, half the newsroom was staring at the newly formed reporting team.

Crumbo leaned forward and whispered to Lacoste. "Honey never tried to poison Leonard. He had high levels of arsenic in his blood from being a farmer all his life and being exposed to arsenic in the pesticides he used on his fields."

Lacoste looked at Crumbo like he expected him to continue. Crumbo paused to let the meaning of his words sink in to the French reporter. It took a minute, but Lacoste finally lit up when he realized the significance of what he'd just been told. "Then why are they running?"

"Because nobody knows this except you and me and Honey's attorney. Honey and Leonard don't even know it yet."

"But Honey must know she didn't try to poison Leonard," Lacoste reasoned. "And Leonard must know he was never poisoned."

Crumbo moved in a little closer to Lacoste. "Actually, they don't know Leonard wasn't poisoned. The arsenic in his blood has even Leonard thinking he might have been poisoned. But they also know the law in Indiana is trying to keep them apart. So, they decided they didn't have time to wait on the law."

"We've got to find them," Lacoste said.

Crumbo opened his arms wide. "Why do you think I came to see you?"

"Oh, right. Yes, yes. I did get a tip just today that they might be heading south. We had a sighting in Dijon."

"Is that where they make the mustard?" Crumbo asked.

"Yes," Lacoste said. "You Americans probably think it's a brand name but it's really a quaint little town in France with big mustard factories." Lacoste checked Crumbo's reaction to make sure the Tribune reporter wasn't taking offense about his reference to Americans. "My guess is they'll keep heading south and be in Avignon by now. All the tourists head there on their way to the Riviera. It's a well-preserved medieval city with the old walls still surrounding it."

Crumbo stood up quickly. "What are we waiting for?"

"Let me tell my boss where we're headed."

"Don't tell him where," Crumbo said. "Just say you're going with me."

Lacoste looked at the ceiling like he couldn't believe he hadn't thought of that himself.

Once the secret mission was authorized by an editor, the two reporters left the building without further discussion, packed their things into Lacoste's car, and took off for Avignon.

EIGHT

LEONARD WAS DRIVING SOUTH of Paris on A5 when Honey spotted the first sign for Dijon. It was, in fact, the exit sign for Dijon and they were almost past it when Honey said, "Leonard, turn here. Turn now. Take this exit. Look, it's for Dijon. That's got to be where they make the mustard."

The tires squealed as Leonard cranked the steering wheel to make the exit. The truck he cut off to make the turn blasted its horn. Leonard turned to Honey and said, "Pumpkin, please, don't scream at me like that. You're going to get us both killed."

Honey apologized but thanked him for being such a good driver and for following her spur of the moment directions. Then came the first of many signs for Dijon.

"Dijon," Leonard said, "that's where they make the mustard."

"Yes, sweetie, that's what I just said. That's why we're going there, to see the mustard factory."

The second sign for Dijon appeared on the side of the road in about three kilometers. Leonard said, "Dijon. That's where they make the mustard."

Honey patted him on his right shoulder. "Leonard, you just said that a minute ago. We both know Dijon is where they make the mustard."

By the fifth time they passed a sign for Dijon with Leonard saying the exact same thing each time, Honey decided to ignore. him. There was no use telling him not to repeat himself.

He forgets what I say as much as he forgets what he says. So, if he can't remember what he says, how is it that he repeats the exact same thing every time, like he remembers what he said before? It's like a broken record, repeating the same thing, over and over.

Despite the repeating issue, the couple arrived in Dijon with high hopes of learning how mustard is made. After a few inquiries, though, they learned that the mustard factory did not allow tourists to visit.

Leonard clapped his hands together. "They must have something to hide."

Honey put both hands on the dashboard and gave Leonard a sly, sideways glance. "Or maybe it's not that exciting to watch mustard being made."

Not being allowed inside the mustard factories did not dampen Leonard's mood for long. He shifted into tour guide mode, even though he'd never seen the city before. He wasn't repeating himself. He was showing off for his girlfriend and trying to lighten her mood.

"I tell you what we'll do," he said. "Since we can't tour the factories, we'll go to a shop and buy a bunch of those little mustard jars we've been seeing everywhere. Then, we'll go to a restaurant and sample them at dinner. How's that sound for a plan? I'm hungry, aren't you?"

Honey put both arms around his waist, relieved to see Leonard back to his old, playful self. "Yes, I'm famished and that sounds like a wonderful plan." She was falling more deeply in love with this resourceful man every step of the journey, even if she was troubled and becoming more mystified by his absent mindedness. It was beginning to dawn on her that Leonard's memory might keep getting worse no matter how much she loved him or how much quality time they spent together.

At dinner, Leonard borrowed her glasses to read the label on one of the mini mustard jars. "Looky here. Dijon mustard began in 1856 when some guy substituted the juice of not-quite-ripe grapes for vinegar."

Honey was paying more attention to the menu than to Leonard, so he pressed his point. "Don't you think it's funny how one little difference in the recipe can change the way the world thinks about mustard?"

Honey looked over her menu at Leonard and smiled. "I do think that is interesting. But what I find even more interesting is that bright yellow mustard we've got back in the States is called French's."

As they laughed together, the waiter came over to check on them. Once Honey clued him in on the mustard joke, the waiter said, "We do find that funny. But not as funny as calling your grease-fried potatoes *French fries*."

"I'll have some French's Mustard on my French fries," Leonard joked.

"No sir," the waiter said. "For that, I am afraid you will need the tomato sauce the English call ketchup."

Once he left, Honey leaned over and said to Leonard, "Isn't it fun to see how people from other countries look at food?"

"I'm just glad he didn't recognize us," Leonard said. "People seem to be looking at us like they know us from somewhere but they can't quite remember where."

But the waiter had recognized them from their photos in the newspapers. Honey's generous tip did nothing to keep him from calling in a tip of his own to the Paris newspaper. He'd been following the growing story and wanted to be part of it. He didn't get paid for his information but he did get to talk to the rising-star reporter, Corbin Lacoste. The waiter told the reporter he had overheard Honey and Leonard talking about heading south.

Leonard counted down the mileage signs to Avignon like a kid who couldn't wait for Christmas. He told Honey all about the ancient town on the Rhone River. He had been reading travel brochures along the way. "This city was actually the center of the Roman Catholic Church in the 1300's," he said. "Some Pope moved out of Rome and started building palaces and churches in Avignon. From what I hear the old town is surrounded by medieval ramparts with guard towers and gates and the whole bit."

"So that's why they call the wine Chateauneuf-du-Pape," Honey said.

Leonard slapped her left leg playfully. "That's right. The Pope's new castle. My favorite wine in the world, and they make it right here."

Honey grabbed his hand and held it on her leg. "You just like it for the fancy seal and the castle on the label."

Leonard ran his hand higher up her thigh and tightened his squeeze. "You know me better than that. It's the richest, full-body red wine on the planet. And I'll bet it's a lot cheaper here than it is in the States."

Honey pulled his hand off her leg and put it back on the steering wheel. "You better keep both hands on the wheel so we can get ourselves into town and find some of that new Pope wine."

Finding a room in Avignon was confusing and frustrating. The streets were much too narrow for modern traffic. Even the main boulevard, Rue de la Republic, was no wider than an alley in a modern city. Two-way traffic at 4 p.m. was barely moving. It was so slow that Jack Crumbo recognized Honey and Leonard as they drove past him and Lacoste.

Crumbo pointed at the runaway couple and got so excited he

tried to get out of the car without unbuckling his seat belt. "That's them. Stop the car. Let me out. That's Honey and Leonard."

Lacoste slammed on the brakes, as Crumbo unbuckled his belt in a fury and jumped out to try and catch their car on foot. But Leonard was moving away too quickly. A break in traffic allowed him to speed away just as Crumbo was waving his camera at them and shouting at them to stop.

Honey heard the shouting and turned around to see what the commotion was all about. "Keep driving, Leonard. It's that Jack Crumbo from *The Chicago Tribune*. How in the world did he track us down here?"

"How do you know what Jack Crumbo looks like?" Leonard asked.

Honey opened her mouth and covered it with one hand in mock horror. "Why Leonard Atkins. You do sound a little jealous."

"Not jealous, just curious," Leonard said as he watched Crumbo getting smaller in the rear view mirror.

"Well, if you must know," Honey said, "Mr. Crumbo did come to the house while you were still in the nursing home. Against my attorney's orders, I let him in and we had quite the interview. You know that. You read the story."

Leonard turned to give her a blank stare. "I don't remember."

Honey waved off his embarrassment. "Not only that. His photo is now appearing with his articles. He's on television too. He's getting almost as popular as we are. And he doesn't look happy to see us getting away."

"Well, he hasn't tracked us down yet," Leonard said as he sped up and took a right down a blind alley.

"Well this is no good," Honey said as they came to the dead end of the alley. "Back up, back up. We can't just sit here and wait for them to come find us. What kind of getaway driver are you?"

"This is going to be one low-speed chase," Leonard said as he backed out of the alley and managed to get on the main drag, nearly nudging pedestrians with the rear end of the car.

They were stuck in traffic and trying in vain to change direction. Crumbo and Lacoste were nowhere to be seen.

"We've got to get out of town," Honey said. "This place is too small. They'll find us for sure."

"No, no," Leonard said. "That's what they'll expect us to do. So we won't do that." He made a right turn, drove down the side street for about a block, and pulled into a garage that said "Hotel Parking," in English.

"We'll stay here for the night," he said as he pulled up to valet parking for what looked like a high-class hotel. "Come on, we'll let them hide the car for us and we'll get a room."

"Are you sure?"

Leonard got out of the car and came around to open Honey's door. "I'm sure I can't drive any more in this crazy little circle of a city."

By this point, Honey and Leonard each had a small suitcase filled with clothing they had purchased along the way. Honey used a credit card to pay for the room. Until that point she'd been paying cash for everything but the rental car. The rental car people had insisted on payment by credit card in case the car was damaged during the rental.

Honey wasn't paying cash in an effort to keep people off their trail. She and Leonard had no idea that people could track them by looking at their credit purchases.

Seeing the *Chicago Tribune* reporter on their trail in Avignon unsettled them. "What will happen if he catches up to us?" she asked as they settled into their small but elegant room.

Leonard thought about her question for a moment. He had just slipped in and out of a bout of forgetfulness. He was trying to regain his focus. Honey could tell he was not quite with her, but at least he wasn't suffering from one of his spells. She repeated the question.

Leonard comprehended the question the second time she asked it. "The first thing you've got to remember is this. Jack Crumbo is not the police. In fact, I dare say he's on our side. He's in it for the story. Our story is the best thing that's ever happened to his career. He probably won't even give away our location. If he did, the story would be over and his scoop would be gone. No, I don't think we need to run from Crumbo. In fact, let's take a walk tomorrow and see the sights and see if we can find him."

Honey took a seat in front of a large mirror and looked sadly at her tired reflection. "But Leonard, it's not just Crumbo who's looking for us. Our picture is in all the French papers. It's probably on television too."

Leonard considered her comment and said, "You're right. We need to buy some hats and sunglasses to disguise ourselves."

Honey turned around and laughed at him. "Buy some hats and sunglasses? Is that the best you can do? I was thinking something a little more James Bond."

"Like what?"

"Like catch a submarine out of here and head for South America."

"I doubt if the river is deep enough," Leonard said.

Honey got up and gave him a gentle shove with both hands against his chest. "Then maybe a helicopter would do."

Leonard wrapped her into a hug and they fell onto the bed together. In that delicious moment, they were not afraid of getting caught. They weren't afraid of anything. The only thing they cared about was being together. As long as they were together, nothing bad could happen.

The French police had other thoughts. The order to apprehend Honey and Leonard had finally been issued four days after their arrival in France. Politics finally trumped personality. The FBI and the U.S. embassy in Paris convinced French authorities that Honey and Leonard were criminal fugitives, not the latest Romeo and Juliet. Police were looking for the couple in Paris until Gretchen notified them of the Avignon hotel credit card purchase.

The next day, Honey bought a blonde wig and sunglasses at a costume shop. Leonard bought a hat, a fake beard and glasses. They had a good time dressing each other up in the mirrors. In the end, they still looked like themselves, wearing cheap disguises. They didn't care. They hardly recognized each other. They hit the streets of Avignon like two kids, trick-or-treating on Halloween.

Leonard had a glass of Chateauneuf-du-Pape for lunch. Honey had to cut him off before he had a second glass because she knew the wine would drastically worsen his memory problems.

The lack of a second glass of wine didn't stop him from feeling jubilant as he and Honey toured the ancient walls of Avignon. The old city turned out to be more hospitable on foot than in a car. People were friendly, although they did stare at the disguises.

Honey and Leonard strolled on paths atop the battlements. At one point, they heard the heavenly sounds of violin players rehearsing in a nearby university studio. This spurred Leonard to begin waltzing with Honey on the deck of a tower overlooking the Rhone River. They danced together well. Several tourists applauded. Leonard dipped Honey for a big finish and lifted her up for the two of them to take an exaggerated bow.

"Leonard, you shouldn't attract so much attention," Honey said. "People can see us up here for miles."

Leonard held her, cheek to cheek. "Nonsense, blondie, it's you who's attracting all the attention. You're the one who's having more fun as a blond."

They continued walking the ramparts along the river until they saw the Pont d'Avignon, the historic bridge that ends in the middle of the river.

"Now that's something you don't see everyday," Leonard said. "A bridge that only goes halfway across the river. Look, you can walk on it. There are people walking right up to the edge. That looks like fun. Come on, let's go."

Honey and Leonard went down to the bridge and walked it as far as they could. They looked down into the Rhone River, imagining a time when the bridge went all the way across. Back when mounted knights in suits of armor patrolled the premises.

They turned around and looked back at the city of Avignon with its church spires and palace towers. As they were marveling at the magic of the fairytale city, they noticed Jack Crumbo and Corbin Lacoste walking toward them.

"Oh, my dear goodness," Honey said.

"They couldn't have caught us in a better spot," Leonard said. "There is literally nowhere to run."

Honey clung to Leonard as if wild wolves were surrounding them.

"Don't worry," Crumbo called from twenty yards away. "You don't have to worry about us. We're on your side."

"See what I told you," Leonard said.

"We'll see who's on what side," Honey said.

Crumbo approached with outstretched arms. "Honey and Leonard, I am Jack Crumbo from *The Chicago Tribune*. You remember me, Honey. It's so good to see you. Allow me to introduce you to my friend, Corbin Lacoste. He's covering your story for the Paris news. He helped me find you here."

"Nice to meet you, Mr. Lacoste," Leonard said. "And good to finally meet you in person, Mr. Crumbo. Honey has told me a lot about you."

Honey relaxed and gave Crumbo a hug. "Jack Crumbo, how on earth did you find us?"

Crumbo laughed as he broke away from Honey to shake Leonard's hand. "We saw you dancing on the ramparts. The disguises were a dead giveaway."

"But what made you come to Avignon?" Honey asked.

As Lacoste was telling them about the waiter in Dijon who called in the tip, a police radio on his hip came alive with official-sounding, French chatter. He stopped to listen.

"We'd better move to a more private location," he said. "The police have somehow been alerted to your presence in Avignon."

"How would they know that?" Leonard asked.

"Credit cards," Crumbo correctly deduced. "You must have used a credit card here."

"Oh, my stars," Honey said. "I did pay for the room with a credit card. But who would tell the French police about my credit card account?"

"Gretchen would call," Leonard said. "I know she's been tracking us. You must have used my card. She's got access to all my numbers."

"Oh, that might be true," Honey said. "I never know whose card I'm using."

"I know a place we can go," Lacoste said.

"How do we know we can trust you?" Honey asked.

Lacoste patted the radio on his hip. "I'm the one with the police radio who didn't call the police."

━━━━━◆━━━━━

The chapel of a nearby Catholic church turned out to be the perfect hideout. Lacoste was a good friend of the young priest in charge. It was also an ideal location for Crumbo to interview Honey and Leonard and to tell them the news from Indiana.

"Your attorney, Robert Nimmo, has a pretty good handle on your case, Honey," Crumbo said. "He's hired a forensic expert who says the arsenic in Leonard's blood is the result of him being a farmer all his life."

"What do you mean?"

"I mean a lifetime of working with pesticides is what caused him to have high levels of arsenic in his blood."

"So we can prove he wasn't poisoned?" Honey asked.

"That's right," Crumbo said.

Honey and Leonard hugged each other in relief. This was a huge moment for both of them. It's not everyday a possible murder charge against you is discredited. Honey was uplifted by the news. She started jumping up and down to kiss Leonard on the cheek or the forehead or whatever part of his face she could reach.

"So, shame on anyone who ever thought I might be a bad person," she said once she had regained her breath from her victory dance. "My attorney said he would make them print this in the paper even bigger than the first headlines."

"Don't worry, Honey," Lacoste said. "This will soon be worldwide news. You two are the hottest story on the planet. You are so big, I can't believe I'm sitting here talking to you in person."

Crumbo gave Lacoste a flat hand gesture for him to back off the starstruck, hero worship. The younger reporter immediately stiffened to what he hoped was a more professional demeanor.

"Unfortunately," Crumbo said, "the arsenic news doesn't change the fact that there's still a warrant out for your arrest. They filed the felony charge a week ago in Indiana for violating the no-contact order."

"I thought the no-contact order would go away with the poisoning charge," Honey said.

"The order was issued before you left Indiana," Crumbo explained. "That means you still violated the law even if no criminal charges were ever filed.'

"What about me?" Leonard asked.

Crumbo scratched his head to think aloud. "They've got nothing on you. You're just an alleged kidnap victim. You haven't violated any court order. You can go home anytime you want."

Leonard took two steps forward to bring himself eye to eye with Crumbo. "What about Honey?"

Crumbo stopped scratching his head. "Well, that's going to be a major problem. Once the French police take her into custody, it might take weeks to get her back to Indiana. And once she's back, it might be quite a while until her case comes up for hearing. She won't get a bond because she fled the jurisdiction. And she did violate the no-contact order."

"What about me?" Leonard asked. "Didn't I violate the no-contact order?"

"No. The order is only against her seeing you. It says nothing about you seeing her."

"Then I guess we're right back where we started," Leonard said.

"Where's that?" Crumbo asked.

Leonard put his hands on his hips in a determined stance. "On the run."

"Can I quote you on that?" Crumbo asked.

"Absolutely," Honey and Leonard said in unison.

Crumbo and Lacoste did an extensive interview with Honey and Leonard. The reporters explored everything from personal histories to how they ended up on the run and all the way to Avignon.

"What made you decide to leave Indiana and head for France?" Lacoste asked.

"It was the nursing home more than anything," Leonard said. "After the big poisoning scare, they had me all doped up, and I couldn't see Honey at all, not even for a visit. So, I had to leave because I'm not ready to stop living. In fact, it feels like we're just getting started."

"That's right," Honey chimed in. "We're still in our seventies, for heaven's sake. You can tell the world to stop making such a fuss about us. We're not ambassadors of love or Bonnie and Clyde or Romeo and Juliet. We're just Honey and Leonard and we're in love and we'd like to be left alone if you please."

"I can understand that," Lacoste said, "but what I wonder is why did you come to France?"

Leonard held up the index finger on his big right hand. "Number one, we always wanted to come here. But number two, we figured the French people would understand better than anyone why our love is so important."

"And why is your love so important?" Crumbo asked.

Leonard stopped talking with his hands and clasped them together in front of his chest. "Because we're what most people call old, but our love makes us young again."

"I couldn't have said it better myself," Honey added.

Crumbo and Lacoste couldn't believe the story they were getting. At the end of a two-hour interview, Crumbo asked, "I guess the only question left is how will we stay in touch?"

"Give me a number at your newspaper," Leonard said to Lacoste. "We'll check in from time to time."

"So where is your car and your bags?" Lacoste asked. "We've got to retrieve them quickly."

They had previously retrieved the car from the hotel valet,

packed up their things and checked out of the hotel. Leonard kept reminding Honey of the need to keep moving.

"Everything's already in the car," Honey said. "It's only a few blocks from the church."

"Wait a minute," Lacoste said. "There's one more thing I have to ask. My readers will want to know."

"What is it?" Honey said.

Lacoste shuffled his feet and was obviously embarrassed by what he was about to ask.

"He wants to know about our sex life," Leonard said.

"That is exactly right," Lacoste said with a sigh of relief.

Crumbo held up his hand to intervene in the name of privacy but thought better of it. He cast a knowing glance at Lacoste as if to say, "Good question."

"I'll handle this one," Honey said. "The short answer is 'yes,' we still have sex. We get naked and everything. Here's the news flash for your readers; sex is still fun, even into your later seventies. But sex is no longer the main deal. Young people often confuse sex with love. The longer and more complete answer to your question is that love is more a spiritual union than a physical one. Love isn't about two people trying to satisfy each other's sexual needs. Love is when two people stop being selfish and start to care more about the whole of the relationship more than the parts that make it up."

"That is beautiful," Lacoste said. "So what you're saying is . . ."

"Love is greater than the sum of its parts," Honey concluded.

"Can I quote you on that?" Crumbo joked.

"You'd better," Leonard said.

Leonard's side of the story broke the next morning in Chicago and Paris. News outlets from all over the world picked it up immediately. Honey and Leonard were becoming folk heroes for being old and in love and for being fugitives from an unjust legal system. Crumbo's story portrayed Leonard as mentally competent and as being grateful for being given a second chance at love. He quoted Leonard as saying, "Honey shows me everyday what it means to be in love. It's about caring more about the other person than yourself." He also quoted Leonard as saying, "If anyone's doing any kidnapping around here, it's me kidnapping her."

Most importantly, the story broke the fact that Leonard had not been poisoned in the first place and that the high levels of arsenic in his blood were caused by his years as a farmer working with pesticides.

Unfortunately, the police did not believe everything they read in the papers and saw on the news. By noon the next day, Lacoste had French police in his hotel room in Avignon, threatening to throw him in prison for obstruction of justice and not revealing Honey and Leonard's location. Lacoste said exactly what any reporter should say when threatened by the government.

Nothing.

NINE

HONEY AWAKENED in an inexpensive hotel room in Marseilles to find Leonard was gone. She threw off the covers and sprang out of bed while scanning the room and calling his name.

The clock on the nightstand said 7:30 a.m. She checked the bathroom. No Leonard. She dressed hurriedly and checked the hallway all the way down to the small lobby. No Leonard.

"Excuse me," she asked the desk clerk. "Have you seen a man in his seventies walk out the door this morning?"

"Yes, I saw this man leaving," the clerk said.

"What was he wearing?"

"He was wearing a jacket, and how you say, no hat."

"Did he have shoes on?"

"*Oui, madame.*"

Honey charged out into the streets and found the place they had parked the car the night before. It wasn't the same car they had rented in Paris. The priest in Avignon had sold them a used, black, four-door Peugeot from the Abbey. Honey had written a check for $3,000 on the spot.

"This is the perfect cover car," Leonard had said. "It always looks like it's in a funeral procession."

The priest accepted the check as good and promised to return the Paris rental car in two weeks. He offered to give Honey and Leonard confession. Leonard politely declined the ritual, but they did accept the priest's generous donation of a white, summer, nun's habit as a disguise for Honey and a priest's outfit, complete with brimmed hat, for Leonard. The French reporter, Lacoste, had convinced them they needed a disguise upgrade and an immediate change of vehicle. He also convinced his friend, the priest, to part with what is considered sacred clothing by the Catholic church.

"Father, forgive me," the priest said as he handed over the garments. "I can make an exception since these garments would only be thrown away. The fact that they fit you perfectly is very nearly a sign from God. They are quite used but they will serve you well. I would not do this for anyone else. The two of you represent the love of our Savior as well as anyone I have ever known or even read about. Even so, I am breaking sacred rules here, so you must never tell anyone about the car or the clothes."

Memories of the priest and his reluctant generosity made Honey smile even as she was getting frantic in her search for Leonard. He was not at the car. Honey knew he couldn't have driven off because she had the only keys. That was small consolation. She was fighting off panic, worrying about Leonard's whereabouts. Here he was in the main trade port of the former French empire, surrounded by forts and churches and basilicas and seamen who looked like pirates, not to mention immigrant fisherman and dock workers who looked like gangsters.

She walked to the wide boulevard, La Canebiere, and headed for the Old Port. She knew the center of trade and tourism would attract Leonard. She began hurrying down the street and shouting his name until she realized she needed to calm herself. She could not panic. Leonard's life might well depend on her keeping a clear head.

She could not call the police, no matter what.

Marseilles was majestic in the Mediterranean morning. The natural harbor was lined with boats, both modern and traditional. Their blue and green and red reflections gleamed and danced on the water. Ancient stone buildings shined in the sun as they had for centuries. Any other time Honey would have marveled at the cosmopolitan and nautical sights. Not today; her mission was clear. She had to find Leonard. Several times she thought she saw him in the distance, only to be disappointed once she got close enough to realize it wasn't him.

Honey walked and walked and ended up on the south side of the Old Port at the fortified tower of the Abbey of St. Victor. She paid little attention to the abbey, one of the oldest sites of Christian worship. It was nearly ten a.m., and everywhere she went people seemed to be looking at her like they recognized her.

The more she couldn't find Leonard the more angry she became with him for leaving her alone in this dangerous seaport. She knew what could happen to a woman by herself near the docks of Marseilles.

Her worst fear was for Leonard. She knew he could take care of himself in any kind of tough spot. He was big enough and still quite strong. She'd seen him handle an obnoxious drunk or two back in Indiana. But eventually, someone was going to recognize him and report him to the authorities. That would be the end of their honeymoon. And they weren't even married.

Suddenly, her mind took her in another direction.

Maybe he's back at the hotel. He might have found his way back by now. I should not be mad at him. He can't help wandering off.

The city was preparing for lunch by the time Honey made it back to the hotel.

The desk clerk gave her the news before she had a chance to ask. "He is here. I told him you are looking for him."

Honey raced up to the room and found Leonard relaxing on the bed with his back propped up by pillows. She was so relieved to see him that she threw herself on top of him. He groaned and wrapped his arms around her.

"Boy, am I glad to see you," Leonard said. "I thought you got mad and left me. Thank heavens the guy at the desk told me you were out looking for me."

"Where did you go?" Honey asked, starting to tear up in relief.

Leonard gave her that hopeless look he only used for his memory issues and said, "Honey, I don't know what to tell you. I don't remember leaving this morning or even getting dressed. I ended up wandering around the city. And then the strangest thing happened. My mother came to me and so did my daughter, Emma, the one who drowned fifty years ago. I swear they were both with me. We had the best time. It was like a reunion."

"What did your mother say?"

"She told me not to be afraid of what's happening to my mind. She told me not to be angry or sad about Emma dying so young. Emma said the same thing. She said she was fine. It broke my heart to see her. I actually held her in my arms. I felt her tears on my cheek. She called me 'daddy.' She sounded just like my mother. It was like they were both the same person. It was impossible because mother was gone before Emma was born. But it felt so real. And it felt so good."

"Oh, Leonard, it must have been wonderful."

"It was more than wonderful. But then the strangest thing happened."

"What?"

"Emma and my mother turned into the same person and that person started looking more and more like you, and then I remembered you weren't with me. I don't know what made me take a walk and I don't remember anything until I was talking with mother and Emma and then I began to worry about you."

Honey sat up on the edge of the bed. "Did your mother say anything to Emma?"

Leonard straightened himself up on the pillows. "She kept saying how delightful it was for all of us to be together. It was wonderful. It was perfect. It made me realize that everyone you love is part of the same thing."

"What thing is that?"

"I don't know what to call it," Leonard said, squinting his eyes in concentration. "It's hard to put into words. But it kind of goes along with what my mother always says when she appears to me."

"What's that?"

"It's always something about how we're all part of the same thing. And she always reminds me to not be afraid. She says being afraid spoils everything."

Honey threw her head back on Leonard's chest. "I'd have to say your mother is a very wise woman."

Leonard sighed happily. "You're so much like her it's scary."

Honey lifted her head to look at Leonard. "I wish I was more like her. The problem with me is I worry too much. That's one way you and I are so very different. You never seem to worry, even when you should. That's probably why we're so good together. When I get worried, you calm me down. When you should be worried, I'm here to worry for you."

Leonard turned away from her gaze and looked out the window. "You don't think I'm crazy for wandering around this foreign city and talking to people who aren't really there?"

Honey put her head back on his chest and squeezed him with all her might. "I don't think you're crazy. I know you're crazy. And I know I'm crazy about you and I'm so, so glad you came back to me. You have no idea how worried I was. I could see our fabulous trip coming to a terrible end. But tell me, how did you find your way back?"

Leonard reached over to the nightstand. "I had this card from the hotel in my pocket. I must have picked it up at the front desk. I gave the card to a taxi driver, and he took me right back here. I did recognize the place once I saw it again."

Honey sat up and took the card. She turned it over to look at the back, which was blank. "How did you pay for the ride? I've got all our money."

"I got the guy to talk to the hotel clerk. The clerk told him about you and said to come back at noon to be paid. The driver wasn't too happy, but he said he'd be back for sure. What time is it?"

"It's time for us to come up with a plan so nothing like this ever happens again. I've been worried sick about you. This old port city is no place to be lost and alone."

"I wasn't afraid," Leonard said, "and I wasn't alone."

"I'm not talking about you," Honey said. "I'm talking about me. I thought I'd lost you for good. And it sounds like I might have lost you if it hadn't been for that lucky card you found in your jacket."

"Actually, I found it in my pants pocket."

"Oh, so now you're Mr. Smarty Pants," she laughed in relief before sobering quickly. "Leonard, I'm talking about not letting this happen again. You have moments when you totally forget where you are. That's dangerous. It's dangerous for you and terrifying for me. I can't go through what I went through this morning looking for you. I can't go through that ever again."

Leonard smiled wryly. "I guess we'll just have to watch me a little more closely."

"I can't watch you when we're asleep," Honey's lips began to tremble as she was about to cry.

Leonard reached out to comfort her. "Oh, come on now, pumpkin. Don't cry. What's that you always say about the power of love? We'll be fine."

Honey couldn't help but smile at his reference to her unbounded optimism. "I suppose I'll just have to tell the desk clerks to be on the lookout for a sneaky old man who might not know where he's going."

"There you go," Leonard laughed. "I'm okay with that."

Honey did not tell Leonard how close she'd come to calling the police. The thought of Leonard wandering around, lost in Marseilles, was more than she could bear. It might have taken all day. But she would eventually have called the police.

"So, let's go eat something," she said. "I'm famished. I didn't get breakfast. I think I'll get dressed up as a nun. Come on, let's see how you look in your priest outfit."

"I'm not wearing a disguise," Leonard said. "It was nice of that priest to try to help, but I'm not going to dress like him just to go have lunch."

"But what if the police find us? You know they'll be looking here by now."

"Nobody's going to catch us. We'll take the car and find a nice little seaside restaurant. The seafood around here has got to be fantastic."

All through lunch Honey was having a flashback epiphany. As she and Leonard found a four-star restaurant on the rocky cliffs overlooking the Mediterranean Sea, a highlight reel of her love life blazed through her mind at warp speeds to penetrate her subconscious. It began with Daniel, her first love, the boy who broke her heart. She gave herself to him so foolishly and so completely. His desertion hardened her heart in ways she was only now beginning to understand.

She saw herself fifty-five years earlier, walking down the aisle as a bride in her family's church in Mobile, Alabama. Every step took her closer to marrying a man who would protect and provide for her. Every step a calculated move toward marrying a man she trusted and admired but did not really love.

She saw her entire marriage fly by. It had been fun at times but much more a business deal than a romance. By the time the doctor died, Honey had grown into an independent soul who could appreciate her newfound freedom. She had to be free before she could finally fall in love.

As Leonard was ordering grilled lobster for the two of them, Honey was reliving the early days of her marriage to the doctor, particularly the decade of trying to conceive a child. By the time the fertility doctor finally concluded she could not bear children, Honey had already decided not to adopt. She was too busy becoming the reigning queen of a small town's high society. The love of raising children would not be part of her makeup.

"What's up with you?" Leonard asked as dinner arrived at the table. "You feel a little far away."

"I am," Honey said. "But I'm beginning to realize something I should have known a long time ago."

Leonard waited for her to continue as he began trying to dismember the lobster into something he could actually put in his mouth.

Honey spoke quietly. "You're the first man I ever fell in love with."

Leonard kept working on the lobster.

She raised her voice like she was talking to someone who was hard of hearing. "Leonard, did you hear me? I'm pouring my heart out to you here, and you're not even paying attention to me."

He put down the lobster and wiped his hands on the napkin, "I'm sorry, pumpkin. Did you say I'm the first man you ever loved?"

"Yes, I did. And thank you for listening."

Leonard realized he needed to step up his game. "Come here. Stand up and give me a big hug."

Their embrace morphed into a slight dip of a dance move, much to the delight of their fellow diners.

"It doesn't seem fair," Honey said as they sat back down. "Why did it take me this long to finally follow my heart instead of my brain?"

Leonard drank down an entire glass of water in several deep gulps. "I know what you mean. But, in fairness, we didn't meet each other until recently."

"Do you think we would have fallen in love and lived happily ever after if we'd met when we were sixteen?"

Leonard was about to attack the lobster again but thought better of it. "Would you have gone for a farm boy?"

Honey's head shrunk into her shoulders. "Probably not. I was looking for Prince Charming to whisk me away in his golden carriage. I was waiting for Cupid to shoot me with his arrow. I was looking for love to come into me from the outside. It took meeting you, later in life, to realize that true love has to come from within."

"It's better to love and be loved," Leonard said.

Honey looked at him with the deep gratitude of understanding and of being understood. "Exactly right. Love needs to be a two-way street."

Leonard nodded and took a long pause before speaking. "Honey, if we're doing true confessions, there's something I've got to tell you."

"What?"

Leonard wiped his lips with the cloth napkin. "You're the first girl I was ever in love with."

Honey took his work-gnarled, lobster-smeared hands into hers. "Oh, my dear Leonard. You are so sweet. I do love you so.

You make me feel like I always wanted to feel. This is our time. Nobody can take it away from us."

She noticed tears in his eyes as she wiped away her own. "Now, if only the police weren't after us."

Leonard smiled and got himself together. "They'll never catch us. We'll stay on the move."

"But it's not that simple," Honey said. "Now that we're in love and in France, I'm afraid I'm going to lose the man I love, like I did this morning at the docks."

"Oh, that was just a temporary thing," Leonard said.

Honey waited to continue the conversation.

"Okay, what's up?" Leonard broke the silence. "What's on your mind? I can tell something's bothering you."

Honey took a long sip of her wine before answering, "I'm not talking about losing you physically. I'm talking about losing you mentally." Honey fidgeted in her chair and stabbed at her lobster a bit before continuing. "Leonard, let me just say it. I'm afraid you've got Alzheimer's, and it frightens me to death."

Leonard looked out on the sparkling sea and seemed to become lost in watching the endless waves rolling into shore. Honey began to think he might not be willing to address the issue. Then he smiled politely and said, "Honey, I've known about my memory problem for more than a year now. Things are not going to get better for me. They're going to get worse. You deserve better. But I'm going to keep giving you everything I've got until there's nothing left to give. From what I've read, there's nothing anybody can do about the damned disease. Why do you think I gave Gretchen the Power of Attorney and let her talk me into living in that god awful nursing home?"

Honey leaned in to him. "You sound so matter of fact about it. Aren't you scared?"

Leonard smiled more warmly. "No more than I am afraid of

dying. And, may I remind you, that's coming soon to a theater near both of us."

Honey sat up straighter in her chair as if cold water had just dripped down her back. "Well, then, I propose a toast. Are you ready?"

"Of course," Leonard said, raising his glass.

Honey clinked his glass with her own. "I propose a toast to living it up, right here and right now."

"I'll drink to that," Leonard said. "That is exactly what we're doing. In fact, I can't think of any two people on the planet who are doing a better job of it than we are."

The grilled lobster turned out to be a little too dry and way too much work. Honey gave up on it after a couple bites. The rest of their luncheon, however, was as good as the view. The sun reflected on the waves, and the waves pounded the rocky shore. Honey and Leonard sipped their wine slowly and planned their trip down the coast of France, heading east. Their next stop would be Cassis. Nobody at the restaurant seemed to have recognized them, but they knew they had to keep moving.

As they were getting back in the car after lunch, Honey returned to their philosophical discussion. "What do you think happens to you when you die?"

Leonard started the car and revved up the engine before easing off the gas and turning to look at her. "It's going to be a lot like it was before you were born."

Honey found that interesting and funny and comforting. It was so . . . Leonard.

"I think I'll just be happy with what I've got," she said.

"That's my girl," Leonard said as he drove the priest's black sedan down the winding road along the rocky cliffs.

Back in Indiana, Robert Nimmo, was trying to talk Prosecutor Karen Lindvall into dismissing the felony charge against Honey for violating the no-contact order. The prosecutor had agreed to meet with Nimmo in her office.

"So let me get this straight," Lindvall said. "Your client is a suspect in an attempted murder case. She flees the jurisdiction with the man she allegedly tried to poison. She thumbs her nose at the court's no-contact order. She's arguing her case in newspapers and television stations around the world, trying to make us all look like fools. And you want me to say the whole thing has been a big mistake on my part? What I should do is file obstruction of justice charges against Jack Crumbo and *The Chicago Tribune* for refusing to reveal Honey and Leonard's location."

Nimmo realized he had to respond carefully. "I don't think you're looking bad here," he began. "I think you did what you had to do, considering the evidence in front of you at the time. All I'm asking you to do now is consider some newly discovered evidence."

Lindvall looked at Nimmo like she was ready to pay attention.

Nimmo continued, "I have three documents I would like you to review."

Lindvall leaned back in her chair. "You've got the floor."

"Thank you. First of all, here's a report from a forensic pathologist who says Leonard Atkins was never poisoned in the first place. It was his years of exposure to pesticides on the farm that led to high levels of arsenic in his blood."

Lindvall read the report carefully and said, "Has this guy looked at the actual blood work?"

"No, but he will if you convince Adult Protective to turn it over."

Lindvall thought about that proposition for a moment and then said, "All right, what's the second thing?"

"The second thing is this Power of Attorney that Leonard gave to his niece, Gretchen Atkins. This is where the plot thickens. Gretchen got control of his money and now she wants him declared incompetent so he can't get it back. She wants Honey out of the picture because Honey asks too many questions. That's why she used the blood tests against her."

Lindvall took the power of attorney from Nimmo and looked it over carefully. "How did you get this?"

"Leonard gave his copy to Honey and Honey gave it to me with his permission."

Lindvall leaned forward in her chair. "What do you mean she used the blood tests against Honey?"

Nimmo stood up and walked around the back of his chair. "Once the arsenic showed up in his blood, she should have had more tests done on him. Instead, she went right to the police and adult protective."

The prosecutor thought about that argument for a moment before asking, "So what's the deal? Is Leonard competent or is he not?"

"He's more competent than you or I most of the time," Nimmo said.

"What do you mean, 'most of the time'?"

"I mean he has his moments of forgetfulness like anybody his age."

"So why doesn't he just revoke the Power of Attorney and be done with Gretchen?"

Nimmo slapped the back of his chair for emphasis. "Because he's in France with Honey and he can't turn himself in because she'll go to jail on the charge you have filed against her."

Lindvall leaned back in her chair again. She kept her poker face but frowned with her eyebrows and lips as she continued staring at the documents. Nimmo could see he was making progress.

She spoke deliberately. "I can't drop the Invasion of Privacy charge for her violating the no-contact order and leaving the country with Leonard. That's just blatant disregard for the law."

Nimmo couldn't help but press his point. "What if the attempted murder investigation shows Leonard was never poisoned? That would mean the no-contact order was never needed."

Lindvall stood up slowly. "You do know Honey and I have been friends for a long time?"

"Honey has only spoken of you in the most glowing terms," Nimmo said.

Lindvall smiled tightly at that remark as if to say, "I know you're kissing my ass now."

"This isn't about Honey," Nimmo said. "This is about Leonard's niece, Gretchen, a retired school teacher manipulating the system so she can keep stealing her uncle's money."

Lindvall turned around and looked out the window over the bookshelves behind her desk. "You keep saying that but you can't prove it."

"No, but that brings us to the third item of newly discovered evidence I would like you to consider." He knew the final document would be the trump card. He waited for Lindvall to turn around and handed it across the desk ceremoniously, like he was offering an exhibit as evidence in a trial. "This is part of an application for a zoning variance. It shows somebody is trying to turn Leonard's farm into a housing subdivision. That somebody is doing business with Gretchen Atkins, and you can bet Leonard has no idea what's going on."

Lindvall read and reread the document. The prosecutor looked up at Nimmo with questioning eyes. "The only thing that doesn't make sense is why Gretchen would turn on her Uncle Leonard. Those two have been like father and daughter for as long as I can remember."

"The two oldest motivators in the world," Nimmo said. "It's greed and jealousy. Gretchen's been spending her uncle's money like it was her own for years. Now, Honey comes along to steal not only his affections but also Gretchen's entire inheritance. In Gretchen's jealous mind, she's not betraying her uncle, she's protecting him from Honey."

"Very interesting, Mr. Nimmo. But none of this changes the fact that your client fled my jurisdiction in direct violation of a court order. The fact that she's my friend has nothing to do with it. I don't do special favors. The people of Wabash County didn't elect me to play favorites."

"All I'm asking is that you look into the matter," Nimmo said as Lindvall showed him the door. "I'm not looking for a fast answer."

"Lucky for you," Lindvall said.

TEN

HONEY FOUND HERSELF LOST and afraid in the middle of a field of tall corn, calling Leonard's name. The moon was nearly full but its light couldn't help her see anything but six-foot corn stalks. She was eighteen years old again. She was dreaming.

"Leonard!" she screamed. "Stop playing games. You're frightening me."

A tremendous rustling in the rows of corn behind made her turn around quickly. She felt like some beast of the night was about to devour her. She knew what was going on, but that didn't stop her heart from pounding in her chest.

Leonard popped out of the corn with a big laugh and wrapped his strong, young arms around her. She struggled only momentarily before relaxing into the warmth of his embrace and the excitement of his kiss. They were young and in love and alone. The night was their canvas, and they knew exactly what to paint.

Leonard spread out a blanket in the space between the rows of corn and laid her down gently. He began kissing her neck and worked his way down her quivering chest. She made no protest as he took off her top and eased his muscular, bare chest onto her full, naked breasts. Her skin melted into his. He felt better than Clark Gable looked in *Gone With the Wind*.

The moon and all the stars in the world were shining down on their love-nest. They made love slowly and perfectly. They became one. He was gentle and smooth. He filled her with love. She kissed him deeply, tenderly.

There were no bugs. All she could smell was ripe corn, rich soil and Leonard's scent mixing with her own. He was the farmer and she was the field. Hearing herself moaning, Honey awakened from the dream to find herself in bed with a sleeping Leonard. She couldn't remember where she was as she threw her leg and arm over him. It didn't matter where they were. They were together.

"Leonard," she whispered, still buzzing from the erotic dream. "Wake up sleepy head. I just had the most fantastic dream about us."

He rolled over and rubbed his eyes. "Were we in a cornfield making love when we were young."

Honey's eyes widened. She almost choked on her own surprise. *How could he know that? Was he with me in the dream? Have I had that dream before and told him about it? No, I haven't had that dream before.*

"Leonard," she said as she grabbed his shoulders with both hands. "Look at me. Are you telling me you've been making love to me in cornfield dreams? Were you just having that dream?"

"I don't know if I was just now having that dream, but I've had the dream before. At least it feels like I have. By the way, you should see yourself at eighteen. You are one hot little number. Almost as cute as you are now."

"No, no, don't joke. I need to know if we've been meeting each other in dreams. I need to know if it's the same dream or maybe we're just having similar dreams."

"Pumpkin, doesn't it make sense that if you love someone, you love them on all levels, not just the wake-up world."

Honey's eyes opened wide. "The wake-up world?"

"Yes, the wake-up world as opposed to the dream world."

Honey got up out of the bed and went into the bathroom to

splash some warm water on her face. She looked much worse than she had seen herself in the dream. *How can you see yourself in a dream?*

Returning to Leonard, she said, "Just what do you know about the dream world?"

Leonard looked at her with a knowing look in his eye she had never seen before. "I know it might be more real than the wake-up world."

"All right, I get that kind of thinking. But let me ask you, specifically, how do we find the room to make love in the middle of a cornfield?"

"You know. You were there. I just throw down a blanket between the rows. There's plenty of room."

"Leonard, stop. I wasn't there. We were dreaming."

"Honey, the only difference between dreams and what we call reality is what we choose to believe. Dreams don't just come true. They are the truth."

Honey looked at him like she was seeing him for the first time. "I never thought about it like that. I never thought I'd be making love to you in my dreams as a young woman. I'm still not sure what's real about my dreams."

Leonard swung his legs over the edge of the bed and sat up. "I'll tell you one thing, for sure. My thoughts on reality have changed a lot since I started having these spells of forgetfulness."

Honey sat down beside him and looked at him in wonder. "What do you mean?"

"Well, for example, I often see my mother again. She's been gone for years, but I am convinced it is really her I see and it is really her who talks to me. What does it matter if it's really her or if I'm just making her up? She's still there and I still get comfort from talking to her. She loves you, by the way."

Honey leaned against him. "Leonard, I never met the woman, but I'm sure she was, or is, a wonderful person. In fact, next time you see her, tell her I said hello."

"Don't make fun."

She pushed him back into bed and said, "No, I'm not making fun. You just continue to amaze me, that's all."

They cuddled and stroked each other for a delicious half hour until Honey got out of bed. She felt stiff and creaky. Her back was hurting as if she had actually been lying on the uneven ground of a cornfield. She began stretching and remembering where she was.

They were in a villa in Cassis, halfway up the low-slung mountains and overlooking the Mediterranean bay. The room they had rented the night before was the bottom floor of a three-story, stone structure in the middle of a connected row of dwellings on a street barely wide enough for one small automobile to pass. The front windows were boarded for safety so they couldn't see what they knew must be a wonderful view. On a whim, they walked out the back door into a garden courtyard. Near the back of the house, they found a ladder from the garden to the roof.

"I'm not sure about this," Leonard said, looking up the ladder's twenty-two steps. "I'm not as good on ladders as I used to be. I swore off ladders the last time I cleaned my gutters. That was ten years ago. I was sixty-six years old then. I distinctly remember thinking how old that was."

"No matter how old you are," Honey said, "ten years later you'd give anything to be that young again."

Leonard hung onto the ladder without going up. "Isn't that the terrible truth?"

"Let me remind you how it's done," Honey said as she nudged her way around him and started up the ladder. They were both wearing the flannel pajamas they had splurged on in a Paris boutique.

"Don't you think we'd better get dressed first?" Leonard asked as she quickly climbed halfway up the ladder.

Honey stopped and looked down. "We are dressed. These outfits cost enough to show this little town who we are."

Leonard got into position at the bottom of the ladder. "I don't know, pumpkin. Lots of people can see you once you're on the roof. Remember what happened to us in Avignon. Dancing on top of that tower showed those reporters exactly where we were."

Honey teased him as she began climbing again. "Come on, sweetie. It's early. No one will see us. Start climbing and stop stalling. It's easy. Just take the steps one at a time."

"You make this sound like an Alcoholics Anonymous meeting."

"It is an AA meeting," she said, looking down from the roof. "That stands for Adult Adventurers. That's what we are. Come on, sweetie, show me what you got."

Leonard made it to the top with much less difficulty than Honey had anticipated. Her taunting must have given him just the boost of energy needed to make the climb. Honey chuckled as she realized the schoolyard competitiveness that had become part of their relationship. Even at seventy-six, he didn't like the notion of being shown up by a "girl," especially a woman who was a year older than him.

Once they hauled themselves up and onto the roof, they took in the breathtaking view of the ancient fishing harbor, the Gulf of Cassis. The deep blue water was surrounded by giant maritime cliffs that had been sailors' landmarks since ships began to sail. Nestled between the rock walls and the shoreline was a village of pastel-painted buildings. Fishing vessels bobbed and reflected on the water in front of the village along with sightseeing boats and luxury yachts of the wealthy.

Honey pointed to the dock in front of the village. "Look at the masts and sails and wooden decking shining in the sun. It looks like a Manet painting. This is too good to be true. Last night we came in the dark. I had no idea how beautiful this place really is. Let's stay here forever."

She began feeling lightheaded as she spoke. At first, it felt like a natural response to the overwhelming beauty of the scenery. But it was more than that. Before she knew what was happening, Honey was fainting.

Leonard saw it coming and managed to mostly catch her as she collapsed on the roof. Once she was down and Leonard got a good look at her, he realized what was happening.

Honey was not breathing.

Her color quickly faded. Her eyes were closed and she looked lifeless. She was beginning to turn slightly gray as Leonard began administering CPR. Due to his own heart condition and the advice of doctors, he had taken several courses in CPR. Even so, the act of pushing on Honey's chest and trying to give her mouth-to-mouth resuscitation filled him with dread. It took him right back to the terrible time when he had not been able to save his own daughter from her drowning tragedy. He wasn't about to lose another fight with death.

"Honey," he barked as he continued his frantic efforts. "Honey, stay with me."

The gorgeous scenery of Cassis turned into a menacing, medical, no-man's land. There was no way he could summon help, let alone expect any to arrive. He couldn't take the time to go back down the ladder and look for someone who might understand the situation. He knew he had to keep pushing on Honey's chest. He was her only hope. He pushed harder, many more times, waiting several seconds between each push. He stopped to listen, checking inside her mouth with his fingers to make sure she hadn't swallowed her tongue. She wasn't breathing, but her color didn't seem to be getting any worse.

Leonard could see his only daughter dying in front of him all over again. After fifty years, the image was still painfully fresh. He had watched his daughter dying every single day of his life. At least Honey had not taken in too much water. There was still hope.

His life would be empty without her. His life would be over.

"Please, God, don't let her die," Leonard cried as he rested between pushes.

Honey's left hand began to twitch. Leonard wasn't sure if that was a good sign or a bad sign. He kept pushing and trying to talk to her. He felt himself sobbing with every push. He was losing her. He was losing strength. Only by resting for several seconds between each effort was he able to keep going. Honey was running out of time. Leonard was desperate.

"God," he pleaded to the sky. "Please don't take her from me now. I've got so much left to give her. Please, please, help me save her."

On the next push, Honey's eyes opened and she gasped for breath. Leonard's rescue efforts were working. She was coming back. He kept pushing, more gently, until she pushed his hands away.

Her eyes began focusing in anger. "Stop, you're hurting me."

He straightened up, still kneeling, and looked at her through his tears. He was exhausted and emotionally drained, breathing heavily and feeling lightheaded himself. He looked at the sky and said, "Thank you, thank you, thank you."

Honey was still disoriented but she could see Leonard was thanking God for her breathing again. She had always known he was a man of faith but she had never figured out exactly what it was he believed in.

"Who are you thanking?" she asked.

Leonard took her hands into his own. "I'm thanking God you're still alive. I thought you were leaving me."

"What does she look like?" Honey teased, beginning to come to her senses.

Leonard laughed at the notion God might be a female and kissed Honey on the forehead so hard she thought she might pass out again. "I don't know what she looks like," Leonard said, "but I'm sure glad she's there."

Honey's return to the world of the breathing was like Lazarus coming back to life in the Gospel of John. Leonard looked at her in awe and held her hands as if she might be an angel who would soon fly away. He tried to talk her back into full consciousness, "Don't try to move, pumpkin. Just keep breathing."

"What happened?" she asked as she struggled to get up on her right elbow.

"Don't try to move. I'm pretty sure you just had a heart attack or a stroke. We've got to get you to a hospital."

Honey took a couple deep breaths and took a long look around. "Where are we?"

"We're in Cassis, France. We're on the roof. Look, there's the harbor."

"Why are you wearing pajamas?"

"We just woke up and decided to climb up on the roof so we could get a good view of the harbor."

"Why am I wearing pajamas that look so much like yours?"

Leonard felt strange being the one to help Honey with her memory. "We bought them in Paris. Think back. You can remember. Take deep breaths. It will come to you."

"I must have fainted. Oh, Leonard, it's you. I didn't recognize you at first."

"Yes, it's me and I'm afraid you did more than just faint. I think you had a heart attack."

"What makes you say that?"

"I had to bring you back with CPR. You weren't breathing. You were starting to turn blue. We've got to get you to a hospital."

"We're not going to any hospital," Honey said as she began to gather her thoughts. "I remember where we are now. And I remember why we're here. The police are after us. No, we won't be going to any hospital or even to a doctor. That would be the end for us. So listen to me. What you're going to do is go back to the room and get me one of my heart pills. Can you do that? I remember the ladder now. It's not an easy climb. I think it might be the climb that got me. I was showing off. I came up too fast."

Leonard began struggling to stand up. "I can go get you a pill, but I don't think it's a good idea for you to take my medicine."

"Leonard, I've never told you, but I've had this happen at least two times in the past three years. You know what the doctor gave me? It's nitro, or something similar. That's all I need. Now, go get me a pill. I've got my own. I don't need one of yours. It's in a little pink prescription container in the bottom of my purse. My purse is in the bathroom, next to the sink. See how good my memory is? Better bring a bottle of water too. I'm probably dehydrated."

Leonard looked at her like he was getting a new lease on life. "Thank you, Lord," he shouted to the sky.

"Yes, it's all coming back to me now," Honey said. "We had sex in a cornfield last night. It's those wild dreams that are doing this to me. We can't keep going back in time like that. It's hard on my heart."

"I'll go get your pills and some water, but we're going to need a helicopter to get you off this roof."

Honey was able to smile at his desperation. "I won't be needing a helicopter as long as you don't need one to get down and back up that ladder."

Her challenge moved him into action, although completing the errand took much too long. Once he got back to the room, Leonard forgot what he was supposed to be doing. He began wondering where Honey had gone. It wasn't until he noticed her purse in the bathroom that he remembered his mission.

By the time he climbed back up to the roof with the medicine and a bottle of water, Honey was sitting up, looking tired and alarmed but no longer confused.

"You know," she said. "This wouldn't be that bad of a place to die. Just look around. It looks like we're in heaven."

Leonard gave her the medication and water. "There, there; let's not have any talk about dying. Let's talk about living. After all, I'm the one who just saved your life."

"Yes, you did," Honey said. "You most certainly did save my life. Once again, you are my hero." She threw her arms around his left leg, nearly tackling him. "How long was I out?"

Leonard patted the top of her head. "Not that long. Long enough to scare the heck out of me. Maybe a minute, it felt like an hour."

Leonard helped Honey to her feet after she took the medication and drank the entire bottle of water. "I thought I was supposed to be taking care of you," she said.

Leonard took her into his arms to stabilize her. "We're taking care of each other."

Honey looked up at him with love in her eyes. "You know, sweetie, we've been on the run now for what? Maybe it's been nine days. Looking back, it's been the best time of my life. Do you remember all the places we've been?"

"I can't say as I do, pumpkin. I remember bits and pieces, but I couldn't recite an itinerary or anything like that."

Honey backed out of his embrace and stood on her own. "Well, I can and I will do it just to show you I don't need a doctor. We've been to Indianapolis, New York, Paris, Giverny, Dijon, Avignon,

Aix en Provence, Marseilles and Cassis. How about that for somebody who doesn't need to go to a hospital?"

Leonard shook his head in amazement. "Not bad for somebody who didn't know who I was a few minutes ago. You really are something. You're lucky your memory comes back so quickly. Sometimes mine doesn't come back at all. I don't remember that 'X' place you mentioned."

Honey shook her finger at him like a determined school teacher. "Yes, you do. We didn't stay there overnight. Remember, we tried to get into the home of that artist. What was his name? You said he was your second favorite French artist, after Monet."

Leonard's face lit up. "Oh, Paul Cezanne. Yes, I do remember a little now. His old home and studio was closed. I remember the big green door you tried to push open but it wouldn't budge."

"See, your memory isn't as bad as you think."

Leonard took her hands in his at arm's length. "Well, it's certainly not as good as yours."

Honey continued her lesson. "Here's a memory challenge for you. Do you remember the night not so long ago when you came knocking on my door from the nursing home?"

"I do remember that."

Honey nodded encouragingly. "We decided to break the law and leave town together without much discussion at all."

"It was impulse fleeing," Leonard laughed. "If we'd have thought about it any longer, we probably wouldn't be here."

"And look what we would have missed," Honey said, pointing at the storybook land and seascape all around them.

Leonard took a deep breath of the sea salt air. "Yes, I feel sorry for all those people back in Indiana who wish they were here but don't have the guts to get up and do it. I'm proud of us for doing it. But two things still scare me."

"What?"

"Number one, getting caught by the police. There are bound to be plenty of people who've recognized us along the way. We're much bigger news than I ever thought we'd be. Wasn't it strange, seeing ourselves on the television news last night?"

"What was that newsman saying?" Honey wondered. "It was something about us being the Bonnie and Clyde of love. What do the French know about Bonnie and Clyde?"

"American gangster movies are big all over the world. I guess we're on the run like Bonnie and Clyde, but we haven't robbed any banks or done anything wrong."

"Except be together when they told us we couldn't," Honey said. "The French media seem to be on our side. They treat us like celebrities. Maybe we should do a live interview on television to argue our case."

Leonard's face tightened. "That's the best way I know to bring the police down on us."

"So, what do you always say about not getting caught?"

"We got to keep moving," Leonard said. "And right now, that means climbing back down the ladder. Are you up to it? How do you feel?"

"I'm good to go," Honey said. "The ladder's no problem. Going down should be easier than coming up. I think I can make it. I'll take it nice and easy. What's the second thing you're worried about?"

Leonard thought about her question as he began climbing down the ladder first. She looked down at him before beginning her shaky descent. "What's the second thing?"

Leonard raised his voice to make sure she could hear him. "The second thing is our health. Things like what just happened to you make me think we're way too far away from medical care."

"Listen, mister," Honey said as she climbed down slowly. "We're running away from the medical system as much as we're running away from the legal system. If either one of them catches up with us it's already too late."

"What we're really running away from is the nursing home," Leonard said as he helped Honey down the long, last step to the garden. "It's the nursing home that kills you."

Honey took a long nap after her ordeal on the roof. She awakened feeling better but still a little weak. She and Leonard took a slow walk around the colorful harbor. Honey continued to resist Leonard's efforts to seek medical care. "You can stop with all that talk about me needing a doctor. I've had this happen before. I've already taken the medicine prescribed by a doctor. I'll be fine."

"You can't just get up and go on with life after you stop breathing like that," Leonard said. "You need to stay a couple days in a hospital for tests and such."

"What happens to me is not a heart attack. It's what my doctor calls a 'heart event.' It's more like a mini-stroke than anything. It's certainly not a heart attack."

Leonard stopped walking and turned to Honey. "I don't care what your doctor calls it. You should have seen me pumping on your chest up on the roof."

Honey swooned. "Yes, I wish I could have seen you in action. You must have worked me over pretty hard. I'm still sore and getting more sore by the minute."

They found a crowded café with tantalizing aromas and stopped in for lunch. Several diners stared at them as they were escorted to a small table with an unobstructed view of the water. "Ah, this is living," Leonard said as he unfolded his cloth napkin.

Honey stretched her hands in the air and then clasped them together behind her head. "I wonder what the poor folks back in North Manchester are doing right now?"

At the waiter's suggestion, they tried the bouillabaisse. "Now, this is the best fish stew I've ever eaten, anywhere," Honey said once the meal arrived and they started eating. "This is what I need, a big bowl of hot, garlic and pepper broth. Not a bunch of expensive doctors in a hospital where they run too many tests on you just so they can make more money. Don't talk to me about doctors. I know all about doctors. I was married to one most of my life."

Before they could finish the soup or their conversation about doctors, a man in a suit, who appeared to be the owner or the manager of the restaurant, approached the table, leaned down and said in an out-of-breath whisper, "Honey and Leonard. It is you, no?"

Honey and Leonard were too surprised to react. The owner continued without waiting for them to respond. "You must come with me. The police are on their way at this very moment. They will be here in less than five minutes."

Honey and Leonard exchanged a glance that acknowledged they had no choice but to trust the stranger. They got up with as little fuss as possible and followed him through the bar and into the kitchen. He barked a few orders to the busy staff and walked Honey and Leonard out the door and into the back of his restaurant van.

"Where are you staying?" he turned around from the driver's seat once they were on the move.

"Is it safe to go back to the room?" Honey asked.

"Yes," the man said. "Somebody saw you walking near the water and called the police. My waiter heard it on the police scanner and then saw you sitting at his table. The police don't know where you are staying but they are looking for the car you rented in Paris. They say it's a blue, 1992 Ford. Are you still driving that car?"

"No, we switched vehicles in Avignon," Leonard said.

Honey nudged him to not reveal more information.

"Good," he said. "I heard them describe the vehicle on the police radio," he said. "They are looking for the wrong car. But they do know that today you were walking along the harbor in Cassis."

"Won't you be in trouble for helping us?" Leonard asked.

"I'll drop you off at your hotel and then continue on to the market for supplies. I told my kitchen staff I was going out for spices."

The helpful restaurateur drove the speed limit until he dropped Honey and Leonard off at their rented villa. "Why are you doing this for us?" Honey asked as she stepped out of the van.

The man got out of his vehicle and embraced both Honey and Leonard. "I'm doing this for the excellent example you make for the world. Many people are on your side, as you say. God bless you both. I hope they never catch you. They should not be on the chase."

The man got back in his van and drove off before Honey and Leonard had a chance to properly thank him. They looked at each other. They were speechless. How was this happening to them?

Leonard looked at Honey and grinned. "Who was that masked man?"

"It was the Lone Ranger," Honey said. "It's not everyday you get the Lone Ranger rescuing Bonnie and Clyde."

"Hi, ho, Silver," Leonard raised his voice. "Away!"

They hastily packed bags and donned their costumes from the Abbey in Avignon. By now, Leonard realized they needed all the disguise they could muster. Honey looked quite convincing in her habit. She was still pale from her health problem, and she washed off all her makeup. Leonard did not look quite so natural in his cassock and hat but he could pass for a priest in a hurry. Driving away in the black sedan, they looked like a nun and a priest on their way to some church business.

As they drove along the highway overlooking the harbor, they could see the flashing lights of half a dozen police cars down below, along the waterfront.

Leonard took off his broad-brimmed hat and slapped it on the seat in triumph. "You can search all you want down there. You're not going to find us. We're on a mission from God."

"Leonard, don't be sacrilegious."

"I'm not being sacrilegious. I'm just stating the facts, ma'am. And, by the way, you're about the cutest little nun I ever did see."

"Leonard," Honey giggled, "maybe it's better we stay on the mission from God."

"God apparently does not want us to get caught," Leonard said. "He keeps sending angels to help us get away."

"I just wish we didn't have to leave such a beautiful place," Honey said. "We could have stayed there all winter and had a marvelous time."

It had not occurred to Honey and Leonard that their growing celebrity status could attract people with questionable motives. So far, everybody they met had been willing and able to help.

Their getaway from Cassis was not as clean as they thought. Someone who was not with the police was following them.

Meanwhile, Gretchen Atkins was beginning to feel the heat from Prosecutor Karen Lindvall. In fact, the prosecutor had invited her in for an "informal chat." Gretchen knew Lindvall socially and she was curious as to what Lindvall wanted to know from her. *Did she want help in finding Uncle Leonard? Or was she curious about what was happening with his money?*

She knew going to the prosecutor's office without an attorney was probably not a good idea. She also knew that having an attorney would make it look like she felt guilty about something. She finally decided that her approach would be to question the prosecutor on what was being done to find her uncle. She was not prepared for the prosecutor's opening salvo.

"What's this I hear about you selling the family farm to a housing subdivision?" Lindvall asked before any of the usual, introductory small talk.

The question hit Gretchen like a punch in the stomach. She didn't know what to say so she said nothing.

"What?" Lindvall said. "You don't want to answer that question? Do you think you've got something to hide?"

"Not at all," Gretchen tried to recover. "I just don't see what that has to do with finding my uncle."

"Are you, as Leonard Atkin's Power of Attorney, selling his farm?"

Gretchen realized she would have to lie. "Well, yes, if you must know, I am. And you should also know that it is with the full approval of Uncle Leonard."

Lindvall pointed her finger over the desk at Gretchen. "You do realize we will eventually find him and he will be able to either confirm or deny your statements."

Gretchen knew the prosecutor did not believe her. It was time to throw down her trump card. "Uncle Leonard no longer remembers much of what he has said and done."

"Is that why you've filed for guardianship over him?"

"Yes, it is."

"Do you think Honey Waldrop has kidnapped your uncle?"

Gretchen sensed uncertainty from the prosecutor's change of direction. With renewed confidence, she said, "No, I don't think Honey had to kidnap him. I think he went along willingly. It might have even been his idea. The whole runaway thing is just proof that he is no longer competent."

"Have you been reading the paper or watching television?" Lindvall asked. "Apparently, nobody but you believes he is incompetent."

Now, Gretchen felt like she could gain the upper hand. "You, of all people, should know better than to believe what you read in the paper. Especially, the tripe Jack Crumbo's been writing in *The Chicago Tribune*. He's making a career out of this story. Did you see his article in *Newsweek Magazine*? I'm sure his book will be coming out soon."

Lindvall couldn't help but be amused by that comment. "Be that as it may," she said, "we'll have plenty of time to test Mr. Atkins for competency."

"You can test him all you want," Gretchen said. "He can fool you for a while. I'm here to tell you, I know him better than anyone and the man is no longer in control of his own mind. And I'll go you one further. He knows it. Why do you think he signed the Power of Attorney over to me in the first place?"

"You mean this Power of Attorney?" Lindvall waved her copy at Gretchen. "This was signed nearly two years ago, shortly after his wife's death. You know these things can be revoked at any time?"

Gretchen tried not to sound smug. "Only by someone who's mentally competent." She could see the prosecutor was more than suspicious of how she was handling her uncle's money. She decided to say nothing more. "I'll be leaving now. If you have further questions, you can take them up with my attorney."

"Rest assured, I will have more questions," Lindvall said. "But, before you go, be advised there are laws that will hold you accountable for every cent of your uncle's money."

Gretchen couldn't help but respond, "I know you're trying to protect your friend, Honey Waldrop. May I remind you there is still a case against her for attempting to poison my uncle."

Lindvall attempted to conceal her anger at being accused of impropriety. "We both know why arsenic was found in Leonard's blood."

Gretchen left Lindvall's office in a hurry. She did not know why arsenic was in her Uncle Leonard's blood, but she did not want the prosecutor to see her shaking. The weight of the world was suddenly on her shoulders. She felt guilty, guilty, guilty.

Hearing the prosecutor say she would be held accountable for spending her uncle's money, made her realize how criminal her conduct had become.

How could I have known what a comeback he would make once Honey entered the picture? I thought he was on the way out. Now, what am I going to do?

Gretchen realized she was at a crossroads. She could find her uncle and beg his forgiveness. She knew he would forgive everything except selling the farm. She could undo that somehow. But Honey would certainly get in the way. And the law might not be so quick to forgive once an audit revealed how much money she had spent on herself without her uncle's knowledge or permission.

Her second option was to find Uncle Leonard and have Honey prosecuted. She knew the attempted murder charge would probably not stick. Honey would never try to hurt Leonard. But Honey was clearly guilty of violating the no-contact order.

Gretchen knew her uncle really was having memory problems that could only get worse. Time was on her side.

She returned home to discuss the matter at length with her new best friend of late, a bottle of Jack Daniel's whiskey. "Jack Black" had been her father's constant companion in his last years.

By 6 p.m., Indiana time, Gretchen was two-thirds drunk when she got the call from her investigator, Adam Wolfe.

"We're on the scene in Cassis," Wolfe said.

"Who's 'we' and what 'scene' are you talking about?"

"By 'we' I mean me." Wolfe lied, realizing he hadn't told Gretchen about his interpreter and new girlfriend, Simone. "And by the scene, I mean French police are about to arrest Honey and Leonard in Cassis. They're such celebrities in France that people are able to recognize them and report them to the police."

"Why are they celebrities?"

"The French people love them. At least that's what all the papers and television reporters say. They're calling Honey and Leonard the Bonnie and Clyde of love."

"Oh, my God," Gretchen groaned.

"I'm tuned in to the police radio. I was in Marseilles when I heard they were spotted in Cassis. I'm already here. And, by the way, I'm running out of money. Can you send me another $5,000?"

"I'll do you one better than that," Gretchen slurred her speech enough to let Wolfe know she had been drinking. "I'll do you one better," Gretchen repeated. "I'll bring you the money. I'm coming to Cassis. It's time we put a stop to this nonsense."

ELEVEN

"**L**EONARD, SLOW DOWN, PLEASE," Honey said as the Peugeot's over worn tires squealed through the hairpin turns on the steep road down through the orchards to St. Tropez.

"I'm not going that fast, pumpkin," Leonard said. "These turns are just too tight, and the tires are too old."

Honey braced herself with both feet on the floorboard and both hands on the padding above the passenger glove compartment. "You are going too fast. If the tires are making screeching noises, you're going too fast."

"I am not going too fast," Leonard said through gritted teeth. The car hit a dangerous curve and skidded into the oncoming lane.

"Stop the car this instant," Honey yelled. "I am getting out before you kill us both."

Leonard regained control of the vehicle in plenty of time to avoid oncoming traffic.

Honey stomped her feet and pounded her fists. "Stop the car now, Leonard Atkins. I mean it. I am getting out. I'll walk the rest of the way if I have to. My heart can't take this wild driving."

Leonard pulled off the road and got out of the car. He was still wearing the priest cassock. Honey got out of her door and stomped around the car to confront Leonard. She was wearing the nun's habit. To passing motorists, it looked like the Catholic church was coming apart at the seams. Honey was poking her finger in Leonard's chest and he was doing his best to stay out of harm's way.

Honey and Leonard were having the first major fight of their relationship. Her fear had turned to anger, panic morphed into rage. She pushed him with both hands in his chest so hard he actually had to take a step backwards to keep from falling over. "Don't think you can scare me half to death just to have a little fun."

As she came at him again, Leonard sidestepped her with some nimble footwork, learned from training as a boxer in his teens. This only made her angrier. "Don't you run away from me. I will catch you and then you'll be sorry."

Honey was running out of steam as she came at him once more. This time he let her push him, but braced and held his ground. He couldn't help but see the humor in this little nun trying to push her priest around with no success. He laughed out loud, and even Honey began to see how foolish she must have looked.

A mother with two children in her car was so unnerved by the sight of the nun attacking the priest that she pulled over and asked if anyone needed help. She spoke first in French but quickly changed to English when Leonard said, "No Francois."

"Is everything good?" the mother asked.

"Oui," Leonard replied with one of the few French words he knew and then switched back to English. "The sister is just confessing her need for God's help."

Honey waved to the mother that everything was fine and then returned her wrath to Leonard. "You're the one who's going to need God's help."

"Settle down, Honey," Leonard said as the mother drove away. "You're making the whole church look bad."

Honey put her hands on her hips and stared at him with a look that said, "Pay attention, mister, or you will be sorry."

"Hold it, hold it," Leonard relented. "Okay, I'll admit it. I was going too fast. I'm sorry. There, I said it. Are you happy? Here, why don't you drive for a while? We're almost there. You can drive us into St. Tropez."

"I'm not going to drive down this sidewinding road for you or any man," Honey sneered. "We're going to stay right here until you agree to get in that car and drive us slowly and safely into town. I am much too tired to watch you play race-car games behind the wheel."

Leonard turned and looked down on the town in the distance. All he could see was the golden dome of a church, gleaming in the sunshine. He hated to admit it, but he knew she was right. He had been having a bit of fun at her expense. He hadn't driven fast down a mountain road in some time.

He turned around, took a deep breath and said, "All right. I'll say it again. I was going too fast. I'm sorry, but it was fun. So, I'll say it. You are right and I was wrong."

"You don't mean that," Honey scolded.

Leonard wiped the smirk off his face. "Actually, I do mean it. I did not mean to frighten you and I'm sorry I did. I keep forgetting what happened on the roof with your heart." He took another deep breath and said, "Come on, get in the car. I'll drive like a little old lady."

Honey did not appreciate his sarcasm but she got in the car anyway. She was exhausted and feeling light headed. Leonard kept his word by driving cautiously into St. Tropez. They rode in strained silence most of the way, but as they came into the seaside resort town, Honey said, "Let's get a room and book it for a week. I need to stop moving for now. I need to rest."

The tension in the car began to ease up as the glory of St. Tropez enveloped them. Soon they were in the center of the ancient port on a seaside road with a wall of four-story buildings on one side and massive yachts docked in the water on the other side. Leonard drove slowly out of the central chaos until he found an inviting hotel at the base of what looked like the largest hill in town.

"We must be near the old fort," he said. "I think I see cannons up there on the hill."

In the hotel parking lot, Honey changed out of her nun's habit and said to Leonard, "You wait here, and I'll see if we can get a room. This does look like a nice place. And by the way, I am sorry I got so mad up there. But you scared me. I guess I'm a little tired and cranky."

"No need to be sorry," Leonard said. "We're both tired. We need a break from the road."

Honey disappeared into the hotel. She knew they had a much better chance of remaining anonymous if they were not seen as a couple. She was gone for more than fifteen minutes.

Leonard had changed clothes and was basking in the early evening sun when Honey returned with renewed cheer. "I booked us for three nights. We got the last room they had. It was expensive but it's got its own little porch and a view of the water. And, by the way, I paid cash."

Leonard was relieved to see her. "Come here, pumpkin, and give your sweetie a big hug."

Honey threw her arms around him. "You big lug. You know I can't stay mad at you for long."

He kissed her and held her tight. "I don't want you mad at me even for one second."

<hr>

Honey and Leonard entered the hotel in St. Tropez one at a time. After freshening up in the room, they walked out the back door of the hotel and hiked up the hill overlooking the port city and the Gulf of St. Tropez. Honey took frequent breaks on the way up, but her energy level was excellent. She was surprised and pleased by how much of her stamina had returned since the rooftop heart event in Cassis. It felt good to walk and stretch after too much time in the car.

The sun was just setting behind the far side of the harbor when they reached the top of the hill for the breathtaking view. Fishing boats and massive yachts were mingling on the shoreline docks. The town and its famous beaches stretched out for sandy miles. The landscape was overgrown with trees and bushes, still glowing green in the crepuscular light. The golden dome on the church below was beginning to lose its shine.

"Here we are at the Citadel," Leonard said as they took a rest on the large stone remains of the ancient battlements. "You can see why they put the cannons up here. They could control the entire harbor. I read a pamphlet on it in the room. This fort was built a long time ago. I forget the date, but it's hundreds of years old."

A huge destroyer anchored in the middle of the bay looked completely out of place in the idyllic scene. It was ominous and menacing. They couldn't tell its country of origin. It had massive gun turrets all over it with long cannon barrels that looked like they could open fire at any moment. Honey and Leonard stared at it for a long time, neither one of them commenting on the obvious anomaly. They were tired. Tired from walking uphill. Tired of traveling, tired of being chased and tired of being famous, or notorious.

"Doesn't that just say it all?" Leonard finally said.

Honey couldn't help but laugh. She knew what Leonard was thinking. She was thinking the same thing. She grabbed Leonard's arm and said, "You don't have to say it. I'll say it for you. There's a gunboat in the middle of our sea of love."

Leonard laughed with her, and their fatigue began to wash away. Honey saw the twinkle return to his eyes. Knowing what another person is thinking is the romantic payoff for sharing the rigors of the road.

They held hands and watched the lights of the town and on the destroyer gradually begin to turn on and shine in the growing darkness. A peacock wandered into their view, not twenty yards away and slightly down the hill. With a mighty squawk that startled them both, he spread feathers and erected his train to form a shimmering fan of what appeared to be a bright blue arch in the twilight.

"That's the male," Leonard said once he recovered from the surprise. "He looks like NBC. There must be a female nearby. He's putting on his show for someone special."

"Look," Honey said. "There she is. See her? She's behind that large pine tree down there."

As Honey spoke, the female peafowl took flight and landed on a branch halfway up the tree.

"Whoa," Leonard said. "I didn't know they could fly. I've never seen one fly."

Honey grabbed Leonard's arm. "The male must have excited her or maybe he scared her. Look at her. She's looking right at me, like she's trying to tell me something."

Leonard remained still as a hunter. "I don't think she's looking at anything except all those male feathers. Look at that boy. Each feather looks like it's got an eye that can see. He's pulling out all the stops for that girl."

Honey began whispering. "No, she's looking at me and she's saying, 'Look at the boys with all their feathers and battleships trying to impress the world.'"

Leonard hung his head and chuckled in amazement.

"What?" Honey asked.

"Only you could connect peacocks and battleships."

He took Honey in his arms and gave her a grateful kiss and a long embrace. When they uncoupled, the peacock and his potential mate were gone. The battleship was looking more and more sinister as darkness began to fall. Honey and Leonard decided to walk back down while they could still see the pathway.

They walked back into the hotel in St. Tropez as a couple. The concierge did not recognize them. He was busy helping other guests. After they rested in the room, they left out the back door again and changed into their Catholic costumes behind their black, four-door Peugeot in the parking lot.

Leonard tried to hold Honey's hand as they walked down from the hotel to savor the sights and delights of the romantic city by the sea. Honey withdrew her hand and said, "Priests and nuns do not hold hands."

"What if they're Episco*pals*?" Leonard asked, emphasizing the "pals. I think they've got Episcopals in France."

Honey couldn't help but laugh. In that moment, Leonard reminded her of her own playful father who loved to tease her when she was a child. "It's Episcopalians, not Episcopals. And, yes, they are all over the world. But we are Catholic, not Episcopal. Besides, I don't think any kind of nuns hold hands with their priests."

"That's why I hate these costumes," Leonard grumbled.

"Come on, Father, don't be a grump. Let's go see St. Tropez." Honey fluffed up her habit as best she could and turned her attention to Leonard. "Here, let me straighten your hat. There, you look positively priestly."

Leonard played along as they continued walking, but he couldn't resist giving Honey a playful spank on the fanny every now and then.

Even in the dark, St. Tropez was colorful. Most of the streets

were less than twenty feet wide. Five-story, stone buildings
rising on either side of the street made Honey and Leonard feel
like they were walking down canyons of French Riviera culture.
Ornamental streetlights hung off curled-iron hangers from the
second story level. Bright, colored lights identified shops of all
kinds at street level. Narrow sidewalks along the cobblestone
streets were protected by rows of black, metal bumpers that
looked like chess pawns on parade. On many stretches, however,
the sidewalks were unprotected from the maniac drivers in their
little compact cars.

The worst drivers were on scooters, passing cars through the
most narrow of spaces and brushing pedestrians back against
the walls of connected buildings. One particularly reckless Vespa
driver nearly knocked Leonard to the ground with the tip of his
handlebar.

"Hey, what do you think you're doing," Leonard boomed.
"You just about broke my goddamned arm."

People nearby stopped dead in their tracks when they heard
the priest cursing so loudly. They couldn't understand what the
priest was saying but they knew he was saying it with too much
venom to be a man of the cloth. Honey hustled him into a high-
priced gift shop to avoid further scrutiny.

"What do you think you're doing?" she scolded. "Did he really
hurt your arm?"

"Yes, he banged me good. I'll be fine. He just scared me. I know
priests don't curse. But guess what? I'm no priest. Besides, nobody
around here speaks English."

Honey got as close to his face as she could. "They don't have
to speak English to know you don't sound like a priest when you
lose your temper in the middle of the street."

Leonard looked around the shop to make sure nobody was

listening. "The next guy who brushes me back with his scooter is going to lose his head."

Honey shushed him. "Now, sweetie, let's not have you losing *your* head."

They left the shop before the over-dressed employee could try to sell them anything and went off in search of something to eat. "Leonard was hungry and Honey was ready to think about getting something to eat.

They walked at a leisurely pace as the narrow street emptied out into a broad walkway by the bay. It was jammed with pedestrians. On the left, cafés had outdoor seating lined up like expensive box seats at a sports arena. Red and green and blue awnings proclaimed the names of the establishments and the types of food they served. On the right of the promenade was a formidable row of giant yachts, docked side by side, with light-metal gangplanks jutting out the back of the boats and reaching down to the wooden boardwalk.

"Looks like we'll be dining with the rich and famous," Leonard said. "Hard to believe this was a sleepy little fishing village until Brigitte Bardot started getting her picture taken here in the fifties and sixties."

"How do you know that?" Honey asked.

"Oh, I followed Miss Bardot closely in the old days."

"Who do you follow now?"

Leonard smiled and made her wait for what he knew she needed to hear. "I follow the most wonderful and beautiful woman in the world."

"And who is that?"

"It is you," Leonard nearly shouted as he took Honey in his arms and swung her off her feet.

Honey forgot herself for a moment. By the time she could get

Leonard to stop dancing with her, a circle of impressed onlookers had formed around them. Leonard realized he had blown his cover, once again, and walked Honey through a gap in the circle of people to continue along the boardwalk. They didn't realize it, but a crowd was starting to follow them. Word began to spread that Honey and Leonard were on the boardwalk, disguised as a priest and a nun. Honey could feel the world beginning to collapse in on them.

The yachts were floating palaces, mostly three decks tall, with space age communication devices on top. Each had a flag angling off the back and many smaller boats stowed on board. One particularly massive yacht had a helicopter on the upper deck. The largest boats were more than 20 feet wide and at least 150 feet long.

"Now, that's living," Leonard marveled as they strolled by the ostentatious flotilla. "These people must really know how to live."

"Depends on who they are," Honey said. "I'll bet some of the people who own these boats are just as miserable as they can be. And I'll bet some of them are going to end up in jail someday."

"What do you mean by that?"

"I mean there are only two ways you get the kind of money it takes to own boats like these."

Honey paused, waiting for him to ask her to complete her explanation. He didn't seem the least bit interested. He turned away and began walking, seemingly mesmerized by the splendor laid out in front of him. Honey hated being ignored but she could see Leonard's world beginning to spin. Everyone was getting louder and crowding in on him. There was no way to escape the curious crowd.

Honey grabbed his sore arm by mistake and raised her voice to be heard, "Leonard, aren't you listening to me?"

"Ouch. That hurts. But okay, okay. What were you talking about?"

Honey grabbed him by the shoulders and said loudly, "I was talking about the two ways people get the money to buy these boats."

Leonard grimaced in pain. "Hey, watch the arm. It's starting to swell up. It's getting worse by the minute. We'd better get some ice on it pretty soon."

"Don't you dare forget what I'm talking about," Honey shook her finger in his face. Once again, people were forming a circle around the priest and the nun who were obviously having an argument.

"Honey, people are starting to stare," Leonard whispered as he tried to take her hand down from being shaken in his face.

Honey pulled her hand back, hard. When Leonard let go, she went sprawling, backwards, to the ground after tripping on her habit.

Leonard bent down to help her up. He was trying to be of assistance, but it didn't look that way to the crowd. A couple of drunken Belgian bankers stumbled forward to grab Leonard and nearly knocked him into the water. Leonard held his ground. One of the bankers pulled on Leonard's injured arm. The pain instinctively infuriated him. With one swift motion he threw the priest hat to the ground and took a boxing stance, clenched fists and all. The crowd gasped collectively. This was no priest. Leonard looked like a prizefighter, which is exactly what he had been for a short time in his youth.

"Come on, fool," Leonard snarled.

Honey got up and threw herself on Leonard's back, trying to restrain him.

"Hey," somebody in the growing crowd yelled. "It's Leonard. And that's Honey."

"It's Honey and Leonard," somebody else shouted.

"That's no priest. She's no nun," people chimed in.

Everyone froze as the recognition settled in. Leonard dropped his fists. Honey slid off his back. The crowd began inching forward. Word spread quickly. From the back of the crowd, people were straining to get a better view of the famous Honey and Leonard. By now, they had been front-page news in France for more than a week. Anyone who wasn't living in a cave had seen photos of the American couple in print and on television.

Shore police noticed the commotion and tried to force their way through the crowd. This only made the excited onlookers surge forward all the more. Honey and Leonard took a step backward as though recoiling in horror at the mess they'd gotten themselves into. Their backs were against the water. There was no escape.

The police kept coming. People were shouting and pushing each other to get a better view of the action. Whistles were blowing. A woman shrieked in pain as she was knocked to the ground. The crowd became a mob. Honey took a step backward in fear and tripped again on her habit.

"Leonard!" she screamed as she lost her balance and toppled off the boardwalk, falling ten feet into the water with a sickening splash.

The water temperature on that September night was breathtakingly chilly.

Leonard froze momentarily in disbelief as Honey disappeared into the darkness below. He looked at the faces in front of him. They tried to keep their distance but they were being pushed from behind. He looked back at the water. Honey had not resurfaced. He knew what he had to do. The police were about to break through the tightening half-circle of humanity. They would certainly arrest him.

He jumped off the dock and splashed into the water. The crowd gasped collectively. People strained forward to see where Leonard went under. No one could see if he came up for air. It was too dark.

"*Reculer!* Everyone stand back," the shore policeman yelled. That warning wasn't enough to stop the mob's momentum. As the two policemen were staring into the murky water below and wondering what to do next, the human wave pushed them both over the edge and into the water. They howled obscenities on the way down and as they bobbed up, flailing their arms and gasping for air.

More people were pushed into the water. The mob had no mind of its own. People looked like lemmings as they continued to be pushed off the dock and into the water.

Pandemonium broke out along the boardwalk and in the yachts as well. Every five seconds another person was either pushed into the water or jumped in to aid in the rescue. There were twenty people in the water by the time the first policeman to get wet climbed the ladder back up to the boardwalk. Even if Honey and Leonard had come up for air, they could have easily been lost in the confusion.

A man in a white uniform leaped from the upper deck of a yacht and into the water with two life jackets in his hands. He still had his white shoes on as he miraculously avoided hitting anyone. A woman in a black evening gown on the yacht to the right unhooked a long pole and thrust it into the water, yelling, "*Saisir la perche!* Grab the pole!"

It took more police and a good twenty minutes to restore order on the dock and to fish everyone out of the water. By then, there were several rescue boats in the water, continuing to search for Honey and Leonard.

Police stared into the water like they expected someone to surface at any moment. A few swimmers stayed in the water and began diving underwater to search for Honey and Leonard. Scuba divers arrived within a few minutes to search for bodies. The water was twenty feet deep. The divers stayed down for what seemed like a long time. They looked around and under every yacht and into the bay. Their underwater lights could be seen from the dock. One by one, they resurfaced, shaking their heads in amazement that nothing had been found.

A television news crew arrived and set up their cameras just outside the area cordoned off by police. Radio and print journalists were clamoring for information. "Are Honey and Leonard dead?" one pushy reporter kept asking at top volume.

About an hour after the incident, a spokeswoman for the police set up a table and chairs and a makeshift sound system to hold a press conference. Three ranking police officers took their seats as the mayor of St. Tropez used a microphone to address the growing throng of news people and curious members of the general public. He briefly recounted recent events and then announced that the search had been suspended until morning.

"Are Honey and Leonard presumed dead?" the persistent journalist asked for the fiftieth time.

"We are presuming nothing at this time," the mayor said.

"Were police attempting to arrest them when they went into the water?" a television journalist asked.

"The shore patrol and several witnesses have informed us," the mayor said, "that the American couple went into the water when they were surrounded and perhaps pushed by a crowd that had gathered around them on the dock."

"Did the police push them into the water?"

"Who was injured in the incident?"

"How long did it take for rescue boats and divers to arrive?"

Questions were being thrown at the mayor like stones from the angry mob. He held up his hands for silence and waited until the questions stopped.

"We do have reports that the woman fell in first and the man jumped in to rescue her," the mayor said. "We have not found their bodies. The underwater currents in this area can be tricky. We do fear the worst."

A hush fell over the crowd for a full ten seconds as the gravity of his comments sunk in. Then another wave of questions erupted. Instead of trying to provide answers, the mayor indicated the press conference was at an end.

People and press surged forward and surrounded the official table. It took concerted effort from a phalanx of police to extricate the mayor and his aides from the scene.

The dockside promenade turned into a massive, brawling riot of a party. The restaurants were so packed there was no way to get a drink. People started throwing empty glasses at waiters and at nothing in particular. Shattered glass was everywhere. The smell of marijuana was in the air. Wine bottles were being passed around. Men and women who barely knew each other were crying together. People were genuinely upset that Honey and Leonard had fallen victim to the tourists and police of St. Tropez.

Television crews interviewed the revelers and the mourners and even the thugs who used the chaos as an excuse for criminal activity. All sorts of drunken misinformation was spread under the guise of eyewitness testimony. The Belgian banker got his time on camera by describing how Leonard was physically attacking Honey. "I tried to stop him but I was too late. I think he pushed her into the water."

A second, intoxicated witness interrupted the interview. He barged into the camera shot and summed up the feelings of many "The police killed them. They drowned Honey and Leonard. It was police brutality and police incompetence. That's why they won't tell us they found the bodies. Because they killed them and they know it."

TWELVE

JACK CRUMBO was in his inexpensive hotel room in Cassis when he heard the news. He answered the banging door to find his French colleague, Corbin Lacoste, fighting back tears. "It's all over the police radio. Radio and television news are picking it up. There's a riot going on in St. Tropez."

"What happened?" Crumbo asked. "Something about Honey and Leonard?"

"Yes, yes, yes," Corbin answered, his chin lowering closer and closer to his chest. "The worst has happened."

"What?" Crumbo asked again as he waited for his friend to collect himself.

"Honey and Leonard drowned in St. Tropez."

Crumbo straightened up and shifted instinctively into his skeptical, journalist mode. "They drowned? How?"

Lacoste came into Crumbo's room and sat down on the bed. He began crying as he told the entire story about the crowd pushing Honey and Leonard off the dock and all the people and police falling into the water and the divers not being able to find the bodies.

Crumbo was packing his bag to head for St. Tropez as Lacoste finished telling what he knew. The younger journalist was hanging his head in sorrow. Crumbo's mind was already set on getting to the bottom of the story. "So, you're telling me that all those people went into the water and Honey and Leonard were the only ones who couldn't make it out?"

Lacoste raised his head to look at Crumbo with the faintest glimmer of hope in his eyes as he realized where the more experienced reporter was going with his questions.

"And you're telling me they haven't found the bodies?" Crumbo raised his voice in disbelief.

Lacoste stood up. "That's what the police are reporting. The mayor says the currents are strong in the dock area. People are saying the police found the bodies but won't admit it because it was their own incompetence and brutality that caused the drownings."

Crumbo closed his suitcase. "What's the mayor doing in the middle of this story? Since when are currents strong in a harbor? When have you ever seen police try to hide a body they dragged out of the water? Police show off bodies like cats bring dead rodents home to their owners as trophies."

Crumbo's questions made Lacoste realize he'd better start packing his own bag. "So you think they might be alive?"

"The whole thing sounds fishy to me."

"What do you mean, 'fishy'?"

Crumbo had to laugh. "It's not about fish," he said. "It's an Americanism. It means the story doesn't make sense."

"So why do you say it's fishy?"

Crumbo had to think about it for a second before explaining, "Fish don't smell good. If a story doesn't pass the smell test, it's probably not true. It's 'fishy'."

"Oh, I see," Lacoste said, only half understanding. "So, we're off for St. Tropez?"

"As soon as you're ready," Crumbo said as he zipped his bag shut, waiting for Lacoste to catch up.

"You Americans are always in such a rush."

Investigator Adam Wolfe arrived on the dock of St. Tropez with his interpreter/girlfriend, Simone. The riot was winding down. Police had arrested the worst of the bottle throwers and fire starters. Restaurant personnel were starting to clean up their premises, which had been progressively trashed throughout the evening.

Wolfe interviewed hangers on and began putting together a report. Gretchen Atkins was on her way to St. Tropez by way of rental car. She had landed in Paris earlier in the day. Wolfe informed her by telephone of Honey and Leonard's drowning in St. Tropez. She had already heard the story. Her only comment to Wolfe was, "I'll meet you at the police station in St. Tropez tomorrow at noon."

Wolfe had been in Cassis when the story shifted, most abruptly, to St. Tropez. By the time Wolfe was looking into the murky waters that had reportedly swallowed Honey and Leonard, he already had serious doubts as to their alleged demise.

Crumbo and Lacoste arrived at the dock in St. Tropez shortly after Wolfe made the scene. The investigator recognized Crumbo immediately from his photos in all the newspapers. The reporter had a boyishly chubby face that seemed much too young for his nearly bald head. Crumbo and Lacoste had their notepads out and were interviewing a restaurant owner when Wolfe decided to introduce himself.

"So, I finally get to meet the great Jack Crumbo," Wolfe said as he extended his hand for a friendly greeting.

"Excuse me," Crumbo said as he shook Wolfe's hand.

"I'm Adam Wolfe. I'm an investigator from Indianapolis. I've been hired to find Honey and Leonard and everywhere I go it seems you're always one step ahead of me."

"Who hired you?" Crumbo asked. "By the way, this is my French associate, Corbin Lacoste."

"I couldn't believe you guys interviewed Honey and Leonard

in Avignon and then let them go without informing the police," Wolfe said. "How did you get away with that?"

"Are you a cop?" Crumbo asked.

"No, no," Wolfe laughed, realizing he'd come on a little strong. "I've been hired by Leonard's niece, Gretchen Atkins, to find her uncle."

"So, you're a private dick?"

"Only if you're talking about Dick as in Dick Tracy."

"Sorry," Crumbo said. "No offense."

"None taken. And, oh, here she comes now. This is my French associate, Simone."

Crumbo and Lacoste nearly fell over each other trying to shake the hand of the statuesque, young blonde. Simone knew how to break the ice. "Oh, you're the famous Jack Crumbo who found Honey and Leonard in Avignon. And you must be Corbin Lacoste." She and Lacoste chatted excitedly in French for a short time, and then Simone returned to English to address Crumbo. "We've been reading your stories. You are both really quite talented. Are we all so sorry to hear what has happened to Honey and Leonard?"

"Not really," Crumbo said.

"So you don't believe it either," Wolfe said.

"But how could they have gotten away?" Lacoste asked. "The dock was swarming with cops."

"Somebody in a yacht fished them out," Wolfe said. "Nobody saw it in the confusion."

"Yes, but the police did search the boats," Simone said.

"And no boat can leave the harbor," Crumbo pointed out. "Look at those military boats out there. That's what you call a blockade."

"So the police might still find them?" Lacoste asked.

"I doubt it," Wolfe said. "Whoever fished them out probably got them out of here before the blockade got set up. Which brings me back to my original question. Why didn't you two turn them in to the police when you had the chance?"

"Let's get a drink and talk about it," Crumbo suggested. "There's a bar down the way that's still open. Since we're both from Indiana, we should get acquainted. I don't think we're really competitors."

Once they were settled in back of an old fisherman's bar and had their drinks in front of them, Crumbo answered Wolfe's question about letting Honey and Leonard go. "You know, we're not trying to catch Honey and Leonard. We're here to report their story. In fact, we hope they don't get caught. They've had a good run and so have we."

"That doesn't change the fact that she's wanted for attempted murder and violating a no-contact order in Indiana," Wolfe said.

"You do know the poisoning case is bullshit?" Crumbo asked.

"I read what you wrote, if that's what you mean," Wolfe said. "But, forgive me if I don't believe everything I read in the paper."

Crumbo took a long drink of beer to manage a cool headed response. "Well, think about it then. It makes common sense that an old farmer would have arsenic in his blood. It also makes sense that his niece, your employer, would use the blood tests to try to cut Leonard's girlfriend out of the picture."

Wolfe lowered his voice and spoke slowly. "All my boss wants is to see her uncle returned safely to Indiana. He's not well, you know. He might fool you for a while in an interview setting, but we're going to lose him eventually."

"If he's not dead already," said Lacoste.

Simone stepped in to ease the tension and said, "Our boss is worried about Leonard because of his Alzheimer's."

"You have a point there," Crumbo acknowledged. "But I'll wager you wouldn't turn them in either if you had the chance."

"What do you mean by that?" Wolfe asked.

"I mean it looks like you two are having a pretty good time running around France together. If you find Honey and Leonard and turn them in, your job is over and so is your paycheck."

Simone looked at Wolfe to check his reaction. The investigator drained his Scotch on the rocks, set his glass down and allowed a wry grin to slowly soften his rugged jaw. "I have thought about that a time or two."

The booth erupted in laughter. Another round of drinks was quickly delivered and Lacoste proposed a toast. "Here's to Honey and Leonard. Long may they run."

After several more rounds of drinks, Wolfe returned to the subject at hand, "So, how do we find Honey and Leonard before they get arrested by the police?"

"What makes you so sure they're not really dead?" Lacoste asked.

"They would have found the bodies," Crumbo said.

"Here's to no bodies being found," Simone toasted. The booth was getting downright giddy. The more drinks they were served, the more everybody felt like old friends.

"The best way to help them," Wolfe said, "is to go with the story that the police are hiding the bodies to cover up their own problems. Nobody keeps searching for dead people."

"We can't just make up the news," Crumbo protested.

"You don't have to," Simone said. "People are already rioting in the street over the way the police mishandled this whole thing. Everybody I talked to thinks the police killed Honey and Leonard."

———◆———

A part of Gretchen Atkins felt vindicated by news of Honey and Leonard drowning. She knew something bad would happen once the two of them took off from Indiana. She had warned the sheriff and anyone else who would listen.

Another part of her felt vastly relieved. All her fear of being caught misspending her uncle's money could be gone. As Leonard's sole heir, his fortune would now be hers to spend without the need for any troublesome accountings. And there would be no Honey to ask questions and convince her uncle to revoke his power of attorney.

A third part of her felt terrible grief and guilt at her uncle's passing. All the way on the flight to France she couldn't help but wonder if there was a way to make everything right with Uncle Leonard. She still loved him even if that love was now clouded by greed and jealousy of Honey.

The largest part of her, however, wasn't convinced that Honey and Leonard had drowned. For one thing, she knew Uncle Leonard was a strong swimmer. She could never forget his powerful strokes in the water, trying to save his daughter.

She also knew that Honey and Leonard stayed in shape by swimming regularly at the YMCA in a water aerobics program they jokingly referred to as the "ancient mariners."

Gretchen drove on into the night. She had to make St. Tropez by noon and she had no idea how long the drive would actually take. The more she thought about Honey and Leonard, the more convinced she became that they had not drowned. If she'd been told they were killed in a car crash, she might have believed it. But drowning? That didn't sound right.

I've got to get Honey arrested. With her out of the way, I can get Uncle Leonard declared incompetent and everything will be all right. Honey is the problem. I hope she is dead.

THIRTEEN

HONEY DIDN'T HAVE A PLAN until she hit the water and sank a good ten feet. During the fall, she had instinctively taken in a huge breath of air. The water shocked her with its chill, but she was not frightened to disappear into its dark womb of silence. The nun's habit wasn't that much of a drag underwater. It was made of lightweight material for summer wear. She knew she could swim in it. Her adrenaline had taken over. Her mind was racing. The cold and darkness of the water jolted her into thinking beyond her first instinct to resurface for air. Rather than come back up directly, she decided in an instant to take as many strokes away from the dock as possible before coming up for air.

One, two, and three kicking breast strokes and she still had air left in her lungs. Five, six, seven and she began to feel the need to surface. Her lungs were burning. Strokes eight and nine brought her up and gasping for air. She had been in deeper than she thought.

Once she caught her breath and looked around, she could see she was halfway down the length of one of the big yachts and completely out of sight of the confusion on the dock. A few more strokes away from the dock and she reached an anchor line stretched out from the bow of the boat. She hung on and hoped Leonard would know why she hadn't come up for air. Hopefully, he hadn't been apprehended. All she could hear was a lot of shouting and splashing from people and police falling or being pushed into the water.

She waited for what seemed like much too long for Leonard to appear in the water. Certainly, he would come in after her. He must have known what she was thinking. They were on a mutual wavelength of thought. They often completed each other's sentences. She felt certain he would come to her in the water. But what if he came up on the other side of the boat?

Once again, she realized how important this man had become to her. He was more important than any person in her life, including her mother. Falling in love with Leonard had taught her how to live without fear. Her faith in their love was stronger than all her fears. She was no longer afraid to give her love completely.

What would she do without him? Here she was, hiding from a mob while trying to keep from drowning and she was more concerned about Leonard than herself.

Honey was about to dive under the boat to check the other side when Leonard's head popped out of the water about twenty yards away. He was near the stern of the boat but just out of sight of the dock. The boats were backed in to the harbor, stern to dock. "Honey," he called out, his voice echoing between the hulls of side-by-side yachts.

"Leonard!" Honey shouted loud enough to be heard over the din on the dock.

Leonard turned toward the sound of her voice and began swimming to it. He couldn't see her.

"Leonard, I'm right here," she said splashing the water to help him see her. There was just enough light from the dock for him to see the splashes. "Come on, I'm right here. Swim to me. There's a line we can hang onto."

Leonard took a few smooth breaststrokes. "Hold on. I see you.

You can stop the splashing. Let's not let everybody know where we are."

Leonard was laughing by the time he reached the anchor line. "Man, this water is cold. I'm not used to swimming with my shoes on. I'm going to kick them off."

"No, don't do that. We don't want to leave any clues. If they find our shoes but not us, they'll know we swam away. Where is your hat?"

Leonard put his hand on his head and had to think about the hat for a long moment. "It's back up on the dock. I left it there when that idiot wanted to fight."

Honey kissed him hard on the lips. "We can't stay in this water too long. Come on. Each of these boats has anchor lines. We'll swim from one to the next until we reach the pier. I can see it. It's not far. Maybe three boats down."

Leonard swam closely behind her. "You are one clever girl. I knew what you were doing as soon as I saw you didn't come up for air. I waited until the police were almost through the crowd before I jumped in to follow you. That was some jump. It was a lot farther to the water than I thought. I must have gone twenty feet underwater."

Honey stopped swimming and treaded water to listen to the commotion on the dock. "What's happening up there? It sounds like people are going crazy."

"I don't know but I think some people came into the water after me."

"Oh, I'm so glad to see you and your wet head," Honey hugged him, cheek to cheek.

Leonard treaded water with her. "Who would have thought we'd end up in the water at night in St. Tropez?"

Honey's smile made her look young, even in the shadows.

"Anything is possible with you, sweetie. Come on, let's swim for the pier. I'm starting to stiffen up from the cold. How's your arm?"

Leonard kept his head above water as he began swimming. "The arm is fine. Swimming in this cold made me forget all about it. Where's the pier? What are we going to do once we get there?"

Honey thought about the question and turned her head toward Leonard. "I don't know, you'll think of something."

They swam around the bow of the next boat just as a powerful light illuminated the anchor line where they had just been. People were looking for them.

"Better keep moving," Leonard said as they looked back and saw the lights sweeping the water.

"Here we go," Honey said as she began swimming for the next anchor line.

When they finally reached the pier, there was no ladder out of the water. They clung to the inflated rubber side of a dinghy, which was tied to the pier. "What now?" Honey asked as she caught her breath.

Leonard looked up and assessed the situation. "We're going to get you up and into that boat."

Honey looked puzzled. "What about you?"

"I'm going to push you up once you get halfway up."

Honey looked up at the boat and then back at Leonard. "How are you going to get up? I won't be strong enough to pull you by myself."

"There's a ladder in the boat," Leonard said. "You'll throw it down to me."

Honey threw her arms up without asking any more questions even though she knew Leonard had no way of knowing what was in the boat. She grabbed a rubber cord on the dinghy as Leonard boosted her by her butt into the boat from the water. She flopped into the dinghy and got up on her knees to assess the situation. Once again, she marveled at Leonard's strength.

Honey leaned over the boat to look down at Leonard. "Hang on, sweetie. I'm looking for a rope or a ladder in this thing."

As she tried to hide the worry from her voice, a man in a dark uniform jumped down from the pier and into the boat behind her. He was quick and quiet as a cat burglar. Honey tried to jump back in the water, but the man already had his arms around her midsection.

"Relax," he said in perfect English with a British accent. "I'm not with the police. I'm here to help."

He was so strong that Honey had no choice but to stop struggling and relax in his arms. He let go of her and reached over the edge of the rubber boat to haul Leonard out of the water with what seemed like superhuman strength. In one quick motion, he had Leonard on his stomach in the boat, and in another move, he grabbed Leonard by his pants and pulled him into a standing position.

Leonard started to say "Thank you," but he had to lean over the edge of the boat to cough up water. By the time Leonard collected himself and sat down in the boat, the uniformed man had started a motor on the back of the dinghy and was pulling away from the pier at a stealthy pace.

"Where are you taking us?" Honey asked.

"And who are you?" Leonard added as he turned to look at the lights of the harbor.

The man put them at ease with a friendly laugh. "I know this feels like a kidnapping but it is not. Once I get you out of this mess, you shall be free to go, I assure you."

Honey and Leonard said nothing. The uniformed man continued his explanation. "I am an employee of Mr. Luther

Patrick. I've been following you since Avignon. This is one of Mr. Patrick's small boats. We are headed for his very large boat. He has taken quite an interest in you two. He has nothing but your best interest at heart. I was on my way to retrieve this boat to assist in the search for the two of you when I found one of you already on board. Frankly, I'm having a difficult time believing my good fortune."

"Where are you taking us?" Honey repeated her question. "And why are you wearing that gun?"

The man looked down and realized the breeze had blown back his jacket to reveal the sidearm. "Do not be alarmed by the weapon. I am part of Mr. Patrick's security detail. As I said, I'm taking you to Mr. Patrick's ship. It's too large for the dock. He's anchored in the bay. You can't see the ship right now. That French military vessel is in the way. Once we get around it, you'll see *The Sinbad*."

"The what?" Leonard asked.

The man with the gun laughed. *"The Sinbad,"* he said. "That's the name of Mr. Patrick's ship."

"Who is this, Mr. Patrick?" Honey asked.

"He's an international businessman," the man said as he motioned them to get down in the boat. "Lie down, quickly! I see boats launching from the destroyer. They'll be shining lights on us in less than a minute. Here, throw this blanket over yourselves."

Honey and Leonard got prone on the wooden floor of the dinghy and gratefully wrapped the blanket around themselves. They were wet, and the night air was increasingly cold as the dinghy picked up speed.

"Here they come," the man said tensely as he sent some kind of signal with his flashlight to the approaching military boats. Honey and Leonard heard the roar of their engines and felt the dinghy bobbing up and down from their wakes. The military boats passed them by without even pausing for inspection.

"Amazing," the man said. "They think they're assisting in a search for bodies, I'm sure. Little do they know, I've got the precious cargo onboard."

"The man pulled a small radio out of his breast pocket and said, "This is Ivan One. I'm headed to you with quite a surprise. Please tell Mr. Patrick to be prepared to meet his most honored guests."

Leonard unwrapped himself and sat up in the dinghy. "Are we the 'most honored guests'? Pardon me if I feel like a turkey being invited to Thanksgiving dinner."

The man smiled easily at Leonard's sense of humor. "Don't worry," he said. "Mr. Patrick is a most gracious host. He's been anxious to meet you. The first thing we've got to do is get you out of those wet costumes."

"Why do you call them costumes?" Honey asked.

The man didn't answer until after a thoughtful silence. "I spotted you in Avignon at the same time as the news reporters. It wasn't that hard. You were literally dancing on top of the city walls."

"Were you following us?" Honey asked.

"Half of France is following your every move. People love you. You have become overnight folk heroes."

"Following us on the news is one thing," Honey said. "Following us on foot is quite another matter. Why were you tracking us?"

"Mr. Patrick took a personal interest in your story and he assigned me to locate you and find out everything I could and protect you if necessary."

"So you followed us to the church at Avignon," Leonard surmised.

"I saw you leave the church in the same clothes you're wearing now and I saw you switch cars to the black Peugeot. A very good move on your part, I might add. I can't believe the priest accommodated you as much as he did. I am sure he will pay a terrible price for his kindness."

"All I want to know," Leonard said, changing the topic through chattering teeth, "is how long until we can get into some dry clothes. I'm freezing."

Honey nodded her agreement and shivered as she wrapped the blanket around herself.

The man pulled out his radio again, "This is Ivan One. We're coming around the destroyer. You can see my signal. Please have the butler stand by. I need dry clothing for a man about Mr. Patrick's size and for a woman who seems to be about five feet tall, slender build."

"Five, four, 115 pounds," Honey corrected him.

"Make that five feet, four inches tall, 115 pounds," the man said into the radio.

Honey smiled at the correction and then gasped as *The Sinbad* came into full view. "That's bigger than the Queen Elizabeth."

"Not quite. She's 147 meters with room for 50 guests, a crew of 65 and a security detail of 20."

"What did I tell you, Leonard, about the two ways to get enough money to buy one of these yachts?"

"I don't think you ever got time to explain the two ways," Leonard said.

Honey lowered her voice and said, "You either inherit the money or you break the law."

"By the way," the security man said, overhearing her. "My name is Michael Maxwell. And, may I assure you, Mr. Patrick is no common criminal."

"I can see that," Leonard said.

"What I meant to say is that all Mr. Patrick's businesses are strictly legal and above board."

———————

Honey and Leonard waited to meet Luther Patrick in the ship's main barroom, which was well trimmed in mahogany paneling and shining brass light fixtures. Employees dressed in black uniforms with silver buttons and belts provided them with dry clothing and gourmet snacks. A man wearing a black tuxedo brought them a bottle of Chateauneuf-du-Pape and opened it with a flourish that was almost sexual. He used a corkscrew to start the cork out of the bottle and then pried it back and forth with his thumbs until it came out with a gentle pop. He then left them alone in the room.

"This guy is good," Leonard said. "And so is his boss. He knows our favorite wine. I can't wait to meet this guy."

"They've been following us all over France," Honey said. "It almost feels like we've been kidnapped."

"Well, it certainly beats drowning in the harbor of St. Tropez," Leonard said as he drained his first glass of wine.

Honey tried to grab the wine glass out of his hand. "Don't you dare drink that fine wine like it was water. You know how you get. You'll forget where you are."

They were startled when one of the mahogany panels slid open and in walked a man who looked to be in his middle fifties. He was wearing a light blue, silk shirt with dark blue pants and white leather deck shoes. He had a full head of silver, wavy hair. He would have been strikingly handsome except for a hawkish nose, which was too big for his square jaw.

The man paused for dramatic effect and then spoke with a smile as he walked toward Honey and Leonard. "Excuse me, I didn't mean to frighten you, but I just love coming through the secret panel. It's my favorite shortcut on the ship. I am your host,

Luther Patrick, and I am at your service. I did not mean to keep you waiting. I see the butler found you ship's uniforms to fit. Rest assured, we'll find more suitable clothing in the very near future."

Honey turned on the Southern charm, extended her hand and said, "Why, Mr. Patrick, we are thrilled to make your acquaintance. I feel we owe you a deep debt of gratitude. Your man rescued us and now you have made us feel safe and warm again."

Luther kissed her hand and shook Leonard's hand warmly. "I know you have questions, Mr. Atkins. Rest assured I will answer them all over dinner if you will be kind enough to join me."

"You say 'rest assured' quite a bit," Leonard observed.

"Do I?" Luther asked. "Rest assured I'm only trying to make you feel comfortable."

"There you go again," Leonard said.

Luther threw his head back and laughed out loud. "Oh, yes, I see what you mean. Thank you for pointing that out. I'll have to work on mixing it up a bit."

"What flag do you fly on this ship?" Leonard asked.

"Why, the flag of the United States of America, of course. I was born and raised on a dairy farm in Minnesota. You and I have more in common than you might think."

"Your hand is pretty rough for a guy who lives on a fairy tale boat."

"Leonard," Honey scolded.

"No, no," Luther said, "I take no offense. I'm proud to say I do as much real work as anybody on board. Like I said, I was raised on a dairy farm."

"Milk those cows twice every day, come hell or high water," Leonard said, relaxing a bit. "We had cows growing up."

"We would be honored to join you for dinner, Mr. Patrick," Honey said, responding to his invitation.

"Please, call me Luther. And may I call you Honey and Leonard?"

"Please do," Honey cooed.

"That's what they call us in the papers," Leonard said. "To tell the truth, we've been shocked by all this attention. What did we do to get people like you following us all over France?"

"We're old and in love and on the run," Honey said.

"That sums it up nicely," Luther said. "Forgive my surveillance. To tell the truth, I thought about bringing you on board for your own safety. You've come close to being caught several times. Now, here you are, quite by accident. I assure you, you are free to leave at any time. You are strictly my honored guests. We were in the Mediterranean when your story began to take over the news. I come to you strictly out of curiosity and the desire to be of assistance. I heard about a farmer from the Midwest and his lady friend being called the Bonnie and Clyde of love. Who could resist a story like that?"

Honey and Leonard waited for him to continue.

"And may I say neither of you looks as old as I would have thought, particularly after your circumstances of this evening."

"Why, thank you, kind sir," Honey said. "Love is our elixir of youth."

"Well said," Luther commented as he and Leonard shared a sideways glance. "So please, join me for dinner. I cannot believe my good fortune. I've been wondering for quite some time if this moment would ever happen."

"Oh, do take us on a tour of this marvelous ship," Honey said. "I've never seen anything quite like it." She could tell Leonard did not like the attention she paid to Luther, but under the circumstances, what choice did they have but to graciously accept his hospitality?

A valet entered through the main door. Luther directed him,

"Please turn on the television so we can catch up on the news regarding our guests before we head off for dinner. We need to see what's going on back in St. Tropez."

The first thing they saw on the screen was a photo of themselves. This shot cut to a French newsman who was obviously speaking in the hushed tones of someone in mourning.

"What's he saying?" Leonard asked.

Luther interpreted. "He's saying the two of you are presumed dead by drowning off the dock in St. Tropez."

"Look how sad he looks," Honey said. "Isn't that touching? It makes me want to cry, and I know I'm not dead."

"It's not everyday you get to watch your own funeral on television," Leonard said.

Luther smiled broadly in appreciation of Leonard's summation. "Leonard, you and I are going to get along just fine."

"You know what? I think we just might do that," Leonard said. "We do owe you a debt of gratitude for fishing us out of the drink and bringing us onboard. I'd like to thank your man in person if that's possible."

Luther snapped to attention. "Yes, of course. I should have thought of that myself. Valet, please ask Mr. Maxwell to join us in the dining room."

The valet nodded and asked, "Shall I turn off the television, Mr. Patrick?"

Luther looked at Honey, who said, "Yes, I've seen quite enough. It's already starting to repeat itself. Please turn it off. I would have hoped they'd found a better photo of me by now. They keep using that one from *The Chicago Tribune* that makes me look so old. And I don't know why they always have to mention that I'm 77 years old."

"I wouldn't put you a day past 55," Luther said.

"Smart man," Leonard said.

The valet left and Leonard asked, "What can you tell me about this ship? It really is impressive."

"Well, let's see," Luther began. "It was designed by Maierform and built in 1984 by a company in Denmark. I had it secretly commissioned. It's basically the same boat as the one owned by the King of Saudi Arabia."

"Oh, so you're in the oil business?" Leonard asked.

"Among other things," Luther said. "Come, let's head for the dining room. It's at the other end of the ship. I'll give you a guided tour on the way."

Luther knew every inch of his ship and he loved sharing his hands-on relationship with it. He took them down to the engine room where one of his staff informed Honey and Leonard that *The Sinbad* had a top speed of 22 knots.

"How fast is that in miles per hour?" Leonard asked.

"A little more than 25 miles per hour," Luther answered.

As the tour continued on the way to the dining room, Luther got his first clues about Leonard's mental condition. Leonard asked about the boat's top speed at least four times in less than twenty minutes. He was tired and repeating himself. Luther shot a knowing glance at Honey.

"I think we'd better grab a quick bite to eat and get ourselves to bed," Honey said. "It's been a long day."

"I'll have my staff physician give you two a quick checkup after dinner," Luther said. "No doubt, he can provide whatever medications you may have left behind."

"You can do that?" Honey asked.

"We have a rather complete pharmacy on board," Luther said. "Let me know if you have trouble sleeping."

Honey and Leonard looked at each other in amazement. "Does the doctor live on the ship?" Leonard asked.

"Only when we're at sea, which is about one third of the time,"

Luther answered. "I and my mobile staff have living quarters in several locations around the world. We are the doctor's only patients. He'll take excellent care of you. I stole him from The Mayo Clinic in Minnesota. He has the resources of that entire facility at his beck and call."

The tour continued into the dining room, which was open air with glass walls near the stern of the ship. It was large enough to seat at least fifty people but only one large round table was set up with silver place settings and sparkling, crystal glassware on a blue linen tablecloth.

"What do you do if it rains?" Leonard asked.

"We have an automated, retractable roof," Luther said. "Would you like to see how it works?"

"Yes, I would," Leonard said.

Honey intervened, "That won't be necessary. The stars are too beautiful tonight. And look at the lights of St. Tropez. This could not be more perfect."

Waiters appeared. Soup and salad and bread were served and wine and bottled water were poured. Honey and Leonard dug into their food like they hadn't eaten in days.

"Isn't it funny how swimming makes you hungry?" Honey observed.

"So does running from a mob and dodging the police," Leonard said.

"You two must be exhausted," Luther said as plates of steak and seafood and vegetables were set before them.

"We're having too much fun to be tired," Honey said. "And look, here's Mr. Maxwell."

"You've asked to see me, Mr. Patrick?"

Luther stood up. "Yes, Michael. Glad you could join us. Our guests want to thank you for a job well done. So do I, as a matter of fact."

Maxwell bowed in appreciation. "Thank you, sir, but I must say, our guests did all the hard work."

Honey jumped up from the table and threw her arms around Michael Maxwell. "Oh, how I love that English accent. You must be related to James Bond. Thank you so much for saving us."

"You almost didn't let me," Maxwell said.

"I did try to jump back in the water," she explained to Luther. "But he was too quick for me. And then he had Leonard out of the water, and off we went before we really knew what was happening."

Luther shook Mr. Maxwell's hand, more as a friend than an employer. "Fine work, Michael. I've come to expect nothing less from you."

"Thank you, sir. And might I say to our guests they are even more charming in person than in the press. The pleasure was all mine."

"Oh, my, what a perfect gentleman," Honey said.

"Won't you join us for dinner?" Leonard asked. "We've got enough food here for an army."

"No, thank you. I had my dinner earlier," Maxwell said to Leonard. "I really must be on my way." He then turned to Luther and asked, "Will that be all, Mr. Patrick?"

"Yes, but do report to me first thing tomorrow. We need to discuss our plans."

Maxwell left after Honey and Leonard thanked him again. Once he was gone, Leonard turned to Luther and asked, "What plans do you have for us?"

Luther frowned slightly and said, "To be honest, I don't have a plan, which is quite unusual for me. Let's all sleep on it and see what we come up with in the morning."

"I love a man with no plan," Honey laughed. "Particularly one who's not afraid to admit it."

"We'll come up with something," Luther said.

They finished the grand meal and got a quick check up with Luther's physician, Dr. John Laughlin. The doctor was able to provide Honey and Leonard's medications for heart and blood pressure and asthma.

It was after midnight before Luther showed them to their cabin, which was as large and elegant as a suite at the finest hotel. The bed was round and covered with pillows. "Shall I have it turned down for you?" Luther asked.

"Oh, no," Honey said. "We can manage."

Luther left, and Honey and Leonard chased each other around the bed, briefly, as they threw the pillows at each other. They were too tired to keep the slumber party action going for long. Once they figured out how to get under the covers and sheets, they snuggled each other like they had found the sacred womb of love.

Honey fell asleep immediately, but Leonard kept waking her up. He was convinced people were outside the windows, looking in on them. Honey got up again and again to reassure him. Eventually, she gave him two sleeping pills from the doctor so she could get some rest herself.

All night she dreamed of sailing on the sea with Leonard. They were the only two people aboard a very large boat with several sails. Honey kept asking him where he learned how to sail. Leonard kept insisting he had no idea how to sail a boat this size. Each of them became progressively more amazed as the ship made one masterful maneuver after another. Leonard finally concluded, "This ship is sailing itself. Just like life."

Honey awakened to that marvelous thought as morning light began streaming into their cabin. She let Leonard sleep as she explored the sweet-smelling soaps and shampoos and lotions of the master bath.

Dr. Laughlin turned out to be extremely interested in Leonard's mental condition. He spent two hours with Leonard the next day before providing him with an experimental drug called donepezil hydrochloride. "This drug is going through trials," Dr. Laughlin said to Honey. "It's showing good results in treating the symptoms of early Alzheimer's disease. Let's try a moderate dose on Leonard and see how he does."

FOURTEEN

Honey saw a noticeable improvement in Leonard after only a few days on his new medication. He wasn't repeating himself as often and his conversational focus seemed to improve. Leonard spent nearly an hour a day with Dr. Laughlin and he was able to share with Honey most of what transpired during his meetings with the physician.

The doctor met with both Honey and Leonard to share his diagnosis that Leonard had Alzheimer's disease. "I know you already know," Dr. Laughlin said. "I just don't want to give you false hope. This drug I've prescribed for Leonard is not a cure. In fact, I've got to swear you to secrecy because it's not even approved at this point. It has only showed signs of slowing the progression of the disease in its early stages."

"I know there's no cure," Leonard said. "And I know it won't do any good to worry about it. I'm just very grateful for your help, doctor."

"He is having visions of his mother," Honey said. "Occasionally, he forgets where he is and who I am. At first, I thought my love would cure him of all that, but I've been learning the hard way that love does not conquer all."

"Yes, it does, pumpkin. Your love has saved me."

"No, my sweetie, my love for you has saved me."

"The bad news," Dr. Laughlin said, "is that we don't know much about the disease. The good news is everybody's different.

People have good and bad days. The chances are good that you and Leonard have many more good days ahead. Make sure to give him the sleeping medication every night around 9 p.m. Nighttime can be the worst. Or the best, if he's getting a good night's sleep."

"You seem very interested in this disease," Honey observed.

The doctor put down his clipboard and leaned forward. "I lost my father to Alzheimer's last year after a ten year battle. It was the worst thing I've ever been through. My hero became somebody who didn't even know he was a human being. It almost killed my mother. The only comforting thing about it was knowing he wasn't suffering because he didn't know what was going on."

"I am so sorry," Honey said.

The doctor blinked back tears. "Yes, it was hard, especially for my mother, who tried to take care of him herself for much too long."

"Am I hard on you, Honey?" Leonard asked.

"No, Leonard, you silly sweetie. My love for you is the best part of me. You keep me young at heart."

Leonard put his hand on her shoulder. "Will you let me know when I get to be too much trouble?"

Honey put her hand over Leonard's. "We don't have to worry about that now, do we, doctor?"

The doctor picked up his clipboard and stood up to stretch. "No, like I said, you two have many a fine day ahead."

◆

Life aboard *The Sinbad* turned into the most outlandish honeymoon pleasure cruise ever designed. Luther was a most attentive host. He was careful to obtain Honey and Leonard's permission before weighing anchor and leaving St. Tropez. Once underway, the entire Mediterranean Sea became their playground. Luther and his captain knew all the best anchor points along the French and Italian Rivieras. He made sure his guests got in plenty of swimming and hiking on secluded beach spots. He accompanied them everywhere they went and introduced them to the finest local cuisine, wine, and art.

Luther was so careful to protect their privacy that Honey and Leonard almost forgot they were still the subjects of international inquiry. News of their deaths had been largely replaced by Jack Crumbo's theory in *The Chicago Tribune* that they were alive and well and still on the run.

One night, back onboard *The Sinbad*, they saw Crumbo being interviewed on French television. Crumbo was saying, through an interpreter, that he had learned Honey and Leonard were excellent swimmers. "The fact that no bodies have been found leads me to believe they swam away and escaped in the confusion of the mob scene on the dock."

When the French reporter asked whether he had any evidence to show Honey and Leonard were still alive, Crumbo had to acknowledge he had nothing to go on but his own theories. The reporter asked, "Where did they go?" Crumbo could only answer, "We have no idea."

The reporter concluded the interview and gave the camera a smirk that said, "There you have it. Another American who doesn't know what he's talking about."

Honey turned to Leonard and Luther and said, "Oh, wouldn't it be fun to bring Jack Crumbo on board and give him the exclusive story of our survival?"

The two men, who had become good friends in a short time, laughed at the suggestion at first. Then Luther said, "You know, that might not be a bad idea."

"Better to let the world think we're dead," Leonard said.

"Unless you want to begin arguing your case in the press," Luther said.

"You mean the case that I'm not mentally gone yet?"

"No, the case that says you are mentally competent and that nobody ever tried to poison you. Dr. Laughlin has enough data to testify already. That's why he's been testing you everyday."

"Oh, my," Honey said. "You do think of everything."

"Not only that," Luther said. "My accountants have found that Leonard's niece, Gretchen, has been using some dangerously creative accounting with regard to Leonard's fortune."

"How could you know that?" Leonard asked.

"Remember those consent forms we had you sign?" Luther asked.

Leonard looked at Honey with a blank expression that said, "No, I do not remember any such thing."

Honey said, "Yes, we remember those forms."

Luther looked first at Honey and then to Leonard. "Those forms allowed us to access your accounts, and I'm sorry to report it's not a pretty picture."

"What do you mean?" Honey asked.

Luther looked sadly at Leonard before saying, "I'm sorry to say it looks like she's stolen quite a bit of money from you."

"Tell me something I don't already know," Leonard said.

Honey perked up and began bouncing in her chair. "Leonard, why don't we have Mr. Patrick's lawyers revoke the power of attorney you gave to Gretchen?

Leonard looked at Luther who began a legal backpedal. "If I have you sign something prepared by my attorney and approved by my doctor while you're on my ship, your niece could easily argue I exercised undue influence over you. Unfortunately, your legal competence will probably have to be proven in an Indiana court."

Besides growing up on farms in the Midwest, Luther and Leonard quickly discovered they shared a love of art. This led to adventurous outings along the coast to museums, artists' studios, and galleries. They bought paintings and sculpture and ceramics like they were art dealers organizing a grand inventory. They never tried to talk an artist down on the price. They gladly paid full retail.

Luther's favorite line was, "Buying art is investing in your soul." He loved to say it as he was acquiring a new painting. After purchasing a dreamy Italian landscape from a female artist near Antibes, he couldn't help but elaborate, "Everybody wants to know how to buy art that will increase in value. How to make art a good investment. I say it's the thrill of the hunt and the joy of being in the presence of great art that make it all worthwhile. Art is not like money. Money is objective. Art is subjective. Beauty is in the eye of the beholder. Every society has money or some form of exchange. But each society has its own artistic identity. Art defines civilizations. Even the cavemen are celebrated by the drawings on their walls."

Everyone nearby applauded as he finished his soliloquy, even those who didn't speak English. Leonard held up Luther's hand like he had won a boxing match. The two men and Honey were becoming more close with every outing.

Honey loved Luther's attitude toward art and particularly his line about investing in your soul. She was determined to create a signature line of her own. It took a couple weeks of trial and error and a little help from Leonard but she finally came up with a saying that pleased her. "No space is any better than the art within it."

"And that includes the space between your ears," Leonard always added.

Many a struggling artist had his or her financial year made when Luther and Honey and Leonard strolled into town with their enthusiasm and wit and willingness to invest. Between the three of them, they bought at least twenty pieces per outing. Once each purchase was completed, Luther had Michael Maxwell and his team pick up the art and transport it back to *The Sinbad.*

Several artists recognized Honey and Leonard. They never said anything, but Luther could always tell when they'd been spotted. They became obsequious. At that point, Luther took them aside and made them promise to keep the transaction a secret if they hoped for repeat sales. He knew their promises would not last long.

"I knew you weren't dead," one painter said in English with a midwestern accent. "You couldn't be dead or they would have found your bodies. And now I can see you're alive. This is so far out. And, hey, I'm from Indiana too. I've been following your story since you landed in France. Way to go. Elderly couple from Indiana goes global in France. You guys are so far out. I can't believe you're actually in my studio. I've been painting in Italy for years and you're my first celebrity guests. How about signing my palette?"

"We can't sign anything for obvious reasons," Luther said. "But we do love your work. In fact, I would like to purchase the large painting of the harbor. How much is it?"

"It's $5,000, but I would be willing to give you a great deal."

"That won't be necessary," Luther said. "Will cash be acceptable? I have U.S. dollars."

"Yes. Yes, of course," the artist stammered. "I can't believe I'm selling a painting to Honey and Leonard. I suppose you want me to keep quiet about this?"

"That would be very much appreciated," Luther said.

"I'll take this one of the castle in the moonlight," Leonard said. "I love your purples. How much is it?"

"It's $3,500, but I would be happy to give it to you," the artist said.

"That won't be necessary," Luther said, peeling off more bills. "Your work is some of the best we've seen. It's funny to have the finest art in Italy coming from an Indiana painter."

"I tell everybody back in the states I'm an Italian painter," the artist said.

"I'll bet they eat that up," Leonard said.

The artist couldn't help but count the money. "You bet they do."

Honey was not about to be left out of the action. "I'll take the one of the big orange lobster on the plate. I love, love, love that painting. It must be new. I can still smell the oil paint. And I don't see a price."

"The price for you, my wild and crazy Honey, is nothing. And I insist. No more money. You have been more than generous. I need to return the favor so I can always say I gave a piece to Honey and Leonard."

"And Luther," Honey said, giving her sea captain an inclusive hug.

"Yes, yes, Luther," the artist said. "How have you kept your name out of the papers?"

Luther laughed and pointed to another painting he wanted to purchase. "I don't suppose it will take long before they're after me too."

They had great fun in the studio as the artist regaled them with tales of a Hoosier in Italy. Once Maxwell picked up the art, Honey and Leonard and Luther continued exploring the town with the Indiana artist as their tour guide. They went straight to a corner bar where the artist proceeded to guzzle down half a bottle of wine, straight from the bottle, in celebration of his recent sales. Luther quickly moved the party to a back room to avoid making too much of a scene.

"What are you guys doing, just traveling around buying art and dodging the law?" the artist asked.

"You might say we enjoy collecting," Luther said.

"I almost feel decadent, buying all this art," Honey said.

"No need," Luther said. "We're supporting the art world. And guess what we'll do with it in the end?"

"Donate it to worthy causes," Leonard answered.

"Perfect," Honey said. "It's the circle of art."

———◆———

Luther was beginning to realize he never had such fun as with Honey and Leonard. The only problem was it made him want to have a love of his own. He had resigned himself to living alone until he saw how much fun Honey and Leonard were having.

Leonard and Luther were studying maps and drinking coffee one morning, planning their next adventure. Honey was getting her nails done in the ship salon. Luther said, "You know, I envy you two. Being with you makes me realize I need somebody in my life."

Leonard took a sip on his coffee and looked over the cup. "Luther, I'd think a guy like you could get any woman he wanted."

Luther turned his cup slightly on its saucer. "I could and I have, but that's not what I'm talking about."

"I hear what you're saying," Leonard said. "It can't be easy when they're all after your money. I'll tell you what. You'll never meet anybody sailing around in this boat. You've got to get out there and start helping people before you'll find someone to love."

Luther took a careful sip of coffee. "What do you mean?"

Leonard lowered his head and raised his eyebrows. "Well, take Honey and me. We met at a Halloween fundraiser dance for the United Way. After my wife died, I was in a bad place until I decided to get out there and get involved in some good causes. That's how I found my girl, trying to help other people."

"That statement has the ring of truth to it," Luther said. "I do give tremendous amounts of money to important causes."

"Are you bragging or complaining?" Honey asked as she breezed in from the salon.

"Luther, here, needs a woman in his life," Leonard said.

Honey showed off her nails. "You mean I'm not enough for the both of you?"

"Of course you are," Luther said. "But these past days have been such fun, you've made me see what's missing in my life. I thought I had it all until I met the two of you."

"Oh, my dear, dear boy," Honey said. "The girl of your dreams is already on her way. Don't you see? That's why you met the two of us. So you'll be ready when you meet her."

Luther looked at Honey incredulously, amazed he understood exactly what she was saying.

About two weeks into their friendship, Luther introduced Honey and Leonard to his helicopter. Leonard had been asking about it every day. Luther had a Black Hawk helicopter waiting on the ship's forward-deck launch pad with a pilot and a maintenance crew on board and in a constant state of readiness. Leonard wondered out loud why they always took a boat to shore when they could have flown.

"Can you fly that thing?" Leonard asked one morning at breakfast.

"Why do you ask?" Luther sounded defensive.

"Well, I've heard you talking to the crew, and it sounds like you know about everything there is to know about that helicopter."

Luther paused before answering. There were many aspects of his life he had not revealed to Honey and Leonard. At this moment, however, he decided to let them in on a major part of his background. "Yes, not only can I fly it, but I could do most of the repairs by myself if I had to."

"When did you learn how to fly helicopters?" Leonard asked.

Honey thought Luther wasn't going to answer until he gave a solemn, one-word reply, "Vietnam."

Leonard was not surprised. He had already done the math. He knew Luther was born in 1948, which would have made him of military age during the war in Vietnam.

"I'm sorry," Honey said.

"No, don't be sorry," Luther said. "I learned a lot and I survived. Much of what I do today is a direct result of what I learned in Nam."

"What is it, exactly, that you do?" Leonard asked.

Luther sighed and took a long sip of coffee before answering. "Leonard, my good friend, we'll leave that conversation for another time. But, I'll tell you what. We can take that Black Hawk for a ride today. It's a lot more fun than the ones I flew in Vietnam. I know a great place to land near the most romantic little beach town you ever saw. What do you say? Are you in?"

"We're in," Leonard said.

"How long will we be gone?" Honey asked.

"As long as we want," Luther said. "We could fly to Switzerland if you'd like."

Honey and Leonard packed a quick beach bag and boarded the helicopter with all the enthusiasm of kids at the carnival. "I just took my first plane ride a few weeks ago," Leonard said. "Now, here's another first. I can't believe I'm going up in a chopper."

Luther took the pilot's seat and began his pre-flight routine while a crewmember strapped in Honey and Leonard and gave them helmets with radios. Before anybody had time to get anxious, they were lifting off the ship and hanging over nothing but salt water. Luther banked the Black Hawk sharply and headed for the coast. "How you two holding up?" he asked. "Can you hear me?"

"Loud and clear and roger that," Leonard said.

"Who is this Roger?" Honey joked.

"He's the guy who keeps the radio humming," Luther said.

Once they leveled off, Luther got downright chatty on the radio. "You know, every time I take off in a helicopter I go right back to Vietnam. I can feel the jungle right now. I can see it. I can smell it. I can smell the blood and the body odor of the guys we hauled on medevac. Some of them died in my helicopter. That was the worst, watching bloody boys dying right in front of me. I'll never forget the bodies. I was lucky. I got shot up a lot but I only got shot down once."

"That sounds like more than enough," Leonard said.

"They only got our fuel line so we were able to get out of the zone and make a pretty rough emergency landing. We got picked up pretty quickly."

"What happened to your helicopter?" Leonard asked.

Luther chuckled. "It's probably still there. We were on a secret weapons run to Cambodia. That was actually my introduction to selling weapons, thanks to the United States government. Now, they're my biggest clients. How do you think I got this chopper?"

"You sell weapons for the U.S.?" Honey asked.

"Our country is the biggest arms dealer in the world," Luther said. "I made my first fortune helping the U.S. sell Saddam Hussein an unbelievable arsenal in the 1980's for Iraq's insane war against Iran."

Honey gave Leonard a look that said, for the first time, she was beginning to feel uncomfortable about Luther.

"I know," Luther said, responding to the stunned silence of his guests. "Selling weapons is evil. I see that now. You'll be glad to know I don't have to do that anymore."

"How'd you go from weapons to oil?" Leonard asked.

"Boy, Leonard, there's not much wrong with your memory," Luther laughed. "But to answer your question, there's not much difference between guns and oil. Whoever has the military power gets the goods."

Luther turned and looked at Honey, who was wide eyed at his recent comments. "I can see I've said too much already," he said. "Let's change the topic. See that mountain over there that looks like a volcano? Our landing spot is at the base of that mountain. Prepare for landing."

Michael Maxwell was waiting with a car at the site when Luther made a perfect landing. As the whirling blades slowed and dust began to settle, several men with what looked like automatic rifles reported briefly to Maxwell and then disappeared into the hillside terrain. Honey and Leonard got into the backseat with Maxwell driving and Luther in the front passenger seat. Honey turned around in her seat and noticed they were being followed by a large van. She tapped Luther on the back and asked, "Why are we being followed?"

Luther directed a quick scowl to Maxwell, who got on his radio immediately. The van fell behind and disappeared. "We are never supposed to see the security detail," Luther explained. "If we can see them, so can everybody else."

"Why do we need security?" Honey asked. "I don't think I like that."

"We've had it all along," Luther said. "It's something I got into the habit of doing a long time ago."

"Who's out to get you?" Leonard asked.

"Nobody, actually," Luther said. "It's really more for you than me. You two are the ones being chased."

"So, what are you going to do? Shoot somebody who gets too close to us?" Honey asked.

"No, no," Luther said. "I can see this has upset you. Really, it's more about keeping a lookout than anything."

Honey rode on in silence until they arrived in the fishing village Luther had scheduled for exploration. It was as perfect as he had described; colorful boats on a narrow beach tucked into a rock wall harbor. The three of them walked down to a cinder block restaurant with a large porch overlooking the stunning view. Maxwell stayed with the car. Honey was uncharacteristically quiet. She couldn't help looking around for the security team.

"You won't see anybody," Luther said. "I've sent them back to the helicopter. That does need to be guarded. But, Honey, please, talk to me. I can see that you are troubled."

"Luther," Honey launched into what sounded like a prepared speech, "I saw a side of you come to life as soon as you got into that helicopter. It's your military side, something I suspect you'll be trying to get over for the rest of your life. It divides the world into two parts, friend and foe. It seeks out the enemy and destroys it. It has no mercy and it has no love."

"Honey," Leonard intervened, "don't be so hard on our man."

"No, please," Luther said. "Let her finish."

"Luther, my dear man," Honey said, putting her hand on his shoulder. "You have been so good to us. And we've had such fun with you. It's just that I suddenly realized why you are so alone in this world. And why it's so perfect that you let Leonard and me into your life. Don't you see? We're here to set you free. Free from the war you never stopped fighting."

Luther put his hand on top of Honey's hand and started tearing up. "You have incredible intuition, Honey. I thought I was helping you two, but I'm starting to realize it's really the other way around."

"That's the way it always is when you help people," Leonard said.

"You've opened up your heart to us," Honey said. "Once you let us in you can start letting the rest of the world in. See?" She pointed at their idyllic surroundings. "It's easy. Life can be a perfect picnic in paradise."

The air was cleared. The tension among them vanished. They got back to being carefree friends and traveling buddies. The food arrived and it was delicious; fish in lemon and garlic butter sauce with pasta and fresh salad and white wine in a bottle with no label.

"What is this?" Leonard asked, holding up the breadbasket. "French bread in Italy?"

The waiter almost spilled the water he was refilling. "French bread?" he joked. "Ha. Ha," he grabbed the basket and held it over his head as he began prancing comically. "The bread is Italian. The French steal their bread from Italy. The French take all their cooking lessons from the Italians."

They laughed hard at the impromptu show. When they were coming out of the comic relief, Luther took the conversation in a new and bold direction, "I've been thinking about inviting that journalist, Jack Crumbo, onboard for an exclusive interview."

Leonard leaned forward and asked, "Are we ready for that?"

"Well," Luther began, "I can tell the two of you are beginning to think about heading home. And I've been wondering how I can help."

"What do you mean?" Honey asked.

"First of all, we can prove Leonard was never poisoned. Secondly, Dr. Laughlin can testify that Leonard is competent because he has shown so much improvement from the experimental drugs he's been taking."

Leonard looked at Honey like he was pretty sure he wasn't making all that much progress in the memory department.

"What about me violating the no-contact order?" Honey asked.

"And what about you getting in trouble for helping fugitives or harboring known criminals or whatever they call it?"

"We'll let our attorneys work that out," Luther said as he raised his glass in a toast, "Here's to Jack Crumbo. May we have him aboard *The Sinbad* by noon tomorrow."

"And here's to you coming to Indiana," Honey toasted back. "We might have just the girl for you."

With that, Honey and Leonard stood up like a couple vaudevillians and broke into their spirited version of "Back Home Again In Indiana." It was a song they sang together every chance they got.

They sang it well as they always did. Even though they sang the same notes, it sounded like harmony because of the two-octave difference in their voices. By the time they finished the song, the entire restaurant staff had come out to listen. Honey and Leonard were applauded and cheered by the cook, the bartender, the waiter, Luther and two other tables of their fellow diners. Honey and Leonard took their bows and gave each other a kissing hug.

One thing was readily apparent to even the most casual observer: Honey and Leonard were homesick.

And they were getting careless about being recognized.

FIFTEEN

MICHAEL MAXWELL ESCORTED Jack Crumbo and Corbin Lacoste into the multimedia room of *The Sinbad*. The journalists had black bags over their heads but were not bound in any way. The first thing they saw when Maxwell removed the bags was Honey and Leonard, beaming at them from across a wooden table. No one else was in the room.

"Surprise," Honey said. "We're alive."

Crumbo's mouth dropped open as his eyes adjusted to the light. He knew it was Honey by the sound of her voice, but he was too shocked to speak. Lacoste was in a similar state. They had been under their hoods for nearly two hours.

"Were the hoods really necessary?" Leonard asked Maxwell. "We trust these guys."

"I'm afraid so," Maxwell said. "It's for their own protection. They agreed to it."

By the time he finished his sentence, Honey was around the table and giving both Crumbo and Lacoste a big hug. "Thank you boys so much for coming. Those hoods must have been terrible."

"Not to worry," Crumbo said, returning her hug. "A small price to pay for seeing you two again.." He backed out of the hug. "So, let me look at you and Leonard." Crumbo was beaming. "Now the world will have to admit I was right. You are alive."

Leonard embraced his two favorite journalists. "You're probably wondering why we've invited you here."

"No, I've got a pretty good idea what you're up to," Crumbo said. "But I don't know where we are. In the last couple hours we've been in a car, a helicopter and a boat, and now it feels like we're on a bigger boat. I must say, the gentleman who showed us the way has been more than polite."

"We knew he would be," Honey said. "And I'm glad to see you've brought your cameras and a copy of today's newspaper. We're ready for our photoshoot to prove we did not drown in St. Tropez. Please try to take a better photo than the one everybody's been using. As you can see, we dressed for the occasion."

Honey and Leonard were wearing matching blue flight suits with gold trim and purple zippers. They looked like commanders from the Starship Enterprise.

"You both look fantastic," Lacoste blurted out. "I can't believe Mr. Crumbo let me come along. This is the biggest story of my life. Not only are you alive but you look even younger than I remember."

Honey and Leonard had marvelously deep tans from their travels with Luther.

Crumbo was trying to be all business in getting his camera ready for the photoshoot, but Honey could see tears rolling down his face. "Why, Jack Crumbo," she teased. "You old softy. You're so happy to see us you can't hold back the tears."

"Now, pumpkin," Leonard said. "This is a pretty emotional moment. It's not every day somebody gets to come back from the dead."

Crumbo put down his camera and held his arms out in triumph. "I knew you were alive. I knew it deep down in my bones. You guys are too ornery to die young."

"Oh, my boy," Honey said. "Flattery will get you the news scoop of your lifetime."

Crumbo and Lacoste began taking pictures as Honey and

Leonard held up copies of daily publications to prove the date. Crumbo turned on his handheld tape recorder and began questioning. "Leonard, how are you doing?"

"Better than I have the right to expect. Doc has me on some new drug that helps some with the memory. Go ahead, ask me anything. I'll know the answer."

"How long since you left Indiana?" Crumbo asked.

Leonard looked at Honey helplessly and then said to Crumbo, "You would have to ask me a tough one right off the bat. But wait. I know. Give me a minute. I'm going to say it's been about a month and a half."

"What drug do they have you on?"

"That, I couldn't tell you. All I can say is Doc has me taking it twice a day."

Crumbo asked what he thought would be an easier question to answer. "Who is the doctor?"

Leonard looked at Honey and shifted uncomfortably in his chair. "I'm pretty sure the doc doesn't want his name in the papers."

Crumbo did not press the issue. "Well, I'm no doctor, but you sure sound good to me. And I've got to say it. I've never been so happy to see somebody looking so good."

Crumbo and Lacoste continued the interview, which turned into more of a reunion among friends as they were served a seven-course feast for lunch. Maxwell joined them for the meal. "I promised these gentlemen we would feed them well. They weren't sure they could trust me until I showed them Honey's handwritten note."

"You do know the French police are hot on your trail," Lacoste said. "My connections tell me the Honey and Leonard sightings are coming in quite regularly. Fortunately for you, they're coming from all over. It's like people saying they saw Elvis alive. Most of the reports are clearly not reliable. But lately, the reports are starting to focus on the Italian coast, west of Genoa. Right about where Mr. Maxwell had us meet him."

Honey raised her glass of iced tea in a toast. "You can tell the police they won't have to look for us much longer. We're headed back to Indiana to meet this thing head on. We're not running anymore."

"We never were running," Leonard said. "We were just having fun."

Honey continued with her toast. "So, here's to the Bonnie and Clyde of love, still alive and heading home at last."

Glasses were clinking as Doctor Laughlin walked into the room carrying a thick folder under his arm. He introduced himself to the reporters by his real name. Honey and Leonard were shocked.

Leonard rose to greet the doctor. "I thought you didn't want us to use your name."

"Don't worry," Dr. Laughlin said. "I changed my mind. Once the facts get out, none of us will have to worry." He handed the folder to Crumbo and said, "Here's everything you need for your story. My blood tests clearly show the arsenic levels in Leonard's blood are from years of farming and exposure to pesticides. Also, results from a complete battery of mental examinations showing Mr. Atkins is quite competent, although he is in the early stages of Alzheimer's disease. In addition, my work has been confirmed by a team of talented researchers at the Mayo Clinic."

Crumbo tried to ask questions, but the doctor left the room, saying, "It's all in the reports. Sorry to interrupt your interview."

Honey and Leonard and the reporters were speechless. Crumbo was the first to recover. "So when will you return to Indiana?"

"I can't say exactly when," Honey said. "But it will be soon. Let's just say we'll be home for Halloween."

"It's not going to be as easy as the doctor seems to think," Crumbo said. "Leonard's niece, Gretchen, has her own doctors from the nursing home, and they're all ready to testify that Leonard is not competent."

"I'll set them straight in a hurry," Leonard said. "I'm feeling sharper than I have in a long time."

"You certainly seem competent to me," Lacoste said. "Why don't you revoke the power of attorney right now? Wouldn't that take Gretchen out of the equation?"

Leonard put down his knife and fork and attempted to explain. "We can't do that, not while the guardianship is pending. And, besides, the real problem is the no contact order they say Honey violated."

Crumbo let the answer sink in and decided to change the topic. "So, tell the story of how you kept from drowning in St. Tropez? And how you got away. That's what everybody wants to know."

Gretchen Atkins was back home again in Indiana when she read the shocking banner headline on the front page of *The Chicago Tribune*.

HONEY AND LEONARD ALIVE AND WELL

She was even more amazed by the photos accompanying the story. Honey and Leonard looked tanned and youthful and happy as they held up an Italian newspaper dated October 15, 1992.

Jack Crumbo's byline was on top of the story, and the first paragraph was unmistakably his writing style. Nobody could cram more information and drama into a couple of lead sentences than Crumbo.

Honey and Leonard are alive and living in high style on a luxury yacht somewhere on the Mediterranean Sea. The couple plans to return home to Indiana in the near future to establish Leonard's competency and to defend Honey in criminal court.

Gretchen had to put the paper down after the opening paragraph of the story to catch her breath. She was so emotionally conflicted she was hyperventilating. Learning that her Uncle Leonard was alive was such a relief it made her cry. Knowing that Honey was also alive and by his side, filled Gretchen with enough hatred and jealousy to sink a yacht in any sea.

That bitch! Look at that smug smile. She's mocking me. We'll see who laughs last on this one, Miss Honey.

Gretchen's phone rang. She answered it after five rings. It was the investigator, Adam Wolf. He was still in St. Tropez with his "interpreter," Simon. He needed more money.

"You're fired," Gretchen shouted into the phone.

Wolf said nothing.

"Have you seen *The Chicago Tribune* this morning?" Gretchen asked.

"I'm in France."

"Jack Crumbo has an interview with them on the front page. He's got photos to prove they're still alive."

"Where are they?"

"You're asking *me*?" Gretchen shrieked. "You're asking me?" she screamed again as she hung up the phone with an angry slam.

She looked back at the newspaper in disbelief. Honey and Leonard looked so happy. How could they look so good together? The photo was making her physically ill. Everybody was in love but her. Even her investigator had fallen in love. And she had unwittingly financed the courtship. Or Uncle Leonard did.

What was happening to her? Gretchen was feeling alone and

filled with guilt. No doubt, her theft from Uncle Leonard's fortune would soon be discovered. She would be exposed and ruined. She might even go to jail.

The phone rang again. Gretchen couldn't answer. It had to be Adam Wolf. Her anxiety became full-blown panic as she ran upstairs and threw herself on the unmade bed, sobbing in fear and frustration. A bottle of Jack Daniels whiskey was hidden behind her bed frame. There was less than a good gulp left. She swilled it down and threw the bottle against the wall. It made a dent in the drywall but didn't shatter the glass bottle. She buried her head in the pillow. If only she could suffocate herself to death.

Why did Honey have to come along and ruin everything?

In less than a minute, Gretchen stopped crying and pulled her head out of the pillow. It was as if she had seen from an overhead camera how pathetic she looked. She got up and dusted herself off emotionally.

Come on, girl. He's still your uncle and she's still breaking the law. This game is far from over.

SIXTEEN

HONEY WOKE UP alone in a private white room. At first, she thought it was a cheap hotel. But there were no windows and no furniture except for the single bed in which she had been sleeping. The only light in the room came from indirect fixtures in the high ceiling that emitted a dim gloom. She struggled to a sitting position and immediately became so dizzy she had to lie down again.

She tried to remember where she was and how she got there. Her mind was sluggish. The world felt fuzzy and out of focus. Thoughts were developing as though coming out of a fog. She held up her right arm and studied the palm of her hand. A blurred memory eventually came into focus. Someone in a white uniform was sticking a needle into her arm. Looking up the inside of her arm, she could see the bruise where the needle entered.

It must have been a sedative.

Falling back to sleep, Honey slipped into a troubling dream. It was the dream she always had when she was worried about something. In the dream, she was in the newsroom of her high school paper and couldn't remember the story she had been assigned to write. The old Underwood typewriter was no help at all, and her editor kept asking if she could meet the deadline. She didn't want to ask anybody what story she was on for fear of looking like an idiot. It was her dream of confusion; like her mind could not get itself into gear. Finally, someone slammed a door in the back of the room.

She awoke with a start and was once again confused by her surroundings. There was no color in the room. Something told her it was time to get up. A sense of dread began to fill her. She sat up in bed, more slowly this time, and tried to collect her thoughts. She noticed what looked to be a camera in the upper corner to the right of a single door in the center of the wall. She waved half-heartedly and swung her legs over the edge of the bed. She was wearing a gray, cotton nightgown with nothing underneath. Instinctively, she pulled the bed sheet over her exposed legs.

Looking over the edge of the bed, Honey could see her feet were nearly a foot above the floor. It felt like a long way down. She looked around the room and took several deep breaths. There was no alternative. She slid slowly off the bed to the cold, tiled floor. The shock to her bare feet brought another vague vision into her consciousness. She was looking down on Paris from the top of the Eiffel Tower. The image was so vivid it made her lean back up against the bed. The urge to jump came and left as fast as the memory itself.

"Is anybody there?" Honey said, waving once more at the camera. "I'm up, but I'm not sure I can walk. Where am I?"

The camera provided not so much as a blink in response.

Honey decided to walk to the door. It was only a few steps from the bed, but the distance seemed much further because of her wobbly condition. She wondered about the Eiffel Tower vision before proceeding. Then the entire scene came into recollection. She and Leonard were on top of the Tower, marveling at the majesty of Paris and feeling swept away by the romance of it all. She felt herself swooning in his arms and then falling through his arms as she passed out and hit the deck hard. *I must have had another heart event.*

The mental fog descended on her again, and she had to refocus her efforts at reaching the door. She put her hands over her head and stretched. She moved her arms in circles to get her circulation going. She faced the bed and used it to support a few shallow knee bends. Finally, she turned back to the camera and said, "Here I come, ready or not."

Honey felt quite drunk as she staggered to the door. She was grateful for the support once she grabbed the single doorknob. It wouldn't turn, either clockwise or counter clockwise. Honey put all her weight into the effort. She shook the doorknob for all she was worth. It took a whole lot of shaking before she realized the obvious. The door was locked.

There was no locking mechanism on her side of the door. It was locked from the outside. She was a prisoner.

"Oh, no you don't," she shook her fist at the camera. "You can't keep me in here. I'm an American citizen. I know my rights. You need to let me out of here right now."

Once again, the camera had no reaction.

Honey felt herself beginning to cry and then held back the tears. She had never been locked up beyond the occasional bathroom door malfunction. The cold fear of her circumstance kept her from crying. She had no idea why she was being held or who was holding her. She had done nothing wrong.

The truth hit her like a glove-smack in the face, challenging a duel.

Oh, my goodness, I've been arrested. They caught me when I passed out. What about Leonard? Where is Leonard?

Honey started banging on the door. She didn't care about the camera anymore. She wanted someone to answer the door and to answer her questions. "Open this door right now," she yelled. "You can't keep me in here alone. I need medical attention. I'm having another heart attack."

With that, she stumbled into the camera view and pretended to be collapsing in a medical emergency. The floor was cold. It brought back another fleeting memory. She and Leonard were sitting on the deck of *The Sinbad* with Luther Patrick, reading Jack Crumbo's interview, notifying the world that Honey and Leonard were still alive. Honey could see the new picture of her in the Tribune. She was pleased they finally had a shot that didn't make her look too old.

She faded back out of cogent thought. Her memory was coming in and out like a weak radio signal. She was still on the cold floor waiting for someone to open the door.

No one came, and then no one came some more.

Maybe the camera isn't working.

The floor finally became too uncomfortable. Honey got on her knees and slowly rose to her feet. The struggle left her lightheaded again as she climbed into bed. It was so much softer than the floor. She faded out and slept for another hour.

When she awakened, the fear of being held prisoner was beginning to give way to her need to urinate.

Honey got up on her knees and peered over the top of the headboard. There was a small door that blended into the wall in the rear of the room. She slid down to the floor and walked carefully to the door. It was unlocked. Inside was a bathroom with a shower stall and a toilet that looked like it had been waiting for her for some time. The light revealed another camera above the door facing the toilet.

"Have you no decency?" she muttered as she raised her gown to sit down on what proved to be an icy cold, metal seat. There would be no stopping her answering the call of nature.

As she was finishing in the bathroom, Honey heard the door to her main room open. Someone walked in and quickly crossed the room to knock firmly on the bathroom door.

"No one is in here," Honey said.

The door to the bathroom opened as Honey was standing

up. She found herself face to face with a sternly attractive French policewoman who quickly revealed herself to be fluent in English. "Honey Waldrop, I am Officer Claire Lebeau. I am your liaison officer while you are here at the hospital for observation."

"Am I under arrest?" Honey asked.

"Yes, you are."

"What are the charges?"

"You are being held on a warrant from the United States for violating a no-contact order regarding Leonard Atkins. I believe you know quite well why you are being held."

Honey hung her head. "Where were you when I was collapsing on the floor?"

Officer Lebeau took a quick look around. "I don't know anything about that. All I know is the alarm sounds when the bathroom door opens."

"I didn't hear any alarm."

"Of course not," Lebeau nearly smiled.

Honey gathered the nightshirt around her. "Would you mind terribly if we continue this conversation outside of the bathroom. What do you call it in French?"

"We say toilettes," Lebeau said as she allowed Honey out.

"Everything sounds so perfect when you say it in French," Honey said, turning on the charm and grateful to have human company. "It almost always seems to rhyme."

"I am pleased to see you up and about," Lebeau said. "We thought you were dying on the Tower, but it turns out to be not so serious."

"You know who I am?" Honey asked.

With that, the sternness came out of Lebeau's voice like she was letting down her hair from its tight bun on the back of her head. She sounded like a music fan talking to a rock star. "Oh, yes, I know who you are. You are the one and only Honey of Honey and Leonard fame. You are the talk of the town, of all France, of all Europe, of the world."

Officer Lebeau forced herself to regain composure. "Even so, you are my prisoner for now. I will try my best to make your stay as pleasant as possible. In fact, I am authorized to take you to dinner whenever you are able."

"What time is it?"

"It's 10:30 p.m., Oct. 19, 1992."

Honey crossed her hands over her heart. "Oh, my goodness, I've lost two days. How can that happen? Where am I?"

Lebeau's tone became businesslike. "You are in a lockdown room in a hospital in Paris. You spent one day in intensive care and then you were brought here once your condition stabilized."

Honey held on to Lebeau's left arm. "I'm still feeling a little groggy, but come to think of it, I would love to eat something. I am hungry. But first, I have to get dressed."

"Come with me," Lebeau said. "I have everything you need in a room across the hall."

"Wait," Honey said, grabbing Lebeau's arm more tightly as they were about to walk out of the room. "Tell me about Leonard. Is he good?"

"He is very worried about you," Lebeau said. "He wasn't happy at all when we told him you were under arrest. He made such a scene he almost got arrested himself. He rode in the ambulance from the Tower with you. He had a fit at the hospital when they took you away without him. He tried to run up to your room even though he had no idea what room you were in. There was a man with him who helped us get him under control."

Honey's eyes were wide. "Was that a British gentleman named Maxwell?"

Lebeau cocked her head, trying to remember. "Yes, now that you mention it, I believe that was his name. He walked Leonard out of the hospital like he was placing him under arrest. He used just enough force to get the job done. Leonard seemed to listen to him."

"Oh my dear goodness," Honey said. "Leonard will not do well with any of this. He needs me more than any of you can understand. I keep him on a steady course. He looks to me for cues on what to do and how to act. He won't be in his right mind without me."

"We can't think about that right now," Lebeau said, walking Honey across the hall. "We've got to get you dressed and off to dinner. We won't be in the main dining hall. We'll have our own private space. You'll be pleasantly surprised by the food here. It's not at all like hospital food."

Lebeau handed Honey a black and white prison jumpsuit.

"You've got to be kidding," Honey said. "And look, white socks and black sandals to match. Is this the latest fashion in Paris?"

"I'm sorry."

Honey slipped into the prison outfit and went into the bathroom to check herself out in the mirror. "Oh, my stars, I look 100 years old. It looks like they've been trying to kill me."

Lebeau handed her a small, clear-plastic bag. "I'm not authorized to give you this, but I'm giving it to you anyway. It's a makeup survival kit."

Honey's eyes lit up as she opened up the bag and held up a lipstick identified by a single rose. "Oh, my, you are so fancy."

Lebeau was pleased by Honey's appreciation. "Lancome–L'Absolu Rouge."

Honey forgot about Leonard for a moment. "Unbelievable. I've read about this for years. Funny, I had to go to prison in a Paris hospital before actually trying it."

"I knew you would need it," Lebeau said. "I mean, I knew you would want it."

"You were right the first time," Honey laughed as she explored the contents of the makeup kit. "I'll be careful to keep it light. That way you won't get into trouble. No one will know the difference. They'll think I'm a natural beauty. Of course, that used to be true. I never used a lot of makeup."

"I know," Lebeau said. "I've read so much about you and seen so many photos of you as a young woman that I almost feel like I know you. You and Leonard have had quite an impact on France. You've given new hope to my mother and all her friends. The photographers are everywhere around the hospital. We've never had such a security issue. I'd hate to have somebody get a picture of you not looking your best."

Honey broke into her best southern belle smile. "So, let me ask you something. Why all the fuss about Honey and Leonard? We really don't understand it at all."

Lebeau looked at Honey like she would have to think about that question before answering. Her brow furrowed for a moment and then she responded. "It's because you're in love. And because you are older . . . what do you call it? Senior citizens."

"We're certainly not the only seniors in love," Honey said.

"No, no," Lebeau agreed. "But most of the pictures we see are people having their fiftieth wedding anniversary and they never look to be very happy. You and Leonard give the world hope that love never has to grow old."

"Don't look now," Honey said as she concentrated on her eyeliner, "but I'm getting older every time I look in the mirror."

"You are young. Only young lovers run from the law to elope and get married."

Honey turned away from the mirror to look at Lebeau. "Who said anything about getting married?"

"I read that you were getting married to help with your legal problems."

"Hmm," Honey murmured as she returned to the mirror. "I hadn't thought about that. Maybe it would help fight the guardianship that Gretchen is trying to get over Leonard. Yes, it probably would. I'm not sure how or why, but it makes sense that a wife would have more say-so in court than a girlfriend. I think you're on to something there, Miss Lebeau. May I call you Claire?"

Lebeau winked at Honey in the mirror. "Yes, please do. But not when anyone else is around."

"Of course not. It will be our little secret. Like the makeup."

Lebeau began whispering. "Yes, and now we have a secret strategy too."

"What's that?" Honey asked.

"For you and Leonard to marry. It would be such a smart thing to do right now. I must tell you, I am studying law when I'm not working."

"Oh, so you're not just your everyday matchmaker?"

Lebeau frowned, afraid Honey was mocking her.

"Now, dear, I'm just teasing," Honey said. "But aren't you forgetting something?"

"What?"

"I'm in jail," Honey laughed as she pointed to her black and white jump suit. "It's tough to get married when you're in prison."

"You won't be in jail for long."

"What makes you so sure?"

"What have you done wrong, really? Was anybody killed? Was anybody robbed?"

"They are suggesting I tried to poison Leonard."

"That doesn't make sense," Lebeau said. "If you wanted his money, you would have gotten him to marry you and make a new will before you killed him."

Honey put both hands on Lebeau's shoulders. "You really have thought this thing all the way through, haven't you?"

Lebeau smiled, and Honey noticed for the first time what a beautiful young woman she was. "Oh, look at that smile. You look like Sophia Loren when you smile like that. You don't want to be an attorney. You need to be a model or an actress."

Lebeau shook her head in a little pout. "No, I don't want to be another pretty face. When I grow up, I want to be just like you."

"Why would you want to be like me?"

Lebeau took Honey's hands off her shoulders. "I want to be in love. Really in love. Not just caught up in the heat of the moment. I want to find the man of my dreams and run away from everything."

"Oh, my dear girl," Honey said. "Does my life look that romantic to you? Love isn't running away. Love doesn't solve your problems. Love is caring about someone else more than yourself."

"How does it feel to be in love with Leonard?"

Honey gathered her thoughts in the mirror before answering. For the first time, she realized these questions would be coming at her from a thousand different angles.

I don't look half bad with the makeup on, even in my prison suit. But do I look like an expert on love?

Before leaving *The Sinbad*, she and Leonard had talked extensively with Luther Patrick and Dr. Laughlin about not giving interviews. "Number one, it will hurt your case," Luther said. "And number two, we've got a book deal in the works for you."

"Claire, you don't have a man in your life, do you?" Honey tried to turn the conversational table.

Lebeau hung her head. "I thought I did."

Honey knew that look. "He cheated on you?"

Lebeau looked up quickly, surprised Honey could read her so well. "Of course. That's what men do, isn't it?"

Honey hugged Lebeau. "I'm so sorry. Did he break your heart?"

Lebeau shook her head to keep from crying. "Not really. He was never going to be my Leonard. I've never had that. I want to know what it's like to really be in love."

"All right, then. Let's answer the burning question. What is being in love? Let me begin by saying I am no expert. I can only testify from personal experience. I don't know where to start except to say that, being with Leonard, our whole is greater than the sum of our parts. There is goodness to the two of us being a couple that we could never achieve on our own. I felt that the first time we were together. We were made for each other. We completed each other.

"Being in love makes you feel like you're part of something bigger than yourself. It does more than sweep you off your feet. It sweeps you out of the room and out the door and down the street.

"It's fun being in love, but it's so much more than fun. It's uplifting. It makes you want to do the right thing. It makes you try to do things for the other person, things that will make you happy as a couple. I suppose that's why we left Indiana. Once you get to that place as a couple, nothing can keep you apart."

Lebeau stared at Honey in the mirror, waiting for her to continue.

"Let me digress a bit to say this," Honey explained. "It's taken me quite a while to figure this out, but now I think I can say it with some authority. Are you ready?"

Lebeau nodded for Honey to continue.

"Okay, then. Here it is. Each of us is trapped in a prison. Not like the one we're in now. I'm talking about a prison of self. Everywhere we turn, our eyes tell us we are the center of the universe. Everything we touch and taste and smell and hear tells us we are the epicenter. But we are not. We are part of a universe completely beyond our understanding.

"Being in love with another person is the best way to escape your selfish ways. Once you find the person who can make you forget about yourself, you are on your way."

Lebeau's mouth was slightly open in amazement. "Wow," she said. "You make it all sound so perfect."

Honey laughed, "Perfect? It's anything but perfect. You have to remember, there's a dark side to love."

"What do you mean?"

"The dark side of love is what makes you want to control the other person. The jealousy and the lack of patience and the wanting to make the other person into something he's not. There's a dark side of love that makes you afraid you're going to lose it. It makes you want to take command of the relationship. It makes you want to direct the movie instead of acting in it."

"So how do you keep from doing that?" Claire asked.

"You can't keep from doing it part of the time. You just try to do it as little as possible. You have to remember that you can't have your cake and eat it too. If you consume the other person with your need to control or direct, then the love is gone and you're left alone with your selfish self."

Lebeau nodded. "Men have always tried to control me."

"I know you wouldn't let that happen."

"I know the right person is out there, somewhere," Claire said.

"So how do you find this person?" Honey asked rhetorically. "Here's the tricky part. You don't find the person until you stop looking. Stop looking for someone to make you happy, or fulfill your sexual fantasies, or provide for you, or make you laugh. Stop looking for Prince Charming. He won't appear until you're ready to get over your self and love unselfishly.

"He might be an old man with a bad memory and a lot of legal baggage. But you take what you get and you've got to be happy with what you got. That's what Leonard says. 'Be happy with what you got.' Which reminds me, when can I see my precious boy?"

Lebeau stared into her own reflection. She had not heard Honey's question. She was still trying to wrap her head around what had just been said.

"Claire? Did you hear me?"

"Oh, yes. Yes, I heard you. I did not understand it completely but I heard you loud and clear. Especially the part about not looking for Prince Charming."

Honey leaned into the mirror. "What about the part where I asked about seeing my Leonard again?"

"Oh, yes. I'm so sorry. There I was, thinking of myself again."

"Well?"

Lebeau straightened up her uniform. "We'll see what we can do, but I'm afraid that's going to be a problem."

"What do you mean?"

Lebeau sighed deeply. "The problem is that you are a prisoner for transport, in transition, if you will. Technically, there is no visitation for prisoners en route to another location."

"But you'll see what you can do?

"I'll see what I can do."

Honey looked away from the mirror and directly into Lebeau's eyes. "How about you help me escape?"

Honey thought she saw a flash of conspiratorial recognition in Claire's eyes as she said the word 'escape.' But the police officer quickly lowered her eyes and said, "You wouldn't want to get us both into trouble would you?"

SEVENTEEN

LEONARD WENT INTO A STEEP emotional decline in the days following Honey's arrest. Life without Honey felt empty and pointless. He kept seeing the medics hauling her away from him at the hospital. They banged him up pretty well when he tried to follow them. His left shoulder was still sore.

He blamed himself for letting Honey talk him into visiting the Eiffel Tower. Luther Patrick had arranged a private flight to Indianapolis, but Honey wasn't about to leave Paris without going to the top of the Tower with her sweetie.

All the progress Leonard seemed to have made on the experimental memory drug was forgotten as quickly as a dream once his grief took over. He was lost without Honey. No one could make him understand where she had gone or why he couldn't go see her. He slipped into a depression much deeper than the one that had consumed him after his wife's death. He didn't say one word to Maxwell on the helicopter ride back to *The Sinbad*. He wouldn't even look at Luther once they landed.

"How bad is he?" Luther asked Maxwell once Leonard was below deck with Dr. Laughlin.

"Worse than I could have imagined," Maxwell said. "The first day he was mainly angry. I had to muscle him out of the hospital. He made quite a scene. Then, he didn't want to stay in the hotel. I couldn't let him out. Reporters surrounded the place. He was in no shape to make a public statement. He kept saying they were going to kill her in the hospital and that he was the only one who could save her because he had done it before. I gave him a couple sleeping pills and he slept for fourteen hours. I heard him talking to his mother in his sleep on several occasions. When he awakened, he demanded to go see Honey. I tried to make arrangements, but it was impossible. The hospital has her under complete lockdown. He hasn't spoken to me since I told him we couldn't go see her."

"Honey has a Paris police liaison named Claire Lebeau assigned to her," Luther said. "Lebeau volunteered for the job. She's a big Honey and Leonard fan. We might be able to get to her. Honey's probably got her on our side by now."

Maxwell looked Luther in the eye. "Would you help Honey escape?"

Luther turned away and looked out a window. "I thought about it, but then realized the best thing we can do is let the French police and the F.B.I. transport her back to the States as soon as possible."

Maxwell became agitated. "How long will that take? What are we going to do about Leonard in the meantime? What happens once they go back to Indiana?"

Luther turned around and looked at Maxwell like a patient professor looks at a student. "That's a lot of questions all in a row, Mr. Maxwell."

Maxwell stiffened into his apology, "I'm sorry, sir. I'm afraid I've gotten too personally involved with Honey and Leonard."

Luther put his hand on Maxwell's shoulder. "No need to apologize. It seems the whole world has gotten too personally involved. But let me answer your questions. First of all, Honey should be back in Indiana in less than one week. Our sources tell us she is in fine health. At least she's not in prison. The hospital is a much better place to stay. Secondly, Leonard should do much better once we tell him. Honey will have a $100,000 bond set for her by the Indiana criminal judge. The prosecutor there has already agreed to it. I've made arrangements to post the entire amount in cash. That way we'll get it all back once the proceedings are concluded."

Maxwell did not seem relieved. "What about Leonard's competency hearing? I wouldn't bet on him doing too well at this point."

Luther walked away from Maxwell and began pacing back and forth in front of the window. "Hopefully, he'll get better once he realizes he'll be reunited with Honey in the near future."

Maxwell couldn't stop asking questions. "What about the no-contact order in the guardianship proceeding?"

"We're working on that as well," Luther said.

"Very good, sir."

Luther raised his chin and his eyebrows as though pleased to have the questions stop. "Have you seen Jack Crumbo on the news?"

"Not really."

"Whatever *The Chicago Tribune* is paying him isn't enough," Luther said. "Here, let's turn on the video. I've had a tape made of all his interviews."

Luther and Maxwell watched Crumbo on video for nearly half an hour. He was talking to what seemed like every news source on the planet. The reporter had dropped all pretense of impartiality. He was openly arguing against Honey's arrest and deportation.

"What it is," Crumbo said, "is ridiculous. The no-contact order was issued on the basis that Honey tried to poison Leonard. That point has been soundly refuted. The arsenic in Leonard's blood was from a lifetime of being around pesticides as a farmer, not from any attempted murder. And the guardianship petition is unnecessary because Leonard is clearly competent. What you've got is a bogus charge, leading to a bogus petition, followed by a bogus no-contact order. The whole thing should be dropped."

"He likes that word, 'bogus,' doesn't he?" Maxwell observed.

Luther applauded the television screen. "I'm telling you, I get a kick out of Jack Crumbo. The guy is down to earth. Ever since he came on board to interview Honey and Leonard, I've been following him closely. The man tells it like it is. I could use a man like that."

Dr. Laughlin walked into the room, looking grave.

Luther crossed the room to see what was the matter. "What is it, Doctor? How bad is Leonard?"

The doctor spoke in the hushed tone of a professional with a bad diagnosis. "He's in shock. He's not making any sense. He's grieving like Honey has died, and there's nothing I can say to make him believe she's going to be fine."

Luther nodded and then shook his head. "What can you do for him?"

The doctor hesitated, watching the Crumbo tape until Maxwell turned it off at Luther's direction.

"What can we do?" Luther repeated.

Dr. Laughlin raised his voice and spoke with renewed confidence. "The very best thing we can do is get him back together with Honey as soon as possible. The grief is aggravating the Alzheimer's in a way that is problematic. He has become an excellent candidate for having a stroke. His blood pressure is elevated dangerously and his breathing is labored. We might be looking at heart trouble if we don't act quickly. The man is in physical danger. His mind is writing checks his body can't cash."

Luther looked to Maxwell for suggestions.

"I know the layout of the hospital," Maxwell said, "if you can enlist the support of Officer Claire Lebeau and her superiors."

Luther smiled at Maxwell and then grinned at the doctor. "I'll handle Lebeau and her superiors. Gentlemen, pack your bags. The three of us are taking Leonard back to Paris. We're going to break Honey out of jail."

Honey could not believe the familiar knock on her hospital door. Before she could respond, Leonard burst into the room and swept her up into his arms. He lifted her off her feet and squeezed her so tightly it took her breath away. When he backed off the hug to kiss her, Honey could see tears rolling down his face.

"Leonard. I can't believe it's you. How did you get in? As if I didn't know. Look at you, you're crying," she said, wiping away her own tears of joy.

Leonard squeezed her again and then let her go. "Let me look at you."

Honey put her forehead on his. "Don't you dare. They've got me in this horrible black and white thing. Did you come to break me out?"

"I don't know, pumpkin. I'm not sure what we're doing. They just let me in for a short time to make sure you're okay." He hugged her again, "You don't know how much I've missed you. Or, maybe you do. I'm afraid I've been a little out of sorts since they took you away. I honestly thought you might not make it. And, let me tell you, if you don't make it, I don't want to make it either."

Honey kissed him and held him at arm's length. "Now, Leonard, don't talk like that. Everything's going to be fine. Claire tells me this is only temporary. I should be out of here in a jiffy."

Leonard grabbed her backside with both hands. "Listen to you, trying to make me feel better. I'm the one who should be making you feel better. You're the one who's in jail. How is it in here? And who's this Claire I keep hearing about?"

Honey took his hands off her *derriere*. "She's my new French friend. Actually, she's my private warden."

Leonard could not keep his hands off Honey. He rubbed her shoulders. "I figured you'd have the guards in the palm of your hand by now."

Honey relaxed to his touch. "She's a dear, young lady. But you know what I've learned from talking to her?"

"What?"

Honey grabbed his arms and hung on tight. "The whole world now regards us as experts on love. Once we go public, people are going to be asking us about love and what it's like to be in love and how do you find love?"

"Don't worry about that. Luther's already got us a literary agent. All we have to do is keep our mouths shut for now. Meanwhile, give me another hug. I can't get enough of you."

"I've got a private shower," Honey teased. "And it looks like Claire has decided to leave us alone for awhile."

Leonard's eyes lit up and his mouth fell open. He looked like a man who just realized he'd died and gone to heaven. "You smell so good. I'd guess you just had your morning shower."

"That doesn't mean I can't take another one with you," Honey purred. "How long do we have?"

"They said they'll check back in half an hour," Leonard said.

Honey wrapped her arms around him and grabbed his behind. "Ooh, then it looks like it's time for prison sex."

"Never in my wildest dreams," Leonard said as they went into the bathroom and undressed each other quickly. Honey threw her prison outfit over the camera and turned out the light. "Oh, my goodness," she murmured as she gently squeezed his manhood. "You feel like the Eiffel Tower."

The shower was nice and steamy but quite small. It didn't matter. The two lovers became one. They laughed and moaned and giggled and groaned. A better shower was never taken by anyone, anywhere.

After the shower, they tenderly dried each other off and crawled into Honey's bed for a quick cuddle. "Now, this is what I call a conjugal visit," Leonard said.

"You know, sweetie," Honey said. "I've been thinking."

"Thinking about what?"

"About us."

"Uh, oh," Leonard said. "Sounds like trouble."

Honey whispered in his ear. "What would you think about getting married?"

"If that's a proposal, I accept," Leonard said.

"Just like that?"

"No, not just like that," Leonard said. "We usually don't talk much before we rush off to save the world. But this time I do have something to say."

With that, he got out of bed, naked, cleared his throat and got down slowly on one knee. "You'd better sit up for this."

Honey sat up, covering herself with a sheet, and threw her legs over the side of the bed. Leonard took her hands into his and said, "Honey Waldrop, you are the love of my life. Without you I am nothing. I've realized that in these last couple of days. I never want to live without you again. That's why I'm asking this question: Honey Waldrop, will you marry me?"

Honey looked up at the prison ceiling and shook her hair over her shoulders. Then she looked down again with loving eyes. "Leonard Atkins, yes, I will marry you."

Leonard grinned broadly, then groaned as he began getting up from his kneeling position. "You've just made me the happiest man on Earth."

Honey grabbed his hands and tried to help pull him up. "You don't sound so happy, groaning to get off the floor. But, sweetie,

I must say, you can turn a prison cell into the honeymoon suite at the Ritz. When will we have the ceremony? And where?"

Leonard got to his feet. "Let's do it right here in the hospital, as soon as possible."

Honey looked around the room and then at the camera. "Oh, Leonard, you are so impetuous. Aren't you forgetting something?"

"What?"

She pointed at the camera. "You're not supposed to be here. I'm sure you're breaking several laws at this very moment. By the way, how did you get in?"

Leonard looked at her blankly. He had clearly forgotten the details of his arrival. Before he had time to be embarrassed by his memory lapse, there was a knock on the door.

Officer Lebeau poked her head in. "I'm sorry to interrupt you lovebirds, but I'm afraid I have to ask Leonard to leave right away. The doctor is on his way to check on Honey. You two better get dressed."

No sooner had they gotten dressed, than Michael Maxwell appeared in the room and whisked Leonard out the door.

"Hello and goodbye, Honey," Maxwell said as he was leaving. "I'll have you back with him in no time."

He did not notice that Leonard was not wearing his shoes.

Officer Lebeau saw the shoes and kicked them under the bed as the doctor walked into the open door, studying his charts.

"So, you are the famous Honey Waldrop," the doctor said, checking her pulse and looking her over. "It's good to see you up and looking well. I've been in touch with your heart specialist, Dr. Laughlin, from the Mayo Clinic in the United States. After reviewing your medical history and checking you out today, I believe we will be able to release you from our care."

"So I can get out of here?" Honey asked.

"Medically, you will be discharged, but I understand there are legal considerations over which we have no control."

Honey nodded. "So, you are saying I am cleared to travel back to Indiana?"

"That is correct."

She put her hands together and clapped once. "Then I guess we'll call this good news."

"Yes, and might I say that my wife and I are big fans of you and Leonard. In fact, she made me promise to introduce her to you." The doctor's crisp professionalism had turned into an awkward, awestruck admiration.

Honey was taken aback. "Why, doctor, I would be honored to meet your wife. Under the circumstances, however, that might prove difficult."

The doctor turned to gesture to the door. "Well, actually, she's waiting in the hall if you would be kind enough to make yourself available."

"Of course; I would be delighted."

The doctor's wife spoke very little English but she was obviously thrilled to be in Honey's company. She spoke excitedly and at some length about what a dream come true it was to finally meet the woman she'd been reading about and admiring for the last several weeks. Honey nodded graciously, although she did not understand much of what the woman was saying. The doctor's wife handed Honey a pen and a blank piece of paper, obviously looking for an autograph. Honey asked the doctor and his wife their names and wrote in large letters, "Jacques loves Marie," surrounded by a heart with an arrow through it. Beneath the heart she signed, "Honey and Leonard." The doctor and his wife thanked Honey profusely and then grabbed her for a three-way hug. It was obviously a photographic moment, but no camera was available. The doctor left with his wife, arm in arm, nearly skipping out the door.

Once they were alone again, Honey looked at officer Lebeau in wide-eyed amazement. "Oh, my goodness, I've become the patron saint of couples everywhere."

"Especially couples who might be wondering if love is something that might not last," Lebeau said. "That was perfect, surrounding their names with a heart and signing it 'Honey and Leonard.' That should be your trademark autograph."

Honey thought about having a trademark. "The world is certainly quite desperate if people are looking to me and Leonard as proof that love can survive old age."

Lebeau corrected and encouraged Honey. "It's not just age that worries people about love. It feels like love is fleeting at any age. People who seem great together cheat on each other and end up in hateful divorces. Politicians and preachers have their hapless wives by their sides when they confess to all sorts of infidelity. Love is an endangered species these days."

"No, no, Claire," Honey said. "The world is filled with love. Every day people are loving each other and taking care of each other. It's what holds the world together. The problem is, the news doesn't report much on love until it becomes a heartless headline. That's why Leonard and I are so unusual. The media is finally focusing on a love story instead of a war or some natural disaster. We're giving the world a chance to believe in love."

Leonard and Maxwell rushed back into the room, both slightly out of breath. Leonard handed Honey a pile of clothes. "Here's the finest Paris has to offer, pumpkin. It's all your size. Go ahead and change. We've got a private flight to Indianapolis in Luther's jet."

Honey was dumbfounded. "How is that possible? I'm in jail."

Maxwell took her hand to reassure her. "Luther has arranged for your escape. Don't worry, it won't be dangerous. The entire second shift of hospital staff and security have been well compensated."

"It looks like this is goodbye," Claire said. "It has been such an honor getting to know you."

"What do you mean?" said Honey.

"We're going to sedate her so she can't be accused of helping you escape," Maxwell said, talking about Officer Lebeau. "Don't worry. She won't be hurt. We'll catch her before she hits the ground and then lay her on the floor like she was injected by surprise while on duty."

Honey gasped and grabbed Lebeau by the arm. "You're okay with this, Claire?"

"I'm more than fine with the plan," Claire said. "Mr. Patrick has been so generous with me I'll be able to pursue my law studies full time. Of course, I won't resign until after the inquiries are complete. But they shouldn't take long. I have the feeling Mr. Patrick's generosity has gone all the way up my chain of command."

Maxwell motioned Honey to the bathroom as if to say, "We really do need to be going."

Honey hugged Officer Lebeau. "You have been such a dear. Please tell me you'll bring your new man to visit with us in Indiana."

Lebeau looked at her through tears. "When is this new man coming into my life?"

Honey patted her on both cheeks. "He's already on the way."

Honey headed for the bathroom, paused at the door, and said to Maxwell, "You're sure you won't hurt her?"

"Positive," Maxwell said. "Blow her a kiss. She'll be out by the time you get dressed."

Honey ran back to Claire and hugged her. "You are such a brave girl."

"You're the brave girl," said Claire.

Honey changed and put on some lipstick before stepping out of the bathroom like she was in a fashion show. Leonard let out a wolf whistle and took her hand. Claire was passed out on the floor. Maxwell was waiting at the door.

"Oh, my dear girl," Honey said as she walked around Officer Lebeau's limp body on the floor. "I do hope you will be okay."

"She'll be fine," Maxwell reassured. "Eight hours from now, she'll be as good as new."

The hallway was eerily empty as they made their way to a utility elevator. The three of them moved swiftly, but they did not run. The elevator door was open. They got on at the fourth floor and quickly descended into the lowest level of the building.

"This is how they take the bodies out," Maxwell explained.

"What bodies?" Honey asked.

Maxwell lowered his voice. "Dead bodies. People who die in the hospital need to be removed and taken to the crematorium or to funeral homes for burial."

"That is so awful to think about," Honey said. "But I guess it does happen all the time."

Leonard laughed and squeezed her hand. "These boys have thought of everything. I wouldn't be surprised to see the prime minister on the plane."

Honey looked confused. "Do they even have a prime minister in France? I thought that was just in England."

Maxwell explained that both countries have prime ministers as he hustled Honey and Leonard into the open door of a waiting limousine. Once inside, they realized Dr. Laughlin and Luther Patrick were waiting to greet them with open arms. It was such a reunion of hugging and kissing that Honey completely forgot she was in the middle of a jailbreak.

"At first, we thought it would be counterproductive to have

you escape," Luther said. "But then Leonard became so upset at having you in jail, and we got to thinking how long it would take two governments to get you back to Indiana. So we decided to have a little jail break party."

Honey threw her arms around Luther and said, "Oh, thank you so much. I don't like being a prisoner."

"Looks like we're all on the run now," Leonard said. "How does it feel, Luther?"

"Not bad, Luther said. "Not bad at all. In fact, I think it's time we had a little celebration." He pulled a bottle of champagne out of a built-in cooler under his seat. "Mr. Maxwell, would you do the honors?"

EIGHTEEN

"**C**OME IN, IF YOU MUST," Prosecutor Karen Lindvall said to Honey's attorney, Robert Nimmo. "I know, the internationally-famous lovebirds are back."

"The Eagle has landed," Nimmo joked as he sat down in one of two wooden chairs facing the prosecutor's desk.

"I'm surprised you didn't bring all your co-counsel along for the ride," Lindvall said. "They wouldn't all fit in here from what I've heard."

"I've got lawyers crawling out of the woodwork," Nimmo said. "I'm not exactly sure who's paying them. Don't worry; I'm still the point man on the criminal case. I suppose you've seen my brief on why the charge against Honey for violating the no-contact order should be dismissed."

Lindvall dropped her head and then raised it to look at Nimmo in exasperation. "Not only have I seen it, Mr. Nimmo, but I've read the entire 132 pages. It is very impressive. I can tell you didn't write one word of it."

"I read the first fifty pages and lost interest," Nimmo said.

Lindvall smiled and then became stern. "I assume you understand I will not be dismissing the charge. She deliberately violated a court order to stay away from Leonard."

"Here's the situation," Nimmo responded. "We both know the judge has set bond at $100,000. Honey will post that amount in cash tonight. I can get her in and out of jail in about two hours.

The court will hold the initial hearing tomorrow and set the case for a status hearing in about two months. That means she'll be out on bond."

"But the no-contact order will remain in place," Lindvall said.

"No," Nimmo said. "The judge in the guardianship proceeding has agreed to suspend the no-contact order until the competency hearing can be held. Once Leonard is found to be competent, we can talk about what to do in Honey's criminal case."

Lindvall stood up and seemed ready to pounce on Nimmo from across her desk. "I find it hard to believe that the judge in the civil guardianship case would suspend a no-contact order without consulting me first about the pending criminal case. And what makes you so sure Leonard will be found competent? I've seen solid evidence showing he's got Alzheimer's disease."

Nimmo remained relaxed in the face of adversity. "He's in the early stages. He still knows the difference between right and wrong. He knows what he's doing most of the time."

"Most of the time?" Lindvall began to get off her high horse.

Nimmo continued trying to soothe her. "Hey, nobody knows what he's doing all the time. He's better than Ronald Reagan was in his last year as president of the United States."

Lindvall ignored Nimmo's Republican baiting. "So, if he knows the difference between right and wrong, what's he doing running off to France in violation of a no-contact order?"

Nimmo tried to remain calm but he came off sounding cocky. "That no-contact order says nothing about Leonard seeing Honey. It only prohibits Honey from seeing Leonard."

Lindvall sat down and raised her voice. "Okay, so why's he getting his girlfriend in legal trouble? How competent is that?"

Nimmo spoke carefully. "Leonard knows Honey never tried to poison him with arsenic. Everybody knows that. Even you concede that much. If there is no poisoning case against Honey, then there should be no problem with her seeing Leonard. The only reason the no-contact order was ever issued in the guardianship case is because there was a short period of time when the court was afraid Honey might have tried to poison Leonard."

"But it was in that 'short period of time,' as you describe it, that the court order was violated," Lindvall argued.

"If a court order is found to be unnecessary, and therefore, wrongfully issued, it should never be enforced," Nimmo countered.

Lindvall began to soften. "I love the way you say a court order is not really a court order. It's that kind of circular reasoning that keeps criminals thinking maybe crime does pay. But yes, I've always known Honey would never do anything to harm Leonard. In fact, she's got a love for him that I can only envy. I just wish she and Leonard would think things through before they get themselves into so much trouble."

"Love is blind," Nimmo said, "just like justice."

Lindvall laughed out loud. She couldn't help herself. "Oh, that's a good one. It's not often you hear love and justice used in the same sentence."

"It's ironic," Nimmo said. "It's so ironic you could press your pants with it."

Lindvall stood up to begin showing Nimmo the door. "You'd better get out of here before I press your pants with your own bull shit."

Nimmo took the not so subtle hint and got up to make his exit. "There is one more thing. You should know that Leonard will be filing suit against his niece, Gretchen, in the near future. He's already revoked the Power of Attorney he gave her. He's going after her for misspending his money."

"How can he do that if he's incompetent?"

"He hasn't been found incompetent in any court of law,"

Nimmo said. "And a Power of Attorney can be revoked at any time."

"What about this lawsuit against Gretchen Atkins?"

"I don't know much about it," Nimmo said. "But from what I hear, the New York law firm has already uncovered a ton of missing money."

Lindvall stopped before reaching the door. "How can they know that?"

"Leonard authorized them to investigate his accounts."

"I guess he can do that."

"That's right," Nimmo said. "Just because he gave Gretchen a POA doesn't mean he can't act on his own behalf at any time."

Linvall paused and tugged a little on her right ear. "I wondered why Gretchen has been so scarce lately. Nobody's seen her since she got back from France. I hear reports that she's hitting the bottle again."

Nimmo nodded that he'd heard about Gretchen's drinking. "She'd better be getting herself damn good legal counsel. You don't suppose she'd use Uncle Leonard's money to defend herself against Uncle Leonard? She probably would if it wasn't for one thing."

Lindvall was no longer showing Nimmo the door. "What's that?"

Nimmo smiled at regaining the prosecutor's attention. "Leonard has closed her access to his accounts. He issued written notice to the banks and brokers that he has revoked the POA."

"Did Leonard do all this on his own or is Honey doing it for him?" Lindvall asked.

Nimmo looked carefully at Lindvall. "I can see you haven't heard the really big news."

"I've heard all the news I can stomach for now," Lindvall said.

Nimmo looked at the ceiling in disbelief. "You really don't know, do you?"

"Know what?" LIndvall grabbed his right arm with her left hand.

Nimmo grabbed her right arm with his left hand. "Okay, I'm going to tell you something that's going to rock your world, and you must always remember that I'm the one who told you first."

Lindvall squeezed his arm. "What?"

Nimmo made her wait for it.

Lindvall backed away from their awkward embrace. "All right, I'll remember who told me. Now, what?"

Nimmo made her wait twenty long seconds before he finally said, "Honey and Leonard were married on the plane as soon as they landed in Indianapolis yesterday."

"Oh, my God," Lindvall shouted as she stepped backwards in shock. "This Honey and Leonard thing gets crazier by the day. I can't believe you didn't tell me this sooner."

Nimmo held both hands up like a touchdown had just been scored. "I was waiting for just the right moment."

"Good for them," Lindvall recovered. "I can't believe I didn't see this coming. But, of course, it makes sense on so many levels. Now, I see why the guardianship judge is so willing to suspend the no-contact order."

The prosecutor walked back to her large, oak desk and went to look out the window at the falling leaves. "I suppose I'm a little jealous, although I can't imagine marrying a man who's losing his mind. I guess all men are constantly losing their minds. Even so, Honey never was one for beating around the bush. She always went out and got what she wanted."

Turning back to Nimmo, she asked, "Has the press found out about this?"

"It should be on the evening news." Nimmo tried hard not to gloat.

"They'll have a field day with this," Lindvall said. "Did they have a prenuptial agreement?"

"Nope. They're in love. They say money doesn't matter."

"I hope they realize that, if he's found incompetent, the marriage will be void, along with everything else Leonard is trying to do."

"Everyone is well aware of that," Nimmo said.

News of Honey and Leonard's marriage took the world by storm. It was bigger than Hollywood and the British Royal Family combined. The international media descended on North Manchester, Indiana, like a plague of locusts from the biblical book of Exodus.

Once Honey posted bond and was released, she and Leonard were no longer fugitives. They were now prisoners of their own celebrity in Honey's home. They were surrounded, but at least they could live together legally since the no-contact order had been recalled.

Luther Patrick and Dr. John Laughlin had accompanied Honey and Leonard on the flight to Indiana, along with Michael Maxwell and his security team. They planned to remain at Honey and Leonard's service until Leonard could prove his competency. Luther and the doctor stayed well removed from the scene at Honey's home, but Michael Maxwell secured the site with a security detail of five uniformed men. Coordinating his unit with local police, Maxwell was barely able to keep the media circus off Honey's property. The neighbors, of course, were not so fortunate.

Only Jack Crumbo was allowed inside.

"Jack," Honey greeted him with open arms as he hurried in the door. "Only you gain access to the inner circle."

Crumbo was flushed and out of breath. "Thanks for letting me in. I didn't think you saw me. I've been out there for at least an hour. Your phone's been completely jammed."

Honey hugged him. "Mr. Maxwell spotted you and we had him bring you in. Honestly, Jack, we still can't believe our story has gotten so out of control. What's so interesting about a couple of old folks getting married?"

"Hey, Leonard," Crumbo said, giving Leonard a hug before answering Honey.

"Good to see a friendly face, Jack," Leonard said. "We haven't seen you since *The Sinbad*. We read everything you write about us, and I must say, we approve of most of it."

"Most of it?"

Leonard chuckled and said, "We think you could have left the part out about me proposing to Honey in the nude while she was in the hospital jail."

Crumbo pretended to be surprised by Leonard's comment. "You know my readers love those juicy details. But, hey, what's this about not inviting me to the wedding?"

"You know us," Honey said. "It all happened so fast we weren't that sure it was really happening."

Crumbo got back to being a reporter. "I heard the ceremony was on the plane right after you landed. What was that about?"

Leonard seized the moment. "I decided to make an honest woman out of her. I got tired of people calling her my girlfriend. That made her sound cheap. Now, everybody knows she's my wife, plain and simple."

"How does it feel?" Crumbo asked Honey.

"I am quite happy to be Mrs. Leonard Atkins," Honey beamed.

"We did things a little differently than most folks. We went on our honeymoon before we got married. It turned out better that way."

"What say you, Leonard?" Crumbo asked.

"I feel great," Leonard said. "I've never been much for being a single man. A man needs a woman. When you find one like Honey, it's time to snatch her up before somebody else does."

Honey threw her arm around his waist. "Leonard, you know you're the only one for me."

Crumbo looked at them with envy. "You two are so lucky to have found each other. Congratulations on getting married. You're setting a great example. Everybody wants to be you."

"I'm not so sure about that," Honey said. "It feels like we've made a mess out of everything. We can't go anywhere without armed guards. That's no fun."

"So you decided to get married to really bring the pot to a boil," Crumbo said.

Leonard waved his hands like Crumbo had just said something unacceptable. "We got married because it was the right thing to do."

"Now, sweetie," Honey said, "don't take offense. Jack is just stating the obvious. Our quiet little ceremony on the plane has apparently caused quite a stir."

"You've got a mob scene on your hands," Crumbo said. "And it doesn't look like it's going away any time soon. What are we going to do about it? You can't live like goldfish in a bowl."

"So, back to my question," Honey said. "Why all the fuss?"

Crumbo looked at her to make sure she wasn't being sarcastic. When he saw she really was looking for an answer, he said, "Mind if we sit down at the table for this? I've been standing too long."

"Of course," Honey said. "I am sorry. I'm so overwhelmed I've forgotten my manners. Here, we'll sit at the dining room table. What can I get you to drink? How about some tea? Yes, I'll make us some tea. That will help us think."

Once they were all sipping cups of Earl Grey tea, Crumbo said, "You two are the greatest story ever. All the elements are there. You've got elder love, elder law, arsenic poisoning, Alzheimer's, running from the law, romance in France, being dead and then not dead, mystery yacht rescue, Eiffel Tower arrest, Paris jail break and now, airplane wedding. You've got it all. You can't make this stuff up. You've made me the most popular writer on the planet. Thank you very much, by the way."

"You make it all sound so thrilling," Honey said. "But, honestly, we didn't try to make any of this happen. It seemed to grow on its own. It's all a big blur to me now. It almost feels like none of it ever really happened. Except for the wedding, of course."

"So, why did you get married on the plane?" Crumbo asked.

Honey looked at Leonard to make sure she should take the lead in answering the question. "I don't know. We wanted to come back married. Kind of like we eloped."

"And we knew it wouldn't hurt at the competency hearing," Leonard said.

Crumbo took out his notepad. "What do you mean by that?"

"I think a wife's testimony has a little more meaning than a girlfriend's testimony."

"That makes sense to me," Crumbo said. "But speaking of the competency hearing, how are you feeling in that regard? How's your memory holding up?"

Leonard scratched his head. "Not that great, to be honest. It's like I'm all the time walking into a room and forgetting what I came in for."

Honey took his hand and patted his arm. "That happens to everyone."

Leonard motioned to Crumbo's notepad as if to make a correction. "I'm not saying I'm incompetent. I'm just saying I have to remind myself a lot about where I am and what I'm doing."

"You know who I am," Crumbo said.

Leonard patted Crumbo on the shoulder. "My favorite reporter of all time. How could I forget? But, see, now, here I go again. I don't remember your article about the wedding."

Crumbo tapped his notepad on the table. "That's because I haven't written it yet. It just happened yesterday. In fact, I'm interviewing you for it right now. Who performed the ceremony?"

Leonard turned to Honey for help. "Some pastor from Indy. What was his name, pumpkin?"

Honey smiled politely. "Now, see, I don't remember his name. But let's think; it's on the marriage certificate. Where did I put that thing?"

"I'll save you the trouble," Crumbo said. "I already know. It was William Fishbaugh from the First Presbyterian Church of Indianapolis."

Leonard pretended to remember as soon as he was told. "Oh, yeah, Rev. Fishbaugh. He did a good job. The pastor was a friend of the pilot's. The whole thing took about ten minutes. Luther Patrick was my best man and Dr. Laughlin was the maid of honor. It was a good time. We laughed a lot. We didn't have any vows written out. We just said, 'I do,' and that was it."

Crumbo paused to take notes, impressed by Leonard's recollection of detail. "Could the pilot have married you?"

"I don't know about that," Leonard said. "At this point, we're not taking any chances. We wanted it done legally and in the good old United States. I'll tell you what. We had a wonderful time in France and Italy, but it's good to be back home again in Indiana."

Honey said, "Hey, we haven't sung the song yet. Come on, we've got to sing the song. I can't believe we haven't sung it."

Honey and Leonard sang "Back Home Again In Indiana" with Crumbo joining in on the words he remembered.

"So what are your plans for the immediate future?" Crumbo asked once they'd finished congratulating each other's singing efforts.

"I'll tell you what we're going to do," Honey said, making things up as she went along. "We're going to have a big church ceremony followed by a carriage ride to the new reception hall. We're going to have a massive party and invite everybody. That's what these people want, isn't it? We can't just sit in here and hide. I'm already getting cabin fever. So, we'll give them a great big show, and hopefully, they'll be happy and leave us alone to get on with our life of wedded bliss."

Gretchen was beginning to feel like a cornered animal. News of Honey and Leonard's marriage and return to Indiana made her feel like she would soon be exposed for spending her Uncle Leonard's money like it was her own. Media coverage of the Honey and Leonard story and her role in it had forced her into hiding. She was holed up in a hotel in Warsaw, Indiana. She had less than $1,000 to her name and no way to access Leonard's accounts. To make matters much worse, she was drinking at least a quart of Jack Daniel's whiskey every day.

Everything had changed for Gretchen once she obtained a Power of Attorney over her Uncle Leonard. That one legal document had changed her life more than she could have imagined. With access to her uncle's considerable fortune, Gretchen retired from being an educator. Her teaching income seemed a sad joke in light of the multi-million dollar estate she controlled and was soon to inherit. But leaving her students and fellow educators effectively severed her last remaining ties to society. She became more and more reclusive.

The Midas touch turned her cold as gold.

Uncle Leonard had been her only companion. Once Honey took him away, Gretchen's only friend was the bottle. The drinking started as a cure for loneliness but always ended up making her feel lost, alienated, and alone.

Attorney Alice Chambers had helped Gretchen file the petition to have Leonard declared incompetent and to have a guardian appointed to take care of his affairs. The case had been simple at first. Leonard was in the nursing home and Gretchen seemed to have his complete cooperation as well as control of his considerable estate. Lately, however, the case had taken on international proportions under the spotlight of the world press. Attorney Chambers found herself facing hordes of lawyers from New York and Chicago, who all had local counsel from Fort Wayne, Indiana. Uncle Leonard was no longer cooperating. He was fighting back. She was clearly outgunned. She needed to hire a litigation team to handle what was shaping up to be an epic court battle over Leonard's mental competency and Gretchen's handling of his financial affairs.

Gretchen arranged to meet with Attorney Chambers at her hotel room in Warsaw. The attorney had only agreed to make the hotel call once she realized Gretchen would not, under any circumstances, come to her office. In fact, Gretchen had just begun to drink herself out of a wretched hangover from the night before when the attorney arrived at noon.

"You look terrible," Chambers said as she got a good look at Gretchen, who hadn't bathed or combed her hair or changed her clothes in three days.

"I'm even worse than I look," Gretchen moaned, pouring herself another glass of whiskey from a nearly empty bottle. Her hands were shaking badly.

"Give me that bottle and the glass too," Chambers said. "I'm not going to waste my time talking to a drunk." With that, she grabbed the glass and the bottle and poured their contents down the drain in the bathroom sink. "Now get in here and take a shower while I search the room for the bottle you've probably stashed somewhere."

Chambers had plenty of first-hand experience handling drunks and she knew Gretchen well enough to take matters into her own hands. The two had taught together for several years before Chambers went on to law school.

Gretchen complied with Chambers' demands without saying a word. Too exhausted to argue, she took a shower and reemerged looking slightly more healthy and alert. She even managed a smile as she said, "You didn't find another bottle because there isn't one. I was going to stay sober last night for our meeting, but then, at the last minute, I ran out and got one last blast."

"Let's skip the small talk," Chambers said. "They've filed a suit against you, claiming you've stolen nearly a million dollars from your Uncle Leonard's accounts. I only hope that number is accurate because that means you'll have plenty of money to pay your legal fees."

Gretchen said nothing. She looked like a cocaine dealer who had just snorted her entire inventory.

"Don't tell me the money's gone," Chambers said.

Gretchen looked down at the floor for the better part of a minute, then looked up and said, "I've got a little left."

Chambers jumped up out of her chair, strode to the window and flung open the avocado-colored curtains. The room was suddenly much too bright for Gretchen, who shielded her eyes from the glare of sunshine. "Let's go ahead and shed a little light on the situation. How did you blow through a million dollars in two years? I know some of it went to me, but I'm beginning to feel like I haven't billed you nearly enough."

"Don't worry," Gretchen said. "I'll get the money to pay you.

I spent almost $350,000 paying off the mortgage on my house. I can remortgage it to get you whatever you need. I've got to win this competency hearing. I know Uncle Leonard is not in his right mind. Why else would he run off and marry that little gold digger, Honey Waldrop?"

Attorney Chambers sat back down and began to take a much softer approach. "Gretchen, I can see how hurt you are because you feel like Honey took away your Uncle Leonard. And I know that he was all you had. But don't you see? There is another way out of this. You can go to your uncle and beg his forgiveness and drop the petition for guardianship. He's a good man. He'll forgive you. It's not too late to stop the deal on the family farm, is it?"

"The housing developers own the farm. The money is in Uncle Leonard's bank account. I can't touch it. They've frozen me out. And that's not right. I closed that deal. We made $2.5 million on that deal. That's my money. I'm his only heir."

Chambers reached out and began massaging Gretchen's back. "Gretchen, Gretchen, Gretchen. You're forgetting one thing. You're forgetting one very important thing."

Gretchen gave her attorney a doleful look. "What's that?"

"Your Uncle Leonard is not dead yet."

It took a while for the gravity of this comment to settle in on Gretchen, but it eventually left her dumbstruck. She looked at her attorney as if she had been gravely wounded. Chambers had seen the look before. It was the "deer in the headlights" look that alcoholics get when it first dawns on them they might need help with substance abuse.

"What am I going to do?" Gretchen moaned. "I've betrayed Uncle Leonard. He's the only man I ever really cared about. He's the only one who ever tried to teach me anything. He took care of me. Now, I've let him down. I've been so bad. I'm probably going to end up in jail. I feel terrible. The only thing that helps is the whiskey, and now that's starting to kill me. My hands are shaking and my head is pounding and my insides feel like they're trying to be my outsides. What am I going to do?" She slid out of her chair and fell to the floor, sobbing.

Chambers let her cry for a minute, then helped her up for a hug. "You don't need a lawyer," Chambers said, "you need a sponsor."

"What do you mean?" Gretchen asked.

"Chambers wiped away Gretchen's tears. "I mean it's time for you to check into Mapleton, my *alma mater.*"

Gretchen sniffled. "You went to school at Mapleton? Where's that?"

"It's in Minnesota, a little north of St. Paul. It's not a school. It's an addiction rehabilitation center. One of the best. I went there for a month, 12 years ago. I haven't had a drink since. Mapleton saved my life, and it can save yours too if you'll give it a chance."

Gretchen shook her head in denial. "I don't think of myself as an alcoholic and I know I'm not a drug addict."

"Alcohol is a drug, Gretchen."

"I guess I knew you were an alcoholic."

"I'm a recovering alcoholic," Chambers corrected her.

Gretchen became sheepish. "Do you think I'm an alcoholic?"

Chambers took a deep breath. "Let's think about it this way. Say you're driving down a road and it's getting more and more narrow and it goes from blacktop to gravel and then to dirt. As you're driving, the car is running out of gas and the snowstorm is getting deeper every minute. Finally, you reach the end of the road and you're out of gas and the car is totally buried in the snow."

Gretchen nodded her head repeatedly and wiped a tear off her cheek. "That is, pretty much, me."

"So, you hear a knock on the car window. You try to use the automatic window, but it won't work because the car's not running. You open the door and you see it's a woman in a furry parka. And the woman asks you if you'd like a new road, a full tank of gas and sunny weather."

Gretchen raised her eyebrows hopefully, silently asking her attorney to continue.

"I'm that woman in the furry parka, knocking on your window."

NINETEEN

HONEY AND LEONARD DID NOT DO WELL in captivity. Being a celebrity turned out to be nothing but trouble.

Even going to the grocery store proved to be an impossible task. Rude, excited reporters kept pressing microphones and cameras in their faces. Maxwell's bodyguards couldn't keep them away. One photographer popped out of a cooler and got a tabloid shot of a horrified Honey, clutching a quart of skim milk, with her mouth and eyes open as wide as they could be.

On day four of their return to Indiana, Honey and Leonard managed to sneak out of the house, undetected, in the back of a plumbing truck. Luther had a car waiting for them at the edge of town.

"What did we do to deserve the never-ending kindness of a man so wonderful as you?" Honey asked.

Luther laughed gleefully as he handed the car keys to Leonard. It was plain to see that the captain of *The Sinbad* got a major kick out of any caper involving his famous friends. "Nice work, sneaking out of your own house. You can pull this car back into your garage anytime. The door opener is in the glove box."

Leonard opened the driver's door. "We might not be back for a day or two."

Luther walked around the car to open the door for Honey. "That's fine by me. Just remember, Dr. Laughlin's got both of you scheduled to be at the Mayo Clinic on Sunday for complete physicals."

"You're asking an Alzheimer's patient to remember his doctor's appointment?"

"I'm talking to Honey."

"Don't worry, father," Honey teased Luther, "I'll have us both home by dinner time. There will be no more running away for us."

Leonard drove Honey out to the family farm for a long-overdue visit. He was having an excellent day. He wasn't repeating himself at all. No one else was in the car, although they both knew that Maxwell's men had to be nearby. They talked about how strange it was to have achieved such sudden fame and how even more strange it was to have one of the world's wealthiest men taking care of them.

"I think Luther might have been getting a little bored with his life before we came along," Honey mused. "Plus, I think he feels good, rolling up his sleeves and getting dirty to help someone else."

As Honey was speaking, Leonard brought the car to a complete stop in the road before making the turn down the lane to his old farmhouse. He almost didn't recognize the turn. On either side of the road were huge billboards proclaiming the area as the future site of the Silver Creek Housing Addition. The mighty oak tree that had been a roadside landmark was gone.

"What the hell is going on?" he wondered out loud as he slowly turned down the lane. "Somebody took down the oak tree. What kind of fool would do such a thing? That tree's been around since before I was born. And what are they calling Silver Creek? There's no creek on this land, just the lake we built. And there sure isn't any silver. Who thinks he can put a housing subdivision on my farm?"

Honey looked back at where she remembered the giant oak tree had been. "I don't even see a stump."

Leonard didn't say a word for at least 100 yards. He finally broke his shocked silence by muttering, "I thought the lawyers said they could stop this from happening."

Honey leaned forward in her seat. "Maybe they haven't done anything except put up the signs."

Driving down the lane, hoping against hope, they saw a grim parade of giant machines. From a distance, they almost looked like the vehicles of harvest. But that was wishful thinking. These were not combines and grain wagons. They were road graders and front-end loaders and bulldozers.

Once they turned onto the farmhouse lane, they saw that Leonard's once elegant and endless cornfields had been graded into piles of dirt and long stretches of flat, naked ground. The smell of freshly turned soil clogged the air. A silent scream of sorrow filled the sky. The farm had been raped.

Leonard stopped the car in the middle of the lane and got out to stare in disbelief at what had happened to his cherished heritage. He'd known every furrow and slope of that ground. He'd plowed and tilled every inch of it hundreds of times. Now, he barely recognized the land. The gentle rolls of the terrain had been flattened. The only thing that allowed him any perspective was the forest in the distance to the west. The maple trees were turning red and orange and gold.

Honey got out of the car to join him as he began walking into what had once been his most fertile cornfield. He couldn't let her hold his hand. His fists were clenched in rage. He was breathing hard. He choked back a scream.

Tears rolled down Honey's face. "Oh, Leonard, what have they done?"

"They've killed me."

She grabbed his arm and they walked on, across the uneven ground, in a pallbearers' shuffle, as though they were carrying a casket of grief. It was hard for Honey to imagine the barren landscape had once been a successful farm.

She stumbled on a dirt clod and almost took Leonard down with her until he managed to keep them both from falling. He was still a sturdy man. His shoulders were broad and his back was strong. Honey kissed his hand, partly to thank him for keeping her upright and partly to comfort him from the trauma he was facing. His hand had character. The fingers were long and thick with calluses. The knuckles were swollen from arthritis. Dark blue veins wound down from the top of his hand like ivy branches. Age spots on his skin could no longer pass for freckles. The hand was rough but clean. His fingernails were precisely clipped.

She held his hand to her cheek. He was her hero in so many ways. It was hard to watch him suffer such obvious pain. He winced to hold back tears as his gaze took in the entire panorama of developmental devastation. He fell to his knees then collapsed further, palms on the earth. His shoulders shook with sobs of helpless sorrow.

Leonard didn't raise his head until one of the road graders passed by about thirty yards away. "What the Hell do you think you're doing?" he cried out.

The operator held a hand to his ear, obviously unable to hear over the din of the thunderous engine. Leonard got up and walked toward him with Honey close behind. The man kept driving away, unwilling to be interrupted from the task at hand. Leonard waved his arms at the driver until he reluctantly brought the machine to a creaking halt.

"What can I do for you?" the driver said, annoyed at having to halt progress.

Leonard walked up to the grader and took the first step up to the cab. "You can tell me who you work for."

"Why should I do that?"

Leonard took another step up the ladder, face to face with the driver. "Because this is my farm you're destroying."

The driver sat up straight in his seat, realizing he had trouble on his hands. "Hey, buddy. I'm not looking for trouble. I work for Briggs Construction. I'm just doing my job. I'm just doing what they tell me to do."

With that, he put the machine in gear and began driving away, forcing Leonard to jump clear of the machine. The driver looked over his shoulder with fear in his eyes, expecting Leonard to chase him. Leonard didn't follow. He could see the driver talking into his radio.

"He's calling his boss," Leonard said to Honey, "and his boss will call the cops and they'll come arrest me for trespassing on my own property."

"Maybe we should leave," Honey suggested.

Leonard looked at her sternly. "You can leave if you want to. I've got some looking around to do."

Honey stayed by his side as they continued walking deeper into the farm. They came to the top of a hill and saw that the lake on the other side had been filled in and was being turned into an artificial creek.

Leonard stared at the scene in shocked silence and anguish. He looked like he'd been shot.

Honey grabbed his shoulder and tried to comfort him. All he could do was breathe heavily, making loud, sighing sounds of disbelief. When he finally turned his head to look up at Honey, his eyes were full of tears. "That was where I lost my daughter," he said, pointing at the land. "All that empty bowl of ground used to be a lake. That was the lake that took my daughter. It wasn't a bad lake. That lake used to tell me everything was going to be all right, even after my daughter died."

Leonard hung his head and cried softly. His entire body shook with a lifetime of grief. He shook his head and tried to regain his composure. His eyes were still streaming tears when he looked up at Honey. "Has Gretchen done this to me? How could she?"

Honey looked at him helplessly. She didn't know what to say. Leonard had told her so many stories about the farm. She had walked through rows of corn with him and seen how he came alive talking about the secrets of growing corn and beans. This farm had been his life. Now, it was gone.

Honey wasn't ready to let it go without a fight. "Don't give up, yet, sweetie. We can still get this land back. We can buy it back if we have to. We'll replant the fields and fill the lake back up and make it even better than before."

Leonard tried to smile. He loved her spunk. She made him feel resilient, even in this most crushing moment of defeat. He hated to have her see him so devastated. "I love you, pumpkin," he said as he kissed her tenderly on the forehead. "I love your spunk. You make me feel strong They can't keep a good man down as long as he's got a good woman by his side."

He squeezed Honey hard. "I'll tell you what we'll do. We'll plant this entire field in pumpkins. We'll call them Honey pumpkins and sell them for $20 a piece."

A man in a suit wearing a hard hat, came walking through the dirt to ask if he could help them. He was already on his radio, calling for help. It looked as though the elderly man might be having a heart attack. "Do you need me to call an ambulance?"

"No," Honey said. "This is Leonard Atkins, and I'm his wife, Honey Waldrop . . . I mean Honey Atkins. Excuse me. We're new-lyweds and I keep forgetting I've got a new last name. Anyway, he doesn't need a doctor. He's just upset, that's all. This is his farm."

"Oh, my God," the man said. "It is you." He held out his hand to Leonard, "I'm Don Granger, sir, and I can't tell you what an honor it is to meet you. My wife and I have been following you two on the news since you ran away to France. Are you sure you're okay?"

Leonard shook his hand and said, "Nice to meet you, but as you can see, I'm having a terrible time here. I thought we were coming out here to visit my farm."

The man opened his mouth in surprise. "You mean you didn't know about the development?"

"We thought it was in the middle of a legal battle," Honey answered. "We didn't realize things had gotten this far out of hand."

"I am so sorry to hear that," Granger said. "This must be quite a shock. I work for the developer, Wabash Homes, and they're in a hurry to get this thing going before the ground freezes."

"Is the farmhouse still standing?" Leonard asked.

"Yes, the house and all the barns are still intact right over that hill. I'm not supposed to let you on the property, but considering the circumstances and who you are, I don't think there will be any problem letting you look around."

"If anybody gives you trouble," Leonard said, "you can tell them I'm considering repurchasing the entire development."

"Oh, my, are you serious?"

Leonard was regaining his composure. "Maybe. I'm not sure yet. But thank you for letting us look around and reminisce. I promise we won't steal the barn."

Granger laughed and turned to walk away but then stopped. "Let me ask you one thing while I've got you all to myself."

"Go ahead," Honey said.

"Okay. Here it is. What's the real story on how you got out of the hospital jail in Paris?"

"You have been following us in the news," Honey said.

"You want the real answer?" Leonard asked.

"Yes, of course."

"The real truth is we walked out the door and there was nobody in the hall to stop us. Then we got into an empty elevator and went down to the basement to walk out another empty hall and into a car that was waiting for us."

"Where were all the guards?" Granger asked.

"They all took a break at the same time," Honey giggled.

"I see," Granger nodded knowingly as he walked away.

Once Granger was back in his truck and out of hearing distance, Leonard said, "I guess celebrity does have its privileges."

"Yes, but don't you think it's funny what interests people?"

"At least he didn't ask about our sex life."

"What would you say if he did?" Honey asked.

"I'd tell him I can't keep up with you."

Leonard brightened considerably as they walked over the hill and saw the farmhouse, looking exactly as it had looked when he grew up there as a child. It had been at least temporarily spared since it was located in a wooded area on the edge of the farm. He quickened their pace as they walked to the house.

"Maybe they'll turn it into a museum now that we're so famous," he joked.

"Don't laugh," Honey said as she turned the handle on the side door. "Look, it's open. Can we go inside?"

"Without hesitation," Leonard said as he led the way.

Once inside, Leonard was instantly submerged in waves of nostalgia. His deep sadness at the destruction of the farm was momentarily suspended as he felt childhood rushing toward him like it was running out the main door on the last day of school.

"This is the kitchen," he said as he went over to the cupboard above where the stove used to be. "Ah, I can actually smell my mother's bacon and eggs in the morning. She used to mix in Parmesan cheese and parsley. They were delicious. She called them 'French eggs.' We never had anything like that in France, did we?"

"No, we didn't," Honey said.

"The sad thing is, she never made it to France."

"I would love to have met your mother. She must have been quite a woman," she said, wrapping her arms around Leonard's waist. "She certainly did a fine job on you."

Leonard hugged her back and then continued the tour. "Come on, I'll show you the studio where she used to paint. It's in the next room. Here it is. Look at this bay window. Talk about letting in a lot of light. See that love seat right over there? I used to sit there and watch her paint for hours in that wonderful light. Evenings when the sun got low was always her favorite time to paint. The light was 'rich' then she used to say. It was the best time to watch her paint because I could smell dinner in the oven."

Leonard lingered for a moment at the bay window. He was listening to something. He went into a trance, transfixed before the glory of the window light, which seemed much more brilliant than it had moments earlier. Honey stepped away.

Leonard held his arms open and laughed heartily like he was having a wonderful reunion. He didn't say anything but he was obviously listening quite attentively.

The event lasted nearly five minutes. When it was over, Leonard lurched back into everyday consciousness and turned to look at Honey. He seemed surprised to see her at first but he quickly recovered.

"Did you see her?" he asked.

"Your mother? No, I couldn't see her. But I could tell you were having quite a visit. What did she say?"

"She was telling me all about our trip to France, like she was there with us. It was so wonderful to see how happy she was that we finally made it to France. And she was very, very pleased with us getting married. She says I've found the right girl."

"Did she say anything about the farm and what's happening to it?"

"No, she didn't. All she did was act like everything was going to be all right. She did say something about how I shouldn't be angry. She always used to say all anger is foolish. She said people mainly get angry when they can't get their own way. Anger is selfish. That's what she always used to say and she said it again, just now. Isn't that amazing?"

"Yes, my sweetie, it is amazing. You are amazing. Your mother is the most amazing of all. I can feel her presence in this home. You are so lucky to still have her in your mind and in your heart. Come to think of it, I've still got my mother too. Maybe it's time I had a little talk with her. But not now. Come on, show me the rest of this place."

Leonard led Honey up a wide staircase with an oak newel post and carved, cherry balusters. The newel post was crowned with a large acorn.

Leonard rubbed the carving like it was a crystal ball. "Mother had an old German craftsman come in to hand carve the acorn. He seemed old at the time. He was probably no more than fifty. It took him the better part of two days. She loved that acorn on top of the post. She always said the acorn doesn't fall too far from the tree."

Leonard showed Honey the bedroom he had shared with his brother. "This is where Gretchen's father, Daniel, and I slept growing up. Hard to believe two brothers coming out of the same room could turn out so differently."

"What was he like?"

"He was the funny one. He could always make us laugh. Even

after the booze got hold of him, he was always in a good mood. He was a happy drunk until about two years before he died."

"What happened then?"

"He got mean all of a sudden and for no good reason. It was like the drunk inside him finally killed the clown. He got pale and sick and thin. He took it out on Gretchen. She was the only one around. She spent lots of nights at our house toward the end."

Honey and Leonard toured the old farmhouse until it started getting dark. Leonard had a story for every nook and cranny in the creaking, wood frame home. Honey marveled at how sharp his memory was when reminiscing

When they were heading out back to the barn, Honey asked, "So what are we going to do about Gretchen?"

Leonard stopped in his tracks. "That, my pumpkin, is the big question. Out there in what used to be my fields I was thinking about blowing her head off with my shotgun. Now, I'm starting to feel different. Somehow, being in the house has settled me down. Maybe it's the spirit of my mother. She was always a big one for forgiveness."

"Could you ever forgive Gretchen for what she's done?" Honey asked.

"I suppose before I could forgive her I'd have to try to understand why she's done what she's done. For the life of me, I can't understand how or why she would treat me this way. All I ever did was love her and try to make her happy. I was like her father, especially after my brother drank himself to death. She became like my own daughter, like the daughter I lost had come back to life. Years later, when my wife died, she became almost like a wife to me."

"And then I came along," Honey said.

"I know she couldn't handle being second fiddle. But I got the feeling I was losing her a little even before you came along."

"How's that?"

"Well, she started drinking too much. By the time she turned fifty, she was having a tough time making it to school to be a teacher. I talked to her about it. Told her she was starting to remind me too much of her father. Of course, she wouldn't listen. She liked to say I was the one losing my mind, not her. And I'll say this. I was losing my mind after my wife died. I didn't know what to do until I found you. Hell, Gretchen had me in a nursing home, doped up, half out of my mind, when I met you."

"So Gretchen hated the fact that I could help you and she couldn't."

Leonard took Honey by the hand and they began walking again. "She hated the fact that she couldn't be the queen bee once you came along. I know she was already spending my money like it was her own. Here's the funny thing. She didn't have to spend it behind my back. All she had to do was ask and I would have given it to her. I was going to give it all to her anyway once I died."

Honey danced around to walk, backwards, in front of Leonard. "What are you going to do now?"

Leonard stopped to take both her hands. "I don't know. Give it all to you, I guess."

"How about we both give it all to charity?" Honey said.

"That's exactly what Gretchen is afraid will happen."

Honey sided up to Leonard and got him walking again. "What if we give her enough to get by and forget about all the money she's taken? Maybe, then, she would drop the petition to declare you incompetent?"

Leonard thought about that concept for a couple steps and then shook his head. "I don't think I can ever forgive her for what she's done to the farm. Not to mention what she's done to my reputation. Half the world thinks I've got Alzheimer's and I can't even remember my name. And now I've got to go to court to prove I'm competent."

"The problem is, you do have Alzheimer's," Honey said. "Even Dr. Laughlin says so."

"Then I'll have to prove that the early stages of Alzheimer's doesn't make you incompetent."

Honey followed Leonard into the barn. He started telling stories about the animals he had taken care of and learned to love. He was having a good afternoon, memory-wise. It was as though the jolt of seeing the farm destroyed had sharpened his focus. Honey didn't say much.

"What's the matter, pumpkin? Why are you so quiet?"

"Oh, nothing. I'm just listening."

"All right. I know you're still on the Gretchen thing. What do you think I should do?"

Honey walked over to lean against the gate to one of the abandoned horse stalls. "I'm not sure what you should do," she said. "But I do know this. Forgiving Gretchen might be the best way to show the world how truly competent you still are."

TWENTY

PROSECUTOR LINDVALL was working at her desk when her secretary burst through the door without knocking. "I'm so sorry to interrupt," she said. "But Luther Patrick is here to see you."

Lindvall looked up with a start. "Luther Patrick? Luther Patrick of Honey and Leonard fame?"

The secretary was out of breath. "One and the same. And he looks much younger than I thought."

Lindvall rolled her chair back from the desk and took a deep breath. "Tell him I'm busy and I don't generally see people without an appointment, but I'll make an exception in his case if he'll wait a few minutes."

The secretary left to deliver the message. Lindvall stepped into her private bathroom and freshened her hair and makeup, wondering who this guy thought he was, coming to see her unannounced. Returning to her desk, she made herself wait three full minutes before buzzing her secretary to say, "Please show Mr. Patrick in."

Luther entered like an eighth grader who had been sent to the principal's office. His head was slightly bowed and he seemed to be looking mainly at the floor.

His meek behavior was in stark contrast to his confident attire. He looked like he had just stepped out of the pages of a men's fashion magazine. His blue blazer had cuffs and epaulets that matched perfectly with his tan slacks and deck shoes. He wasn't wearing a tie and only one button on his light purple shirt was undone.

"Come in, come in, Mr. Luther Patrick," Lindvall said, standing up and walking slowly around her desk. "I've been looking forward to this moment for some time. I hope you're not here to talk about the case against Honey."

"Most assuredly not," Luther said as he extended his hand. "I know better than that. As you can see, I come without legal counsel."

Lindvall shook his hand firmly. "You've been hiring lawyers left and right."

Luther was careful to relax his grip first. "Technically, Honey and Leonard have hired their legal counsel. But I'm not here to talk about the law. I come bearing gifts, and I was hoping you could help me share them."

"Is this bribery you propose?" Karen laughed, relaxing in Luther's presence much more quickly than she would have imagined possible.

Luther was encouraged by the warmth of her touch. "Actually, Honey and Leonard have told me so much about you that I just wanted to meet you in person."

"How are they doing? I just hate it that I can't talk to them." Lindvall caught herself letting down her guard too quickly. "Please sit down."

Luther took a seat on one of the wooden chairs in front of her desk. "They're having a tough time dealing with how big their story has become. They've come home to a place that did not exist before they left. They're famous now and they don't like it very much. All they really want is some peace and quiet."

Lindvall sat down in her chair. "What brings you to North Manchester?"

"I'm here to help them any way I can."

"How are they physically?"

Luther hesitated a few beats before revealing their medical status. "Actually, we're taking them to the Mayo clinic tomorrow for complete physicals."

"Who's 'we'?" Lindvall began her questioning.

"Myself and Dr. John Laughlin."

"Who's Dr. Laughlin?"

"Wait a minute, counselor," Luther laughed. "You've slipped into cross-examination mode."

Lindvall slapped herself lightly on the forehead. "Oh, yes, I suppose I do that all the time. Please excuse me. So, let's go back to the beginning. You said you come bearing gifts?"

"Yes, I do," Luther said. "As you probably know, Honey and Leonard and I became good friends collecting art in the south of France and Italy. Now, we're looking for a good cause and a place to hold an art auction. I am told you are a collector yourself and might want to get involved."

Lindvall smiled tightly. "I obviously can't do it while the case against Honey is pending."

Luther waved his hands to say he wasn't on a sales call. "No, I understand. This would have to be some time in the future."

Lindvall relaxed in her chair. "Now, Mr. Patrick. I know you have much better connections in the art world than me. And North Manchester, Indiana, is not exactly an art center. Why would you want to do anything with me?"

"For starters, Honey and Leonard love this area more than life itself. You should have seen them in all the splendor of the Italian Riviera, pining for Indiana and singing that catchy tune."

"Back Home Again In Indiana?"

"That's the one."

"It's hard to believe how big their story has become," Lindvall said. "They're bigger than Bogie and Bacall. How did you happen to meet them? I've heard you saved them from drowning in St. Tropez. What's the real story?"

Luther straightened up in his chair like the teacher had asked him a question he could answer well. "I started following them in the French news. I had my head of security tail them to see what was going on. I had a hunch they were about to get themselves into trouble. Actually, I thought they might be kidnapped."

"Some people say you did kidnap them."

"Honey and Leonard wouldn't say that."

Lindvall put both elbows on her desk, folded her hands and rested her chin on top. "I know they wouldn't. I'm teasing. Please continue."

Luther could see he might as well start selling popcorn. "Very well. My man, Mr. Maxwell, found them hanging on the side of his dinghy, well on their way to escaping a mob and the police off the dock at St. Tropez. He was running to his boat to join the search for them when there they were, shivering and soaking wet. Honey was in the boat but Leonard was still clinging for dear life. It was nothing but good luck. Quite a bit of swimming and athleticism involved on their part, by the way."

Lindvall caught herself being captivated by this worldly soul who had just walked into her office. She tried to hide it with a question. "How do they do it at their age?"

Luther was quite happy to respond. "They're in better shape than most thirty-year-olds. They stay incredibly active. They've walked me into the ground on many occasions. And they swim quite a bit for exercise."

"How did they elude the harbor police? I heard they secured the area pretty quickly in their search for the bodies."

"The French military boats drove right past Maxwell's dinghy as he was headed to my boat, *The Sinbad*. Honey and Leonard were in the boat, covered by a tarp and some blankets. The military was in such a hurry they never stopped to check."

"Yes, *The Sinbad*," Lindvall said. "The most famous bad-boy boat in the world."

"Why would you call it a bad-boy boat?"

Lindvall pointed both index fingers at Luther. "Maybe because it's called *The Sinbad*."

"Sinbad was a heroic sailor," Luther countered.

"Fictional as I recall."

"Fictional but heroic. The name has nothing to do with sin."

"How many voyages did Sinbad take?" Lindvall asked.

"I'm not sure," Luther said. "But you might want to read *The Seventh and Final Voyage of Sinbad*."

Lindvall laughed. This Luther was fun.

She listened intently as Luther told story after story about Honey and Leonard, revealing quite a bit about himself in the process. He was down to earth, charming without trying too hard. He was obviously excited to share the scoop on Honey and Leonard.

Before she knew it, Lindvall's staff had gone home for the night. She and Luther were alone. She considered offering him a shot of Scotch from the bottle in her desk but then thought better of it. After all, it was their first meeting.

Luther saved the day before she had time to think things through.

"I've got a great idea," he said. "Let's continue this conversation over dinner. I'm famished and I could use a drink. Would you care to join me? Or better yet, direct us to the finest dining establishment in the region? I could have us in Chicago in less than an hour."

Lindvall raised her eyebrows in mock admiration. "That's right. You've got a helicopter, and probably a jet as well."

"Does that offend you?"

Lindvall pursed her lips into a pout that apologized for making fun. "No, I guess not. It's just that I've never gone out with a guy who had his own helicopter. Not that we're going out, per se."

"Of course not. We'll just have a cocktail and a bite to eat. We don't need the plane."

"You know what?" Lindvall stood up and stretched her arms wide. "I could be talked into a Scotch. And I know a great Italian place right around the corner."

TWENTY-ONE

GRETCHEN SET HER SUITCASE on the linoleum floor and looked around the small but comfortable room. There was a single bed along the left wall and a table with two chairs on the other side. A doorway on the right led to a bathroom that looked like it could also be used by the room next door. The front wall of the bedroom was a sliding-glass door that afforded a nice view of a private patio and garden.

This won't be too bad at all.

It was a sunny day. Gretchen walked to the glass door and grabbed the handle to open it. The door wouldn't open. She pulled harder. It wouldn't budge. She bent over to examine the handle. There didn't seem to be a lock or a switch to open. She put both hands on the handle and used her body weight.

A nurse in a crisp, white uniform walked in without knocking and saw Gretchen pulling on the door. "You can stop pulling on that thing. It won't open. It's locked from the outside. You're in a lockdown detox unit. Sit down, I've got to take your blood pressure and ask you some questions."

As Gretchen slowly took her seat in one of the chairs, the gravity of her situation hunched her back and made her shoulders slump.

Has it really come to this?

The nurse got her to sit up straight and told her it would only be a few days before she could leave detox and join her fellow addicts and alcoholics on the unit. "That doesn't sound like much to look forward to," Gretchen said.

"It's better than where you were headed," the nurse said. "Your blood pressure is dangerously high."

This was the beginning of four miserable days for Gretchen. The vomiting and sense of impending doom weren't the worst part of alcohol withdrawal. Neither were the imaginary skin bugs. It was the nightmares that really dished out the punishment. Her dreams of Uncle Leonard were the most terrible psychological suffering she had ever endured. In these dream hallucinations she inflicted unspeakable physical torture on him until he finally had no strength to even cry out in pain. She beat him like an evil horse trainer breaking a stallion.

Gretchen awakened from each dream drenched in the sweat of her own guilt. She had never before suffered dreams of violence.

The dreams became less frightful as the days and nights crept slowly and painfully by. The icy fingers of alcoholism gradually stopped choking her. On the fifth day, she was released from the detox unit and assigned to a room with five roommates.

As soon as she arrived, she wanted to return to detox. Being forced to interact with others would be a new kind of nightmare. The only time she ever had a roommate was her freshman year at college, and that had been a disaster. Gretchen had always needed to get her own way. She was an only child. And a spoiled one.

The unit was a suite of sleeping rooms around a large living space with couches, a television, and a snack area with a kitchen. There were 26 women in the unit and each of them was at a different point in her 28-day stay.

The first woman she talked to was a crack addict out of Boston with ten days in the program. She was a prostitute, thin as a rail.

Gretchen could not relate to her tales of doing tricks and staying up for a week at a time.

The woman in the bed next to Gretchen was on her twenty-fourth day. She saved Gretchen from the Boston girl by introducing herself as a "wild whiskey woman from Washington." Gretchen felt an immediate affinity for her.

"Name's Barbara," she held out her hand. "I'm just about out of here. Don't worry. I know how you feel. Right about now you're beginning to wonder why in the world you let them talk you into rehab. This place feels like prison. It's hard at first but it does get better as you go through it. What brings you to Mapleton?"

"Jack Black."

"Oh, yes, I know him well. Too well."

Gretchen hung her head and confessed. "Also, it looks like I'm about to get busted for embezzling money from my uncle and selling his farm."

"We do the damndest things when we're drunk," Barbara said. "For me, it was always about the sex. Get me drunk enough, I'd roll with a buffalo."

Gretchen laughed like she thought her new roommate was joking. She wasn't.

"It's all the same," Barbara continued. "Drugs, booze, sex, money. They're all symptoms of the disease of addiction. The real core of addiction is the self-centeredness. That's what the twelve steps are all about. It's not about quitting booze. It's about not being selfish. It's about surrender."

Gretechen raised her head with the slightest glimmer of hope in her eyes. "Surrender to what?"

"Surrender to the fact that you can't drink alcohol like a normie."

"What's a normie?"

Barbara let Gretchen think about it for a moment before explaining. "Normal person."

Gretchen laughed a little for the first time since her arrival. "Oh, brother. You people have a funny name for everything."

Barbara bent down to put her forehead on Gretchen's. "What do you mean, 'you people.' Don't look now but you're one of us."

"I'm not as bad as her," Gretchen said, pointing to the Boston girl.

"Don't say that to her. She'll scratch your eyes out," Barbara laughed.

The Boston girl came over and said, "Don't think I don't know you're talking about me. I see you doing your little pointing and giggling. You white girls might think you're better than everybody, but last time I checked, we all ended up in the same place."

"I'm sorry, I didn't get your name," Gretchen said.

The Boston girl took two steps back and put her hands on her hips. "Oh, so now you want to play nice. Well, that's all fine with me. It's Shaniqua. My name is Shaniqua. I know it's gonna take a while, but you'll learn how to pronounce it."

"Come on, Shaniqua," Barbara said, "sit down and talk with us. I've got to warn Gretchen how you fart in your sleep."

"Me?" Shaniqua loosened up as she sat down. "You're the one who turns the room blue every night. It's you old girls got the problem."

It took several days, but Gretchen's worldview broadened considerably as she learned to live in close quarters with roommates of all ages, races, and social status. Their common bond was addiction, and they were learning how to help each other.

Barbara and Gretchen became such fast friends that it was difficult for both of them when it was time for Barbara to go home. Her twenty-eight days were up. Gretchen was on day nine.

As they were hugging each other goodbye, Barbara said, "Stay writing on your steps. And don't wait too long to get to Step Nine. That's the one about making amends. If you try to make amends to your Uncle Leonard, you'll be amazed what happens."

After Barbara left, Gretchen began helping a new woman on the unit. That was the beauty of the 28-day program at Mapleton. Everyone arrived raw and disoriented, but they soon learned the value of helping others. In ten days, they could help new arrivals on the unit. In twenty-eight days, each woman had progressed from rehab rookie to fledgling recovery counselor.

The woman Gretchen took under her wing was a 41-year-old art teacher from Tulsa, Oklahoma. Her name was Bobby. She had been caught using art supply money to support her cocaine habit, which turned into a crack cocaine addiction. Bobby was a hot, skinny mess when she came in, convinced that her life was over.

She sat down on the bed next to Gretchen and cried. "I can't believe I stole from my school. That's the last thing I'd ever do. I love my kids. They mean everything to me. I can't believe I let them down."

Gretchen felt like she was looking into a psychic mirror. "I know how you feel," she said. "I stole a lot more money than you and I did it to the one man who really loved me."

"You stole from your husband?" Bobby asked.

Gretchen shifted uncomfortably on the bed. "No, I stole from my uncle. I've never been married."

"Are you gay?" Bobby was brusquely straightforward.

"No," Gretchen answered after too long a pause. "I just never found the right guy. To be honest, I never even had a long time boyfriend."

Bobby fell back on the bed. "I had a husband. He divorced me about a year ago. Thank God I'm still on his health insurance to pay for this place. How is it you never had a boyfriend?"

Gretchen laid back with Bobby, their arms touching. "I guess it was growing up on the farm, being an only child. We kept pretty much to ourselves out there. By the time I got to college, I was already a loner. I never felt comfortable with myself until I started teaching school. I found my calling and my true self as a teacher. I was good at it. My kids were everything to me. I never had time for men. But I started drinking. My daddy taught me how. Before long, I was taking a nip between classes."

Bobby took Gretchen's hand. "How did you not get caught?"

Gretchen felt an instant relief from Bobby's warmth. "I mixed the booze into a coke bottle and ate tons of breath mints."

"Yeah, I used to do a bump for lunch."

"What do you mean?" Gretchen asked.

"I'd snort a line of cocaine instead of eating lunch. Cocaine makes you not hungry. But it's an expensive diet plan. I figure it cost me about $10,000 a pound."

"How did you afford it?" Gretchen asked.

Bobby stood up and began pacing. "I stole from anybody I could. My husband, my parents, and eventually, even the kids at school. That's why I'm here. They caught me. It was rehab or jail. So what goes on around this place?"

Gretchen got up, feeling better than she had in months. "For starters, it's time to eat. The food is great. It's cafeteria style and you can go back as many times as you want. They've even got ice cream. You look like you haven't eaten in a month. Let's go."

Helping Bobby and the other patients on the unit turned out to be the best medicine for Gretchen. She was older than most of the women. By her twenty-fifth day, she had become a virtual housemother on the unit. She took to recovery with such enthusiasm that her counselor began suggesting she might have a career in the recovery industry.

One afternoon at the pool, she heard herself counseling Bobby.

"You've got to find a way to forgive yourself so you can move on with your life."

Bobby dunked herself underwater and came up slowly. "I don't think I can."

"Oh, come on," Gretchen said. "You're not that important. Everybody makes mistakes. The whole point of the twelve-step program is getting over your self. It's the self-centeredness that keeps us using and drinking and stealing, not the drugs or the alcohol."

Bobby waited for her to continue.

Gretchen grabbed her by the shoulders. "You're the only one who can forgive yourself."

As the words came out of her mouth, Gretchen realized she was talking to herself. She had been taking herself too seriously. She did need to let go of the past and put some faith in a higher power. Let go and let God. The words finally made sense to her.

She needed to let go of her need to be so controlling. She needed to forgive herself so she could move on and do what she needed to do. A new resolve came over her as she made the decision she knew she had to make.

I've got to make things right with Uncle Leonard.

———

Honey and Leonard were sitting close together in hospital gowns on a wooden bench against a blank grey wall, waiting for another round of tests to begin at the Mayo Clinic. "I hate all these doctors," Honey said. "Everybody treats me like a little old lady. I don't feel old. Do I feel old to you, sweetie?"

Leonard missed his cue. He was lost in that place he went from time to time. It was a terrible time for his mind to wander. His wife needed reassurance and she needed it now.

Honey wasn't one to suffer in silence. She punched him hard on the arm to bring him around and grabbed his head with both hands to turn his face toward hers. "I said people are treating me like an old lady. Do I feel old to you?"

Leonard instantly realized the importance of giving the right answer. He kissed her on the lips and stood up to formally proclaim, "You are not old in the slightest. You are my sweet, baby, pumpkin. When you're mad, you're my sweet, baby, grumpkin."

Honey stood up to throw her arms around him. The motion raised up his hospital gown and exposed his bare bottom to a couple passing nurses, who giggled and kept moving. Honey grabbed his butt with both hands. "Leonard Atkins, you are one smart man. But, right now, your rear end is hanging out to dry."

Leonard adjusted his gown. "Was I wandering for a minute there?"

"Yes, you were."

"That's scary," Leonard said as he sat down. "It seems to be happening more and more."

Honey sat down with him. "No, you just haven't had your medicine today. The doctors want to test you without that new drug you're on. They don't really need to test you. I can tell them it's working wonders for your memory and for your attitude in general. For all I know, they're getting close to a cure."

"Wouldn't that be grand?" Leonard said and then fell thoughtfully silent.

Honey put her arm around his shoulder. "What are you thinking?"

Leonard turned his head to look at her with tears in his eyes. "I'm thinking I wish we would have met fifty years ago. We could have danced all night."

"We can still dance all night," Honey said. "We just don't want to."

"I know," Leonard sniffled and began to brighten up. "That's not what I mean. What I'm talking about is why it took us so long in life to find each other. Why didn't we fall in love when we were kids?"

"Do you think we would have had as much fun?"

Leonard turned to smile at her. "Maybe not. They say every age has its compensations. For us, being older has freed us. It's almost like we had to go through a lifetime of struggle to become free enough to find each other."

Honey hugged him and marveled to herself how insightful her man could be in his moments of lucidity. He had made remarkable progress in the six weeks since getting on the experimental Alzheimer's drug. Now, being off the drug for twenty-four hours before testing, she could feel him slipping into the dark world of the forgetful mind. She knew he didn't remember his most recent profound remark.

"What's that you say about every age having its compensations?" she asked.

Leonard gave her that blank look that told her he had no idea what she was talking about.

Honey reminded him. "You were saying we had to go through a lifetime of struggle to become free enough to find each other."

Leonard picked up on her point, although he didn't remember making it himself. "What I think," he said to recover, "is it's a darn shame we didn't meet each other much younger in life."

"Are you saying I'm too old for you?"

"No, no. Not at all. I guess all I'm saying is I'm so grateful we got together. For the first time in my life I feel complete. I really don't know how I went so long without you."

Honey gave him a big kiss on the lips and breathed in through her nose his smell of Old Spice deodorant. "I love the way you smell. And I love the way you kiss, especially since you are now the most famous lover boy on the planet."

"Tell that to my little man," Leonard said. "As much as I love you I honestly feel like he's not down there anymore. It's strange. He used to lead me around like a dog on a leash. Now, I'm off leash and I don't even want to run away."

"Sweetie, I do not feel deprived in any way. We still have our moments. But your hugs and kisses are all I need. Like you say, every age has its compensations. One of the main benefits of getting older is not thinking about sex all the time. Men confuse sex with love, but the two are not even related. Sex is love's evil stepmother."

"Oh, that's a good one," Leonard said. "I'd better write that one down."

Honey hugged him. "Maybe we'd both better be happy with what we've got."

Dr. Laughlin came walking down the hall with three nurses and introduced them to Honey and Leonard. "Leonard, you'll be going with Susan and Laura here, and Honey, you'll be going with Sandra. I'm sorry to break up this little party. I'll get you back together before lunch."

As the doctor spoke, Jack Crumbo came walking down the hall, unescorted.

"Hello, Jack," Dr. Laughlin said. "How'd you get in without a pass? Not that I'm not happy to see you."

"People let me in anywhere these days," Crumbo said. "It seems everybody knows I'm with Honey and Leonard. Hi, guys. You look cute in your little hospital gowns. How's it going?"

"It's a little breezy," Leonard said. "What brings you to the hospital? Is everything all right?"

Crumbo looked at the doctor as if requesting permission to proceed. Once Dr. Laughlin nodded approvingly, Crumbo said, "I thought you ought to know that Gretchen has checked herself into rehab. She's less than an hour drive from here."

"Good Lord," Leonard gasped. "Is she okay?"

"She's better than ever," Crumbo said. "She hasn't had a drink that anybody knows about for 24 days. It looks like she'll be checking out in four more days."

"Can we go see her?" Leonard asked, looking to Dr. Laughlin for an answer.

"You could go tomorrow," he said. "Your testing will be completed and I'm pretty sure they allow family visits. She's at Mapleton, right?"

"That's right," Crumbo said. "Nobody knows it yet. I called her attorney, Alice Chambers. She wouldn't confirm it but she wouldn't deny it either. She knows Gretchen is in trouble about your money, Leonard. And she knows rehab might help her client's position. She just doesn't want to break the story herself."

"How did you find out?" Honey asked.

"Gretchen called me one night in a big drunk and let it slip that she was in a hotel in Warsaw, Indiana. She wanted to set the record straight about how incompetent her Uncle Leonard was and how the evil Honey had him under her spell."

"What did I ever do to make her hate me so?" Honey asked.

"You stole her Uncle Leonard," Crumbo said. "You should have heard her on the phone. She was spitting fire."

"So how did you find out about the rehab?" Dr. Laughlin asked as his nurses listened, wide-eyed.

"I tracked her to the hotel. There's not that many in Warsaw. Then I found a maid who was mad about the mess she left without leaving a tip. Sure enough, the maid overheard her talking with a woman who came to pick her up. She said they were talking about going to a hospital called Mapleton."

"Did you tip the maid?" Leonard asked.

Crumbo winked. "Twenty bucks, but don't worry about it. I'll put it on your bill."

"So who talked at Mapleton?" Dr. Laughlin asked. "That place has pretty high confidentiality standards."

"It just so happens," Crumbo said, "that one of my fellow reporters, who shall remain unnamed, happens to be a guest at the same facility. The reporter is female and she's even had a conversation with Gretchen. She says Gretchen is doing quite well with her program of recovery. It might be a good time for you to go see her."

"Why do you say that?" Leonard asked.

"She might be ready to make amends," Crumbo said. "From what I understand, that's a pretty important part of rehab and recovery."

"That's not why we would go see her," Honey said. "We'd go see her because we want to help any way we can."

Everybody stared at Honey like she had just suggested something completely crazy.

It took Honey a long moment to realize what they were thinking. "Oh, so you don't think I should go. Is that it?"

"Wherever I go, Honey goes," Leonard said.

"Well that settles that," Dr. Laughlin said. "When are you going to break the story?" he asked Crumbo.

"I'd like to file it today, but I thought I would talk to Honey and Leonard first."

"Why don't you wait until we can talk to her," Leonard said. "I don't want her to feel like we've got her cornered."

"That's a good idea, sweetie," said Honey. "I want to show her we can still be friends and stop all this nonsense. Now that Leonard and I are married, she is technically my niece too."

"She's the one who wants to get your marriage declared illegal," Crumbo said.

Honey stomped her foot and pointed a finger at the reporter. "We'll see about that."

TWENTY-TWO

"ALL RISE," the uniformed bailiff shouted as Judge William Fee walked into the Wabash County courtroom in a full-length, plain black robe.

Leonard stood up to face his most terrible fear. He was losing his mind. He had no idea what he was doing in front of a judge. The two men who stood up with him were apparently his attorneys, but he couldn't remember their names or why he had hired them.

He looked around behind him at the crowded gallery and saw Honey in the first row. She kept dabbing at her eyes with a handkerchief.

Judge Fee took his seat behind a raised wooden desk in front of a marbled wall. The artistic backdrop had pillars and bas-relief sculptures of soldiers fighting Indians in one panel and having peace talks in the next. Leonard couldn't help but focus on another panel to the far left depicting a single pioneer being burned at the stake by a war party of dancing Indians.

The Indiana flag was on one side of the judge's bench with the United States flag on the other. A court reporter sat at a smaller desk in front of the judge, recording the proceedings. The witness stand was between the judge and the jury box. There was no jury. Leonard racked his brain, trying to remember how he had gotten into this predicament. And why was there no jury?

The judge had a gavel but he didn't bang it on his desk before taking charge of the hearing with a booming voice. The nearly 200 people in the large room with a 30-foot ceiling could all hear him well.

"You may be seated."

The courtroom resonated with the creaking and rumpling of people taking their seats. The old, wooden chairs were attached to each other in long rows. A wooden railing separated the courtroom proper from the spectator section.

Leonard was at a table facing the judge's bench. To his left, he could see his niece, Gretchen, seated at opposing counsel's table. She would not return his gaze.

"We are here today in the matter of the Petition for Guardianship over Leonard Atkins," the Judge said. "Are counsel ready to proceed?"

Gretchen's attorney, Alice Chambers, was first to speak since she had filed the petition. "We are, your honor."

Leonard grabbed his attorney's arm and whispered into his ear, "If this is about my guardianship, I'm not ready. I'm having a really bad moment here. I can't remember my own name."

Michael McNamara was a New York City attorney with 30 years of litigation experience. Never had a client put him in such an awkward position. Nonetheless, he barely missed a beat before saying to the court, "Excuse me, your honor, but my client informs me he is having a medical emergency."

"Shall I call for emergency services?" the Judge asked.

"May we approach the bench, your honor?" McNamara asked.

"Please do," the judge said.

As the attorneys talked to the judge, Leonard looked around the courtroom. He could see reporters and people he knew he should recognize but could not. He did know Honey, who gave him a weak, thumbs-up signal. And then he saw something he thought he would never see again. There, in the third row on the left, sat his long-deceased, only daughter. She smiled and waved happily.

At that point, Leonard knew he was in serious trouble. He was having visions. He scanned the gallery for any sign of his mother.

The lawyers finished talking to the judge and came back to their respective tables and talked some more. Leonard heard their voices but he couldn't understand what they were saying. He was in a daydream he could not shake. The world was out of focus and slipping away. It felt like he was sliding backwards, down a tunnel, with nothing to help regain his footing. Once again, he wondered what he was doing in a courtroom in front of a judge. He heard his name called.

The judge had not allowed a continuance based on the witness's lack of memory since that was the very issue before the court.

Leonard's attorney had to help him take the witness stand. He had become so disoriented it was difficult to walk.

"Are you able to proceed, Mr. Atkins?" the judge asked.

"I think so."

"Very well, raise your right hand."

Leonard raised his left hand.

"Your other right hand," the judge said.

The judge waited until Leonard's correct hand was in the air. "Do you swear to tell the truth, the whole truth and nothing but the truth, so help you God?"

"I'll do my best," Leonard said. The room had fallen completely silent. He felt like everyone could see he was disoriented to the point of being in a daze. Leonard felt suffocated by their attention. He tried to breathe deeply to regain his bearings. It didn't help.

"Please state your name for the record." Attorney Chambers moved in for the quick kill. She had planned to make her case with testimony from the nursing home doctors, but once she saw Leonard's condition, she decided to call him as her first witness.

Leonard looked to the judge for help. "I can't remember it right now, your honor, but I'm just having a bad moment. I'm not always this bad."

"Mr. Atkins," the judge said. "I can't help you answer the questions. Just do your best. If you don't know the answer, just say you don't know."

"My name is Mr. Atkins," Leonard answered. Nobody laughed at the fact the judge had helped him answer the question.

"We know that," Attorney Chambers said. "The judge just told you that. But I want to know your full name; first, last and middle."

The respondent thought about being cute. That wouldn't work. He wasn't thinking very well at all. He couldn't remember his own name. It was humiliating. Losing your mind isn't usually too hard because you don't know what's happening. But now, the confused man was being made keenly aware of his memory deficit. He hung his head in shame.

"I can't remember it right now," he said.

"Do you know where you are?" Chambers asked.

"I'm in a court of law."

"And what are you doing in this court of law?"

Leonard looked helplessly at the judge, who made a hand gesture for Leonard to return to the question.

Leonard took a big sigh and said, "I don't know why I'm here."

As he spoke, the silent courtroom rumbled into a collective murmur of disbelief and pity. Honey jumped out of her chair and ran to the witness stand, grabbed Leonard by the shoulders and tried to shake some sense into him. The bailiff grabbed her from behind. Leonard held on to her arms. Other officers rushed in to assist in the human tug of war. Leonard cried out in anguish as they pried Honey's arms out of his grasp. It felt like he was losing her forever. He heard himself beginning to sob. It was awful to be crying in front of so many people.

He could see Honey being taken away, but at the same time, he could feel her shaking him. How could that be?

"Leonard, wake up," Honey said. "Wake up. You're having a terrible dream."

Leonard came out of his troubled sleep with a massive snort. He looked at Honey, trying to get his bearings. His cheeks were wet with tears. It took him several seconds to recognize her. "Oh, Honey, thank God it's you. I was having a terrible dream. I was losing my mind in a court of law. I couldn't remember my own name. I was losing you. They were dragging you away. You were trying to save me."

Honey wiped away his tears on both cheeks. "There, there, sweetie. You're with me now. You know who I am, don't you?"

"Of course I do, pumpkin. And I know my name is Leonard."

Honey sat down on the bed. "So everything is fine."

"No, everything is not fine. I am losing my mind, slowly but surely. The dreams remind me all the time. It won't be long before this damned Alzheimer's takes me away from you. It's not fair to you and it's not fair to me. It's not fair at all."

Honey put her head on his chest. "Life's not fair. We both know that. The only thing fair is the State Fair. Come to think of it, after the big stage collapsed at the Fair and killed all those people, I'm not even sure the State Fair is fair anymore."

Leonard couldn't help but chuckle at her sense of humor. It always picked him up. He got out of bed and got dressed. They were still in the hotel near the hospital. It was almost 6 a.m. They went out for breakfast and found some great waffles at a hole-in-the-wall diner.

"Let's go see Gretchen," he said as the waitress poured him a second cup of coffee.

"Are you sure you're ready?" Honey asked.

Leonard put his nose to the coffee cup and let it warm his face. "After dreams like I just had, it feels like the sooner I go see Gretchen, the better off we'll all be."

Honey reached across the table and took his hands in hers. "What are you going to say to her?"

Leonard looked up at her and smiled wryly. "I don't know. That depends on what she has to say to me."

Honey and Leonard said nothing to each other as they waited nervously for Gretchen to arrive for their 11 a.m. private meeting.

Gretchen walked into the huge room and saw them from a distance. She wanted to run to her Uncle Leonard and throw her arms around him and hug him like the long-lost love he was. But Honey was sitting right next to him at the round table in the back of the recovery center cafeteria. Gretchen was not ready to embrace Honey. An unforgiving corner of her heart still regarded Honey as the bitch that ruined her life.

Still conflicted, but twenty-seven days sober, Gretchen breathed deeply in an effort to appear relaxed as she approached her visiting couple. They looked much younger even than their newspaper photos. They looked happy together. They were holding hands on top of the table.

Yes, I can see your wedding rings. You don't have to rub it in.

"Congratulations, Mr. and Mrs. Atkins," Gretchen said, extending her hand to Leonard.

"No, no. That won't do. Come give me a hug," Leonard said. "And congratulations, yourself. You're doing what I could never get your father to do. We're very proud of you."

Gretchen hugged Leonard warmly and then Honey more formally. "They told me I had visitors, but I never dreamed it would be you two. You're famous now. How did you get in here without a mob of reporters following you?"

"We made arrangements with the management here," Leonard said. "We told them what car we'd be driving and they let us in through the loading dock behind the kitchen."

Gretchen waited for him to continue. Honey remained silent.

Leonard looked into Gretchen's eyes as though searching for her soul. Gretchen couldn't help herself. She started crying and sat down at the table. Leonard took her hands in his and let her cry.

Gretchen finally looked up and asked, "Can you forgive me, Uncle Leonard?"

She could see her uncle was having trouble holding back his own tears so she continued, "I'm sorry for spending your money like it was my own. I started out small and always meant to pay it back and then I got mad about Honey and I started spending it to hurt you and I don't know why I did all the things I did. I am so, so sorry."

Leonard wrapped his arms around her and gave her the kind of hug he always gave her as a child. They were both crying. Honey was crying too.

They were both laughing in embarrassment by the time the hug came to its emotional conclusion.

"Of course, I forgive you," Leonard said. "What kind of uncle would I be if I couldn't forgive my favorite niece? But there is one thing I need to know."

"What's that?" Gretchen asked.

Leonard folded his hands on the table in front of him. "What about the farm?"

Gretchen wasn't quite ready to take complete responsibility for her actions. She had been lying to herself so long she almost believed herself when she said, "The farm? You told me to sell the farm. You said it was too close to town and the highway. You said it would only stand in the way of progress."

Gretchen watched her uncle's response. This was her private test of his competency. He might think his memory had gotten so bad that he had forgotten what he had said to her.

Leonard looked at her sternly. His eyebrows formed a deep furrow of a frown but his mouth was slowly developing the first signs of a sarcastic smirk. "Gretchen . . ." he said in a warning tone.

"No. You wanted me to help find a buyer for the farm. That's why you signed the Power of Attorney in the first place."

Gretchen studied her uncle's eyes. He obviously knew he had the moral high ground. His steady gaze pierced her heart. She knew the truth and now she could see he remembered the truth as well as she did. She lowered her head. She couldn't look him in the eyes. He said nothing, waiting for her to come clean.

"I know I shouldn't have done it," she confessed. "It started when you were in the nursing home. Most of it happened while you were away. I finally went through with the deal when everybody was saying you were dead."

Leonard waited for her to raise her head. "What about after they found out we were alive?"

Gretchen looked at him briefly then lowered her head again. "I am so, so sorry. I know what I did was wrong."

Leonard said nothing. The silence was overwhelming.

Finally, Honey couldn't take it anymore. She had to speak. "We can fix all this, you know."

"You stay out of this," Gretchen said without raising her head.

"Gretchen," Leonard said. "Honey is my wife now. You're going to have to get used to it. I don't want her staying out of anything. But us getting married doesn't mean I don't love you as much as I always did. Come on, look at me." Gretchen raised her head. "You're still the little girl I taught how to ride horses and drive tractors."

Gretchen's body shook in a convulsive sob. "No, I'm not. I'm the drunk who stole your money and sold your farm."

Leonard rubbed her back. "Come on now, Gretchen. It's only money. Nobody got killed. What the hay, I got married out of the deal. Who knows? Without you churning up the butter, Honey and I might never have run off to France."

Gretchen looked at her uncle in amazement. Then she looked at Honey, who was smiling back at her hopefully. Gretchen felt the world turning inside her head. She looked Honey in the eyes and saw kindness. She felt like she'd just fallen off a high tightrope and been saved by a sagging safety net.

Honey and Leonard joined hands with her. Gretchen sighed deeply. Leonard finally broke the silence and said it all. "It's good to have you back, my dear."

TWENTY-THREE

THE WEDDING WAS an international sensation. People came from all over the U.S.A. and from as far away as China. The story of old people in love, beating the legal and medical systems, had captured the world's attention. It rang the planet's bell so well that one overzealous CNN commentator called it, "The largest celebration of love the world has ever seen."

Honey had decided to give the people what they wanted. With the help of Luther and a team of wedding planners, she and Leonard decided to reenact their wedding in grand style on the grounds of Manchester University. Honey wanted a church wedding, but there was no church large enough for what she had in mind. The town would not be big enough. No matter, Honey was determined to have a hometown wedding.

On New Year's Day, they announced the wedding would be held June first. That gave Honey and Leonard fans plenty of time to make travel arrangements. Any hotel within 100 miles of North Manchester was completely booked by the end of March. State and local police were scheduling reinforcements and getting plenty nervous by the end of April. An invasion of food vendors, souvenir hawkers, and portable toilets began in the middle of May.

The French press had been the first to call them the Bonnie and Clyde of love. But they hadn't been riddled with bullets in the end.

They survived the chase to lead the world in a new celebration. Now, they were simply Honey and Leonard. They were larger than life. They didn't need last names or clever monikers.

The sudden fame did not go to their heads. Honey was too busy trying to keep Leonard in his right mind. Both she and Leonard did realize, however, their responsibility to show the world that love works for all ages.

When the wedding day finally arrived, the weather was sunny and a perfect 72 degrees with no breeze. News and entertainment media was everywhere, except in the sky above the ceremony. Luther Patrick had found a way to keep helicopters from hovering over the event. His high-ranking friends in the U.S. military had intervened and established a no-fly zone.

The event was held in the largest park in North Manchester. A massive stage was set up on the north side of the park. It was decorated in a French theme with a fifty-foot Eiffel Tower in the middle, serving as a canopy for the exchange of vows. The sound system would have suited a major rock band on tour. Trees throughout the park were rigged with speakers.

Pre-ceremony music included an all-star gospel choir from Detroit, a headliner jazz band from Chicago and half the philharmonic orchestra from Indianapolis. Each performance unit had a stage and sound set up. There was no break between the acts. The 45-minute wedding warm-up was a seamless presentation of musical heritage and excitement from the heartland.

The crowd of an estimated 10,000 people was stunned by the concert. It took nearly five seconds after it was over for the audience to start an applause that morphed into wild cheering.

People had flocked to North Manchester like it was Mecca. Most couldn't get anywhere near the stage. All roads leading to the small city were badly congested. Busloads of people were stranded along highways. All-wheel-drive vehicles damaged fields and lawns as they created new bypasses and detours. Well-prepared wedding pilgrims parked their vehicles in nearby towns and rode bicycles into what quickly became known as "ceremony central."

"This is Woodstock for old people," an NBC reporter crooned. "The town has been completely overrun by visitors for more than a week now, but amazingly, there has not been a single arrest for anything more than a parking ticket. In fact, I'm told the police stopped writing parking tickets days ago."

An area in front of the wedding tower was cordoned off for the 750 invited guests. Honey had to turn down requests for invitations from A-list celebrities in order to preserve seats for friends and family and selected guests. Those specially selected were mainly volunteers and beneficiaries of charitable organizations.

Luther Patrick was front and center in the invited section with the woman who had obviously become much more than his date for the event, Prosecutor Karen Lindvall. They were both dressed in deep blue formal wear and she was clinging to his arm in a most un-prosecutorial manner.

"How did you keep the helicopters away?" Lindvall asked as they took their seats.

"Friends in high places," Luther said.

"High as the sky?"

"Even higher than that."

Lindvall put her head on his shoulder. "Luther, you are the most amazing man I have ever met."

Luther rested his head against hers. "And you are the most beautiful woman at this wedding. Don't tell Honey I said that."

Across the center aisle from Luther and Karen were Gretchen Atkins and her attorney Alice Chambers. The two arrived at the ceremony and walked down the aisle like it was their own wedding. Gretchen looked happier than ever. She had lost thirty-five pounds since getting sober. She wore a long, black gown and a purple Greta Garbo slouch hat. Alice wore a matching purple Fedora and a black silk pants suit. She and Gretchen were camera-ready and in a celebratory mood.

They certainly had reason to celebrate. A deal had been struck for Gretchen to drop all guardianship proceedings regarding her Uncle Leonard in exchange for his forgiveness of any debt she incurred while acting as his power of attorney. Gretchen and Leonard started working together again. By the time of the wedding, they had nearly completed the process of repurchasing the family farm.

The prosecutor agreed to dismiss charges against Honey for violating the no-contact order. That meant Honey's legal problems were over. The attempted murder investigation had long ago become nothing but an embarrassment to local law enforcement.

Leonard signed a will. Gretchen would remain in her uncle's will as a fifty-percent beneficiary, the other fifty-percent going to Honey. He trusted each of them to eventually give her estate to charity.

As the legal wranglings wound themselves down to satisfactory conclusions, Gretchen and Alice realized their feelings for each other had evolved into something much more confidential than the attorney-client privilege.

Honey and Leonard left a trail of lovers united in their wake. A significant part of the invited section at the wedding was a who's who of Honey and Leonard's French adventure.

A beaming Jack Crumbo showed up in a tuxedo, escorting none other than Jennifer Johnston, the flight attendant who helped Honey and Leonard get from Indianapolis to Paris. Jack and Jennifer had become friends as he interviewed her for the Honey and Leonard story. Now, they held hands as they paused for interviews.

"What's a nice girl like you doing with a reporter from *The Chicago Tribune*?" a CBS reporter joked.

Jennifer kissed her man on the cheek. "I knew he'd help me get through the traffic."

"I got her a helicopter ride from the Indianapolis airport," Crumbo said. "She never would have made it otherwise."

"And look who's here," Crumbo said as Corbin Lacoste walked down the aisle with Claire Lebeau, the French policewoman. Corbin wore a formal blue suit with a red and orange tie. Claire looked smashingly stylish in a high neck, sequin dress, wrapped tightly around her attractive figure.

"We're not really together," Corbin said. "We just thought we'd save money if we shared a hotel room."

Crumbo and Jennifer laughed. Corbin elaborated. "Actually, we've been together since Claire woke up in the Paris hospital jail. It was I who kissed her and brought her back to life."

Claire threw her arms around him. "You are my Prince Charming."

The two looked like they were about to kiss until they saw an old friend walking down the aisle. "Look who's here," Corbin said. "We've got celebrity company. It's the one and only Father Girard. We might have to let him share our room."

"Father Girard, *ici*, come join us," Corbin called out. "This is the guy who gave Honey and Leonard a new car and church clothes in Avignon," he explained to Jennifer.

The priest held out his arms in greeting. He was pleased to be recognized amidst the sea of strangers. "I've been walking for miles to get here. I had to show my invitation five times to get through all the security. So good to see you, Corbin."

Corbin hugged his old friend. "Do you need a place to stay?"

"Oh, no, I'm all set up at the church in Fort Wayne. It took a while for the bishops and my fellow Catholics to forgive me for giving away ceremonial, church garments, but they did forgive me because it was Honey and Leonard. Now, I'm a big celebrity."

Michael Maxwell, Luther Patrick's head of security, was coordinating safety efforts from the main stage. He had become director of the event. When the prelude music came to a flawless end, he waited for the thunderous applause to die down and then cued Leonard and his groomsmen to take their places alongside the Eiffel Tower replica. Luther Patrick and Jack Crumbo left their seats to become part of the ceremony. The crowd came to an absolute, expectant silence. It was time for the bridesmaids to make their appearance.

One by one, Honey's bridge club and charity volunteer friends and Claire Lebeau entered stage left and took their place opposite the groomsmen at the tower. Each wore a unique dress, designed by the best in the fashion industry. Honey had always hated the notion of matching dresses for bridesmaids.

The philharmonic orchestra played processional music as the wedding party was assembled. Then silence. It was time for the bride to make her entrance. The crowd craned their neck to see how Honey would make her entrance. Would she appear from the side of the stage or would she walk down the long, grass aisle?

Leonard left his place on the stage and began walking up the aisle. It looked like he would be the one to escort Honey to the stage. As he was halfway up the aisle, Honey emerged from a ring of security guards and waited to greet her groom. The jazz band broke into a rousing rendition of "Here Comes the Bride."

Honey wore a sleek, white dress with a modest train. She wore no veil and had no one to tend the train. Her blonde hair shined in the sun like gold. She was beaming as bright as the glorious reflective glint of her diamond tiara.

The bride looked like she'd just been crowned Miss Universe.

She looked like the Queen of Love, ruling over her subjects by unanimous proclamation.

As Leonard came closer, he could not control his pace. He began running toward his bride. Honey rushed into his arms and kissed him as the crowd broke into a victorious cheer.

A thousand cameras captured the moment. It was a shot for the ages. It was the shot seen around the world. It was unrestrained and unabashed love.

The glow of that embrace was immediately beamed around the planet. Anyone with a television could feel the triumphant glory that one loving moment can have over all the evil in the world.

The people of the world cried mutual tears of joy. French celebrated with Germans, Serbs with Croats, Moslems with Jews, Arabs with Eskimos, teenagers with their parents, cops with criminals, and even doctors with lawyers.

For years to come, poets would use every language available to celebrate the moment that changed so much for so many. True, it was just a moment. But if one moment can do it, why can't all the rest?

Honey and Leonard promenaded down the aisle as the crowd surged to touch them as they walked by.

The actual wedding ceremony was short and sweet. There were no long vows or letters, no speeches or long-winded prayers. Once the minister said, "You may kiss the bride," the choir burst into a spirited version of "Back Home in Indiana."

As the song was concluding, Honey and Leonard walked off the back of the stage and got on top of a fire truck. The rest of the wedding party followed behind on the top of a double decker bus from England. They turned the celebration into a Mardi Gras parade.

Honey and Leonard got as many people into the act as they

could. They threw commemorative beads and chocolates to the crowds. They accepted gifts until they ran out of room. The fire truck and bus had trouble inching through the throngs of well-wishers and adoring fans.

It seemed the party would never end. Mass euphoria reigned in the streets. The parade went on until sunset, making frequent stops for interviews, refreshments, and photo opportunities. Honey and Leonard never ran out of energy and smiles for the crowd and cameras.

As the sun went down, people started pointing at the fire truck. Honey and Leonard weren't there anymore. They were gone. They left without saying goodbye. They simply disappeared. They vanished into their own, private dimension.

The party went on without them.

TWENTY-FOUR

SIX MONTHS AFTER THE WEDDING Honey was having serious difficulties with Leonard's memory. The medicine prescribed by Dr. Laughlin wasn't working. Leonard was frequently forgetting where he was and what he was supposed to be doing. At least once a day, he looked at Honey like he didn't know who she was. During these half hour periods of confusion, his eyes moved rapidly from side to side like a cornered animal.

Some days were better than others but evenings were becoming a persistent problem. The sundowner's issue had been escalating for some time. When Honey and Leonard disappeared off the fire truck during the wedding parade, most people assumed they had pulled off another clever escape. That was not the case. As the sun went down, Leonard became increasingly paranoid and anxious about the crowd. Honey tried to calm him but her efforts only seemed to agitate him. Leonard became so frightened and angry he decided his only course of action was to flee the scene. Michael Maxwell caught him clambering off the truck and hustled him into a car with tinted windows.

Two more members of Luther Patrick's security detail grabbed Honey off the truck and whisked her into the car. She welcomed the escort since she had seen the panic building in Leonard. He had shaken his fist in her face and raised his voice to an angry snarl. "Don't wave and smile at these people. Can't you see we're surrounded?"

She joined Leonard in the back seat. The car took off and slowly made its way through the crowd. Tears were streaming down his face. "I'm so sorry, Pumpkin. I don't know what happened to me. I had to get out of there."

Honey wrapped her arms around him. "Oh, my dear Sweetie. Don't you worry. It's all been too much. Believe me, I understand. It's all been too much for me. I was ready to get out of there too."

Leonard was not about to be mollified. "You know the best thing about this wedding?"

Honey winced and played straight man. "No, what?"

"It's over," Leonard grumbled as he looked out the window at all the people trying to look inside the car.

The car stopped before Honey had time to cheer him up. Luther Patrick got in the front seat and Dr. Laughlin got in the back with Honey and Leonard. The doctor looked in Leonard's eyes and began taking his pulse. "What's this I hear about you having a little trouble?"

Leonard had already forgotten his episode on top of the fire truck. "No trouble, doc. It was just time for us to get on about our honeymoon. This being famous is not what it's cracked up to be. It's too much work."

The doctor smiled and reached over the seat to get Luther's attention. "Let's swing by the hospital. We need to examine the patient. I'm afraid his blood pressure might be a little high."

Leonard checked out reasonably well at the hospital. His heart rate slowed and his blood pressure dropped as he began to relax. The doctor gave Honey a prescription for an anxiety medication.

Luther Patrick kept checking his watch. Once the doctor signaled that Leonard could be released, Luther took Honey by the shoulders and looked her in the eye. "Sure you're okay?" Honey nodded. "Good, then we'll take you back to the farmhouse. I'll say goodbye for now. I've got to get back to the party. I wouldn't want to leave the prosecutor alone on your wedding night."

Honey hugged him. "You devil. I'm so glad you and Karen are getting together. I knew you'd be perfect for each other. And I don't know what we've done to deserve such kindness from you and all your people. Thank you, Luther. Thank you so much."

Leonard embraced Luther. "Thank you, my friend. We'll see you tomorrow. I've got a feeling it's way past my bedtime."

<hr>

Honey and Leonard renovated and redecorated the farmhouse shortly after returning to Indiana. Crowd control was impossible at Honey's house in the city. Luther's security detail on the farm kept the curious public at bay even during the frenetic buildup to the wedding. Luther tried to talk them into a honeymoon cruise on *The Sinbad.* "I've got a great place in Uvita, Costa Rica. We could disappear indefinitely."

Honey held up one hand like she was stopping traffic. "Hold it, Luther. Before you even get started on how wonderful this place is, Leonard and I aren't going anywhere. We've traveled more than enough for this year. Right, Leonard?"

"Right you are, Pumpkin. We're glad to be back home again in Indiana." He looked at Honey like maybe it was time to sing the song again. Honey told him no with a quick wave of her hand.

Leonard could still fool most people in casual conversation, but his memory declined rapidly in the months following the wedding. One night, Honey found herself frantically searching for him at 4 a.m. in the aisles of an all night grocery store. They had taken to late, late shopping to avoid the paparazzi.

She hurried through the frozen food section, thinking he might be looking for ice cream. Then she pushed her cart through the produce department, the bakery, and the meat section. No

Leonard. She was out of breath by the time she reached the check out lanes and questioned the only store employee in sight. "Excuse me, ma'am, have you seen an older gentleman in a black coat and stocking cap?"

The sleepy cashier said nothing but pointed out the door to the parking lot.

Honey left her cart and ran through the doors and into the parking lot. It was beginning to snow so she had to slow down on the slippery asphalt. There were only two cars in the lot. The spot where her car had been parked was empty but the pavement was still dry. Leonard had driven off without her.

She scanned the darkened horizon for signs of their car but saw nothing. Her fears turned to anger, which quickly became sadness. She was crying by the time she went back into the store to ask the cashier if she could use the phone. She called Michael Maxwell on the emergency number he had given her for just such an occasion. Maxwell answered right away and was not pleased by what he heard. "I've got people following him now. They should know you're not in the car. Stay where you are. I'll have someone there momentarily."

Honey walked into the farmhouse where Leonard was waiting for her at the kitchen table. "Where have you been?" he asked.

She took off her coat, laid it on the counter and sat down with Leonard, trying hard to remain calm. "I was at the store. The store where you left me, high and dry, without even saying goodbye."

Leonard's eyes widened in surprise and then narrowed in denial. "No I didn't. I don't remember anything like that. I wouldn't leave you stranded in a million years."

Honey knew better than to argue with his scrambled recollections "Well, I'm home now and everything is just fine. I brought us home a beautiful cherry pie. The groceries are on the front porch. Come on, help me get them in the house."

Leonard went to the porch and picked up a full grocery bag. "You were at the store. How'd you get there? The car's been here with me."

Honey helped him carry the food into the kitchen and began putting things away. "Leonard, you drove me to the store and then came home without me."

Leonard sat down at the table and stared at the grocery bags. He shook his head in disbelief. Then he put his head in his hands. "Oh, no, no, no. I can't believe this is happening to me. I see the groceries and I have to believe you. But I can't think I would go off and leave you at the grocery store. Honey, I'm afraid to say it but I think I'm losing my mind. No, I know I'm losing my mind. It's been happening for a while and now it's getting worse."

Honey took his hands and directed him to stand up and give her a hug. She pressed her face into his chest. "Sweetie, you might be losing your mind but you're not losing me."

Leonard kissed the top of her head. "I don't want to make things hard for you."

Honey backed out of the hug, grabbed the cherry pie and set it on the table between them. "I'll tell you what let's do. Here's two plates and a knife. You cut the pie and dish it up on the plates. Then you let me pick the one I want."

The time came when Honey needed to convince Leonard he should not take the car out on errands by himself.

Leonard stomped his feet as he walked out the front door. "What are you talking about? I've been driving a lot longer than you. And a lot better too."

Honey followed him out and got between him and the 1990

Ford Taurus he was about to take to town. "Where do you think you're going now?"

Leonard stopped to think about it and realized he couldn't remember where he was going. He improvised. "I thought I'd go see Gretchen."

Honey moved to the left as he tried to get around her. "Gretchen's out of town. She and Alice left for New Zealand two days ago."

Leonard lowered his head like a bull getting ready to charge. "Tell you what. Maybe it's none of your business where I'm going."

Honey took him by the hand. "I'll tell you what. Why don't we go into the kitchen and do a little test. If you can pass it, then I won't ask where you're going. Sound fair?"

Leonard held his ground for a minute, then decided to walk into the house with her. "What kind of test?"

Honey sat him down at the kitchen table and wrote three words on a piece of paper: horse, car, and building. "I'm going to turn this paper over for five minutes. If you remember the three words, you can go anywhere you want. Sound fair?"

"Of course it does. Horse, car, and building. No problem."

Honey looked at the battery clock over the stove. "Okay, Leonard, it's 1:35 p.m. Sign this paper by the words and note the time. We're going to see if you can remember three words for five minutes. Can you do it?"

Leonard laughed out loud as he signed the paper and noted the time. "Of course I can do it. Horse, car, and building. How bad do you think I am?"

Honey laughed with him and turned the paper over. She began talking about the farm and the weather. Leonard commented on how cold it was getting. At 1:38 p.m., she said, "All right, it's only been three minutes. Let's see how you do."

Leonard tilted his head to a questioning angle. "How I do at what?"

Honey pointed to the piece of paper on the table. "How you do at remembering the three words on the back of that paper."

Leonard furrowed his brow. "What three words?"

Honey spoke slowly. "Leonard, when I turn over this paper there's going to be three words you said you could remember for five minutes. You'll see your signature and your note that it was exactly 1:35 p.m. Now, it's only three minutes after that and you don't even know what I'm talking about. I'll tell you this. The words are horse, car, and building."

She turned over the paper to reveal the words with his signature and time notation. Leonard instantly recognized his own signature and realized he had forgotten the words. He covered his face with his hands and let out a slow, deep moan. "Oh, my God. This must be so hard for you."

Honey got up and hugged him from behind. "It is hard and it's going to get harder. But that doesn't mean we're going to give up."

Leonard uncovered his face and turned around to look at her. "Is it too late already?"

Honey grabbed his head and clutched it to her bosom. "It's never going to be too late for us."

"Finally," she thought. "I've proven to him how bad his memory is. I've finally won the battle for the car keys."

Her feelings of being so very clever were short lived. An hour after the demonstration, Leonard announced he was taking the car to town. The entire game of three-word proof had been completely forgotten.

———

Honey and Gretchen became good friends while learning to cope with Leonard's Alzheimer's. At first, they were reluctant allies, but that changed once they realized how much they had in common. They both loved their Indiana town and the farm. Honey accepted Gretchen's new partner, Alice, without hesitation. The three women enjoyed their girls' nights out. And they all loved Leonard.

But taking care of him was becoming a full time job for both Honey and Gretchen. One afternoon Gretchen dropped by the farm to find Honey crying in the kitchen. "What's wrong? Where's Leonard?"

Honey stood up and tried to dry her eyes with a Kleenex. "He's in the parlor talking to his mother."

"Oh, dear," Gretchen said as Honey led her into the parlor. Leonard was muttering something to the light coming through the window. He did not notice his wife and niece.

Honey tried to shake his arm gently to bring him back to reality. He angrily jerked away from her. Gretchen grabbed Honey's hand and walked her back into the kitchen. "How long has this been going on?"

Honey sat down and used another tissue. "It's happening more and more, at least twice a day."

They sat back down in the kitchen and stared at each other, wondering what to do. As Gretchen reached across the table to comfort Honey, Leonard walked in like nothing was amiss. "Why, Gretchen. Hello and welcome. I didn't see you come in. Why didn't you tell me she was here, Pumpkin?"

Honey knew better than to remind him of his trance. She smiled instead and stood up to give him a hug. "How about we all have a bite of chicken salad? I just made it this morning. It's delicious if I do say so myself."

The three of them had a snack and took a leisurely walk through a trail in the woods behind the barn. Once they got back to the house, Leonard excused himself and went upstairs to take a nap. As soon as she heard Leonard close the bedroom door, Gretchen zeroed in on Honey. "You can't go on like this much longer, Honey. How can you love a man who can't love you back?"

Honey looked at Gretchen with tears in her eyes. "How did you feel when you fell out with your Uncle Leonard?"

Gretchen sat up straight in her chair. "I felt worse than I ever have in my life."

Honey took Gretchen's hand. "You know he never stopped loving you. So, the reason you felt bad is because you stopped loving him."

Gretchen nodded her head. "I suppose that's right. I never thought about it like that."

Honey squeezed Gretchen's hand. "And you feel better now that you're loving him again?"

Gretchen's face lit up in understanding.

"That's the secret," Honey said. "It's more important to love than to be loved. That's why I won't stop loving Leonard no matter what happens. I used to think love conquers all, that my love for Leonard would make his memory better. That fairytale did not have a happy ending. Then, for a while, I lost faith. I began to think love couldn't conquer anything."

Gretchen thought she knew where Honey was going. "And now you're back to knowing that love conquers all."

Honey shook her head. "No, I'm not back to where I used to be. What I'm saying is I need to love him even more than I need him to love me. I know he loves me. But there are times when I get tired of loving a man who can't remember my name. Those are the bad times."

Gretchen leaned in closer to Honey. "I saw you crying in the kitchen today."

Honey shook her head and laughed gently. "I'm not saying loving Leonard is always easy. But I know it's the most important thing I can do. For me and for him."

Honey closed her eyes and thought about Leonard. They were standing alone on top of the Eiffel Tower. It was cloudy and windy and beginning to rain. Her hair was out of control. She didn't care. They looked so deeply into each other's eyes that they forgot where they were. Leonard kissed her like there was no tomorrow.

ABOUT THE AUTHOR

Mark Paul Smith has been a trial attorney for over thirty years. After returning from a life-changing hitchhike in the '70's, chronicled in his first book *The Hitchhike*, he became a newspaper reporter for four years and then played in a rock band on Bourbon Street, New Orleans, for three years. He and the artist Jody Hemphill Smith, his wife, now own Castle Gallery Fine Art in Fort Wayne, Indiana.

ALSO BY MARK PAUL SMITH

Rock and Roll Voodoo

During the 1970s on a magic mushroom harvesting adventure in the Bayou, a young, aspiring rock and roll musician discovers the voice of Voodoo, which not only alters his life, but the life of his band, the Divebomberz.

When the band is on the verge of making it big, tragedy strikes and Jesse is confronted with the hard truth that life is often a spiritual obstacle course designed to see if you can get over yourself.

A book for rock and rollers of all ages and for restless souls who have chased a dream only to discover that what they really needed was with them all along.

The Hitchhike

In 1972, Mark Paul Smith, an officer in the U.S. Air Force, hitchhiked around the world and came back a conscientious objector. In his journey he discovered some basic truths about all mankind and their desire for peace. This Vietnam era book is his true story.

"When I left on my journey I wasn't sure if I was an intrepid explorer or just another fugitive from justice. I had no idea I would end up meeting John Lennon, hitchhiking through The Iron Curtain, . . . nearly dying in a storm at sea, smoking opium in Iran, finding my soul in the music of Afghanistan, smuggling turquoise over the Khyber Pass into Pakistan and nearly dying from dysentery and the dagger of my Argentinian lover in India."

—From the preface